PRAISE FOR *NEW YORK TIMES* BESTSELLING AUTHOR LYNSAY SANDS!

"*The Key* is a happy surprise...a whimsical tale that never sacrifices smarts for silliness."
—*The Romance Reader*

"Readers are swept up in a delicious, merry and often breath-catching roller-coaster ride that will keep them on the edge of their seats and laughing out loud. A true delight!"
—*Romantic Times* on *The Deed*

"Delightful and full of interesting characters and romance.... Skillfully played out. A well-crafted addition to this series."
—*Romantic Times* on *Tall, Dark & Hungry*

"Readers will be highly amused, very satisfied, and eager for the next Argeneau tale."
—*Booklist* on *Love Bites*

"*Love Bites* is an intelligent, witty barrel of laughs."
—*Huntress Reviews*

"With its whip-smart dialogue and sassy characters, *Love Bites*...is a great romantic comedy worth tasting!"
—*Romance Reviews Today*

"A cheeky, madcap tale...vampire lovers will find themselves laughing throughout."
—*Publishers Weekly* on *Single White Vampire*

MEMORABLE PROPOSALS FROM THE SANDS

The Scots ... "Gently now. Be creative, very light concentration of ... blows sits of course."
Blast Passage

LETTING HER GUARD DOWN...

"There ye are then!" Angus Dunbar slapped him on the back and chuckled. "They've disarmed the lass, so ye should be able to get the deed done."

Blake's eyes widened incredulously. They'd had to disarm her? Good God. This was ridiculous. Women did everything they could think of to seduce, lure, or trick him into their beds, yet his bride had to be disarmed for him to bed her?

"Go on then." Angus gave him a push toward the door. "We'll be below fer a bit. If ye find yerself in difficulty, give a shout."

The crowd began to move off then. All but Lady Wildwood who, after a slight hesitation, stepped closer and whispered so that the others could not hear, "I trust you shall be gentle with her? All that teasing at sup tonight was not her fault and while the girl may seem strong and fearless, she is as overset as any virgin on her wedding night."

The CHASE

Lynsay Sands

LEISURE BOOKS NEW YORK CITY

A LEISURE BOOK®

October 2009

Dorchester Publishing Co., Inc.
200 Madison Avenue
New York, NY 10016

ISBN 10: 0-505-52842-8
ISBN 13: 978-0-505-52842-1

The name "Leisure Books" and the stylized "L" with design are
trademarks of Dorchester Publishing Co., Inc.

Printed in the United States of America.

10 9 8 7 6 5 4 3 2 1

Visit us online at www.dorchesterpub.com.

The
CHASE

Prologue

Seonaid laughed with exhilaration as she rode her mount through Dunbar's gates and across the bailey. Bringing it to a halt at the steps to the keep, she leapt to the ground, then turned to grin triumphantly at her two cousins as they rode up.

"Well, and doona ye look pleased with yerself?" Allistair commented as he dismounted. "I was hoping that letting ye win would put a smile on yer face. Glad to see it worked."

"*Letting* me win?" Seonaid echoed with affront. "Ye ne'er did! I won fair and square and ye ken it, Allistair Dunbar!"

"If you say so, love," he quickly agreed.

Seonaid narrowed her eyes with irritation on his smug smile. He was trying to rile her up. She knew he was. And it worked.

Growling, she launched herself on his back as he made to strut past her. Grateful for the plaid braies she wore, she caught her legs around his waist and slung one arm over his shoulder and down across his chest while she smacked the top of his blond head.

Seonaid was a tall woman, large enough that many men would have been overset by such an attack, but Allistair came from the same stock, was taller than she, and built like a bull. Chuckling with amusement, he caught her under her legs to keep her from slipping off and turned to face his sister as she dismounted and moved to join them.

"You two are a right pair," Aeldra said with amusement. "But you can't fool us with claiming to have let her win to make her smile, Allie. She's been smiling ever since we came up with a way to avoid the Sherwell."

"Aye. So there!" Seonaid gave his long hair a tug.

"Hair pullin'," he snorted, bouncing her on his back. "That's a female's technique if ever I saw one." A shout came from the wall, past the gates they'd just ridden through, and he paused to look.

Seonaid followed his gaze, her eyes widening as a wagon and at least twenty riders came slowly into the bailey.

She frowned at the sight of her father at the head of the party, then spotted her brother riding with his young wife, Iliana, mounted before him. The couple were keeping apace of the open wagon. Seonaid could see at least one head poking out of the wagon, but couldn't see much else.

"What's about?" Aeldra asked.

Unhooking her ankles, Seonaid patted Allistair on the arm to get him to release her, then let her legs drop. Once on her feet, she moved around to the man's side to eye the riders. "I doona ken. I dinna ken they'd left the castle."

"I wonder where they are coming from," Aeldra murmured.

Seonaid shook her head. "It couldna ha'e been far. We werena gone long and they were here when we left."

"They went to fetch Lady Wildwood," explained the breathless maid who was now rushing down the stairs toward them. Seonaid thought her name was Janna. She was one of the new women Iliana had hired from the village.

"Lady Wildwood?"

"Lady Iliana's mother," Janna explained, looking worried. "She fled that Greenweld fellow that forced her to marry him and headed here, but it appears she fell ill or something, for she made it as far as the border of Dunbar but no farther. A servant rode to the castle to say a wagon would be needed to bring her the rest of the way. Lady Iliana and Duncan headed right out with Lord Angus and twenty men to fetch them back."

Seonaid nodded at this news, then turned back as the small party came to a halt before them. She watched in silence as her brother lifted his wife off his mount. The moment her feet hit the ground, Iliana was running around to the back of the wagon. Duncan was quick to follow her. Seonaid saw her brother climb into the back of the wagon and stoop to pick up what at first appeared to be a bundle of heavy cloth. It wasn't until he

was back on the ground and walking toward them that
Seonaid could clearly see that his burden was a woman.
It was only her hair, trailing across his arm and toward
the ground in lank salt and pepper waves, that revealed
her gender. There was no way to tell from her battered
features.

If Lady Wildwood normally looked anything like her
lovely daughter, there was no sign of that now. Her face
was puffy and blotchy with bruises, her lip split, and her
nose was swollen so badly that Seonaid could only as-
sume it was broken. From the way the woman was whim-
pering and flinching with every careful step Duncan
took, the rest of her body had not faired any better. It
must have been a hellish journey for her.

Seonaid's gaze slipped away from the woman's rav-
aged face to her brother's expression. Any questions
she might have asked him were immediately swallowed
back. He was furious. Curious now, Seonaid caught her
father's arm as he made to follow Duncan up the stairs.
She held him back and waited a moment before asking
quietly, "Janna said that was Iliana's mother?"

"Aye." His voice was sharp and short with the same
anger Duncan was carrying.

"What happened to her?"

"Greenweld," Angus said with disgust. "The English
took his fists to her. She was forced to flee for her life."

"And came all the way here?" Seonaid asked with
amazement, thinking that surely there was somewhere
closer in England that she might have sought sanctuary.

"We're kin now through Iliana. She knew we could
keep her safe from that bastard husband of hers, and

wouldn't turn her back over to him when he comes to demand her back," Angus said grimly, then followed the rest of the party up the stairs and into the keep.

The bailey seemed unnaturally quiet once the doors had closed behind them.

"I'm thinkin' 'tis a shame ye werena leaving today," Allistair commented quietly, drawing Seonaid's attention away from the closed door.

"Aye," Aeldra agreed. "Distracted as they are with Iliana's mother, they may no notice our being gone for a bit."

Seonaid nodded slowly in agreement, then shook her head. "Nay. We'll stick to the plan. We ride out tomorrow. They most like still willna notice our absence fer a bit. Greenweld's treatment of Lady Wildwood will have them all fired up for a few days."

"Hmm." Allistair scowled at the closed doors and shook his head. "Bloody English. Cowardly bastards taking their fists to women." He turned a hard look on Seonaid, his eyes burning. "If Sherwell ever—"

"He'll not," Seonaid interrupted firmly.

"Aye." Aeldra nudged her brother in an effort to jolly him out of his sudden dark mood. "Seonaid'll no be here for him to treat in any way. We're seeing to that, if ye'll recall."

"Aye." Seonaid forced a smile. "He tarried too long. I'll no be sitting about here waiting for him."

That just seemed to irritate Allistair more. "Bloody idiot. He'll be sorry when he finally sees ye and realizes what he's tarried so long to collect and thereby lost. He'll try to woo ye then."

"Oh, aye," Seonaid said dryly and started to walk toward the practice area. "A Scottish Amazon. Every Englishman wants one to wife."

Allistair caught her arm and jerked her back around to face him. His expression was hard and angry. "He should have claimed ye at least six years ago. And he wid ha'e too, if he'd bothered to come see ye, if he'd kenned how beautiful ye are."

Seonaid gave a slight shake of her head and tried to turn away, but he caught her by the chin, holding her in place and forcing her to meet his gaze. "For ye are beautiful, Seonaid. I ken how ye've suffered from his neglect. He humiliated ye with his refusal to claim ye. I ken ye felt there must be something wrong with ye to make him tarry so. I've watched ye; I've seen it pains ye."

Seonaid dropped her eyes uncomfortably as the pain and embarrassment he spoke of threatened to overwhelm her. She'd been betrothed to the Sherwell as a child. And Allistair was right; the man should have come to claim her years ago. But he hadn't, and with each passing year, her humiliation had grown. She'd hidden it carefully, pretending she didn't care. Who wanted to be married anyway? Marriage would restrict the freedom she enjoyed. She'd have to wear dresses rather than the braies she and Aeldra ran about in. And no doubt he wouldn't wish her practicing with bow and swords in the bailey, or let her ride into battle with the men. She'd scoffed at the idea of getting married to all who would listen. But of course, Allistair and, no doubt, Aeldra too, hadn't been fooled. They'd seen her pain and the uncertainty that Sherwell's neglect had raised in her. They'd seen her confusion. Had he heard about her? Seen her from a distance without her realizing it? Did he find her repulsive? Was that why he did not come?

Aye. Her outward confidence had hidden a bundle of pain, humiliation, and uncertainty. And then she'd learned he was finally coming to claim her to wife . . . because the king had ordered it so. Seonaid's pain and humiliation had bundled itself into rage. He was coming to get her because the king ordered it so? To devil with that! She wanted no man who did not want her, who had to be forced at the end of the king's sword.

And she'd be damned if she would sit about and wait for him like some dutiful dolt.

Taking a deep breath, she held it for a minute, then exhaled it slowly and forced a smile. "Well, and mayhap that was so, but 'tisn't now. And I'll no be here when he finally does make it here to claim me, will I? Aeldra and I ride out first thing on the morrow."

When Allistair remained still, his expression grim, she cocked an eyebrow and grinned as she asked, "Are ye sure ye'd no like to accompany us?"

For a moment she was afraid he wouldn't let go of the dark mood she was trying to banish, but then he slowly released her arms and forced himself to relax. He even managed a slight smile.

"To the abbey? Oh, aye," he said dryly, then shook his head. "While the idea of being the only man amongst so many women is charming—I'd no wish to have to don a nun's gown to do so." His smile widened when Seonaid and Aeldra both burst out laughing at the idea, then he shook his head. "Nay, as sore as it'll make me heart to be without ye, I'll have to stay here."

"Oh, aye, sore me arse," Seonaid teased. "No doubt ye'll be relieved to have some peace from us."

"Nay, I'll not," he assured her solemnly. "I'll miss ye, that I can promise."

Seonaid smiled as Allistair draped an arm around her shoulders and drew her into his side, then grinned when he caught Aeldra with his other arm and drew her into a three-way hug, adding, "You, on the other hand, I'll no miss at all."

"Aye. Well, I won't be missing you either, brother," Aeldra said dryly.

"Hmm." He started to walk them toward the practice area. "Ye two look after each other, and stay out of trouble."

"What kind of trouble can we get into in an abbey?" Seonaid asked with amusement. "I'm more worried about ye. Without us here to distract ye, there's no end to the possible trouble ye could get up to."

Chapter One

"What does she look like?"

Rolfe ignored the question as they crested the hill and Dunbar keep came into view. He sighed his relief. The castle symbolized an end to the sorry task he'd been burdened with, an end he would be happy to see. Though loyal to the king, he was beginning to think Richard II was going out of his mind. Rolfe Kenwick, Baron of Kenwickshire, was no cupid; and yet he had already been forced to arrange two weddings, was seeing to a third at the moment, and no doubt would have another to see to on returning to court. If he returned to court, he thought grimly. 'Twould serve Richard right if he did not. There were far better things he could spend his time on than arranging weddings and chasing after unwilling grooms. And this groom was definitely not eager.

It would have been smarter to simply send one of the king's messengers to Blake, ordering him to travel to Dunbar. It certainly would have been easier. At least then he would not have been forced to listen to Blake's constant protestations or to suffer his many delays. He also would not have had to answer Blake's constant and repetitive questions as to the fairness and disposition of his soon-to-be-bride, or lied in the matter of both.

Grimacing, Rolfe raised a hand in signal to the two long rows of men-at-arms at their back. The king's banner was immediately raised higher to make it more visible to the men guarding the wall.

"What does she look like?" Blake repeated, his gaze moving anxiously over the castle on the horizon.

Rolfe finally turned to peer at the strong, blond warrior at his side. Blake Sherwell, the heir to the Earl of Sherwell, one of the wealthiest lords in the kingdom. He was called "the Angel" by the women at court. The name suited him. The man had been blessed with the appearance of an angel; not the sweet innocence of a cherub, but the hard, lean, pure looks of one of heaven's warriors. His eyes were as blue as the heavens themselves, his nose acquiline, his face sharp and hard and his fair hair hanging to his shoulders in long glistening golden locks. He was just over six feet in height, his shoulders wide and muscular, his waist narrow, and his legs long and hard from years of hugging a horse. Even Rolfe had to admit the other man's looks were stunning. Unfortunately, Blake had also been blessed with a tongue as sweet as syrup; honeyed words dripped from his mouth like rain drops off a rose petal, a skill he used to his advantage with the ladies. It was said he could have talked Saint Agnes into his bed had he lived in her time, which was why the men generally referred to him as "the devil's own." Too many of them had wives who had proven themselves susceptible to his charms.

"What does she look like?"

Rolfe put aside his thoughts at the repeated question. He opened his mouth to snap at Blake, then caught the expression on the face of the over-large man riding a little behind the warrior.

Little George was the giant's name. A friend and knight, he had decided to accompany Blake on this journey. An odder pair could not be found; the two were as opposite as fire and water. Where Blake was blond, Little George was dark; where Blake was handsome, Little George had been cursed with the face of a bulldog. But what the man lacked in looks, he made up for in strength. The fellow was possessed of incredible height and bulk. He stood somewhere in the neighborhood of six-foot-eleven and measured a good three and a half feet across at the shoulders. He was a rock; silent, solid, and usually expressionless, which made the way he was now rolling his eyes and shaking his jowled face particularly funny. It seemed he, too, grew impatient with Blake's constant questioning on the appearance of his soon-to-be-bride.

Regaining some of his patience, Rolfe turned back to the man beside him. "You have asked—and I have answered—that question at least thirty times since leaving Castle Eberhart, Blake."

"And now I ask again," the fair-haired man said grimly.

An exasperated tsking drew Rolfe's attention to the bishop, who rode at his other side. The king had dragged the elderly prelate out of retirement to perform several weddings in the recent past. The marriage between Blake Sherwell and Seonaid Dunbar was the third he'd been called to officiate in as many months. If they ever got it done. Rolfe wasn't all that sure that they would. It had been nothing but trouble from the start.

Although the betrothal had been contracted some twenty years earlier, no one seemed to wish the wedding to take place.

While Seonaid's brother, Duncan, had forced the marriage with his demand that the king finally see it take place, he'd made it obvious he'd prefer to see the betrothal broken and his sister free to marry elsewhere. As for the father, Angus Dunbar had managed to avoid him for days, then made him talk until he was blue in the face before agreeing to the wedding. The moment he had, Rolfe had sent a message to the groom's father, the Earl of Sherwell, informing him of the upcoming nuptials and the necessity of attending, then he'd headed off to collect Blake. Rolfe could have simply sent a messenger to the son as well, but he'd needed the break from the Dunbars.

Damn. Rolfe had almost pitied the poor man for marrying into the cantankerous bunch—or at least he had at the outset of their journey. However, after the way the fellow had dillydallied using every excuse he could think of to delay on the journey here, then pestered Rolfe throughout the entire week of the trip with his repetitive questions about his betrothed's looks, intelligence, and nature, Rolfe was fair sick of the lot of them. He could not wait to show them his backside on accomplishing the deed.

"Well?" Blake growled, reminding Rolfe of his question.

Giving a long-suffering sigh, he answered, "As I have told you—at least fifty times since starting our journey—she is tall."

"How tall?"

"Mayhap a finger shorter than myself."

"And?"

"Lady Seonaid is well-formed, with long ebony hair, large blue eyes, a straight patrician nose, high cheekbones, and fair, nearly flawless skin. She *is* attractive . . ." He hesitated, debating whether it was time to warn the other man of the less than warm greeting he was about to receive.

"Do I hear a howbeit in there?" Blake asked, drawing Rolfe from his thoughts.

"Aye," he admitted, deciding if he were to warn him at all, the time was now.

"Howbeit what?" the warrior prompted, eyes narrowed in suspicion.

"She is a bit rough around the edges."

"Rough around the edges?" Blake echoed with alarm. "What mean you she is rough around the edges?"

"Well . . ." Rolfe glanced at the bishop for assistance.

Bushy white eyebrows doing a little dance above gentle green eyes, Bishop Wykeham considered the question briefly, then leaned forward to peer past Rolfe's bulk at the groom. "Her mother died when she was young, leaving your betrothed to be raised by her father and older brother. I fear she is a bit lacking in some of the softer refinements," he said delicately.

Blake was not fooled. The bishop was a master of understatement. If he said she was lacking some softer refinements, she was most likely a barbarian. He turned on the younger man accusingly. "You did not mention this afore, Kenwick!"

"Well, nay," Rolfe allowed reluctantly. "Nay, I did not. I thought mayhap it would set you to fretting, and there was no sense in doing that."

"Damn!" Blake glared at Dunbar Castle as they approached. It appeared cold and unfriendly to him. The Scots had not exactly rolled out the welcome, but then he had not expected them to. They wanted the marriage no more than he did.

" 'Tis not so bad, son," the bishop soothed. "Seonaid is a bit rough and gruff, but rather like your friend Amaury is. In fact, I would say she is as near a female version of that fellow as 'tis possible to have."

Amaury de Aneford was Blake's best friend and had been since they'd squired together as children. They got on well and had even been business partners until Amaury's recent marriage and rise in station to duke had forced him out of the warring business. Bishop Wykeham thought he was offering a positive comparison to the young man. He thought wrong.

"B'gad," Blake muttered in horror. In his mind's eye he was lifting his bride's marriage veil and having to kiss a tall, black-haired version of his good friend. It was enough to near knock him off his horse.

Shaking the image away, Blake tossed a glare in Little George's direction as he burst out laughing—no doubt under the influence of a not dissimilar vision. When his glare had little effect, he slumped miserably in his saddle. He would dearly have loved to turn around and head straight back to England. However, it was not an option. The blasted betrothal had been negotiated when he was but a boy of ten and Lady Seonaid just four. His father—the earl—had regretted doing so almost before the ink had dried on the scroll. He and the Dunbar—once the best of friends—had suffered a falling out. They had not spoken to each other since two weeks after completing the betrothal, some twenty years ago. Both had been more than happy to forget all about the contract, but neither of them had been willing to break it and forfeit the properties and dower they had put up against it. Their reluctance had left the possibility of the king ordering the fulfillment of the contract if he so wished. Unfortunately, he wished.

Blake could not turn and head back to England. His future was set. By noon on the morrow, he would be a married man.

Life was a trial, and what little freedom a man enjoyed was short-lived. He forced himself to straighten in the saddle as he realized they were about to pass through the gates into the bailey of Dunbar keep. He would present a strong, confident front to these people. His pride insisted upon it.

Blake lifted his head and met the silent stares of the guards watching from the walls, but soon found it difficult to keep his face expressionless when the men began shouting to each other.

"Which one be he, diya think?" shouted one man.

"The poor wee blond one, I wager," answered another, an older soldier. "He be a fair copy of his faither."

There was a brief silence as every eye examined him more thoroughly, then someone commented, "A shame, that. I be thinkin' the dark braw one might have a chance, but the wee one'll no last a day."

"I say he'll no last half a day!" someone else shouted.

"Whit diya wager?"

Blake's expression hardened as the betting began. Indignity rose in him on a wave. Never in his life had he been called *wee* before. He was damned big next to the average man, though he supposed he appeared smaller next to Little George. Still, he was of a size with Rolfe and by no means small. He also didn't appreciate the fact that they doubted his ability to handle one lone woman, taller than average or not. A glance at Rolfe and the bishop showed both men looking uncomfortable as they avoided his eyes. Little George, however, was looking a bit worried. It seemed he was letting the men on the wall unsettle him.

Well, Blake had no intention of doing so. Stiffening his back a bit more, he led his horse up to the keep's front steps. The absence of his bride, who should have been waiting on the stairs to greet him, was an added insult. 'Twas damned rude, and he would be sure to say so when he met the woman. He had just decided as much when the men in the bailey gave up all pretense of working and began to gather around their party to stare. Being the cynosure of all eyes was discomfiting, but their mocking smiles and open laughter were unbearable.

Blake was relieved at the distraction when one of the large doors of the keep creaked open. A young boy appeared at the top of the steps, turned to shout something back behind him, then bolted down the stairs.

"Thank you, son." Blake slid off his mount and smiled as the lad took the reins of his mount. His smile faded, however, as he noted the mixture of pity and amusement on the boy's face. The child retrieved the reins of Rolfe, the bishop, and Little George's horses as well, then led them away.

Shifting uncomfortably, Blake raised an eyebrow in Rolfe's direction. The other man merely shrugged uncertainly, but worry crossed his features before he turned to give instructions to the soldiers escorting them.

Scowling, Blake turned to peer up the steps at the closed double doors of the keep. The upcoming meeting was becoming more intimidating every moment, and he took the time to mentally calm himself and gird his courage. Then he realized that he was allowing himself to be unsettled by a meeting with a mere female.

Blake paused and gave his head a shake. What the devil was he worried about? Women had always responded well to him. He was considered quite attractive by the opposite sex. He wouldn't be surprised if his soon-to-be-bride melted into a swoon at the very sight of him. Her gratitude at being lucky enough to marry him would know no bounds, and her apologies for not meeting him on his arrival would flow unending.

Being the Angel, he would gallantly forgive her; then they would be married. After which he would have done with the business and head home. There was no law and no line in the agreement stating he had to take her with him. Blake thought he would leave her here, making regular if infrequent visits, until he had a home where he could put her and forget her.

His usually high confidence restored, Blake smiled at an anxious Little George, then jogged jauntily up the front steps to the keep doors. He pushed them open with a flourish, then led his much slower and somewhat less confident companions into the keep. His steps slowed when he spied the men seated at the trestle tables in the great hall. They were wolfing down food and laughing with loud ribaldry. If he had thought the hundred or so men guarding the wall and going about their business in the bailey were all Laird Dunbar ruled, it seemed he had been sorely mistaken. There were at least as many men enjoying a rest and repast inside. 'Twas a lot of men for such a small keep.

Blake did a brief scan of those present, searching for the woman he was to marry and spend the rest of his life with, but there seemed to be none present. Other than a servant or two, the great hall was entirely inhabited by men. It mattered little, he reassured himself. He would meet her soon enough.

Blake moved toward the head table, slowly gaining

the attention of man after man as they nudged each other and gestured toward him.

Ignoring their rude behavior, he moved up the center of the room until he stood before the grizzled old man he suspected was the laird, Angus Dunbar. The room had fallen to silence. A hundred eyes fixed on and bore into him from every angle and still the man did not look up. Blake was just becoming uncomfortable when Rolfe moved to his side and cleared his throat.

"Greetings again, Lord Dunbar."

Angus Dunbar was an old man with shoulders stooped under years of wear and worry. His hair was gray and wiry, seeming to stand up in all directions. He took his time about finishing the chicken leg he gnawed on, then tossed the bone over his shoulder and raised his head to peer, not at the man who had spoken—but at Blake himself. Blake immediately had to revise his first opinion. Had he thought the man old? Worn down by worry? Nay. Gray hair he might have, but his eyes spat life and intelligence as he speared Blake where he stood.

A brief flash of surprise shot across his face, then his mouth set in grim lines and he sat back. "Soooo," he drawled. "For guid or ill ye finally shoo yersel'. Ye look like yer faither's whelp."

Blake took the time to translate the man's heavily accented words. Once he was sure he understood, he gave an uncertain nod.

"Weell, 'tis too late." His pleasure in making the announcement was obvious. "Clockin' time came an' went an' the lass done flew the chicken cavie, so I ken ye'll be thinkin' linkin'."

"Cavie? Thinkin' linkin'?" He turned to a frowning Rolfe in bewilderment.

"He said hatching time came and went and the girl flew the chicken coop, so he supposes you'll be tripping along," the other man explained, then turned to the laird, anger beginning to show itself. "What mean you the girl flew the cavie? Where is she gone?"

Dunbar shrugged a dismissal. "She dinna say."

"You did not ask?"

Angus shook his head. " 'Twas nigh on two weeks ago noo, the day after Lady Weeldwood arrived—"

"Lady Wildwood is here?" Rolfe's surprise was obvious. "She was to wait for us to fetch her back to court."

"Aye, weell, an' surely ye've taken yer time about it, have ye no? We expected ye back more than a week ago."

Rolfe tossed a dirty look at Blake, muttering, "We were unavoidably delayed."

"Weell, while ye were 'unavoidably delayed,' Lady Weeldwood was forced to flee fer her life."

"You do not mean Lady Margaret Wildwood?" Blake interrupted, and was surprised when the Scot nodded. He had met Lord Wildwood and his wife several times at court. Lady Margaret had been there often while the queen had still lived. From what he had seen and heard, the couple had been happily married for some twenty years. Lord Wildwood would never have hurt his wife when alive and certainly could not now he was dead. Blake knew the older man had died in Ireland but a few short months ago. "Lord Wildwood is dead," he spoke his thoughts aloud. "Who would threaten Lady Wildwood?"

Rolfe frowned and seemed to debate what to say, then sighed. "Know you Greenweld?"

Blake nodded at the mention of the Wildwood's neighbor. He was a greedy, immoral bastard, not well liked by anyone.

"He forced Lady Wildwood into marriage," Rolfe told him. "He separated her from her daughter, Lady Iliana, and used the girl's safety as a means to keep Lady Wildwood from protesting the marriage and to keep her in line."

Blake was stunned by the news. "Surely he didn't expect to get away with it?"

"But he did get away with it," Rolfe said. "Until Lady Wildwood managed to get a letter to the king through a faithful servant. The message recounted her predicament. Richard immediately arranged for Iliana to marry Duncan, Lord Angus's son," Rolfe explained, with a nod toward the seated laird. "Thereby removing her from Greenweld's grasp and threat. The king is even now seeking to annul the marriage Greenweld forced."

"Which is most like what got her beat," Angus commented grimly. "He wid see her dead ere givin' up Wildwood."

"Aye." Rolfe nodded. "That may be the case, if he caught wind of it." He considered the situation before glancing at Angus. "She headed here for protection, I presume? Why did she not head for court? The king would have protected her."

Angus shrugged. "I doona yet ken. She fled here with her maid an' the maid's son, but she fell under a fever along the way. She's been restin' since arrivin' an' I have no yet spoken to her."

"I see," Rolfe murmured, his expression tight with displeasure. "Is she well?"

The Dunbar pursed his lips. "Alive. Barely. He near knocked the life out o' her. 'Tis why she anticipated yer rescuin' her an' fled here to the safety we could offer as kin."

Rolfe and the bishop exchanged a glance, then the younger man asked, "Have you sent a messenger to the king with news of her presence here?"

"Nay. I thought to wait for ye to arrive. 'Twill be best to give him all the news at one time. He may wish ye to escort her back to court once she's recovered."

Rolfe nodded. "You are a wise man, Angus Dunbar."

The laird's lip curled. "An' yer a fair diplomat, lad. 'Tis why yer king sends ye out on such fool chores."

"Hmm." Rolfe's displeasure at being saddled with such chores was obvious as he peered at Blake. "We had best see to this one now."

Angus grimaced. "Aye. Weell now . . . that could be a problem. As I was tellin' ye, Seonaid took advantage of the uproar Lady Wildwood's arriving caused. The day after the lady arrived, the men an' I took to bowsin'. The chit waited until I was fou, then come gin nicht she flew the cavie."

"What?" Blake asked, with both confusion and frustration.

"He said she left the day after Lady Wildwood arrived—"

"I understood that part," Blake snapped irritably. "What the devil is gin nicht?"

"Nightfall. Laird Angus and his men were drinking and Lady Seonaid waited until he was drunk, then at nightfall she flew the—"

"Coop. Aye, I understood that." Turning back, he glared at the older man, who was eyeing him with open satisfaction. Blake liked to think of himself as something of a master of words. He used them often and well to gain his way in many things. It was the height of irritation for him to find himself unable to understand what was being said, and he suspected the Dunbar knew as much and was enjoying himself at his expense. "Am I to take it, then, that you are breaking the contract and are willing to forfeit her dower?" he asked.

Dunbar sat up in his seat like a spring. "When the devil sprouts flowers fer horns!" he spat, then suddenly went calm and smiled. "To me thinkin', 'tis ye who forfeit by neglectin' yer duty to collect yer bride."

"But I am arrived to collect her." He flashed a cold smile.

"The lass has seen twenty-four years," the Dunbar snarled. "Ye should have come for her some ten years back."

Blake opened his mouth to respond, but Rolfe touched his arm to stop him and murmured smoothly, "We have been through all this, Laird Angus. Been and back. You agreed to the wedding taking place here, and Lord Blake has come as requested to fulfill his part of the bargain." He frowned. "I do not understand why you are being difficult. You had agreed to the wedding by the time I left. Duncan agreed also. Only Seonaid was wont to argue the wedding taking place when last I was here, yet now you appear to be against it as well."

Angus shrugged, amusement plucking at his lined face. "Aye, I agreed to it. Howbeit, I dinna say I would be makin' it easy for the lad. He's tarried a mite long for me likin', an' 'tis an insult to every Dunbar."

There were murmurs and nods of agreement all around. Rolfe sighed. It seemed the laird would see the deed done, but not aid in the doing, which was not good enough in his opinion. "I understand your feelings, my lord, but I fear Lord Blake is right. By aiding your daughter in escaping her marriage, you are breaking the contract, her dower will be considered forfeit, and—"

Laird Angus silenced him with a wave of disgust. "Oh, save yer threats. I'd see the lass married soon as you would, 'tis well past time." He glared at Blake. " 'Sides, I'd have grandbabies from her, even if they are half-English." He paused to take a long draught of ale from his tankard, then slammed it down and announced, "She ran off to St. Simmian's."

"St. Simmian's?"

" 'Tis an abbey two days' ride from here," he explained with amusement. "She asked for sanctuary there an' they granted it. Though, I canna see the lass in there to save me soul."

"Damn," Rolfe snapped; then his gaze narrowed on the Scot. "I thought you knew not where she was."

"I said she dinna tell me," he corrected calmly. "I had one o' me lads hie after her when I realized she was gone. He followed her trail to Simmian's but had no luck in gettin' her out. Men're no' allowed inside, ye ken."

"Aye, I know," Rolfe muttered irritably.

Angus Dunbar turned his gaze back to Blake, his eyes narrowing on the small signs of relief he saw on the man's face and in his demeanor. "Well? Ye ken where she be now, lad, why do ye tarry? Go an' fetch 'er; she must be bored by now an' may e'en come out to ye."

Blake glanced at Rolfe. He had been thinking that he might have just slipped the noose they would place on his finger, but the expression on the other man's face and his would-be father-in-law's words told him he had thought wrong. They expected him to fetch her out of the abbey to wed. To his mind, it was rather like asking a man to dig his own grave, but it seemed he had little choice.

Sighing, he turned to lead the bishop and Lord Rolfe from the room, but at the door to the keep he paused and waved them on before he returned to face the Dunbar. "You say the abbey is two days' ride away?"

"Aye. Two days."

"Over lands friendly to you or not?"

Angus Dunbar's eyebrows rose in surprise. "Friendly to me. Though no always friendly to the King o' England," he added with amused pleasure. "So I wouldna be wavin' yer banner o'ermuch."

Blake nodded. He had suspected as much. It would no doubt please the Laird of Dunbar and his daughter no end if he died in the attempt, forfeiting the lands promised by his father should he fail to marry the wench. "I would have your plaid then, sir," he said with a predatory smile of his own.

Angus Dunbar blinked at him in surprise, then frowned. "Now, why would ye be wantin' me plaid?"

"If the lands we cross are friendly to you, I would wear your colors to prove we travel under your protection."

There was dead silence in the room and even a bit of confusion; then the men seated at the tables began to murmur amongst themselves, whispering something through the hall until it reached the man to the left of the bewildered laird. His bewilderment seemed to clear as soon as the man leaned to whisper into his ear. Whatever the fellow had said, Angus Dunbar found it vastly amusing. Throwing back his head, he roared with laughter, as did every other man in the room.

Still laughing, the grizzled old man stood, and with little more than a tug and a flick of the wrist, drew the plaid off. Left wearing only a long shirt reaching halfway to his knees, he tossed the brightly colored cloth across the tabletop.

His laughter slowed to a stop as Blake caught the plaid and grimaced at the stench rising off the blanket, then turned to leave again.

"Here!"

Blake paused and turned back. "Aye?"

"Would ye leave me standin' here in naught but me

shirttails?" Laird Angus asked, his brows beetling above his eyes.

Blake stared. "What would you have of me?"

"Yer doublet and knickers there."

Blake glanced down at his gold doublet and braies with dismay. Both were new. He supposed he'd thought to impress his bride-to-be with the fine new outfit. " 'Tis a new doublet," he protested. " 'Tis but a few weeks old."

Angus Dunbar shrugged. " 'Tis a fair trade for me colors." He and the other men laughed again.

Sighing, Blake reluctantly handed the plaid to Little George, who had followed him back to the table, then began working at removing his clothes.

"He be bigger than he first looked," one of the men commented as Blake shrugged out of his doublet and tunic to stand bare-chested before them.

Glancing at the man, Blake recognized him as the older man on the wall who had said he favored his father in looks. It seemed some of the men who had lined the wall had followed them inside, though he had not noticed.

"Hmm," was all the Dunbar said. Taking the vestments from Blake, he handed them to one of the men to hold and quickly shrugged out of his own shirt. Tossing the stained and soiled top to his would-be son-in-law, he took the tunic back and tugged it on.

Blake caught the shirt and nearly groaned aloud at the smell coming from it. He would guess it had not been washed since being donned. Probably some three years ago, he guessed, then braced his shoulders and tugged the shirt on before turning his attention to removing the braies and hose he still wore.

"A mite tight, but no' a bad fit."

Blake glanced at Angus Dunbar as the older man finished doing up the doublet over the tunic. His eyes widened as he saw the truth of the words. It seemed his would-be father-in-law was of a size with himself.

"Quit yer gawkin' and give me the braies, lad. My arse is near freezin'."

Realizing he had been staring at the older man, Blake turned his attention back to removing the rest of his clothes. He gave them up to Laird Angus, then took the plaid back from Little George and began wrapping it about his waist.

"What the devil be ye doin'?"

Blake glanced up to see a mixture of dismay and disgust on Angus Dunbar's face.

"Ye doona wear a plaid like that, ye great gowkie! Ye insult me plaid in the wearin'." Finished tying the braies, he reached out and grabbed one end of the cloth. He tugged it from Blake's hold, then dropped it on the floor and knelt to fold it in pleats. Blake watched closely, amazed at the speed the man displayed in the action and wondering if he would be able to replicate it himself. Doubtful, but if he did, it certainly would not be with the same speed.

"There!" The Dunbar sat up straight and looked up at him. "Lay on it."

"Lay on it?" Blake asked with confusion.

"Aye. Lay on it."

Blake gaped. "Surely you jest?"

"Lay on the demn thing!" the older man roared impatiently.

Blake muttered under his breath and lowered himself to the ground to lay atop the pleated plaid. As soon as he had, the laird began tugging at the material. A mere second or so later, he stood and gestured for Blake to rise as well, then finished fitting the plaid about him.

"There." He peered over his handiwork, then shook his head. "I fear it doesna look as good on ye as it does on me," he announced, and there were mutters of agreement all around. "Ye look like a Sassenach atryin' to look like a Scot. Ah, well . . ." Shrugging, he glanced down at the new clothes he wore. "I daresay I suit your clothes much better. What diya be thinkin', lads?" Holding out his arms, he turned in a circle to model the outfit. "Think ye I'll be impressin' Lady Iliana's mother, the Lady Wildwood?"

There was a rumble of approval, then Angus Dunbar turned to take in Blake's sorrowful expression. "Doona fash yerself over it, Sassenach. Ye have enough on yer plate just now. Go fetch yer bride." He grinned, some of his grimness falling away as he added, "If ye can."

Blake stiffened, his face flushing at the chuckles the last three words caused. He was not used to being the butt of someone else's humor and did not care for it, but there was little he could do about it at that moment, so he whirled on his heel and strode toward the door, Little George at his back.

Angus Dunbar pursed his lips and watched Blake stride away. He waited until the men had left the keep, then moved back to his seat and took a long swallow of ale as he glanced around at his men. His gaze finally settled on Gavin, one of his finest fighters and most trustworthy of men. He called the soldier to his side.

"Aye, me laird?"

"Take two men and follow them, lad," he instructed. "The young Sherwell's just fool enough to get hisself killed, and then his fool English father and the English king would blame us. See he finds his way there without gettin' lost."

Chapter Two

"I cannot take it! I simply cannot!" Lady Elizabeth Worley—abbess of St. Simmian's—snapped the words with frustration as she dropped onto the cushioned seat behind her magnificent oak desk.

Biting her lip anxiously, Sister Blanche grabbed up a piece of parchment and fanned the woman's face as she searched her mind for the correct words to calm her superior. Lady Elizabeth's short temper was well known, as was her tendency toward precipitous action when she lost that temper. It was always best to soothe her if one could.

"Forbear, Mother, we must forbear," she said at last, adding hopefully, "God has seen fit to trial us thusly and he would not trial us with more than we could bear."

"Poppycock!" Elizabeth waved her efforts away with irritation. The abbess was an Englishwoman through and through. She had become a nun to avoid marriage to a particularly odious English nobleman over twenty years earlier. Unfortunately, the nunnery was a popular escape for women unhappy with their marital options, and there had been few positions in England at the time that she had not felt beneath her. Hence she had ended up an English abbess in a nunnery in the center of savage Scotland. 'Twas better than a position as a mere sister in an English abbey, or so she had thought back then. She no longer thought so. The speech of these heathens grated on her nerves like sand in her slippers. Lady Elizabeth was heartily sick of their barbarous ways and language. After twenty years of living here, she was fresh out of the patience needed to deal with the Scottish female who now sought sanctuary, and she would in no way believe it was the will of God that she should.

" 'Twas by no will of God Seonaid Dunbar was sent here." She slammed one hand flat on her desktop. " 'Twas the devil!"

Sister Blanche's eyes widened, her worry deepening. "Oh, surely not!"

"Aye." The abbess nodded firmly. "She is the spawn of the devil, I tell you. Sent to trifle with our goodness and lead us unto temptation."

"Temptation?" Sister Blanche didn't bother to hide her doubt.

"Aye. To break one of the commandments."

"Which of the ten commandments, my lady?"

"Thou shalt not kill."

Blanche's jaw dropped, her eyes near popping out of her head. "Oh, sweet Jesu! You should not speak so!"

" 'Tis true." The abbess smiled grimly at the fear and anxiety in the other woman's face. "I would delight in spilling her blood."

"My lady!"

"Aye, well . . ." Lady Elizabeth sighed. "Let us just hope her Englishman follows quickly and saves me from my sinful thoughts." Reaching into her desk, she searched out a skin of whiskey as she added in a mutter, " 'Ere I actually do the deed."

Sister Blanche frowned at the sight of the abbess partaking of spirits. "She will not go to her betrothed willingly. 'Tis why she is here."

"Nay, but he can fetch her out."

"Fetch her? But how? 'Tis a house of God. Men are not allowed here."

The abbess took a large swig of whiskey, then recapped the skin before commenting dryly, "Men often do things they are not *allowed* to do."

"Aye, but the gate is metal and always barred. And the wall—He will not be able to breach—"

"You will unbar it."

"W-what?" Blanche stammered.

"When they are spotted coming, you will unbar the door."

"I? But—" Blanche peered at her, at a loss. She simply could not believe what she was hearing. "But you promised Lady Seonaid sanctuary. She paid a—"

"She did not pay nearly enough. The coins she gave may have covered what she broke on her first day here, but no more."

"Surely you exaggerate, my lady," Blanche argued

quickly. " 'Tis true she overset one or two things at first, but that was because her sword knocked them as she passed. Now you have taken it away, she has broken hardly a thing."

"I would not call Sister Meredith's foot, 'hardly a thing.' "

Blanche grimaced at the reminder of poor Sister Meredith's foot. "Oh, aye, but Lady Seonaid never meant to harm Sister Meredith. It was an accident."

"*Everything* is an accident with Lady Seonaid." Lady Elizabeth grimaced her disgust.

Unfortunately, it was true. Lady Seonaid did seem particularly accident-prone, so Sister Blanche tried a different approach. "She has a good heart, Mother. 'Tis just she is so uncomely tall, and not very comfortable with it, and having grown up in the company of her father and brother she is unsure in a female environment."

"I swear by my faith in the holy God, Blanche, you would have a kind word and a pint of sympathy for a viper," she muttered, then glared at the woman. "You have my instructions, Sister. When the Englishman is seen to be approaching, you will send the workers from the gardens. Once everyone is indoors, you are to unbar the gate."

"But—"

"Do not 'but' me, Blanche! I have given you your orders and you shall carry them out, else I will send you back to England in disgrace."

Blanche went still. She too was an Englishwoman, though she had joined the order on a calling, not simply to escape an unpleasant marriage. As the daughter

of a lesser baron, she had not been given a choice of
where to serve her Lord. She had been sent to Scotland
because it was where she had been needed. Blanche
had served her Lord and the people here as well as she
was able. Unlike the abbess, she found the Scots color-
ful and brave and had made many friends among the
other sisters, most of whom were Scottish. She had no
wish to return to her family in England in disgrace.
However, neither did she wish to betray Lady Seonaid.
Despite the woman's rough ways and clumsiness,
Blanche found she liked her. In her opinion, there was
a certain feistiness and honor about Seonaid Dunbar
she found admirable. The Scottish maiden also had a
rough charm and good sense of humor.

Perhaps there was a way to do as she was ordered
without betraying the woman.

"Diya hear that?"

Aeldra paused and cocked her head. "Someone's
aweepin'."

"Hmmm." Moving forward, Seonaid followed the soft
sobs until she reached the chapel door. She paused
briefly, hesitant to intrude, but found she couldn't just
ignore the heartrending sounds. Heaving a sigh, she
opened the door.

The chapel was where all the nuns and lay sisters met
to recite Matins and Lauds, which Seonaid had sat
through dutifully for two weeks. Five hours a day of
prayer in this huge cave of a room lit only by an array of
candles on the altar and along the side walls. The
amount of candles used would have lit up the average

chamber to the brightness of daylight, but only ever seemed to give the chapel a soft glow.

'Twas probably a good thing, Seonaid thought, averting her eyes from the walls as she had since the first time she had entered and dared to glance at them in the dim light. From the brief perusal, she knew she would not wish for better lighting to look at the tapestries. They were all religious in nature, depictions of Christ and several saints. Unfortunately, they seemed to portray the more gruesome aspects of their lives or, more to the point, their deaths. There was the crucifixion of Jesus, the beheading of Saint Barbara, the massacre of Saint Ursula along with 11,000 virgins, and a portrayal of Saint Catherine being broken on the wheel.

The making of the tapestries was what the sisters occupied themselves with while not praying. Seonaid knew they were presently working on a piece depicting the stoning of Saint Stephen. Finished with the most gruesome martyrings of the female saints, it seemed they were moving on to the men.

Ah, well, 'twas not her concern, she supposed; then her eyes widened in surprise as she finally spied the woman kneeling before the altar. She had expected it to be one of the sisters, weeping over a punishment by the abbess, but instead it was the only other woman presently seeking sanctuary besides Aeldra and herself. Lady Helen. The woman was English and had arrived just the evening before. Seonaid had heard little about her. No one had told her why Lady Helen sought sanctuary, but she suspected it was something to do with a nasty, overbearing husband or some such thing. Had it just been an untenable marriage she was avoiding, the woman surely would have sought sanctuary in an English abbey rather than run all the way up here to the middle of Scotland.

A nudge from behind told Seonaid she had tarried too long in the door and Aeldra was becoming impatient to see what was about. Seonaid stepped into the chapel, aware that the smaller woman followed as she walked up the center aisle toward the altar and the woman kneeling there.

"How do you plan to get her out of the abbey?"

Blake gave a shrug of unconcern. "The moment she sees me she will come out."

"She will?" Rolfe sounded dubious.

"Certainly."

"I see." He pondered the idea briefly. "Then why ever did she flee to the abbey in the first place?"

"She had yet to see me and had no idea what I looked like," Blake responded promptly.

"Ah." Rolfe nodded. "So, as soon as she sees your fair visage—"

"She shall drop to the ground like a ripe plum and prostrate herself at my feet."

"Of course, she will," Rolfe agreed with amusement.

"Women have always reacted with favor to my looks."

"So I have heard."

" 'Tis a curse, really."

"Hmm. You have my sympathies," Rolfe said dryly, then added, "There is just one thing that concerns me."

"What?"

"How is she going to see your fair visage and be over-come? She will be within the abbey walls, and we with-out. Only holy men are allowed past the gate."

Blake scowled. "I do not yet know. I have been thinking on it since leaving Dunbar Castle, but—" He shrugged before glancing at the man riding beside him. " 'Tisn't re-ally my problem anyway. You are the one who was sup-posed to arrange everything. I was simply to travel to Dunbar for the execution."

Rolfe's lips turned up in amusement. "An execution, is it?"

"It might as well be."

" 'Tis sure I am Amaury thought 'twas something sim-ilar he was traveling to as well," Rolfe said with a shrug. "Yet look how happy he and Emma are now."

A reminiscent smile claimed Blake's mouth as he thought of his friend, Amaury de Aneford, his little wife, Emmalene, and their fond farewell to him. "Aye, 'tis happy enough he is. He was sure Emma would be a hag. Did you know?"

"Nay."

"Aye. He swore her first husband killed himself rather than go home and perform his duty."

"Really?"

Rolfe sounded irritated. Glancing at him sharply, Blake noted the tightness around his lips and reminded himself the man was little Emma's cousin. "Of course, that was afore he set eyes on her. Once he saw how pretty she was, he was fair relieved. Howbeit, that was Amaury and Emma, Lady Seonaid is hardly the same tankard of ale."

Rolfe rolled his eyes. "You have not yet even met her."

Blake shrugged. "She is a Scot. And a Dunbar," he added tightly. " 'Tis all I need to know."

Gaze curious, Rolfe asked, "What caused the falling out your father had with Angus Dunbar? I understand they were as close as brothers at one time."

Blake was silent for a moment, then admitted, "I am not sure. Father would never speak on it. Howbeit, it must have been a fair filthy deal, for he has, as far back as I can recall, called the man horrid names and slighted him at every turn."

"Hmm." Rolfe stared at the trees they passed through, then shrugged his curiosity aside. "As to gaining your bride from the abbey, mayhap Bishop Wykeham could be of some assistance there."

"What was that, my son?" Catching mention of his name, the bishop urged his mount up between the two men and peered from one to the other expectantly.

"Blake and I were just discussing how to get the girl out of the abbey. I thought mayhap you could aid in the endeavor?"

"Hmmm." Bishop Wykeham's gentle face turned thoughtful as he considered the problem, then his bushy gray eyebrows rose and a wry smile came to his face, tugging upward at the wrinkles residing there. " 'Tis true that as a man of God, they would allow me in where the gates 'twould be barred to you. I suppose I could talk to the chit, but 'tis all I can do," he warned. "I cannot force her from her sanctuary."

"Thank you, Bishop," Blake said, and wondered if he might yet escape the marriage. If he did, he would owe the little Scottish wench his thanks. Mayhap he could send her some bonbons, or a bolt of fabric.

"There 'tis."

Blake glanced up at Rolfe's announcement as they rode out of the trees. They were only about fifty yards from the stone wall surrounding the abbey. Tensing in the saddle, he nudged his horse and urged him forward. In the next few minutes he would either gain his bride or fail and continue to be a happy man. It was time to determine his future.

Reaching the gate, Blake dismounted and moved swiftly to the bell pull. He was about to give it a tug when a crack between the door and the wall caught his attention. Frowning, he reached up and gave the wooden door a tentative nudge. It gave a squeal of protest but slid an inch open. Blake stilled, little currents of unease running up the back of his neck. This was not right, and it brought a grim frown to his face as he reached for his sword. "The door is unbarred."

"What?" Rolfe dismounted to join him.

"Nay." The bishop shook his head. "You must be mistaken, Blake. The gate is always barred. There are too many who seek sanctuary within to—" His words came to an abrupt halt when a gentle push from Rolfe sent the door sliding open a little farther. The prelate stared in amazement, then muttered with disgruntlement, "Well! That is not very secure."

Blake pushed the door the rest of the way open. His gaze ran over the empty flower and herb gardens before turning to the building beyond. "Nay. 'Tis not safe at all."

"Damn me!" The bishop scrambled off his own horse and joined the other two men peering through the opening.

"What think you?" Rolfe asked. They all stared at the lush and flowering vegetation revealed.

"The gardens are empty. Should they be?" Blake glanced over his shoulder. The bishop was craning his neck, peering inside even as he shook his head.

"Nay. The servants or lay sisters should be tending them at this hour. Lady Elizabeth Worley runs St. Simmian's, and she is a fair virago of a woman who would put up with no—"

"Look you," Rolfe said, cutting off the bishop. "There are baskets scattered about. 'Tis as if they had been working and left suddenly."

"It sounds worrisome." Little George's rumble drew Blake's attention to the fact that every single man who rode with them had dismounted and was crowded around, trying to peer into a sanctity they would normally never get a chance to see.

"Oh dear, oh dear, oh dear." The bishop shook his head, his eyebrows turned down in concern. "Something is not right; something is simply not right."

"You said many seek sanctuary here. You do not think someone actually broke in and—" Rolfe left the rest of his theory unsaid.

Blake pushed the gate the rest of the way open and started resolutely inside. 'Twas one thing for the little Scottish wench to flee from marrying him; 'twas another for someone to steal or harm her. He would not stand idly by and see that done. 'Twas not in his nature.

* * *

Seonaid was a bit surprised by the wariness on the other woman's face. She was a redhead, her skin pale and powdered with a light sprinkling of freckles. Her face was blotchy from crying and scrunched up in distrust as she watched them approach. Pausing before her, Seonaid glanced uncomfortably away. She wanted to turn around and leave but simply could not. 'Twas due to her one failing; in her heart, Seonaid was soft. 'Twas a fault she and her brother had worked hard to eradicate over the years. They had failed at the task. She could not walk away from an injured animal or man, could not ignore cries of pain, and could not leave the Englishwoman to sob her heart out as she had been doing.

"Yer Lady Helen. I'm Lady Seonaid," she announced abruptly by way of a greeting.

"Lady Seonaid? Aye, Sister Blanche mentioned you to me." There was relief on her face as the woman got to her feet. The emotion turned to surprise as she took in Seonaid's height and realized she was a good foot taller than herself. "You have been here two weeks, have you not?"

"Aye. I be attemptin' to avoid marryin' an English dog," Seonaid announced with feigned boredom.

Helen looked startled, then started to laugh. "And I am endeavoring to escape marriage to a Scottish pig."

"Nay. Really?" Seonaid grinned, then asked, "Well, why did ye no go to an English abbey then?"

Helen grimaced. " 'Twas in Scotland I escaped. I sought the closest haven I could find."

"Oh, aye." Seonaid nodded. "Well, never fear, ye'll be safe here."

"Aye." The word was one of agreement, but her expression was doubtful.

When Aeldra shifted on her feet beside her, Seonaid suddenly recalled her cousin's presence and grimaced at her own bad show of manners. " 'Tis rude I am. This is me cousin, Aeldra. She insisted on accompanyin' me here to keep me safe should I run into trouble."

When Helen stared at the woman in question, Seonaid turned to examine Aeldra, seeing her as the other woman must. Her blond cousin was her opposite in coloring and height, shorter even than Helen herself. Seonaid supposed her cousin's insisting on accompanying her to "keep her safe" would sound odd to anyone who had never seen her fight, but Aeldra was a wildcat in battle.

"She's a fair bloodthirsty wench," Seonaid felt she should explain. "An' nimble too. Show 'er," she suggested.

Nodding, Aeldra turned as if to leave the chapel, took several steps away, then suddenly did three backflips in a row. She landed facing Helen on her last spin, a small knife drawn and at the Englishwoman's throat.

"Oh, my," Helen breathed faintly.

Seonaid and Aeldra both laughed as the smaller woman stuck her blade back in her deerskin boot.

"Can you teach me that?"

Aeldra shrugged. " 'Tis fair impressive to see, but no verra helpful in a real battle. An archer would ha' shot me down in mid-flip 'ere I ever got me dagger near yer neck."

"Oh. So you will not teach me." Helen's shoulders drooped. Seonaid and Aeldra exchanged a glance.

"But I could be teachin' ye something a bit more useful," Aeldra said.

Helen's attitude brightened at once. "Truly? Would you?"

"Aye."

"Oh, my, that would be marvelous. Then should Cameron come for me, I could defend myself."

Seonaid's eyes widened. "Cameron? Lord Rollo?"

Helen grimaced. "Aye"

She considered. "I have heard nothing to say he be so bad. Now, the man I was to marry, he's a dog of the first order."

"Who were you to marry?" Lady Helen asked curiously.

"Sherwell."

"Lord Blake Sherwell?"

"Aye, do ye ken him?" Seonaid asked.

"Aye. Well, nay, I have never met him, but I have heard of him. They call him the Angel. He is said to be fair handsome, and quite charming. 'Tis said he has the looks of an angel and the tongue of the devil, and betwixt the two could have lured even Saint Agnes to his bed." Helen frowned. "Why would you not wish to marry him?"

"He be English." When the woman looked taken aback, Seonaid threw her an apologetic smile. "Well, 'tis no just that he be English. He's a cur as well."

"Oh." Helen hesitated, then asked, "Have you met him?"

"Nay, but me father kenned his father. They were once friends. 'Twas why the marriage was arranged, but then the earl showed hisel' to be the cur he is an' . . ." She shrugged.

"What did the Earl of Sherwell do?"

Seonaid pursed her lips. "Well, now, I dinna rightly ken, but it must have been something fair rude, for me father has hated him ever since an' curses him at every opportunity." When Helen continued to frown and seemed about to comment, Seonaid shifted uncomfortably and asked, "Why are ye fleein' Lord Rollo? S'truth I have heard naught against him."

"Aye." Helen's expression darkened. " 'Tis sure I am, you have not. He hides his true nature well. He fooled even my father, so much so he agreed to the marriage, but on the way to Cameron Castle, I overheard him talking with one of his men. We had stopped to make camp for the night and they thought I was sleeping. They were discussing how he planned to end the marriage as quickly as he could once we reached his stronghold, so that he could marry another woman."

Seonaid raised her eyebrows. "If he planned to end it anyway, why marry at all?"

"For my dowry. My father is quite well off and was generous with my dower."

"But, if he ends the marriage, he canna keep the dower."

"He could if the marriage ended because I had died."

"Nay!" Seonaid gaped at her. "He wouldna!"

Helen nodded grimly.

"Did he say so?"

She nodded again. "They were discussing how best to do it. They could not decide between breaking my neck and throwing me down the stairs to make it look as if I broke it in the fall, or breaking my neck in the woods and saying I fell off my mount."

"The cur!" Turning to her cousin, Seonaid gestured. "Can ye imagine, Aeldra?"

Aeldra shook her head. "Nay. 'Tis lucky ye truly werena sleepin'."

"Aye," Seonaid agreed. "What did ye then?"

"Nothing at first. I had to continue pretending to sleep so they would not know I knew of their plans."

"Oh, aye."

"But soon as I had the chance, we escaped."

"We?"

"My maid was with me."

"Was?"

"Aye, well, I sent her toward home to tell my father. Once he realizes Cameron's plan, he shall come to my aid at once."

"But what if they catch her afore she reaches him?"

Worry crossed briefly over her face, then she shook her head. "Nay. I set all the horses free ere we left."

Seonaid and Aeldra shared a glance; then the smaller Scot arched her eyebrows. "How did ye manage to do all that? I ken well no Scot would sit about while ye packed, let loose their beasts, an' fled."

"Aye, well." She hesitated, then said, "Had they been

able to stop me I am sure they would have, but my maid, Madge, has a special knowledge of herbs. The morning after I overheard them talking about killing me, I told her what I had heard and that we had to escape. She made the sup that night and drugged it so they fell into a deep sleep. While they were unconscious, we packed, let loose the beasts, and fled. I sent her on home alone and made my way here, trailing a second horse so they would think she traveled with me. I made sure they could follow my trail. They will not even need bother looking for it. Madge will make it back home and bring Father to me."

"Ye deliberately left a trail for them to follow?"

Helen nodded. "Well, if I had headed home with Madge, they might have caught us up 'ere we could reach there. They would know I knew of their plans. They would make sure I could not escape again, and most like have seen to the killing at once, on the spot."

"Aye, I ken, but ye dinna have to leave them a way to trail ye here, did ye?"

"I wished them to follow me to be sure Madge would reach my father safely," Helen said plaintively. "Besides, I feel sure once he is made aware, all will be well. At least I did. I thought surely I would be safe here, but now I am not so certain."

Seeing the slight tremble to her lip and afraid she would burst into tears again, Seonaid hurried to reassure the woman. "Oh, aye. 'Tis safe ye are here. No even a murderin' dog like Rollo Cameron appears to be would dare storm sacred ground. An' even did he, the abbess wouldna let him in. Ye're safe here 'til yer father arrives. As am I." Still seeing the fear on the Englishwoman's face, Seonaid searched about in her mind for a way to distract her. "We werena doin' ought. If ye have time, mayhap ye'd like Aeldra an' I to teach ye a thing or two about defendin' yersel'?"

"Would you? Oh, that would be grand. I realized not how ignorant I was of such things until I found myself in danger. I dearly wished I knew how to handle a sword the night I lay listening to Rollo's plans for me. I would have sat up and run him through on the spot."

"Come then, we'll move to the garden, where there's more room." Seonaid led the way to the chapel door and pulled it open. She started into the hall, froze, and stepped back, her hand moving automatically to her empty scabbard.

"What is it?" Helen asked anxiously when Seonaid eased the door closed and wheeled to peer about the room.

"Come." Expression grim, she grabbed the smaller woman's arm and urged her toward the left side of the dim room, sure Aeldra would follow without question.

"What is it?" Helen stumbled along at her side. "What did you see?"

"I saw a man in the hall." Pausing by the first tapestry, Seonaid released the woman and pulled the mammoth decoration away from the wall. Sensing her plan, Aeldra moved up in front of her and slid behind the image of Christ on the cross. Seonaid peered at Helen.

"Get in," she ordered. When the woman hesitated, she grabbed her arm again to urge her forward. "Aeldra shall protect ye from the other side. I shall be on this side."

"But why would I need protecting?" She stilled halfway behind the tapestry and whirled to face her. "Was it Rollo you saw?"

Seonaid shook her head. "I didna' recognize the man, but 'twas a plaid he wore, an' since we are the only two seeking sanctuary here and the man who seeks me is English . . ." Letting the rest of the sentence fade, she shrugged.

Helen needed no further explanation. Panic wreathing her face, she slid the rest of the way behind the tapestry, leaving just enough room for Seonaid's larger frame.

"How do you think they got in?" the Englishwoman asked as the tapestry settled against them. It was not flat and would not hold up well as a hiding spot under close examination, but Seonaid was hoping it would not need to. With the dim lighting in the room and the gory images on the tapestries, she hoped whoever searched would simply give a quick glance and leave. Seoniad was not willing to confront the enemy without her sword, especially when she did not know their numbers. All she had glimpsed was one man, but he had been standing sideways at the end of the hall, talking to someone she could not see. Or several someones.

"There was no warning. I heard no cries or screams. Think you they—" Helen's frantic words came to an abrupt halt when Seonaid reached out and covered her mouth with one hand.

"Lesson number one in defendin' yersel'," she hissed. "When one is hidin', she must remain quiet, else there is no use to hidin' at all. Do ye ken?" When she felt the woman nod in the dark, Seonaid eased her hand away, then stiffened as the chapel door was opened.

'Twas dark and stifling behind the tapestry, the air heavy with must and dust. Seonaid was straining to hear footfalls, but the silence was as heavy as the dust behind the image of Christ.

Releasing the breath she'd been holding, Seonaid drew a fresh one, then immediately covered her mouth and nose with one hand. She had inhaled dust, and a sneeze was forcing its way to life. Silently cursing, she bit her lip and pinched her nose in an effort to distract herself, or at least delay the sneeze. Sweat had broken out on her forehead from the effort when she finally heard the soft click of the door. Her explosive sneeze immediately followed, and Seonaid stepped out from behind the curtain, waving a hand in front of her face to remove any traces of dust still clinging to her skin. Aeldra and Helen followed.

"Damn me! That one near blew me head off."

" 'Twas close." Aeldra eased to the door and pressed an ear to it briefly. Apparently not hearing anything, she inched it open enough to peer out with one eye. " 'Tis clear," she said quietly as she closed the door.

Nodding, Seonaid gestured her back.

"What are we going to do?" Helen asked as Aeldra rejoined them.

Seonaid was silent for a moment, then frowned. "We need to get to our rooms."

"What for?" Helen peered from one woman to the other when Aeldra nodded.

"Me sword." She grimaced. "The abbess took it away. Aeldra's too."

"But if she took them away—"

Aeldra shrugged. "We took 'em back. Pinched 'em while she snored away in drunken ignorance."

"In drunken—? Nay! The abbess drinks?"

"Aye." Seonaid did not appear the least concerned by the fact. "She can toss it back like the best of warriors."

"Aye." Aeldra grinned.

Helen shook her head at the raw admiration in both women's voices.

"Come along, then." Seonaid followed Aeldra toward the door, then suddenly stopped and wheeled on Helen. "Mayhap ye should wait here. We could come back for ye."

"Nay." The Englishwoman shook her head firmly. "I feel safer in the company of you two ladies than I have since overhearing Lord Rollo's plans for me. I wish to stay with you."

Seonaid pursed her lips and considered her for a moment, then nodded. "All right, then let us go." She gestured to Aeldra, who still stood by the door. The smaller woman pressed her ear to the wood surface, then frowned and turned quickly back.

"Someone comes."

Cursing roundly, Seonaid grabbed Helen's arm and hurried her back to the tapestry. She paused there just long enough for Aeldra to slide behind it, then shoved Helen in and quickly followed just as the door opened.

Chapter Three

Seonaid pressed herself against the wall and cursed the fates for allowing this to happen when she didn't have her blade. She held her breath and tried to listen to what was happening in the room but could hear no sound over the pounding of her own heart. When the silence seemed to go on interminably, Seonaid opened her mouth and took a cautious breath, remembering well what had happened the last time she had breathed in through her nose.

After several minutes of silence, she decided whoever had opened the door must have merely peered in and moved on. Seonaid was about to tug the tapestry aside and slip out when a scuffling sound reached them. Someone's foot had knocked against one of the pews. Had their hiding place been discovered?

"Lady Seonaid?"

She stiffened at the whispered query from the other side of the tapestry, then tugged it aside as she recognized the voice.

"Sister Blanche!" Her gaze shot about the empty room; then she grabbed the woman's hand and tugged her behind the tapestry with them. "What do you? There are men in the abbey."

"Aye, I know." Sister Blanche sighed. "I have been looking for you for near half an hour to warn you. The Englishman is come."

Seonaid blinked in the darkness behind the tapestry. "Nay. They are Scots."

"Nay. I saw them when they crested the hill; 'twas Englishmen. They carried the king's banner. 'Tis sure I am."

"Ken you many Englishmen who wear plaids?" Seonaid asked, and sensed the woman's shock in the darkness.

"Plaids?"

"Aye, the man I saw wore a plaid."

"A plaid? Nay." She shook her head fervently, stirring up the dust. "You must be mistaken."

"He stood not ten feet away, Sister. His knees were naked, I tell ye. 'Tis Scots who have breached the abbey; 'tis why we've hidden Lady Helen. 'Tis the Cameron, I'm sure. We must see her out of here. Ye ken what'll happen to her if she falls into Cameron's hands."

The silence following her announcement was long and thick; then Sister Blanche began to move. She was out from behind the tapestry in a heartbeat. Following her, Seonaid watched with amazement as the woman began to tug at her clothes, dragging the habit off with little thought or warning.

"What are ye doing?" she asked with amazement.

"I left the door unbarred," was Sister Blanche's grim answer. "Mother Elizabeth ordered it. She hoped your Englishman would take you away. She is still upset about her crystal. And Sister Meredith."

Seonaid cursed. She had knocked the abbess's crystal decanter from her desk on her first day here. She had tipped her scabbard backward to avoid hitting a glass on a table beside the desk only to knock over the decanter instead. As for Sister Meredith, Seonaid had been kneeling at the altar saying her prayers when the good sister had walked by, tripping over her feet, which—in truth—did stick out farther than anyone else's. Sister Meredith had broken her ankle as she fell.

"I *am* sorry," Blanche said with obvious distress. "She ordered me to watch for your betrothed's arrival, empty the garden, order everyone to the big chapel, and unbar the door. I could not refuse her order. She threatened to return me to England in shame. I did think to warn you, but I could not find you." She glanced at Helen as the woman slid, white-faced, out from behind the tapestry. "I thought they were Englishmen," she said plaintively, guilt flushing her own face as she took in the other woman's fear. Then she shrugged her own feelings impatiently aside and pushed her dress into Helen's hands.

"Put on my gown."

Seonaid's eyebrows rose at the snap of authority in the sister's voice. She wasn't at all surprised when Helen responded to it and immediately began removing her own clothes.

"We will switch clothes, then I shall show you a secret way out of here." Sister Blanche helped Lady Helen disrobe as she spoke. "Should we run into them, the habit may keep you safe. Men do not even really look at nuns. We may fool them with the switch."

Turning away as the women set about exchanging clothes, Seonaid moved to the door and listened for sounds in the hall. Aeldra followed, and they stood silent for a moment, listening. Then Seonaid suddenly glanced down at herself and frowned at the long gown and plaid she wore. Her outfit would hamper her movements if they encountered trouble, and it did appear trouble was brewing.

Gesturing for Aeldra to take her place at the door, Seonaid removed her plaid and used her dagger to cut a slice into the plain white shift she'd worn beneath the plaid. She cut a couple of inches below waist level, then tore the cloth all the way around her body until the bottom of the gown fell away to land in a soft pile around her feet. She then tucked the much shortened shift into the top of the plaid braies she had been wearing beneath the gown and plaid. Seonaid and Aeldra usually ran around in the plaid braies and a short tunic at home. They had only donned the gowns for their stay at the abbey to keep from shocking the abbess and nuns. But now that trouble had arrived, the nuns' sensibilities were less important than practicality. Should they need to fight or run, they could do both much easier in braies than long gowns.

Finished with her own garb, Seonaid quickly used a

bit of cloth to tie her long black hair back, then took
Aeldra's place at the door. She would keep watch while
Aeldra made the same alterations to her own dress.

"Where the devil is everyone?"

Blake shrugged at Rolfe's muttered question. The
gardens had been empty, as had the entry, the hall, and
every other room they had peered into thus far. The
abbey was as silent and vacant as a tomb. It was down-
right eerie, he thought, as he came to an empty side
hall.

Pausing, he turned and peered at the men following
him. Rolfe, Little George, the bishop, and twenty men-at-
arms, curiosity and concern on every face as they peered
about the inner sanctity of the abbey. He could not blame
them. 'Twas not a place they were likely to see again.

Sighing, he shook his head and peered back toward
the main hall.

"What is it?" Rolfe asked, looking back the way they
had come.

"The chapel," Blake said. "I swear I saw the door close
as I stood at the end of the hall."

"Aye, but we looked in there. It was empty."

"Hmm." He continued to stare up the hall. His instincts were telling him to check it again. A warrior
quickly learned to rely on his instincts. Turning
abruptly, he headed back the way they had come, pausing after only a few steps to order the men-at-arms to
continue searching the passage for any of the abbey's
inhabitants. When he continued on, he was aware Rolfe

was following him, with Little George and the bishop close behind.

Seonaid straightened from peering into the hall when her cousin nudged her. Aeldra had finished repairing her clothes so that she too was no longer hampered by skirts, and Sister Blanche and Helen had finished exchanging garments and were moving to join them.

"Your gowns," Lady Helen said with surprise as she saw that they had changed their clothing as well. "You look so . . . different in braies."

Seonaid smiled at the comment as she eased the door closed and turned to properly examine the two women. She could have said the same to them. Both of them had been transformed by the switch. With her hair hidden beneath the nun's habit and every inch of her body hidden as well, Helen had an ethereal beauty. She had been attractive before, but her beauty was somehow transformed to a pure and innocent sweetness. Sister Blanche, on the other hand, looked a perfect mess, her usually serene expression tense and pinched, her shorn head odd without its covering.

Seonaid glanced about, then moved toward the front of the room to snatch the pristine white cloth off the table holding the candles.

"What are you doing?" Sister Blanche hurried after her as the candles tumbled to the floor.

"Should anyone see the two of ye together, they would recognize the switch at once," Seonaid pointed out. "We must cover yer head."

"Oh." Sister Blanche reached up to self-consciously feel her own shorn head, but Seonaid brushed her hand aside and draped the cloth about her head. She then tied the fine linen beneath her chin, and paused to frown over her handiwork. Unfortunately, her efforts revealed how little knowledge she had of primping and fashion. Muttering under her breath, she fussed a bit, relieved when Helen nudged her out of the way and took over the duty. Once the Englishwoman had finished, Seonaid eyed the sister and nodded her satisfaction.

"Let us go. We must gather the blades from our rooms, then find the exit you speak of."

"The blades from your rooms?" Sister Blanche peered at her, bewildered. "But Mother Elizabeth took them."

"We took them back an' we needs must have them to escape."

"Nay, we cannot risk it," the sister protested at once.

"Would ye send us out with naught to protect us?"

Biting her lip, Sister Blanche peered unhappily about, then sighed. "I shall fetch them for you, then."

Seonaid shook her head. "I'll no let ye risk yerself for us."

" 'Tis my fault you are at risk," Sister Blanche argued. "Besides, they would not dare harm a bride of God."

Seonaid smiled slightly. "Ye look little like a sister right now, Sister."

The nun glanced down at her clothes with a start. "Oh, aye, well, but if I had any difficulty I could remove this." She gestured to the cloth on her head. "They would know I was a sister then."

Seonaid opened her mouth to argue, but Sister Blanche shook her head. "I will not argue with you. I am going and that is final."

"I shall go as well," Helen announced, hurrying to follow the sister as she moved toward the door.

"Nay!" Sister Blanche turned on her at once. " 'Tis not safe for you."

"They would not recognize me dressed in your clothes," Helen pointed out. "In truth, I shall probably be safer than you yourself. Besides, Sister, you surely cannot carry the swords by yourself. They will have to be concealed beneath your skirts, and two would be too awkward for one woman."

The words were true, of course, and Seonaid's lips twitched with amusement as Sister Blanche realized it herself and gave an unhappy nod.

Admonishing them to be quick and quiet about it, Seonaid told them where to find the swords and led them to the door. After pausing to listen for anyone approaching, she opened the door to let them out, then watched until they had turned the corner at the end of the hall. She had started to close the door again when a sound from the other end of the hall drew her eyes. 'Twas the first man she had seen, the fair-haired Scot. He had come around the corner at the end of the hall even as Helen and Sister Blanche disappeared around the other. She didn't think he had spotted the other women, but he had definitely seen her.

Cursing her bad luck, Seonaid slammed the door and turned to warn Aeldra.

* * *

Reaching the hall in question, Blake stepped into it, then paused in surprise. The hallway was as empty as it had been the first time he had walked down it, but a long-haired Scot now leaned out of the chapel door, his back to them as he peered toward the opposite end of the passage. Curious, Blake glanced along the hall himself and missed his opportunity to get a look at the fellow's face. The sudden slamming of the chapel door told him that his presence had been discovered.

Cursing, Blake pulled his sword from his scabbard and charged toward the door just as Rolfe reached his side.

He half expected the door of the chapel to be barred when he reached it and was surprised when it gave way abruptly beneath his touch. Turning the knob, he crashed into the room, sword at the ready, aware the other men entered behind him.

For a moment they all stood staring blankly about, for as before, the room appeared empty.

"Empty." Rolfe frowned around the room. "What did you see to make you hie back here?"

"A Scot standing in the doorway. He saw me and slammed the door."

"Hmm." Rolfe glanced around again. "Well, he is not here now."

Blake paused by the pew nearest the door and picked up one of the two plaids that had been left there. "Aye. But I didn't imagine him."

The bishop frowned at the sight of the plaid. "Well, where did he go?"

Blake dropped the cloth. "Could there be a secret passage in here?"

The bishop frowned over the possibility, his gaze moving to the walls and the tapestries hanging there. "I do not know. Of course, 'tis possible one of the tapestries hides a secret passage or—"

Blake raised an eyebrow when the prelate suddenly stilled. Following his wide-eyed gaze to the image of the crucifixion of Christ, he stared at it curiously for a moment before he realized what had caught the other man's attention. The tapestries in the room all reached from floor to ceiling, as did the one the bishop was staring at, almost. It fell an inch or so short of the floor due to the way it bulged out from the wall. Beneath it, two sets of boots showed.

Blake raised his sword and gestured to the other men, then moved toward the tapestry. Pausing a foot or so before it, he waited until the other men had arranged themselves around him, then spoke. "Come out of there, you."

Seonaid cursed under her breath. She had feared the hiding place might not bear up well under close inspection, but there had been little time to find a new one after closing the chapel door. Glancing toward Aeldra, they shared a grim glance, then stepped to the side, half-revealing herself to the enemy and getting her first really good look at them. Well, one of them. Unfortunately, her attention was focused on the man who stood in front, so she did not notice the others accompanying him. The one in front was enough to keep anyone's attention.

Seonaid had never met the Cameron, but if the man

before her was Rollo, God had been truly kind when fashioning him. His hair—as she had noticed earlier—was blond, but 'twas truly a poor description. A touch shorter than her brother's darker tresses, it hung to his shoulders in golden waves that caught and reflected the candlelight in the room. It was glorious, a shade of spun gold she was sure only an angel could possess. His face was equally impressive, with wide, deep blue eyes, and long gold lashes brushing his cheeks as he blinked. A straight strong nose, firm full lips, and a short golden beard and mustache made him as attractive a man as Seonaid had ever seen. She almost expected to see wings sprouting from his back and a halo above his head, but she supposed angels did not have quite so wondrous a body. At least not any of the images of angels she had seen. In the paintings and tapestries sporting visions of angels, they were a thin, small-boned crew. The man before her could never have been so described. He was taller than her own six feet, his shoulders twice the width of her own, his upper arms probably as big around as her thigh. Nay, bigger. And his legs were strong and well formed where they were revealed by the short plaid he wore.

Damn. She released a small sigh. 'Twas almost worth it to die for one night in his bed, she thought, recalling what Helen had said about his plan to kill her.

Blake stared at the creature peeking around the edge of the tapestry and frowned. The lighting in the chapel was poor and the Scot had only leaned his upper body partly out from behind the tapestry, revealing one arm and one eye, but it was enough to tell him this was no soldier. He was lean and sleekly muscled, but was lacking in the bulk that identified a warrior. The fellow did not make his way by the sword. Blake supposed he should have guessed as much when the man had chosen to hide rather than confront him in battle. He shifted impatiently when the silence continued and the man stayed half-concealed behind the cloth.

"I said come out," he snapped, shifting his position threateningly. The Scot seemed to give a start at his words, then glanced back behind the tapestry.

Seonaid was confused. While she had been hidden behind the tapestry, the man's words had been muffled and she had not noticed his accent. It was English, not Scot. She glanced back to Aeldra in confusion.

Aeldra too looked slightly surprised at his accent, then shrugged.

Seonaid peered back to the man, opening her mouth to speak, then paused. Mayhap he had been raised in England. It wasn't at all uncommon for such a thing to happen. Many Scottish heirs were raised there, either by rich relatives or at court itself. Shrugging such considerations aside, she glanced toward Aeldra again, her hand rising behind the tapestry to grab it higher up. She gave her an expressive look, then stepped farther out from behind the tapestry even as Aeldra caught what she meant to do, raised her own hand, and slid out from the other side.

Blake was about to repeat his order for the Scot to show himself when he suddenly did just that. Or, *she* did, he realized with dismay, taking in the ice blue eyes and obviously womanly features. Movement from the other side of the tapestry drew his attention, and he peered at the petite woman slipping out from the other side. Short, blond, shapely, and pretty. Blake was just turning his eyes back to the taller woman when Rolfe suddenly let out a gasp of dismay behind him.

Blake glanced away to see the alarm on the other man's face, then turned quickly back, but it was too late. As they moved out to the sides, both the small female and the taller one had grasped hold of the tapestry and jerked it forward. The heavy rug was even now pulling away from its position on the wall and crashing down atop them. Blake barely managed a step to the side as the tapestry fell. It was not enough to save him completely and the heavy ornament caught his shoulder, sending him tumbling to the ground.

As soon as the tapestry came loose from the wall and began to flap out over the men, Seonaid yelled to Aeldra and raced toward the door, intent on escape. An enraged shout from her cousin made her whirl around, dismay on her face as she saw the tapestry had not come down to cover all of the men. One, a mountain of a man, had been a step or two behind the bishop, guarding the other men's backs, and had entirely escaped the dusty old tapestry entangling the others. He had also managed to catch Aeldra as she raced past him and stood holding her off the ground from behind, his arms around her waist, seemingly impervious to her scratching fingernails as she clawed at him and kicked her feet furiously. She was caught.

Cursing, Seonaid glanced briefly around for something to help her cousin with, but she couldn't find anything appropriate. Giving up the search as Aeldra screeched again, this time in warning, she glanced around to see that the man in the plaid had made his way out from beneath the tapestry and was moving toward her.

Seonaid grabbed up a pew and hurled it at him just as the chapel door opened and Lady Helen and Sister Blanche hurried in. Excitement and victory were on their faces as they entered, but dismay soon followed as they spied the chaos they had walked in on. Not bothering to explain what should have been obvious, Seonaid grabbed up both swords as the women held them out and ordered them to get out of the room before turning back to confront the fellow in the plaid.

Blake slowed his forward impetus as he spied the two blades with which he was faced. Surprise was his first reaction. She held the blades as if she were comfortable with them, which drew his attention to the fact that they were smaller than the average sword and of lighter weight. They had obviously been made specifically for the woman before him and the one giving Little George such a rough time.

"Hold," Blake said as the pieces fell together. He had first assumed the Scot in the chapel a man, and no doubt the one who had broken into the abbey, but now that he knew she was a woman and one who exactly fit Rolfe's description of his betrothed, Blake began to realize he faced none other than Seonaid Dunbar. She fit the description far too well to be anyone but her. Ice blue eyes, glorious blue-black hair, well-formed. Aye, he was finally confronting his betrothed. And she was wearing braies.

"I mean ye no harm," he murmured once he had her attention.

"Nor I you," she answered sweetly, then lifted one of the swords and had at him.

The viciousness of her attack took Blake by surprise, and at first he was kept busy fending off her blows. By the time he recognized that she was directing the battle so that they shifted position, the two of them had already turned enough that she was approaching the spot where Little George and her friend struggled. Before Blake could do anything about it, she had closed the last of the distance between herself and his first and had kicked out to the side with her right foot. Blake winced as her foot connected viciously with Little George's left leg.

The giant grunted in pain and released the woman he held, reaching instinctively to brace himself as he tumbled toward the floor of the chapel. The petite woman threw herself to the side to avoid being crushed by his weight, but was on her feet and at the dark-haired woman's side in a flash, reaching for the smaller second sword to arm herself.

"What goes on here?"

Sister Blanche and Lady Helen straightened guiltily

from their bent positions before the door of the chapel. They had listened to Seonaid's order but hadn't fully obeyed. They had gone so far as to leave the chapel, but it was as far as either of them had been willing to go. Pausing in the hall, they had cracked the door open and watched the commotion within as Lady Seonaid and her cousin faced off against the plaid-clad man inside. Now Blanche and Helen whirled to face the abbess as she strode down the hallway toward them, the skirts of her dark gown flowing out behind her.

"Mother!" Sister Blanche peered at the woman in dismay, then glanced guiltily toward the door to the chapel before straightening her shoulders. "Scots have infiltrated the abbey. Lady Seonaid and Lady Aeldra are fending them off."

"What!" The abbess stared at her askance. "It was the English you were to let in, not the Scots. My God, Blanche, what have you done?"

"What indeed," Lady Helen muttered bitterly. "Just opened the door under your direction to allow men to have at the women who sought protection within these sacred walls."

Lady Elizabeth stiffened at the accusation, sending an accusing glare toward Sister Blanche. She then strode stiffly to the door and threw it open, surveying the battle taking place in the heart of her abbey as Little George found his feet and joined Blake to face the armed women.

"What goes on here? This is a house of God! Would you battle here as if 'twere a tavern?"

Seonaid froze at the harsh shriek, as did the other

combatants. Still facing the two men squared off against them, she cast a quick frown toward the abbess, her disdain obvious. "Open the door to the devil and he's like to walk in," she snapped impatiently. "Ye ordered the door unbarred; do not now cry foul because the wrong suitor entered and we now defend Lady Helen from the man who would murder her."

The abbess glanced sharply toward the two armed men, her gaze quickly taking in the fairer, smaller man's Scottish garb and the larger man's English clothes. She also noted the confusion on the men's faces as they took in Lady Seonaid's words. "How know you they are Camerons? One wears English dress."

Seonaid glanced toward the larger man, for the first time taking in the English clothes he wore. She had neglected to note that fact while in the heat of battle.

"And one wears the plaid," she pointed out, then sneered at the woman standing so self-righteous in the door of the chapel. "Howbeit, mayhap yer right. While I never would have thought to see a Sassenach in Scottish garb, I also never would have thought to see an abbess who cared so little for her God and her charges, she would be willin' to throw them to the wolves as ye've done."

Lady Elizabeth turned bright red, then suddenly paled as her eyes strayed past her to the room at large. Curious about her reaction, Seonaid turned to find the other men had struggled out from beneath the tapestry and were straightening their clothes. Her eyes widened. She immediately recognized the bishop and Lord Rolfe, though she had never before seen the prelate wearing the expression of mingled distaste and fury with which he was eyeing Lady Elizabeth.

"Bishop—" the abbess began faintly, but the bishop cut her off.

"I heard it all, madam, every word as I struggled to get out from beneath that accursed tapestry. Do not further your sins by spouting lies at me now."

"But I . . ."

"Unbarred the gate so all and sundry may enter?" he finished when her voice faded helplessly away.

"Nay!" she cried at once, reclaiming her wits enough to try to defend herself. " 'Twas Sister Blanche who unbarred the gate."

"At your order," Seonaid stated, unwilling to see the woman escape her fault by pushing it onto another. Resheathing her sword, she turned to glance at the bishop. "Sister Blanche didna wish to unbar the gate but couldna refuse a direct order. She did it only because Lady Elizabeth threatened to return her to England in shame did she no do as she was told. She came to warn us as soon as the deed was done."

The bishop nodded his head in silent understanding. "Sister Blanche has naught to fear; she will not be the one returning to England in shame."

No one mistook the meaning behind his words, least of all Lady Elizabeth, who gasped as she hurried forward to fall on her knees before the prelate.

Seonaid grimaced at the undignified display, then glanced at Lord Rolfe before turning to peer at the two other men. Both of them had resheathed their own swords, though they remained tense and alert. It did not require much effort to work out who the man in plaid was. Her betrothed. Who else would be traveling with Lord Rolfe? Besides, Lady Helen's description of the man had been most apt. Fair-haired and handsome as an angel, or some such rot. He was all of those things and more. A fine specimen of a man. With excellent knees, she noted again, then frowned at her own wayward thoughts. He was the man who had neglected to collect her for so long, the man who had made it obvious he had no interest in marrying her. It took an order from the king to bring him to her, and she wanted no such man, especially an Englishman. Especially a Sherwell.

Besides, even had she been able to overlook everything else, there was no way to avoid the fact that he would no doubt find her sorely lacking as a wife. It took only one look at his handsome visage to realize it. Her betrothed was heavenly, perfect, and no doubt used to heavenly, perfect women. Seonaid suffered no delusions regarding herself. She was too tall, too thin, too unfeminine both in manner and in knowledge to even manage being average. She knew naught about being a lady and doubted she could even pass herself off as a true woman. She'd spent too many years in the company of only men. Men and Aeldra—but then, Aeldra was as lacking in the softer refinements of a lady as herself.

Nay, she thought sadly, he would not want her . . . and she had no desire to hear him say so. While she might lack the finer requirements of a lady, she had more than her fair share of pride, and her pride was unwilling to wait about and hear his refusal. Gesturing for

Aeldra to follow, she turned her back on the man and strode toward the door of the church, then paused to swipe up her plaid. She picked up Aeldra's as well and tossed it to her, then started forward again, only to pause when fingers closed around her upper arm.

"Where do you think you are going?"

Chapter Four

Seonaid paused in her steps, eyes snapping as she glared at the hand on her arm. She had known the moment she'd felt his touch who stopped her, even before she heard the smooth velvet of his voice with its clipped English accent.

"Unhand me or I shall unhand you," she commanded. Her lips curled up with satisfaction when he released her at once, though a glance at his face showed only surprised amusement and no fear. When he bowed to her with mock civility, Seonaid found the gesture most irritating.

"Forgive me, my lady. 'Tis poorly done of me to touch you without at least first introducing myself. Lord Blake Sherwell at your service." The introduction was followed by another of the mocking bows.

Seonaid shifted, her expression darkening before she

forced a sickly sweet smile to her lips. "Am I supposed to ken the name, m'laird?" she asked at last. "Should it mean aught to me?"

Blake blinked in surprise, some of his self-confidence slipping. "What? Do you not recognize the name of your betrothed when you hear it?"

Her eyes widened. "Surely ye jest, sirrah? My betrothed died ages ago, at least ten years ago by my count."

Now he truly looked dismayed. "Died? Who the devil told you such nonsense?"

"Told me? Why no one, m'laird. I reasoned it out fer mesel' when he didna arrive to claim me . . . *ten years ago when I came of age.*"

The man had the grace to color at her words, though he regained himself and his quick smile swiftly enough. "I fear your reasoning was wrong. Tardy I may be, but I am certainly not dead."

"Nay. I fear ye're wrong an' me reasonin' was right," Seonaid retorted. "Me betrothed is dead. To me," she added harshly, then turned away and continued out of the chapel.

Blake stared after the woman in amazement. No female had ever dared to speak to him so, nor had any woman yet turned her back on him and walked away. Good God! Women were more like to sigh and swoon in his presence than to show him their back. He did not know what to do about it. Part of him wanted to order her to return to him at once. He had every right, she was his betrothed, and within a short time she would be his wife and under his order. Yet another part reasoned that he did not wish to marry her anyway. Why not let her walk off and hide herself in the abbey somewhere, refusing him? It would set him free.

Oddly enough, Blake quite suddenly no longer wished to be free, at least not this way. He was the one who was supposed to be reluctant to marry her, yet here he was, hesitant about angering the king and his father and unwilling to break the contract and give up rich lands. His would-be bride appeared not to suffer the same concerns. Losing her betrothal lands didn't seem to worry her. Impossible. He was the Angel; she should have been grateful he had come to claim her, no matter his tardiness. He was here, was he not? Who the devil was she to refuse him? A bloody Dunbar.

"All does not go well, I see," Rolph murmured behind Blake as Lady Seonaid slammed out of the chapel.

"All does not go well?" Blake turned on him irately. "Well! She is . . . she is a barbarian. My God, she is wearing braies! And just look at the way she had at me with her sword!" Gaze narrowing, he glared at him. "Did you know she was trained in battle?"

Rolfe shifted uncomfortably. " 'Tis a valuable skill here in the Highlands, where—"

"She is an Amazon!" Blake interrupted. "God's toes! She is near to as tall as myself."

"Aye, she is quite statuesque," Rolfe began soothingly, only to be interrupted once again.

"She is also as flat as a door. Where are her breasts? And what is she doing in a man's braies? I swear I thought her a man when I first saw her." Frowning, he shook his head, saying aloud what he had thought but moments before. "She should be grateful I even bothered to follow her here, yet she insults me and walks away. Who the devil does she think she is?"

Sighing, Rolfe shook his head for answer and returned to the bishop to see what he intended to do with Lady Elizabeth.

"Lady Helen, please doona take on so." Seonaid tried for a soft tone but feared she sounded more annoyed than anything. She was uncomfortable with strong emotion, and there was no other description for what Helen was presently exhibiting. The Englishwoman wasn't exactly sobbing, and she did try to staunch them, but tears continued to flow down her cheeks in silent testimony to her exhaustion and fear. The worst part was, Seonaid could not blame her. The lass had done nothing but run and hide and suffer the fear of capture for days, and now, when she had thought she'd found a safe haven until her father could come to her, she had been shown the error of such a belief.

"Cameron will find me here. I knew he would eventually. I even left a trail for him to do so, thinking I would be safe within these walls. But I will not be safe. Lady Elizabeth will let him in and he will force me to leave with him. If so, I shall be dead."

Seonaid frowned as she paced the small cell she had occupied since arriving at the abbey. They were all there: Aeldra, Lady Helen, and a rather glum-faced Sister Blanche. Seonaid and Aeldra had come across the other two women outside the chapel and led them here.

"Did ye no hear the bishop? He as good as said Lady Elizabeth'll be sent away. She'll no be in a position to allow anyone into the abbey."

"Aye, he says that now. Howbeit Lady Elizabeth is clever; I could tell that during our interview when I first arrived. I think she would promise him anything to avoid such shame. What if she offers something he cannot refuse? What if he changes his mind and lets her stay? Then she may grow tired of my presence as well and allow the Camerons in. I fear I angered her when she came upon us in the hall. I was most rude and she will most like be happy to hand me over to the Camerons when they come."

Seonaid's frown deepened, but she shook her head. "He will send her away. He's a good man an' she has nothin' to use to convince him to let her stay."

"She has you." When Seonaid stiffened, Helen nodded grimly. "They are here to return you to Dunbar. By rights, they should not even have been allowed to step over the threshold, but the damage has been done. She may agree to turn her head the other way while they steal you out of here in return for being allowed to stay."

Seonaid glanced sharply toward Sister Blanche. The good sister appeared worried. Her doubts made Seonaid decidedly uncomfortable. "Bishop Wykeham's a good man; honest an' gentle an' . . . good," she finished lamely, then shook her head. "He'd no stoop to such to remove me."

"He's under order of the king to see the marriage

done," Aeldra reminded her. "An' yer father signed the marriage contract. It's no as if he'd be stealin' ye to kill ye. His conscience may be salved by that."

Seonaid turned away with a curse, her gaze going absently out of the window in the small cell as she tried to think. The other women were silent as they waited. When she whirled suddenly back, only Aeldra did not start in surprise.

"Helen, go to yer room an' gather yer things."

"Why?" the redhead asked hopefully.

"We leave here at once."

"But your betrothed and the others—"

"They'll be busy fer a bit dealin' with Lady Elizabeth, I think. Long enough at least fer us to make our escape. Aeldra an' I'll see ye safely home, then seek shelter elsewhere." She paused, her gaze running over the flowing nun's gown. "Ye should keep that on in case we come across the Cameron along our way. Hopefully it'll fool him." Her gaze shifted to Sister Blanche. "Ye may come with us if ye wish. If Lady Elizabeth convinces them to let her stay, she'll make it difficult fer ye here."

Sister Blanche hesitated, then shook her head. "Nay. I will stay, but I shall help you to escape. I shall fetch some provisions from the kitchens."

"We'll be in the stables," Seonaid told her as the other woman slipped from the room. A glance back and a nod were enough to tell her she'd heard.

Seonaid turned back to the two remaining women. "Quickly, Aeldra, go help Helen gather her belongings. I'll go to the stables to saddle the beasties." She started

toward the door even as she spoke, only to be brought
up short by Helen's words.

"I have no belongings." When Seonaid turned to
peer at her in surprise, she shrugged slightly. "I sent
everything with my maid so I might travel faster."

Seonaid's eyebrows rose, then turned down in disbelief. She had yet to know a woman besides Aeldra and
herself who did not carry about at least two or three
trunks with her. "Ye brought nothin' at all with ye?"

Helen shrugged. "Just one sack, but I left it in the stables last night. I brought no clothes or anything else."

"Incredible," Seonaid marveled. "Well, lucky us, a
woman with some wit. We'll travel like the wind. Come
along."

"Did you not bring any belongings with you?" Helen
asked in hushed tones as they eased cautiously out into
the hall.

"Only what we always carry with us," Seonaid heard
Aeldra answer quietly from behind. "Our plaids an' our
steel, 'tis all we need to travel."

"Oh. I see," Lady Helen murmured doubtfully as they
moved stealthily down the hall.

"Is he not finished yet?"

Rolfe glanced up at Blake's question and shook his
head on a sigh. "He feels he must interview each of the
nuns here 'ere he decides what to do about the abbess."

"Each of the nuns?" Blake asked with dismay. "Do you
mean to say he intends to interview *every single one* of the
nuns in this blessed place before making a decision?"

"He can hardly banish her without a fair hearing."

Blake grimaced and began to pace the room again, his mind in an uproar. He wanted out of this place; he had never been in an abbey before and much to his surprise he wasn't enjoying the experience. Blake loved women, all women, in every shape and size. Well, almost all, he thought, as the most annoying image of Seonaid Dunbar came to mind. Still, a building inhabited by at least a hundred women was almost a dream to a man like himself, or at least he would have thought so. Howbeit, it seemed he had been wrong. He'd never been so uncomfortable in a place in all his born days. These women were all so pious, so pure-looking, he felt like a wolf let loose among the sheep. A wolf with a conscience.

Amazing, he thought on a sigh. He'd seen very little evidence of a conscience in himself in this life when it came to women. If they were willing, he usually saw no reason to deny them the pleasure of his attentions. After all, were it not him, it would be someone else enjoying their offerings. At the moment, however, he was almost afraid to look at the women moving about around him. They were God's brides after all. 'Twas one thing to cuckold a man, quite another to try some such thing on God.

Seonaid managed to lead the other two women out to the stables undetected. All three of them worked at saddling and preparing the horses, accomplishing the task just as Sister Blanche returned with a sack of provisions.

"I fetched as much as I could, which is more than I expected, since the kitchen was empty."

Seonaid's eyebrows rose as she accepted the food. "Empty? The kitchen's never empty."

"Rarely," Sister Blanche agreed. "Howbeit, the bishop is questioning all the nuns, servants, and lay sisters. He is taking an accounting of the abbess's behavior. I think he may actually dismiss her."

Seonaid and Aeldra shared a glance, then Seonaid sighed. "We canna take the chance."

"Nay," Aeldra agreed, leading her horse and Helen's out of their stalls as Seonaid hooked the sack to her saddle.

Sister Blanche followed as they led their horses out of the stables, worry plain on her face as she said, "You must be most careful. Never forget Cameron is out there somewhere."

"We'll be fine," Seonaid assured her with a smile, then mounted her horse as Helen hurried forward to hug the woman.

"Thank you, Sister. For everything."

Nodding unhappily, Sister Blanche hugged Helen back, then stepped out of the way as the woman mounted her own mare.

"I will try to hide the fact that you have gone."

"Thank you, Sister, but doona do anything that'll see ye in trouble. We'll send ye word when Helen's safely home."

Sister Blanche watched them urge their horses through the gate and race toward the trees. She was a forlorn figure in Helen's gown, with the white cloth over her shorn head. She waited until they had disappeared within the woods before turning and moving sadly back through the abbey gate to find out her fate.

Either she or Lady Elizabeth would be banished by day's end, and neither fate cheered her much. Sister Blanche had a kind heart, and despite Lady Elizabeth's condescending air and shabby treatment of the nuns, it saddened her to imagine the other woman's shame. It might also be better were she herself to return to her home in such a circumstance than Lady Elizabeth. While her own family loved her and would show great understanding of the situation, she was not so sure Lady Elizabeth could make the same claim. There must be some reason she could be so coldhearted.

Blanche's thoughts came to a stumbling halt as she found herself colliding with a large male body. Glancing up in surprise, she gaped at the warrior before her, then took a quick, nervous step back. "My lord."

"You must be Lady Helen." When Sister Blanche's eyes widened, Lord Rolfe smiled slightly.

Sister Blanche stared at him wide-eyed. She still wore Lady Helen's clothes, which explained the confusion.

"Ahem." The bishop cleared his throat, drawing her attention to the fact that Lord Rolfe was not alone. "We were just searching for Sister Blanche. You would not know where we might find her?"

Sister Blanche glanced quickly over the array of men before her. The bishop, Lord Rolfe, Lord Blake, the large one she had heard them call Little George, and at least a dozen other men stood there, all waiting expectantly. Having spent most of her life in a nunnery, Blanche was not used to being the center of attention of so many men. Swallowing nervously and feeling herself flush, she shook her head helplessly and took another nervous step backward.

Lord Rolfe's gaze narrowed slightly. "Where were you coming from?"

The alarm on her face was telling. Frowning, Rolfe glanced past her, his gaze going first to the gate, then to the stable entry not far away. Without a word, he moved past her toward the stables.

Biting her lip, Sister Blanche watched with some distress as he entered the stables.

Blake watched curiously too, then glanced toward the bishop as he spoke.

"It really is necessary we find Sister Blanche. After speaking with Lady Elizabeth and the others, it has been decided it might be best if Lady Elizabeth resigns her position. She is preparing to leave. I would like Sister Blanche to take her place until another abbess can be found. If another is needed. The rest of the nuns seem to think this Sister Blanche would fill the position quite satisfactorily."

Blanche forgot about Lord Rolfe, her mind filled with wonder. "Truly?" she asked breathlessly.

"Aye." The bishop frowned slightly and glanced briefly around the garden. "I should like to tell her of my decision and speak with her myself."

"Oh, of course, I—" Her words were cut off by a sudden shout from behind her. Recalling Lord Rolfe's foray into the stable, she whirled to peer at the man as he hurried toward them.

"I think they have fled," he announced grimly, coming to a halt beside Sister Blanche and facing the other men.

"Who?" the bishop asked with dismay.

"Lady Seonaid and Aeldra. There are at least two horses missing from the stables. Mayhap three."

Every gaze turned on Sister Blanche, and she felt the position as abbess slipping from her grasp. For a moment she struggled with herself, ambition and what was right battling within her. Then she straightened her shoulders, faced them grimly, and did as her conscience bade; she lied to save the women who had sought shelter and been betrayed. "They were my horses. I sold them to one of the lords from a neighboring estate. He just left after collecting them."

"You are a poor liar, Lady Helen," Lord Rolfe told her gently. "But the fact that you bothered to lie tells as much as the truth would have." His gaze turned to Blake and he smiled widely. "It appears we shall not be forced to try to talk your errant betrothed into leaving the abbey. She has flown the cavie again."

Far from looking pleased, Lord Blake grimaced at the news and muttered under his breath as he moved toward the gate. Little George and the rest of the men followed.

Sister Blanche was desperately searching her mind for some way to detain them when the bishop suddenly paused at the gate and turned back, his expression distressed. "Pray, find Sister Blanche and explain what I told you, Lady Helen. If she can see her way clear to running the abbey until an alternative arrangement is decided, it would be appreciated. I shall return as soon as I am able to assure all is well."

The man whirled and followed the others as his

words sank slowly into her stunned mind. Only the click as the gate closed, reminded her that the men were leaving to seek the three women. Giving a little gasp of dismay, Blanche rushed forward, running to the gate and tugging it open. It was too late. The men had mounted their horses and were already riding off. The only thing that kept her from calling after them was the direction they had taken. The men were headed the wrong way. Sister Blanche's anxiety immediately gave way to a slow, relieved smile, and she slipped back inside, then pushed the gate closed.

"Thank you, God," she murmured as she slid the bar back into place. "You are truly most wondrous and merciful."

"Where are we heading?" Helen had been wanting to ask the question for the past several hours but had convinced herself Lady Seonaid and her cousin knew what they were doing. But at last she could not ignore her instincts any longer. All the signs seemed to indicate they were heading east, rather than south toward her home. Seonaid's answer made her heart sink in dismay.

"Fer the moment, east."

"East? But my home is in England. In the south."

"Aye, but that's also where Cameron'll expect ye to head," Seonaid reasoned calmly.

"But what is in the east?" she asked at last.

"Dundee."

Helen raised her brows. "And what is at Dundee?"

"Nothin'."

"Nothing?" She gaped at her. "Well, if there is nothing there, why—?"

Sighing, Seonaid drew her horse to a halt and turned to peer at the woman. "We're bein' pursued by two groups of men, are we no?"

"Well, as to that, who can say?" Helen murmured. "Cameron may or may not be on our trail, and as for Lord Blake, he may still be at the abbey."

"'Tis doubtful Sherwell is still at the abbey. Even if Sister Blanche manages to keep our absence secret, a mere glance into the stables will tell him that we've fled."

When Helen's eyes widened in realization, Seonaid continued. "As fer Cameron, he may not be on our trail yet, but he's certainly seekin' ye. Now," she began with the attitude of someone teaching a lesson, "should Cameron trail ye to the abbey an' find ye've fled, he'll expect ye to flee south, straight fer England, and no doubt by the most direct route, like a fox seekin' its hole. Blake, if he kens yer quandary from Sister Blanche and that we intend to see ye home, will expect us to take the same route. If he doesna find out about ye, he'll most like expect us to head west, toward me father's castle, or possibly north, where I've some relatives who might be of assistance, and where there's another abbey, one without Lady Elizabeth. Neither of them have any reason to think we might go east, hence, we'll go east toward the coast, then follow the coast southward to England."

Lady Helen smiled suddenly. "That is very clever."

Seonaid smiled slightly at the praise, then turned to urge her horse into a trot again.

"Anything?"

Little George peered up from the area he was surveying to meet Blake's gaze and shake his head.

"Damn." Blake sank back on his saddle with a frown. "I do not understand it. We have ridden hard for several miles. We should have overtaken them, or at least have seen some sign of them by now."

"Mayhap they did not head this way," Rolfe suggested with a frown.

"Where else would they go?" Blake muttered.

"There is another abbey farther north," the bishop suggested when everyone else remained silent.

When Blake glanced at him hopefully, Rolfe frowned. "You do not think she left one abbey for another?"

" 'Tis more likely than that she returned home."

"She's gone east!"

They all whirled around at that shout to find the speaker was a mounted Scot on the trail behind them. Alarmed by not having heard his approach, the men-at-arms whirled furiously, drawing swords as they faced the man. A shout from Lord Rolfe made them still where they sat, but every man retained his grasp on his sword as Rolfe urged his own mount through theirs to face the sandy-haired Scot.

The man had not reacted to the threat of all those swords being drawn, but sat his horse with a slightly amused expression on his face, calmly meeting Rolfe's gaze as he stopped his mount several feet away.

"Who the deuce are you?"

"Gavin. The Dunbar sent me to follow ye to be sure Sherwell didna get himsel' killed 'ere catchin' up with Seonaid." He waited just long enough for the insult behind the words to sink in, then grinned widely and announced, "Yer goin' the wrong way. The lass an' the other two headed east on leavin' the abbey."

Rolfe sensed rather than heard Blake's shifting impatiently in his saddle and could sympathize. He himself was a bit annoyed at the insult but managed to keep the irritation from his expression as he asked, "The other two?"

The Scot nodded. "Aeldra an' a nun were with her. They headed east. I started to follow, but recalled 'twas Sherwell I was to be tendin' to an' turned back to the abbey to be sure ye followed. Ye must have left 'ere I returned, fer yer horses were gone when I arrived back. I asked at the abbey an' was told ye'd gone south. I headed in that direction, but it took little time to realize ye hadna gone that way, then I backtracked an' checked the road. I soon saw ye'd headed back for Dunbar. So I hurried after ye. Yer headin' the wrong way."

"Who told you we had headed south?" Blake asked, urging his mount up next to Rolfe's.

The Scot shrugged. "A lady. I doona ken who she was, but she werena dressed like a nun."

"Lady Helen. She most likely lied to protect the women," Rolfe murmured, then sighed and considered the man's words. "Why would Lady Seonaid head east?"

The Scot shrugged. "Most like she headed the way ye'd least think she'd go. She's a smart lass."

The men glanced at each other.

"Do you believe him?" Blake asked.

Rolfe shrugged. "I do not suppose there is any reason for him to lie."

"Nay."

" 'Sides, we had already decided she did not head this way."

"Aye."

"I suppose we shall have to head east and find out."

"Aye." Blake sighed, and wondered why he did not simply turn and ride for home. Surely that was within his rights? A groom was not generally expected to chase his betrothed all over the country just to marry her. On the other hand, he did not wish to explain his thinking to the king. He would head east. He urged his horse to follow Lord Rolfe and the bishop as they rode toward the waiting Scot.

"Is it Cameron?"

Seonaid glanced sharply at Aeldra when she asked the question, then supposed she should not have been surprised that her cousin had also realized they were being followed. Seonaid herself had sensed they had company even as they had ridden out of the abbey. She'd thought then that it must be Cameron, and had hoped that after following them for a while, the fact that they were headed east rather than south—not to mention Helen's disguise—would fool him and make him turn back to wait outside the abbey. He had not turned, though, but had continued to follow them for the entire day and now into the night.

"I doona ken," she admitted on a sigh. "If 'tis, then he wasna fooled by Helen's dress."

Aeldra grunted her agreement as Helen wearily urged her horse up between them.

"Will we stop for the night soon?" the Englishwoman asked hopefully. "I am fair sore from being on horseback."

Seonaid remained silent for a moment, considering their options. They could not continue to ride the horses indefinitely; the beasts were already showing signs of tiring and she disliked riding them too hard. On the other hand, if 'twas Cameron following, he would make himself known once they stopped. At least he would not catch them unawares. In fact, she and Aeldra just might take him by surprise. Doubtless he would not expect much of a fight from three lone women.

"Aye. There's a clearin' jest ahead. We'll stop there," she decided aloud, then glanced toward Aeldra. "Be ready."

Ignoring Helen's confused expression, the two women nodded at each other solemnly.

" 'Tis lovely," Helen murmured as they slid from their horses moments later and peered around the small clearing.

"Magnificent," Seonaid agreed, her gaze running over the area with satisfaction. One side was taken up with a small rock cliff, another by the river running along the clearing. That left only two sides for attackers to approach from. It would be easier to defend, especially if they blocked off one other side with the horses. She did not like doing so, since it placed the animals at risk of being injured. But she had no idea how large a party Cameron had with him, or just how much danger they were in.

"We'll settle here for the night," she announced, unhooking the satchel of food from her horse's back and handing it to Helen. Nodding, the other woman moved at once toward the spot she indicated and began digging through the contents of the bag. Seonaid and Aeldra saw to the horses, leaving their saddles on in case they had need of a speedy escape, and settled them where they made a third barrier against their would-be attackers. The women washed their hands in the river and sat to eat, their eyes and ears alert to any sound or sight that might warn them of an oncoming attack.

Once they had finished eating, they all stretched out to rest. Or at least Helen did. Seonaid and Aeldra insisted she sleep with her back snug against the cliff, then lay down before her, situating themselves between the woman and the world at large. But they had no intention of sleeping. They were waiting for the attack they were sure would come, now that they appeared at rest and vulnerable.

Chapter Five

"Wake up, sleepy heads."

Seonaid came awake with a start at Helen's call, her body and mind immediately alert. Sitting up, she glanced sharply around and spotted the Englishwoman approaching from the river. Seonaid gaped. Morning had dawned, there had been no attack, and she'd fallen asleep. Worse yet, so had Aeldra, she saw with dismay, as the other woman sat up beside her and frowned around the clearing.

"How the devil did ye slip by us?"

Helen's brows rose at the question. "I stepped over you. You were sleeping so soundly, I did not wish to wake you."

"Ye stepped o'er us?" Seonaid asked with disbelief, then glanced toward Aeldra. "She stepped o'er us."

"A fat lot of good we would have been had we been attacked," Aeldra muttered, getting to her feet. "Why didn't they attack?"

"Who?" Helen asked wide-eyed as she reached them.

"I'd be thinkin' she means us."

All three women whirled toward the deep baritone voice. Seonaid and Aeldra both grabbed for their swords, but they sagged and sighed when they saw who it was.

"Gavin!" Seonaid snapped as she set her sword back down. "What're ye doin' here?"

"Makin' sure the Sassenach doesna get hissel' killed."

Her eyes narrowed. "Is he with ye?"

For answer, Lord Blake stepped out of the trees and into view. Seonaid shook her head with disgust. "Ye could have let yer presence be known last night. Then we wouldna have had to stay awake the night through thinkin' we were about to be attacked."

"It looked to me as if ye slept jest fine," Gavin commented with amusement. "An' so ye should have; ye were watched ower throughout the night."

"Not the whole night," Lord Rolfe corrected, joining the other two men. "We only arrived a couple of hours ago. We stuck to the woods to avoid disturbing your rest."

Seonaid frowned, her gaze moving to Aeldra. The other woman appeared just as worried. They were both convinced someone had trailed them all day. They had felt that presence as they had settled down here for the night. Yet Lord Rolfe claimed the men had arrived only hours earlier.

"Why are you looking so worried?" Blake's question drew Seonaid's gaze back to her betrothed. He did not look overly pleased to have found her. Truth to tell, he looked about as cranky as she felt on the little sleep she'd had. Not that she'd expected anything else, but still it rubbed her pride the wrong way.

Gavin saved her from having to comment by giving a harsh laugh. " 'Cause she kens we're no' the only beasties in these woods."

Before either Englishman could ask what he meant, the Scot pursed his lips and released a piercing whistle. Seconds later the bushes on either side of the men rustled as two Scots slid out into the open. Both of them were from Dunbar. Gavin nodded, then explained, "I left them to trail Seonaid an' Aeldra while I returned to fetch ye."

Seonaid glared at her father's soldier as he made the admission, knowing now who to blame for her betrothed finding her. Turning, she fixed another glare on the Englishman. "What do ye want?"

"What do you think?" he snapped back.

"I think ye want to go home an' forget ye ever heard me name," she admitted. "An' since that's what I'm wantin' as well, why don't ye do it?"

Blake blinked at her surly words in confusion. "What?"

"Ye heard me. I don't want to marry you an' you don't want to marry me, so go home an' leave me be."

Blake gaped at her in astonishment. Her mettle amazed him. The women he knew, and he knew a lot of them, did not often speak so bluntly. They would have mewed and sighed and hinted, but would never have said something so unpleasant straight out. He couldn't believe she'd done it. And had he heard her correctly? Many women had begged Blake to marry them, and still others had threatened to kill themselves for love of him. He supposed in his mind he'd imagined the chit—if he'd ever thought of her at all—pining away the years, wondering when he would come to claim her and praying nightly to God that he should. This was not wholly because of the way women threw themselves at him; it was also because a life of spinsterhood could be so unpleasant. Yet here she claimed to desire nothing more than to be left to that sad state. It must be an act, he decided, and actually smiled at the realization. Women often played games to attract his attention, and—Amazon or not—Seonaid Dunbar was still a woman. Relaxing as he regained some of his confidence, Blake tossed her a charming smile, "Careful, my lady; one would almost think you were not pleased to see me."

"One would think correctly."

Blake's gaze narrowed. "If you expect me to believe you have not been pining away these last ten years—"

"Pinin'?" Seonaid interrupted with a harsh laugh. "Do I look the sort to pine? No, indeed, m'laird, I've been quite enjoyin' my freedom . . . in many an' diverse ways."

Blake's eyes widened, then his face flushed angrily at the suggestion behind her words. "You—"

"Enough," Lord Rolfe interrupted sharply. "We have

wasted enough time. Let us head back to Dunbar and see the deed done."

"Go ahead," Seonaid muttered, turning toward the horses. "Aeldra an' I'll meet ye there after we go to England."

"England!" Rolfe and Blake echoed the word as one.

"Aye, England," Seonaid said firmly. "We promised." She gestured toward Lady Helen, taking in the nun's habit with new eyes. "We promised the sister we'd see her home to England. She wishes to visit her family. We promised we'd see her safely there." She turned to peer at them sweetly. "Ye'd not wish us to break our word to a woman of God, would ye?"

Blake frowned at his betrothed, suspecting her sweet smile and the veracity behind her words. Rolfe's interruption, however, caught his attention.

"That is impossible. It would prolong the ordeal by at least another week, perhaps two."

As Blake absorbed the truth of his words, Seonaid turned on him bitterly. "What do ye propose? Shall we just leave her here in the woods to make her way alone, unattended?"

"Nay, of course not," Blake murmured, suddenly cheerful. "We shall have to see her home." When Rolfe turned on him with dismay, he shrugged. "Well, she gave her word, and as my betrothed, her word is my word. And a promise is a promise. We can hardly force her to break her word." When Rolfe continued to glare at him, too angry to speak, Blake shifted uncomfortably and turned back to Seonaid more sternly. "We shall see her home as you promised, howbeit that is all I will agree to."

Seonaid relaxed and even smiled at him. " 'Tis all I ask, m'laird."

Blake blinked. She really had a charming smile. Quite charming. Why had he not noticed that before? Because she hadn't smiled at him before.

"Nay."

All of them turned toward the bishop as he stepped out of the bushes to join the growing group.

"Forgive an old man for interrupting, but it would seem to me a detour to England would serve little purpose and merely delay a wedding that has been delayed far too long already. We shall hie to Dunbar."

"But what about the sister?" Seonaid asked with a sinking heart, seeing all chance for delaying the wedding slipping away.

"There is a simple resolution," he said soothingly, then turned to Helen. "Sister . . . ?"

"Helen," the woman squeaked.

The bishop nodded solemnly. "Sister Helen, you may travel with us to Dunbar to attend the wedding if you wish. Lord Rolfe and I shall be traveling back to England then, and we would be pleased to escort you on your visit. Or," he added, when Seonaid made to protest, "or we can surely spare three men to escort you now. We presently have three more men than we started out with anyway, thanks to Lord Angus." He nodded pleasantly toward Gavin and his two men as he spoke, then raised his eyebrows and took a listening attitude as he awaited Helen's decision.

For her part, Lady Helen looked rather confused. Turning, she peered uncertainly at Seonaid, then back to the bishop before blurting, "I shall attend the wedding."

"Good, then we shall head for Dunbar." The bishop smiled graciously, then turned and moved back through the trees until they enveloped him, presumably to return to the camp the men had inhabited during the wee hours of the morning.

Blake peered unhappily from the bishop's disappearing back to his would-be bride and sighed, then shook his head and turned to order Little George to bring their horses into the clearing. Rolfe moved to his side.

"We should disarm them," the king's man murmured, considering the women as they prepared their mounts.

Blake raised his brows. "Do you think they would use their swords against us?"

"They already have."

"That was at the abbey, and they knew not who we were then. They did not try to fight their way out of the clearing," Blake pointed out, his gaze slipping over Seonaid's body. While he had, at first, been shocked at the sight of her in braies, he was beginning to appreciate the way the outfit outlined her slender curves and—

"Aye," Rolfe said, interrupting his thoughts. "But they will be less likely to try to escape do they not have their swords."

His words brought a frown to Blake's lips. It still rankled to think his betrothed might actually not wish to marry him. *He* was the one who should, and had, been reluctant to marry *her*, one of the dreaded Dunbars. She should be grateful he had even shown up, no matter how late in the day. Yet she appeared less than eager to be his bride. Fascinating, he decided, then realized she had yet to experience any of the sweet words that normally dripped from his honeyed tongue in the presence of women. Normally he began to spin a verbal web of beauty about a woman the moment he met her. Yet he hadn't had the least urging to do so with his betrothed. In fact, he found himself more prone to curse at her than soothe her with sweet assertions. Most odd.

Shaking his head, he moved forward as she hooked a satchel to her horse and quickly grabbed for her sword. Seonaid must have sensed his approach for she stilled a moment before he reached her but made no movement as he disarmed her. Instead, she waited until he'd stepped away, then turned slowly to face him.

"You could have asked, m'laird."

Blake raised his eyebrows. He'd expected anger, rage, even snarling and spitting fury. Instead she appeared completely calm. She even tossed a glance toward her companion, which caused the smaller warrior to unsheathe her own sword and step forward to offer it to him.

Blake accepted the weapon with some surprise. He took a wary step back as he confessed, "I did not think you would surrender it willingly."

"Why not?" Her lips curved up in amusement as she shrugged. "If 'twill make ye feel safer to have me unarmed, so be it. 'Sides, surely with such big, strong men around we'd have no need to defend ourselves?"

Blake frowned. There was no guile in her expression,

not the smallest sign of sarcasm in her tone, and yet he was positive she was laughing at him. Worse yet, he suspected the little woman, her friend, had caught the joke and was silently laughing as well. Scowling, he muttered under his breath and turned away to rejoin Lord Rolfe.

"Think you it was wise to give up our weapons?" Aeldra asked quietly.

Seonaid shrugged. "They're less likely to expect an escape attempt if we are unarmed. 'Sides, we can replace them easily enough."

"How?" Helen asked, moving to join them.

"We have friends not far from here," Seonaid informed her quietly, then glanced toward the men. The bishop and the big man from the chapel had left the clearing, presumably to gather their animals as well as the rest of the men and clear away the signs of their camp. That left Sherwell, Lord Rolfe, Gavin, and the other two Dunbar men present, but without their horses. There would hardly be a better time to attempt an escape. "Aeldra, help Helen mount her animal."

Catching the meaningful expression Seonaid tossed her, Aeldra nodded and took Helen's arm to lead her around the large beast Seonaid stood before. Moving calmly, Seonaid stepped to the front of her mount's head and began to coo and pet him softly, her gaze shooting first to the men still talking at the edge of the clearing, then to the two women and two horses hidden by her massive animal's bulk. Aeldra helped Helen mount her horse, instructing her to lay her upper body

flat along the animal's neck and head to prevent drawing attention, then moved to her own mount and
quickly slid atop the beast, pressing herself flat on the
animal's neck as well.

Seeing the men hadn't noticed their activity, Seonaid
moved back to her stallion's side, grabbed the pommel
in one hand, jammed her foot in the stirrup, and
quickly pulled with her hand and stepped with her foot
to propel herself upward and sling one long leg over
the beast's back.

She had mounted and was grabbing for Helen's reins
even as the expected cry of alarm went up. Ignoring it,
Seonaid tugged on her horse's reins and pressed her
heels to his belly, urging him into a bolt. The beast immediately shot forward, Helen's horse following. Aeldra
took up the rear.

"Damn! Little George, bring the horses!" Blake roared,
whirling from the sight of the disappearing women and
starting through the woods.

Rolfe followed him closely. "Do not tell me you have
decided to participate in getting the wedding done? I
began to think you would simply trail me about, hampering my efforts as much as possible until it was either
a fait accompli or the lady escaped."

Pausing, Blake turned to face him. "Do not think I
have changed my mind about the wedding. Howbeit,
do I continue to leave the situation in your hands, I very
much fear I shall be bounced around indefinitely, chasing the woman from one end of Scotland to the other.
'Tis far better to see the matter settled one way or the

other by escorting her back to Dunbar, and it appears to me the only way to accomplish the task is to handle it myself." With those insulting words, he turned to continue forward, only to pause as Little George appeared, trailing three horses.

"They made a run for it," Blake explained dryly, answering the question in his massive man's eyes as he accepted his own reins. He quickly mounted, as did Lord Rolfe. His gaze shot to the Dunbar men and he frowned at their solemn expressions. "Mount up and follow with the rest of the men."

Gavin nodded stoically, his expression remaining dignified and grim until the three men had ridden out of view; then his face cracked in a grin. "I can hardly wait to return to Dunbar and tell the laird about this."

"He's sure to get a good laugh oot o' it," one of the other men agreed, then commented, "'Tis twice now the English has lost oor Seonaid. Hoo many more times diya reckon 'twill happen 'ere we arrive home?"

Gavin shrugged and turned to move into the woods, intent on gaining his horse. "Twa or three, I'd wager. Fetch yer beasties and follow me. We'll gather the rest of the English and follow."

The women did not get very far. It was no one's fault, just happenstance. Helen's mount set her foot down wrong as she landed after leaping a log in their path. Releasing a scream of pain, the animal went down hard, sending Helen to the ground with a cry of alarm.

Tugging sharply on her own mount's reins to bring him to a halt, Seonaid glanced back to see Aeldra make good use of her swift reflexes to steer clear of the fallen horse and rider.

Turning her animal, Seonaid urged him back to the fallen mare, releasing the breath she'd been holding when Aeldra reached the girl and horse first and helped Helen to her feet. Apparently, the woman had suffered a fright but was otherwise unhurt.

"Is she all right?" Helen asked anxiously as Aeldra turned her attention to the mare struggling back to her feet.

The shorter woman examined the leg briefly, watching as the mare hobbled lamely a step or two, then glanced up at Seonaid and shook her head.

Mouth tightening unhappily, Seonaid bent to grasp Helen's arm and draw her attention. "Come. Mount behind me. We'll share my mount."

"But my mare," she protested. "She is hurt."

"We have no time to tend her," Seonaid snapped as Aeldra mounted her own horse. "Gavin will see to her."

"But—"

"There is no time to argue. They are comin'."

Sighing, Helen nodded resignedly and struggled onto the saddle behind her with a little help, then clasped her arms around her waist as Seonaid urged her horse forward. They'd taken only a few steps when they heard the thunder of approaching hooves.

Cursing, Seonaid pressed her heels to the horse's belly, urging it to gain speed, but she knew the effort was useless. The approaching riders were pounding toward them at a dead run. And her mount now had the weight of two to carry. Seonaid wasn't surprised when after less than a hundred yards the men caught them up and shot past them, then slowed their own horses and dropped back, two of them crowding her mount and Aeldra's together from the sides. Lord Blake slowed his own before them, forcing them to come to a halt.

Silence reigned for a moment as they all eyed each other; then Blake offered a chilly smile. " 'Tis obvious by your abrupt departure that you are eager for the wedding to occur. Howbeit, I fear your sense of direction is somewhat lacking. I must tell you, you were headed the wrong way once more, my lady. Dunbar is west."

"Ha, what a wit ye are, m'laird," Seonaid said. "I doubt not but ye leave the women laughin' at ye at every turn."

Blake's gaze narrowed. Her words could be taken in either of two ways and he very much suspected she meant it in the most insulting light. "Rolfe?"

"Aye?" The red-haired Englishman urged his horse forward, glancing at him questioningly.

"Mayhap you should take the good sister onto your mount," he suggested.

"She rides with me," Seonaid said grimly, urging her horse backward as the other man moved his own horse toward hers.

"She rides with Lord Rolfe," Blake ordered grimly.

Seonaid opened her mouth to snap at him, then smiled suddenly with a nasty sweetness before asking, "Affeared I might escape ye? Again?"

A wry smile tugging at his lips, Blake nodded. "Aye."

His honesty surprised her so much, Seonaid simply sat there as Rolfe moved forward and lifted Helen gently from her horse to his own, settling her comfortably before him as he moved the horse a short distance away.

Seonaid was frowning her displeasure at Blake when he suddenly smiled and called out to the other man. "Little George."

"Aye?"

"Aeldra rides with you."

Nodding grimly, the large man urged his horse forward to collect the woman, but she was of no more of a mind to make things easy than her mistress. The little hellion kicked the great man in the shin as his horse reached her side, then tried to punch him in the face as he ignored the first strike and lifted her from her own mount to his. In the end, he had to catch both of her small hands in one of his own and hook one of his great legs over both of hers to prevent her from doing herself damage. He managed to calm her as he settled her on the saddle before him, but she glared at him with disgust before throwing Seonaid an apologetic sigh as she sank against his huge chest.

Mouth tightening as she saw her ability to escape slipping away, Seonaid glared at her betrothed, almost daring him to come near her.

Blake picked up the challenge at once and urged his own mount toward hers. Seonaid immediately made her own stallion side step away, and the animal responded at once. Blake's eyebrows rose at the skill, but he urged his horse closer, unsurprised when she again deftly avoided him. Shaking his head, he glanced toward Little George and nodded. Understanding the silent order, Little George moved forward even as Blake did again. When Seonaid automatically began to urge the mount into a side-step, she found herself coming up against Little George's horse. Before she could instruct her stallion to move forward or back, Blake reached out and caught her about the waist, drawing her easily onto his lap.

He wasn't terribly surprised when she immediately began to struggle against him, though he was a bit startled by her strength as she did so. Tightening his arms around her, he hid his surprise with an expression of mixed exasperation and amusement. "We can do this the easy way, my lady, or the hard one. 'Tis up to you."

"Then it'll be the hard way," Seonaid muttered. Elbowing him in the chest, she tugged hard on his horse's reins, so the animal reared up, hooves pawing the air and sending Blake toppling from the saddle behind her. Seonaid grunted with satisfaction as the beast settled back on all fours, then squeezed her knees and sent him into a dead run for the hill ahead.

"Aye, I can see you are handling the situation much better than I," Lord Rolfe commented with amusement, peering down at Blake from his seat on his mount. "No doubt we shall reach Dunbar within the year at this rate."

Cursing, Blake struggled back to his feet, accepting the reins of Seonaid's horse when Little George offered them. Mounting the animal, he didn't even bother to comment to the man, but charged off after his betrothed.

His horse was fast and Seonaid rode him well, but her horse was faster, he saw with interest and not a little disapproval. In his opinion, 'twas a shame to waste such a beast on a woman; a warrior would have got more use out of it. Still, despite the animal's speed, they had gone quite a distance before he managed to catch up to her. Glad he wore the plaid and not encumbering mail, Blake raised his feet to the saddle and launched himself at her. He was a little behind Seonaid but caught her with his left arm as he flew past, tugging her from her mount and bringing her crashing to the ground on top of himself. Her own landing cushioned by his body, Seonaid recovered first from their tumble and struggled to her feet, attempting to flee toward her horse, but Blake regained himself enough to reach out and clasp her ankle before she'd managed a step. His hold on her, pitted against her forward momentum, sent her crashing to her stomach on the forest floor.

Shifting onto his hands and knees, he started to rise, then paused to grab her ankle again when she started to scrabble away from him in the dirt. Falling back to her stomach, Seonaid rolled onto her back to kick at him with her free leg. Catching the second ankle as well, Blake held it fast, then cursed when she immediately sat up to strike out at him with balled fists. Yanking her ankles wide apart, he dragged her along the forest floor until he knelt between her open legs. Then he stopped her struggling by the simple action of launching himself on top of her. His legs quickly stopped the action of her own, and his hands grabbed hers and dragged them above her head so they were unable to strike out at him. Face-to-face and panting heavily, they glared at each other where they lay, then Blake began to feel a sense of awareness stealing through his body.

Frowning over the surprising reaction, Blake managed a wry smile as he regained his breath somewhat, then muttered, "You are a fair handful, my lady."

Seonaid did not smile back. "An' ye're an English dog."

His smile losing some of its luster, he arched his eyebrows arrogantly. "That is a fine thing coming from a red shank."

Seonaid's eyes narrowed at the insulting term the English often used to refer to Scots. She spat, "Better a red shank than the spawn of a Sassenach."

"Methinks your protests excessive, my little roughfoot. Mayhap you are not as adverse to the wedding as you would have me believe." He arched an eyebrow when she merely glared at him, too furious to speak. "Out of words to parry with, my lady?"

" 'Tis sorry I am to admit it, m'laird, but aye," Seonaid admitted with a suddenly sweet smile. Then she added, "But then, I have ever been better with the sword than with words. Shall we try those now instead?"

She began to struggle beneath him again as she spoke, and Blake found himself briefly distracted by the surge of heat her movement engendered within him. It took him a moment for her challenge to sink in. When it did, he shifted his lower body to still her struggles and released a short, deep laugh. "Nay, my lady. The only sword I would use with you is one you have not to use back." He was satisfied by the sudden deep red flush coloring her cheeks. "You are quite lovely when you are not cursing or spitting, my dear. Your mouth is really rather sweet when not spewing filth; 'tis shaped like a heart with full curves and—"

"Do ye intend to lay upon me all day aspoutin' your pretty words, m'laird?" she interrupted in a decidedly bored tone. "Or shall ye let me up?"

Blake stiffened at her words as Little George and Lord Rolfe arrived, their saddles conspicuously empty of women. Turning his head toward them, he raised an eyebrow, and Little George quickly explained.

"The men caught us up right after ye flew after the girl. We left the other two with them while we followed to see if you needed any help. Howbeit, 'tis obvious you have all in hand here."

"Oh, aye," Blake agreed dryly. Shaking his head, he got slowly to his feet before offering a hand to Seonaid. Much to his surprise, she accepted the offer of assistance. He realized his mistake almost at once, for she did not use his hand in order to raise herself up, but instead to pull him down. He'd barely understood the meaning behind the sudden tug to his hand when he felt her foot lodge itself somewhere in the vicinity of his groin. Then he was sailing through the air, somersaulting over her head onto his back with a crash that reverberated through his entire body. He did not even notice she had regained her footing and was charging toward the woods once more.

"Are you all right?" The smile Little George struggled

to hide as he slid off his mount took away somewhat from the concern underlying the question.

"Of course he is all right." Still seated on his mount, Lord Rolfe didn't even try to hide his amusement. "He is handling the matter, can you not see that?"

Groaning, Blake shifted onto his side, then got gingerly to his feet, wincing at the pain in his lower regions as he did. "Which way did she go?" he muttered as soon as the pain had lessened enough to allow speech.

Little George pointed toward the woods and Blake groaned, took a step toward his horse, then shook his head and set out on foot. It seemed to him it would be less painful to run than to set his jewels on a horse's back to be bounced about.

After several moments of running, he had to wonder if he hadn't made the wrong decision. It seemed to him this little jog merely exacerbated the pain he was suffering. And the wench proved quick on her feet, certainly faster than he'd expected. He almost doubted he could catch her up, and it was both a surprise and a relief when he actually managed to close the distance between them enough that he could lunge forward and tumble her to the ground once more. There they tussled briefly before he managed to subdue her using his maltreated body. After the abuse he'd suffered at her hands, it was almost a relief when she gave up struggling and began to spit curse after curse at him. Some of them actually made him flush. Where the devil had she learned such a litany? Good God, she knew more curses than he did.

He gave her a shake to silence her, then sighed and

shook his head. "Your tongue is as sharp as your blade, my lady."

Seonaid's eyes widened slightly at his tone of voice as he made the announcement. "Ye almost sound admiring, Sassenach."

"Aye, for truly I do appreciate your wit." When he saw her eyes narrow, he grimaced and raised an eyebrow. "Are you going to continue this behavior all the way to Dunbar?"

"Did ye think I'd make it easy on ye?"

"Nay, but I fear I should warn you, should you continue to try to escape, forcing me to chase and tumble you, I may be moved to anticipate the exchanging of the bands and consummate the marriage before we even reach your land. 'Tis fair true the feel of your body squirming beneath me fans fires I did not think you could."

As he'd expected, Seonaid stilled at once. Blake smiled widely. "Ah, my lady, you fair wound me. Would you not wish to handfast with me? 'Tis what it is called, is it not?"

She was frowning at him oddly, her nose twitching.

Raising his eyebrows, he lifted himself slightly from her body. "What?"

"Is that you?"

"What?"

"Ye smell like a bloody barn. Could ye no bathe before ye came to fetch me?"

Blake pushed himself away from her at once, then reached a hand down to help her up, pulling it back as he recalled what had happened the last time.

Amusement on her face, Seonaid rose under her own impetus and led him toward the horses as they broke into the clearing. This time, all of them were there; Lord Rolfe and Little George had the women before them again, and the bishop, the three Scots, and the men-at-arms were all in attendance. Ignoring their presence, Seonaid moved to Blake's horse in silent surrender, but paused before mounting him and glanced back at Blake where he still stood watching her. "By the by, about anticipatin' the weddin'? I think ye should be aware of all things afore ye make yer decision."

"Such as?"

"Such as while ye've taken away me sword, I still have me *sgian dubh* an' I'll no hesitate to use it should ye try anything. 'Twould be a fair shame for your lovely deep voice to suddenly start singin' high."

Turning away, she mounted the horse, her expression cold as she waited for him to climb up behind her.

"What is a *sgian dubh*?"

Rolfe, Bishop Wykeham, and Little George peered up blankly from their positions around the fire. They had ridden throughout the day, traveling at a slower pace than usual to avoid taxing the overburdened horses. Now they sat, relaxing about the fire they had prepared as darkness had settled over the land. Seonaid, Aeldra, and Helen were all just beyond the trees, bathing in the cool river water. Blake had considered setting a guard on them but had decided against it. Instead he'd set six guards on the horses. The women could not flee far without horses.

The thought of horses made Blake shift uncomfortably. He did not know how the other two men had faired, but for himself, it had been a hell of an uncomfortable ride, and he was grateful to finally be able to rest. His lower body still ached from the kick he'd received. Eight hours of riding hadn't aided in his recovery much, and he'd spent most of the ride torn between warily watching the woman who sat so stiff and still before him and trying to ignore the odd sensations holding her so close caused.

The whole venture had taken an unexpected turn for Blake. He'd started out as reluctant as a man on the way to the Tower. Now he could not really say how he felt. Part of him still balked at marrying the wench, but another part, the same part presently aching from her kick, showed some interest in at least the consumation of the wedding. Much to his dismay, his Amazon betrothed was extracting all sorts of interest from his body. He'd seen the first signs while wrestling with her in the woods, but his interest had continued and even intensified throughout the day. Truly, he'd cursed himself a time or two for suggesting that the women be forced to ride with the men. Having her bottom firmly pressed against him had been mightily distracting.

Were that all it was, Blake supposed he could accept his reaction as an aberrant desire, take her to wife, then to bed, and forget about it. But his reactions to the female were a bit more complicated. He hadn't been lying when he'd claimed to enjoy her wit. He did. He enjoyed sparring with her verbally. He'd even enjoyed the chase when she'd fled, first on horseback, then on foot. And damned if their brief struggles hadn't set his heart to pumping with an adrenaline that had given him a sort of thrill. Worse yet, he was even beginning to enjoy her refusal of him. She was a challenge. Blake had never been able to resist a challenge and, to date, no woman had truly offered him one.

"A *sgian dubh* is a knife, m'laird," the Scot named Gavin answered his question, drawing Blake from his ruminations. " 'Tis about yeah long." He held his hands about six inches apart. "Some of 'em are quite sharp an' nasty, could slit a man's throat clear through, or castrate him in a flash," he added, the twinkle in his eyes revealing he'd overheard Seonaid's threat.

Chapter Six

Seonaid ducked her head under the cold stream water, then straightened and slicked the hair off her face as she peered around the clearing. She suspected there was a guard somewhere, despite the impropriety of it, but could see no one from where she stood in the river.

Her gaze slid to Aeldra and Helen, who were grimly attending to their ablutions next to her. Both of them looked about as downhearted as a pair could be. Seonaid couldn't blame them. She was a bit disheartened herself. They had been captured. Not once, not twice, but three times. Things weren't going quite according to plan, but she hoped to change that.

Sidling closer to Helen in the water, Seonaid nudged her to get her attention. When the other woman turned, she asked in hushed tones, "Helen? Do ye recall which plant yer maid used to make the Camerons sleep?"

The shorter woman appeared surprised at the question but considered it briefly. Finally, she bit her lip and said with uncertainty, "I think I might recognize it again did I see it. Why?"

"I'm thinkin' me betrothed an' the others might need a rest after all their traipsin' around." Seonaid didn't bother to hide the wicked glint in her eyes. A smile widened her lips when Helen's brows flew up.

"Oh, aye, I think ye may be right." Aeldra's grin matched Seonaid's as she joined the conversation. "They can take a little nap whilst we tend to seein' Helen home."

"Aye." Seonaid removed the smile from her face and glanced warily around, concerned their standing about smiling and talking might raise suspicions in their hidden guards. The three women shouldn't be so happy at the moment.

"I shall need to look about the woods a bit," Helen pointed out, looking concerned.

"Aye." Seonaid nodded, but knew searching about the woods could be a problem. They might manage a quick look about did they claim a need to relieve themselves, but she knew getting a lot of time to hunt up the plant wasn't possible.

"Perhaps we could help," Aeldra suggested.

Seonaid nodded. "Ye'll have to tell us what it looks like. We'll split up as if to relieve ourselves an' each bring back what samples we can. Come."

Helen described the plant in question as they waded out of the water. Once on shore, they were silent as they dried off and donned their clothes, then Seonaid announced, "I've a need to find a handy bush."

"As have I," Aeldra said loudly. "I'll go this way." She moved into the woods on the left.

"I . . . er . . ." Helen cleared her throat, then said a little louder, "I do too. I'll just go over here."

Seonaid watched her disappear into the woods on their right, then peered around slowly. Nothing moved. There was no sign of anyone about, but she felt sure someone was there. Or at least not far away. She rather hoped the latter was true. It would allow them the freedom to look for a few minutes at least. She moved into the brush straight ahead, scanning the ground as she walked.

Helen had been very particular with her descriptions of the plant in question. At least Seonaid had thought so at the time, but as she scoured the ground in search of the proper plant, she began to think they all looked terribly similar. Still, she did the best she could, grabbing up several handfuls of any plant resembling the one Helen had described. She had no idea how much of the plant the woman would need, but she suspected it would be a plentiful amount to manage to send the whole camp to sleep.

Helen and Aeldra were waiting at the river's edge when Seonaid returned. She glanced from them to the surrounding woods as she asked, "Did either of ye spot anyone?"

Seonaid frowned when both women shook their heads. She hadn't either and was beginning to think it might mean there hadn't been a guard posted after all. Propriety might have swayed the Sherwell from posting a guard to watch them bathe, she realized. It wasn't as if they would have been foolish enough to try to escape without the horses. Glancing back to Helen and Aeldra and the collection of plants they were sifting through, she decided to hope for the best. They had to sort the plants. They would have to hope either the guards weren't posted or they were so far away as to not be a concern. Joining them, she dumped the plants she had found in the pile and knelt to help with the chore.

"How did we do? Did we get what ye need?" she asked as Helen examined the offerings.

"I am not sure," the woman admitted. "I found two plants I think might be the one she used. And you have one of them here too." She lifted the plants in question, and Seonaid had to admit they were very similar. One was a slightly lighter color than the other and perhaps a little larger.

"Well, was it the lighter or the darker o' the two?" she asked.

The Englishwoman bit her lip as she considered. "I can not be sure. It was dark when she showed them to me. I—" She shook her head helplessly.

"Perhaps the bigger ones are only a different color because they are older," Aeldra suggested.

"That could be," Helen allowed doubtfully.

They were silent for a moment, considering the plants, then Seonaid shifted impatiently. "Try to remember, Helen, an' pick which one ye think 'tis."

The smaller woman stared at first one, then the other plant, then reached for the bigger-leaved one. "The larger one, I think."

Seonaid nodded, scooped up all the pieces they had
of the larger plant, and tucked it in her plaid. "Come
along, then; we'll offer to cook the sup. How did yer
maid feed it to the Camerons?"

"In a stew."

"A stew it is then," Seonaid announced and led the
way back to camp.

Her plan seemed simple enough. Offer to cook,
make a stew, dump the leaves in, feed the men, wait for
them to drift off, then saddle their mounts, free the rest
of the horses, and set out. Simple.

Not so simple.

"Let you cook the sup, my lady?" Blake actually laughed
at the idea. "What? So you can poison me? I think not."

Seonaid did her best to look properly aghast at the
suggestion. Then she did the only thing she could think
to do. She shrugged and said, "Fine. Sister Helen
merely mentioned she made a fine rabbit stew, which
started me hankering for some. Howbeit, I shall survive
with the stale bread an' old cheese we brought with us
from the abbey. I'm sure you men have something to
make do with too." Then she started to walk away. Much
to her relief, Blake stopped her after two steps.

"The nun was going to do the cooking?" he asked
with sudden and obvious interest.

"Aye." She turned back. "Well, you doona think I ken
how to cook, diya?" she asked with a sneer. "My only
contribution was goin' to be to catch the rabbits she'll
need to feed us all."

Blake remained silent for a minute, then nodded.

"Fine. But you are not hunting the rabbit. I will send a few men out after them. I shall set two men to build a fire and—" He paused suddenly and frowned. "We have naught to use for a pot to cook the stew."

Seonaid found herself flummoxed by the comment. Dear Lord, she hadn't even considered a pot would be needed for the stew. She almost slapped herself in the head for such stupidity, but before she did, Helen stepped forward and blurted, "I have a pot, my lord."

Seonaid turned to gape at the woman in surprise. "Do ye?" she asked.

Helen nodded. "Remember the sack I mentioned leaving in the stables when you asked if I had brought anything with me?"

"Aye." Seonaid nodded.

"Well, the pot is in it. 'Tis why I left it in the stables but collected it when we were saddling the horses. I thought . . . well . . . it saved my life once." She shrugged.

Seonaid could have hugged the woman for such brilliance. Her respect for Helen rose. She was a clever wench.

Aware Blake had started barking orders behind her, sending some men to hunt rabbit and others to start a fire, she shared a smile with the Englishwoman, then said, "Ye'd best ask him to assign some men to help ye root out whatever wild onions and such ye can find around here fer the stew, to cover the taste o' the weed. Do I offer, he's sure to get suspicious I'm tryin' to poison him again."

Helen nodded but didn't move. After a hesitation, she admitted, "I am not sure how much to add."

Seonaid frowned, then shrugged. "Guess."

"But if I add too much it could kill them."

"That would be little loss," Seonaid said with amusement, then sighed when she saw the alarm on Helen's face. The English never had understood the Scottish sense of humor. "I was teasin'," she explained. "Very well, 'tis better to err on the light side, I suppose. Even do they not sleep as long as we'd hope, so long as it is long enough for us to get away . . ." She shrugged.

Helen nodded solemnly, then moved past her to approach Blake.

Seonaid decided to seek out a comfortable spot to settle. It would require a bit of time for the stew to cook, and it seemed to her a nice rest was in order did she wish to travel through the night. With Helen forced to cook the stew, there was little chance of her getting a rest, but if necessary Aeldra and Seonaid would take turns holding her up before them while they rode. It would slow them down, but there was little else she could think to do. She sat on a soft patch of grass, tried to relax, then lay on her side and closed her eyes. She sensed rather than saw Aeldra claim a patch of grass at her back.

"Will you stop glaring at the woman."

Blake scowled at Rolfe's impatient words but merely shook his head, never once taking his eyes off his betrothed. "She is up to something. I can feel it."

"She is sleeping," Rolfe said with exasperation.

"So she would have me believe," Blake said wisely. "In truth, she is plotting. And when she thinks she has me fooled and I have let down my guard, she will rise up and slaughter us all."

Rolfe gave a snort of laughter. "She is your betrothed, not some demon sent to plague you."

"Is there a difference?" Blake asked dryly.

Giving up on him, Rolfe shook his head and walked away, leaving Blake to stare at the woman he felt sure feigned sleep. She looked angelic in repose, but he had a tender set of jewels to prove she was anything but. Seonaid Dunbar was hell's spawn and that was all there was to it. He would not let down his guard around her again. He sat and watched her and could almost believe by the rhythm of her breathing that she truly was sleeping. He felt sure she hadn't yet given up. The woman had already proven herself too damned stubborn to simply surrender. Nay. She was up to something. He just wished he knew what it was.

The scent of the stew cooking eventually began to weave its way around the camp, and Blake found himself inhaling the aroma with growing anticipation. It felt as if he had been traveling forever. He had been forced to make do with moldy bread and moldier cheese for the majority of their meals during the trip. The very idea of a real meal, even something as simple as rabbit stew, was enough to have his mouth watering. The actual aroma of it, delicious as it was, nearly had him panting. He could not wait to eat.

"Well?" Seonaid asked quietly as Helen moved to sit between the women with a portion of stew poured into the last of their stale bread. "Will it work?"

"I am not sure," the redhead whispered anxiously. "I hope I used enough."

Seonaid hoped she had too but merely nodded. They would simply have to wait and see. Her gaze turned back to the men eagerly gobbling up the stew. They claimed it was most tasty fare, and Seonaid had little difficulty believing them. The scent wafting off the portion Helen had dished out for her smelled divine. She was almost tempted to eat it herself. Almost.

"They doona seem to be growin' sleepy," Aeldra murmured with concern as the men began to finish their food.

Seonaid didn't say anything, but slipped her bread bowl behind her back and tipped it over, dumping the stew in the grass. The last thing she wanted was for one of the men to notice they hadn't eaten it. Bringing the empty makeshift bowl back around, she traded it for Helen's full portion, then dumped it as well. She did the same with Aeldra's as she watched the men closely. Unfortunately, her cousin was right. They were all almost done and none were showing the least sign of weariness.

Her gaze turned on Blake with displeasure as she watched him pop the last piece of bread into his mouth. He had eaten the stew as well as the bread bowl holding it. Getting to his feet, he nodded toward the three women. "That was delicious, Sister. You have my thanks. Now I think I shall clean up at the river before retiring."

"How long did it take to work last time?" Seonaid asked Helen as the three of them watched Blake leave the clearing. She began to fear the Englishwoman had gone much too light with the plant in her worry at over-dosing them.

Helen thought for a minute, then shook her head. "I am not sure. I recall it seemed to take forever, but I was frightened at the time. I knew did we fail, I would soon be dead."

Seonaid shifted with impatience. How long would they have to wait? Would it work? Dear Lord, what if they had grabbed the wrong plant and merely mixed a harmless herb in the stew?

She grimaced at the thought. The lost opportunity would be irritating, but almost equally upsetting would be the lost stew she had just dumped. It had smelled mighty fine, and if it was untainted and now feeding the earth . . . well, that was a terrible disappointment. Were their plan not going to work, they might at least have had a good meal out of it.

Her thoughts were disturbed when Aeldra reached behind Helen to poke Seonaid in the side. She glanced at her cousin, then followed her nod to where a couple of the men, the ones who had eaten the fastest, were beginning to rub absently at their bellies.

Seonaid felt a prickle of unease race along her back as she watched the pained grimaces on their faces. They were looking a tad uncomfortable.

"Er . . . Helen . . ." Seonaid began, then paused. Two of the men had lurched to their feet and stumbled from the fire. The distant sound of retching soon followed.

"Oh, dear." Helen sounded shaky as a couple more men suddenly stumbled off into the woods. "Cameron's men did not react this way. I think it may have been the other plant, after all."

Seonaid bit her lip to hold back the nervous laugh that wanted to escape. It didn't help when she glanced at Aeldra and saw her goggling at the woman.

"Ye think?" her cousin asked with disbelief as several more men staggered off. "Ye *think* it might have been the other plant? I'm thinkin' it's pretty certain."

The camp emptied quickly. Seonaid could only be grateful Blake wasn't there to see his earlier suspicions being confirmed. As it was, several glances had been sent their way as the men headed out into the surrounding woods. The only ones not presently showing signs of discomfort were the three Scots Seonaid's father had sent out. They had passed up the stew in favor of their usual packet of oats, she noticed with concern. Damn. She hadn't considered them in this plan. It was an oversight that could be a real problem, she realized unhappily.

"Oh." Helen stood suddenly. Her face was a mask of misery as she watched Lord Rolfe and Bishop Wickham join the burgeoning number of men in the bushes. The men were not quiet in their agony, and the sounds were a torment to hear.

Aeldra stood too, trying to soothe her. "Now, now, Helen. 'Tis sure I am they'll be fine. A little discomfort is all they're sufferin'. They'll be right as rain on the morrow. Or the next day," she added as the cacophony of sounds grew around them.

"If they do not die," Helen moaned.

"Well, an' if they do, their sufferin' will end that

much sooner," Seonaid said practically, drawing a gasp from the woman.

"Well?" Gavin asked.

Seonaid turned to the only men left seated by the fire. The three Scots were grinning fiendishly.

Now that he had her attention, the Scot asked, "Are ye goin' to make guid yer escape while ye can or no?"

Seonaid considered him briefly. "Are ye goin' to stop us?"

He merely shrugged. "The Dunbar didna say to stop ye, lass. Jest to keep Sherwell from killin' himself."

Seonaid felt herself relax somewhat. She hesitated, then told him, "We never meant to make them ill." She had to raise her voice to be heard over the retching taking place in the woods around them. "The stew was supposed to make them sleep."

"But I picked the wrong plant," Helen explained pitifully.

"I'll be sure to tell him," Gavin assured them with amusement.

Grimacing, Seonaid urged Helen to the horses, aware Aeldra followed. She had some trouble getting the Englishwoman to mount. Helen feared she had sentenced the men to death by her poisoning. Seonaid assured her the men would be fine, pointing out that they were purging the stew and whatever poison was in it. Helen didn't appear much relieved but did allow herself to be urged up onto a mount.

Seonaid and Aeldra then conferred over what to do about the horses. Gavin watched them closely and would no doubt raise a fuss did she try to free all of them. He'd not allow her to scare off his or his men's mounts. In the end, they took three horses: Aeldra and Seonaid's own as well as another horse to replace Helen's injured animal. Then they set the rest loose . . . all but the three beasts belonging to her father's men. Seonaid knew she couldn't get away with setting them free. Unfortunately, she also knew that the rest of the horses probably wouldn't go far and would be easily rounded up with the horses she'd had to leave behind. Which meant all this trouble had bought them very little time in the end.

Blake stumbled back toward camp. His body trembled with weakness from an hour of retching at the side of the river and still he didn't feel much better. At least the heaving had stopped. Something in the stew obviously had not agreed with him, though he would not mention it to Sister Helen. The woman had worked for hours over the meal, and it had been quite tasty. Since the meat had been freshly caught, he suspected the culprit must be one of the wild vegetables and herbs the men had scavenged for her. He hoped he was the only one affected by it. The last thing he needed was three weak women on his hands. Blake loved women, but he preferred them warm and willing to ailing and wailing.

He reached the camp and stumbled weakly to the log he had been seated on earlier. He dropped onto it beside Rolfe, who sat, shoulders drooping, as he wiped his mouth with the back of his hand. The man looked rather pale and unwell, Blake noted, then frowned at the sight of the bishop lying on the dirt behind them, holding his stomach and moaning. It seemed he hadn't been the only one affected after all, Blake realized, and glanced around at the rest of the men. A good half of them were slumped around the fire, some clutching their bellies and rocking in silent misery, while more were staggering back out of the bushes to join them. There was no sign of the women.

"Were the women sickened too?" Blake asked with concern.

"The women?" Rolfe glanced around with bleary eyes. "I imagine they were. They must still be in the woods. Women are much more delicate than men. They would require more time to recover."

Blake grunted something of an agreement as his gaze moved to the fire. He sat still for a moment, loathe to move and stir up his stomach again, but the women shouldn't be off alone in the woods. He knew he would have to check on them. After another moment had passed and none of the women rejoined the sufferers around the fire, Blake heaved back to his feet and forced himself to walk to the edge of the clearing. He paused there, really too weary to do a proper search. Instead, he called out into the woods, his only answer the moans of his men. He stood there, confused and shaky and wondering what to do next, when Little George lumbered out of the woods directly before him. In all the years Blake had known the giant of a man, he had never seen him unwell. It wasn't a pretty sight. Putting out a hand in case he took the notion of toppling on him, Blake asked, "Are you all right?"

Disgust flared on the giant's flat face and he shook his head. "I had three portions of the stew 'ere I started to feel poorly. I am paying for it."

Blake nodded in sympathy. He'd gobbled down two portions himself and wished he hadn't been so greedy. "Have you seen the women?"

Little George shook his head. "Have you asked the Scot?"

"The Scot?" Blake turned back to the fire, only then noting Gavin sitting, grinning like a fool. The man obviously wasn't suffering like the rest of them. But more importantly, he sat alone. The other two Scots were missing, and Blake didn't think for a minute they were with the other men in the woods. The Scots had refused to eat the Englishwoman's stew. Besides, the man looked terribly amused. He would hardly be so amused if his own men were ailing. Growling under his breath, Blake moved back to the fire, aware Little George was on his heels.

"Where are they?" Blake snapped without preamble and glared down at the Scot.

"Me men?" Gavin asked with a grin.

"No. The women."

"Hmm." Gavin shook his head. "Ye'd have more luck askin' me where me men are."

Blake hesitated, then decided to play along, "All right, where are your men?"

"Followin' the women."

He stood there for a moment, his face blank, his mind slow to process this news. Then his gaze shot instinctively to where the horses should have been tied. He wasn't sure what he had expected to see. All of the horses were gone, but for one. It seemed a good guess that the one remaining horse was the Scot's mount.

"Damn!" he cursed volubly. "Damn and double damn! They've flown again."

"What?" Rolfe interjected weakly and stood to join him. "They could not if they were as sick as we are. Did they not eat the stew?"

"Nay, they *cooked* it," Blake spat out. "At least one of them did."

"But Sister Helen cooked," Bishop Wickham protested, forcing himself to a seated position. "No bride of God would poison me."

"Seonaid must have convinced her to put something in the stew. She probably told her it would just make us sleep," he reasoned, then shook his head with disbelief. "Damn, the wench would rather kill me than marry me."

The very idea so shocked him, he could hardly believe it. A sudden burst of laughter from the Scot drew Blake from his thoughts.

"It was supposed to make ye all sleep, but the nun was unsure which weed would cause it. She was most distressed that she had blundered so and caused such discomfort, horrified even at the idea she might be responsible fer yer deaths."

Blake had started to relax when the man added, "Seonaid soothed her by pointin' out that should ye all die, ye'd be out o' yer misery."

The Scot burst out laughing at the horrified expressions on their faces.

Blake recovered enough to scowl at him, then strode to the man's horse. He had just laid his hand on the mount's tether when Gavin caught up and stopped him. "Horse thievin' is frowned on here in Scotland."

"I have to go after Seonaid," Blake said grimly.

"Ye'll find her faster with me to lead the way. Ye'd no recognize the trail me men will leave without me."

"Why?" Rolfe asked with bewilderment as he joined them. "Why would you lead us to her? Why did you not just stop her from leaving?"

"The Dunbar didna send me to stop her."

"Then why the hell did he send you?" Blake asked irritably.

"To keep ye from gettin' lost . . . or killed," Gavin reminded him in a tone filled with amusement.

Before Blake could react to the slight, Rolfe intervened, saying, "I suppose we had best hie after them."

"Hie after them?" Blake scowled. "On one horse?"

"Well, obviously we shall have to round up the others. They will not have gone far. Look, there is one there. Is not that your mount?"

Following his pointing finger, Blake saw Rolfe was right. His mount stood not ten feet away, munching on grass. He had owned the animal for several years, and it was a faithful beast. Leaving the others, he walked to fetch the stallion, his mind working over the problem. He had half a mind to let the wench go. Why chase after her? She would just run again.

On the other hand, he would like to see the wench again. Very much so. He would like to catch up to her, drag her off her mount, pull her over his knee, and . . .

Blake stopped his thoughts on a sigh. He felt sick and weary and thought he might be lucky to stay on his horse long enough to catch up to the woman, let alone pull her off her mount. But the idea of doing so was a lovely thing to contemplate. Pushing his fantasies aside, he forced himself to straighten his posture and stride manfully toward his mount as he ordered, "The rest of you follow as soon as you round up the other horses. I shall give chase."

"On your own?" Rolfe and Little George spoke the query at the same time, but in vastly differing tones. Rolfe sounded dubious, as if he thought Blake *couldn't* manage the task on his own. Little George sounded disapproving, as if he thought Blake *shouldn't* do it. The bishop and the damned Scot, Gavin, were holding their tongues, but the laughter in the Scot's eyes suggested he was sure Blake *wouldn't* manage the task.

Always having been a contrary sort, Blake took their reactions as a challenge. He mounted his beast, then forced one of his wicked smiles to his pale face as he turned to salute them. "Happy hunting."

"And to you; you shall need it," Blake thought he heard Lord Rolfe respond. He didn't pause to answer the comment as he was having difficulty staying mounted. After his bout in the bushes, his legs were as weak and trembling as a woman's, as were his arms. His whole body ached and trembled and his stomach muscles were the worst. He had to consider the irony of it all. He had survived countless battles yet been laid low by a rabbit. And a Scottish witch.

It was well past dawn before Seonaid deemed it safe for them to stop. She wouldn't have paused then except for the horses. The mounts had enjoyed little rest, riding a full day, then a full night with naught but a couple of hours' break in between. Worried about them—and Helen, who was just as exhausted, but too stubborn to allow Seonaid or Aeldra to take her up before them on their mounts—Seonaid had waited only until they had reached the relative safety of Comen's croft before stopping.

Comen was a friend to her brother. His home was always open to them on their travels, and this time proved no exception. Comen's wife offered up the only bed in the small hut, but they had chosen to sleep in the barn instead. Twice the size of the hut, it was filled with hay and most likely just as comfortable, if not more so. Besides, Seonaid felt it best to stay close to the horses in case the men caught them up. It was a very real possibility. If they still lived.

Seonaid scowled at the thought and turned on her side in the pile of hay she had made for herself. Aeldra and Helen were sleeping soundly, but Seonaid hadn't yet been able to find that happy state. She needed sleep but felt tense and wound up inside. It had been a tiresome task to ride through the night. Seonaid had constantly had to strain her eyes in an effort to judge the ground they crossed in the moonlight. It wouldn't have done to have another horse lamed on top of everything else.

Then there had been the tension of listening and watching for attack. It wasn't until they were well away that Seonaid had realized they hadn't found and retrieved their weapons before riding off. The three women were traveling unarmed. It was then Seonaid had realized just how rattled she had been by the men's reactions to the stew. She really hadn't wished them ill. Perhaps the Sherwell deserved it, but Lord Rolfe. . . . well, he *was* trying to force her to marry Sherwell, but the bishop certainly did not deserve to be made so ill. Even if he planned to perform the ceremony binding her to the damned Sassenach.

Irritated by her own thoughts, Seonaid rolled onto her back, then froze in shock. There was a man standing over her. Lord Blake. She hadn't heard him approach. Even the horses hadn't made a sound of warning—he must have crept up on them like a ghost. Actually, she realized, he rather resembled a ghost, haggard and drawn and pale to the point of being almost gray-faced. Blake looked exhausted and definitely wasn't happy.

Seonaid instinctively reached for the sword lying on the ground next to her, only to recall that they had fled unarmed. She had no sword.

"You would be clever not to try anything at this moment."

Seonaid opened her mouth to give a witty reply, but he forestalled her, growling, "You would be clever to keep your mouth shut too, else you may move me to doing something we would both regret."

Seonaid decided it might be in her best interests to do absolutely nothing, so she lay there still and silent, watching him watch her. She didn't even move when the tension suddenly slid out of him and he moved to lie down beside her. She did turn onto her side away from him then, but got no further before he caught her around the waist and dragged her back against him. He arranged her so they lay spoon style, then fixed her firmly in place by casting one leg over both of hers.

That was a little too much togetherness for Seonaid. She opened her mouth and took in a breath to speak, but Blake's arm tightened around her waist and he growled by her ear, "Shut up, Seonaid. I am not very pleased with you at the moment. If you know what is good for you, you shall be quiet and let us both sleep."

Seonaid shut her mouth. They both lay silent and still and she soon became aware of his relaxing behind her, his muscles easing. She stared at the streams of sunlight slipping through the small cracks between the barn slats and listened as Blake's breathing slowed to a deep, steady sound. There were tiny dust motes moving through the streams of sunlight and she tried to concentrate on that rather than the way his breath softly stirred the hair on top of her head, or how his hand had shifted as he relaxed so it was now curled just below her breast. Every time she breathed in and her chest expanded, it felt as if he were almost cupping it.

It looked almost as if the dust were dancing in the sunlight, she thought with unaccustomed whimsy, determined not to admit even to herself she was relieved to see him here. That she truly hadn't meant or wished to see him harmed. Despite her cold words to Helen and Aeldra, she *had* worried. She'd felt guilty through the entire ride here. She was glad to see him alive and well. She didn't even mind suffering his hold. In fact, she couldn't help but notice they fit together rather nicely. Seonaid breathed in again and Blake murmured, shifting his arm in his sleep so he was definitely cupping her breast. His hand held her firmly, making her body respond in ways Seonaid wasn't at all used to and wasn't sure she liked.

She tried to concentrate on the dust motes and ignore the tightening of her nipple and the liquid heat pooling between her legs, but nearly moaned aloud when he murmured something incomprehensible by her ear and shifted closer behind her. It was almost too much to bear—his breath, warm and ticklish against her sensitive ear, his hand tightening and squeezing her breast, the feel of his hard body nudging up behind her. She wanted to squirm and arch and writhe against him. But Seonaid's warrior training and discipline held her in good stead and she managed to force herself to remain still. Playing dead, her brother had always called it. Seonaid played dead, but knew—despite her exhaustion—she would not sleep with him pressed against her as he was.

Chapter Seven

Seonaid slept like the dead. When exhaustion finally overtook her, it dragged her so deep into sleep that she didn't awaken when the others stirred and rose, not even when Blake removed himself from her. For one moment, when she finally did wake up, she almost thought the memory of Blake's arrival had all been a dream. But then she noted the crushed straw beside her. It had all been real.

Unsure whether she would prefer it to have been a dream or not, she sat up, then forced herself to her feet. There was much talk and movement coming from outside the barn. Seonaid supposed it meant that all the men had caught up to them now. She hadn't considered the matter when her betrothed had appeared but was pretty sure he'd been alone. She hadn't heard any sounds to suggest a small army of men were making camp outside the barn.

As she had expected, the area between the cottage and barn was awash with men and horses when she stepped out into the sunlight. While Seonaid was sure they hadn't ridden in with Blake, it appeared they had arrived some time ago. Most of them were up and about, but—despite it being late afternoon—some were just rising from sleep.

In the midst of all this noise and commotion, Seonaid spotted Helen and Aeldra. The two women were seated alone and appeared rather uncomfortable under the men's accusing glares. Seonaid almost moved their way to offer moral support, but she had some personal needs to attend to first. She turned her feet toward the path leading to the side of the river.

Much to her surprise, no one stopped her from going or tried to follow her to the river's edge, but she understood why when she reached the edge of the river and found Blake already there, partially submerged in the water. She scowled at the back of his head, but when the man stood up the scowl slid away. Seonaid's mouth dropped open and her eyes widened incredulously. She'd noted Blake's fine figure the first time she'd seen him inside the chapel at the abbey, but he'd been clothed then. He was not now.

Her gaze slid over his wide shoulders and strong arms with appreciation. He had truly magnificent muscles, she saw, as he reached up to slick the damp gold hair off his face. Every muscle in his arms, shoulders, and back seemed to shift with the simple action.

Seonaid knew she should really make her eyes stop there—she felt sure a true lady would have—but she didn't. Instead, she let them drift down over his magnificent back to his equally magnificent behind and pause there to ogle him shamelessly.

It was a wonder to Seonaid that she had reached the advanced age of twenty-four without noticing how beautiful the male body could be. Still, she supposed she was usually too busy noting what idiots men could be, especially when a woman was about. They often seemed to act like brainless twits when a pretty face and figure entered their vicinity. Rather like she was doing at the moment.

The man was gorgeous. Seonaid couldn't recall ever having seen a more delectable behind than the one Blake was displaying. None of the warriors she'd been raised around had seemed so perfect. It wasn't flat and saggy like the one or two she had accidentally caught glimpses of over the years. Blake's behind was round and . . . well, pert was the only word she could think of. It made her want to reach out and squeeze—

"Are you going to stand there ogling me all morning?"

Seonaid stiffened, her eyes shooting upward to find Blake still standing with his head turned away from her. She was sure he hadn't glanced around. There would have been some shifting of muscle to warn her, so it would seem he'd been aware of her presence since her arrival . . . and no doubt his standing up had been an effort to shock her and scare her into rushing back to the camp, as any proper lady would no doubt have done. Instead, Seonaid had stood there and gawked at his nakedness like—

"Well?"

She let her thoughts scatter again and shifted to prop her hands on her hips with irritation. "Well what, Sassenach? How can I stand here all day when the day is mostly over? 'Sides, if yer goin' to put on a show, it seemed only polite to enjoy it."

"Ah, so you *are* enjoying it? That is good to know. Then you will not be using the claim of deformities as an excuse to cancel the wedding?"

She scowled at the smile in his voice.

"But we had best be sure 'tis true of all." On that note, he suddenly turned to face her, and Seonaid found herself presented with a full frontal view of him from the top of his head to his knees. The rest of his legs were submerged under the water.

"God's toes," she breathed, gaping at him. Had he mentioned deformities? Now she understood why. The man *was* deformed. He was huge. Her thighs squeezed together reflexively at the thought of him coming anywhere near her with the monster dangling between his legs. There was no way on God's green earth that he was sticking his sword in *her* sheath. Gad! Coupling had looked unceremonious, undignified, and uncomfortable the few times she'd happened upon couples engaged in the act. Seonaid had always wondered what all the moaning was about. Now she knew. It was pain. At least she was sure she'd be moaning in pain were he to try to—

"You do not look impressed."

The dry comment drew her gaze up to his face. He was frowning.

"In fact, you look rather . . . put off."

Seonaid met his gaze for a moment, but it was all she could manage. Then she merely shook her head and turned to head back to the camp. Her horror at the sight of his member had managed to do what her lack of maidenly modesty had failed at. She'd been driven off from the idea of ducking her head underwater, something she had always found helped to clear her thoughts. Seonaid had hoped it would help her figure out a way to again escape her betrothed, but it would seem she would have to make do with a muddled mind for now. Even more muddled than she had been on first awakening, she admitted to herself. The man had distracted her mightily with his little display. She was now even more desperate to avoid wedding and bedding him, and desperation was always a bad thing when one was trying to form a strategy.

"Are you planning on standing there all day?"

Blake blinked at the question, an echo of his own words to Seonaid earlier. He peered over his shoulder to where Lord Rolfe stood at the river's edge and shrugged for an answer before turning back to the water and his thoughts. He had stood, lost in thought, since Seonaid had hurried back toward camp. The woman was an enigma to him. He felt sure it hadn't been any sense of maidenly modesty that had sent her running away—the woman had stared at him rather boldly until he'd turned and presented her with a view of his front. Blake hadn't been surprised. He'd spoken with Gavin when the two had ridden out alone after the three women and had learned more about her somewhat unusual upbringing.

Gavin had proven to have much to say on the subject of his laird's daughter, and most of it had been praise. Her mother had died shortly after the contract binding Blake and Seonaid together, and while she should have been looked after by one of the women after that, Seonaid wouldn't have it. She seemed to cling harder to her brother and father after the loss of her mother, as if afraid they too might leave her and "go to the angels" were they out of her sight. Angus Dunbar hadn't been able to stand his young daughter's sobs at being left behind and had taken both children with him whenever he could. Gavin had said the pair of them were like his shadows, hand in hand, trailing him about the bailey as he oversaw the warriors in training and took care of other clan business. When Angus Dunbar's brother was killed and his children, Aeldra and her brother Allistair, arrived at Dunbar, they too had joined the party trailing the Dunbar laird about.

When Duncan and Allistair came of an age to begin training, no one found it odd that Seonaid and Aeldra joined in as well. Both females showed impressive skill and talent for battle, making up for their obviously lesser strength with intelligence and speed. Having been around the training field all their lives, and having roughhoused with their brothers for years, neither female shrank from the possibility of being injured. They both took up the sword as naturally as most young girls took up the needle.

Blake had listened with fascination. Here was a woman like none he had ever known. Other than a couple of failed attempts by her sister-in-law, the inestimable Lady Iliana, Seonaid had received no training in the ways of a lady. She'd grown up running, battling, and hunting with the men of Dunbar, taught to fight with the specially made sword she carried, to shoot an arrow as true as her brother, and various other warrior skills.

Seonaid Dunbar was as far from the delicate flowers of womanhood that littered court as his best friend and valued warrior Amaury was. The good bishop had not been far off with his comparison of the two, and while Blake had, at first, been horrified by the idea, now that he'd met the chit, he found her rather intriguing. Certainly she was more interesting than were any of the court flowers he had often dallied with. Beneath their soft petals and sweet scents, Blake well knew that those exotic flowers hid thorns ready to rend a man to pieces if given the opportunity. It was part of the fun for him, enjoying the pleasures they offered while avoiding the thorns, a task he'd found sadly easy to perform.

Seonaid would be an entirely different prospect. She didn't hide her thorns and she had a fine, hard armor to stave off any unwanted approach. She also didn't seem overly impressed with his good looks, which had made conquests so easy for him in the past. Seonaid Dunbar would definitely be a challenge.

A long-suffering sigh again drew Blake from his thoughts.

"Sherwell—"

"I'm coming." Blake interrupted what would no doubt be a complaint or order and turned to wade out of the water. "Are the rest of the men up?"

"Aye. And the women."

"Good. We shall head out directly then, and travel at least a couple of hours before making camp for the night."

Rolfe didn't look pleased. "I would rather travel through the night, as we are now at least three and possibly four days away from Dunbar, thanks to all this nonsense. But I suppose none of us is really up to a rigorous ride today."

Blake scowled over the reminder of their poisoning. Riding after the women with Gavin had been the worse sort of torture for him. They'd been forced to stop several times so he could stand by his horse, dry heaving. There had been nothing left for his body to purge, but it had definitely still felt like purging. Blake was a trembling, exhausted mess when they'd finally tracked the women to the barn where they were sleeping. Had Seonaid decided to fight him, he would have had a hard time stopping her. Thankfully, she'd not caused any fuss at all, but had heeded his warning and stayed put. Blake had almost been moved to thank her for it, but instead he'd merely dropped to lay next to her to recover some of his strength.

He didn't feel much better today. He wasn't quite so weak, but his stomach muscles ached from their unaccustomed efforts the night before and he still felt a bit shaky. The very idea of food made his stomach roil threateningly and he didn't really feel up to traveling today at all. Blake doubted the rest of the men did either, but a slow, easy ride for a few hours this afternoon that would take them closer to Dunbar, seemed a better idea than sitting here all day and night waiting for Seonaid to come up with her next escape scheme.

Blake grabbed his tunic from the branch where it had been drying and tugged it on with a grimace. Angus Dunbar's tunic no longer stank thanks to its washing, but it hadn't fully dried in the short time he had taken to bathe in the river. It was still damp and clung to him unpleasantly, which was better than the stench it had carried about with it earlier, he decided as he next grabbed the plaid. Knowing it couldn't possibly dry in the time it took for him to bathe in the river, Blake hadn't washed the woolen cloth. However, he'd hung it over a bush, hoping the wind blowing through it would remove some of its unpleasant stench. Unfortunately, the airing had done little good, and he wrinkled his nose with distaste as he caught a whiff of it.

Muttering under his breath about the habits of his soon-to-be father-in-law, Blake laid the plaid on the ground and scowled down at it with irritation. It was the first time he'd had it off since trading for it with Angus Dunbar. And he hadn't a clue how to don the bloody thing again. Oh, he knew he had to pleat it and lay on it, but he wasn't sure what Angus had done to pull it on and fasten it for him at Dunbar. He had watched carefully but wasn't at all certain he could repeat the man's actions.

"Need a hand with that?" Rolfe asked, and Blake wasn't surprised to see the other man's lip twitch. Rolfe hadn't been present when Angus Dunbar had helped him don it, which meant Little George might have mentioned what had occurred in the keep after he and the bishop had gone out. But Little George wasn't the sort to gossip, which left only Gavin or one of his men to have told the tale. Bloody Scots! Gossiping like old women, he thought with irritation.

"Nay, I can manage," he answered the question with a touch of resentment. And he did intend to manage the feat . . . one way or another.

However, he was no more clever with his hands when he knelt to pleat the plaid than he had been at Dunbar keep. It didn't help that Rolfe stood there, seeming to loom over him as he knelt to attempt the deed. He was almost relieved at the excuse to stop his clumsy efforts when Little George came stomping out of the trees.

"What is it?" Blake asked, noting the irritation on his first's face. Something had bothered the man mightily.

"A band of men have ridden up. Campbells." He said the word with disgust, as if he actually knew the men in question, though as far as Blake was aware, Little George didn't know anyone in Scotland.

"So?" Blake asked. "They are probably friends of Comen's too, and seeking a spot to rest on their travels."

"Aye." Little George nodded. "But they have joined Gavin and the women at the fire, and Gavin is regaling them with tales of our troubles with keeping the women. The Campbells are finding it mighty amusing . . . and they are flirting outrageously with Seonaid and little Aeldra." The last part seemed to upset Little George more than anything else, and Blake wondered if the man was attracted to Seonaid's cousin. Either way, if Gavin had been regaling the Campbells with tales of their troubles keeping the women in line, Blake would be the laughingstock of Scotland, he realized with a sigh.

"I could do with a hand after all," Blake announced, gesturing to his poorly half pleated plaid. "Send Gavin down to help me with it."

It wasn't until Rolfe had nodded and turned to walk back with Little George that Blake realized that might not have been the most clever tactical move. Now he would add the fact that he couldn't dress himself to the other tales. At least it would get Gavin away from the men and shut him up.

"Bloody hell," he muttered under his breath and set back to work on the plaid. He hadn't given a very impressive showing to date. Every time she managed to escape him, Blake felt as if he appeared that much less able in her eyes. He wasn't used to appearing incompetent. He was a warrior, for heaven's sake. Lords all over England paid exorbitant fees for him and Amaury to bring their warriors out to fight battles for them. And now he was the focus of humorous stories, and couldn't even dress without assistance.

" 'Tis quite odd really." _____

"What is odd, Helen?" Seonaid asked the question in

a desultory voice. Floating on the loch's surface, its cool water lapping at and caressing her naked body, she was too relaxed to work up any real interest in what the woman might be talking about. It was the first chance she'd had to relax since leaving the abbey. After the unfortunate incident with the poisoned stew, she had decided there was little chance the men would let down their guard again, at least not until they reached Dunbar. That being the case, Seonaid had concluded it might be best to simply allow themselves to be escorted back to her home, then try again once they were there.

Fortunately, Blake had allowed Seonaid and Aeldra to carry their swords once again. Unfortunately, he was still insisting that the women ride with the men. Aside from drawing out the trip because they were forced to move at a slower pace to avoid overtaxing the horses, it had also made for a terribly strained ride. At least it had for Seonaid, who found it incredibly discomfiting riding double with Blake. She was terribly aware of his chest at her back, his legs rubbing against hers and his arms around her body. She had sat silent and stiff for the few hours they had ridden yesterday after leaving Comen's cottage behind, and through the whole day today as they had traveled.

When they had come upon this small loch in late afternoon, Blake had decided they would stop early and set up camp for the night. Lord Rolfe had seemed annoyed, but Seonaid had been relieved. It might delay arriving home by a few more hours, but her muscles had been aching from sitting so tensely before Sherwell on his horse, and she had wanted nothing more than a swim in the cool water. She had been so eager for the treat that Seonaid hadn't even minded when Blake and Lord Rolfe had insisted the women needn't aid in making camp, but should go tend to their evening ablutions. Not that she expected the men would ever allow any of them to cook for them again, but the three of them could have helped by bedding down the horses and collecting wood for a fire. Were they traveling with her father and his men, they would have been expected to do so. They had grown up fighting to prove they were as strong, smart, and skilled as the Dunbar men. Treating them like fragile ladies was not allowed.

"Lord Blake," Helen explained what she had been speaking of. "I have heard it said he could talk the birds out of the trees yet have seen no evidence of this skill to date. He has yet to say anything the least complimentary. I can understand why he would not attempt to flirt with or flatter me, as I am dressed as a nun, but why has he not attempted to use his silver tongue on you to make you stop attempting to escape? I think it just seems odd."

A snort sounded behind Seonaid, but she didn't open her eyes or glance around in the water to where she knew her cousin was swimming. Seonaid was busy controlling her expression to hide her own feelings regarding the matter. In truth, it had already occurred to her that his sweet tongue appeared to be missing in her presence. The man certainly had not taxed himself in an effort to try to compliment her, and though she would never admit it, Seonaid found it a touch distress-

ing. Was it that he could find nothing about her to compliment? Or could he simply not be bothered because
he disliked her so? Either possibility was distressing.
While she was trying to avoid it as long as she possibly
could, she knew she would have to marry him eventually. Who wanted to be married to a man who thought
so little of his bride?

"Mayhap he realizes 'twould be a waste of time,"
Seonaid said at last, with forced derision.

" 'Tis possible," Helen allowed. "You are not like
other women, after all. He may realize that sweet words
are not apt to win you."

Seoanid opened her eyes and frowned up at the darkening sky. She had never considered whether fine words
would win her or not. She had never considered what
would impress her. She might like sweet words, though
that would surprise anyone who knew her. Seonaid had
been fighting to make a place for herself in her own
clan her entire life. From childhood she had known she
was betrothed to the Sherwell, and had listened to her
father curse the name just as long. As the Sherwells were
so hated by her father, it had always seemed to her that
being intended to marry one was a bad thing, a strike
against her. She had fought to make herself acceptable,
to make him proud, and the only way she could think to
do that was to be the best soldier she could be. But perhaps sweet words would be nice once in a while. And
the fact that he hadn't bothered with them rankled her.
She almost found it hurtful. What was wrong with her?
Was she not worthy of compliments?

Hurt pride, fear, and anger mingling through her, Seonaid stood up in the water and moved toward shore. She'd had enough relaxation for one day.

"The women seem to be taking their time about their ablutions," Rolfe commented.

"Women always do," Blake said as he added wood to the fire.

"You do not think they have managed to flee again?"

"They will not try to flee without horses, and I have four men watching the animals," Blake reassured him.

"Aye, I know." When his words brought Blake's questioning gaze his way, Rolfe shrugged. "They are the king's men, in my charge to see to these weddings. They check with me on every order you give them."

Blake scowled at the news. He had quite forgotten the men were not under his rule. He was used to having an army of warriors at his service. But he had dispersed most of his own men, allowing them time to visit their families while he saw to this duty. The knights traveling with them were under Rolfe's rule. He would have to try to keep that in mind.

"What if the Dunbars have friends near here we know not about? The women could have slipped away, gained horses from them, and—" Rolfe broke off abruptly when Blake straightened to peer at him sharply.

"Do you know something I do not?"

"Nay." Rolfe's mouth turned down in a frown as his gaze slid around the surrounding trees. "I just have a feeling something is not right."

Blake shifted on his feet, his own gaze slipping around the surrounding forest. He would have shrugged off Rolfe's concerns except that he too had felt a bit anxious since stopping for the night. It was nothing he could give a name to, simply a faint sense that all was not well. Or perhaps a sense that someone was watching them, that they weren't alone.

"I'll go check on them," he said finally.

Rolfe merely nodded, but was obviously relieved. Blake supposed the man was well past tired of the whole endeavor.

A mere gesture to Little George was enough to make the large man take his place at the fire, then Blake headed into the trees. There was a narrow path leading from the small clearing in the woods down to the edge of the loch. It was obvious others had set up camp here on occasion over the years. Blake wasn't surprised. It was quite a handy spot. The clearing rested a good twenty feet away from the loch itself, allowing privacy to anyone wishing to bathe or tend to other personal needs.

He moved at a quick clip at first, but slowed when he knew he was nearing the end of the trees and would soon step out on the narrow clearing along the loch's edge. His ears began to strain then, listening for sounds from the women that would tell him their location. He didn't wish to mortify Sister Helen by catching her in a state of undress. He didn't really think such an occurrence would be all that upsetting to Seonaid or Aeldra. He could be wrong, but his betrothed's lack of maidenly modesty regarding his nudity suggested she had seen her father's men or even her brother and cousin in a similar state a time or two in the past, and perhaps had been spotted herself as well, which he supposed would be quite likely considering her life riding with the men.

Blake found the idea of other men seeing Seonaid's naked body a bit unsettling, so he quickly pushed the thought away and concentrated a little harder on detecting voices or the sound of splashing water, but there was no sound at all coming from up ahead. Blake tried not to let this and Rolfe's comments bother him, but he did pick up his step a bit. If the women had slipped away again, and—

The thought died abruptly as he stepped out of the trees and spotted the women in question. Helen and Aeldra were still in the water. The small Scot was floating on the surface, her eyes closed, and Helen was simply standing in the water, watching Seonaid, who was on the shore and walking toward where her clothing lay in a heap. Blake couldn't take his eyes off her.

In Blake's experience, women were soft. They had soft bodies with curved hips, plump thighs, and gently rounded breasts and bellies. It was one of the things he liked best about them. They were comfort with feet, their breasts soft pillows for his head, their bodies warm cushions he could sink his into. There was nothing soft about Seonaid. Her body was all lithe muscle that shifted and stretched as she moved. He was sure if he touched her, she would be as hard as any one of his soldiers. And yet she was still beautiful, her body as sleek as a cat's, her every move feline in its grace. She might not be a soft rest for his head and body, but she was as much of a feast for his eye as any woman he had ever met.

Blake couldn't look away from her lean length. His mouth had gone dry at first sight of her. When she reached her plaid and suddenly glanced up, Blake found himself helpless to do anything but stare back as her eyes went wide with surprise. While he was still searching his mind for something to say, an apology perhaps, her surprise turned to a flash of what might have been alarm. It was quickly followed by a mask of steely determination.

Nothing in Blake's life had shocked him more than when she suddenly reached down, purposefully grabbed her sword, then strode forward.

He was so stunned at such an aggressive reaction to his presence that he merely stood there, frozen. Perhaps if she had raised her sword or said something, he would have snapped out of his surprise and reacted, instead of just standing there like an idiot—or like a child caught peeking. Then movement in the water drew his gaze in time to see Aeldra come bounding out. Like Seonaid, the short blonde did not even bother with her shift, but grabbed her sword instead. It was at that moment that Sister Helen turned and spotted him there. The shriek she let loose was what Blake had needed to snap him out of his shock.

"I was not—" he began apologetically, but Seonaid had reached him and, much to his amazement, reached out with her free hand and gave him a shove. Caught off guard, Blake stumbled to the side, regained his footing, and started to turn back, just as the clang of metal hitting metal rang in his ears.

Completely alert now, Blake whirled to see that Seonaid was doing battle with a man who had apparently approached him from behind. She hadn't been reacting to him at all, or perhaps the first surprised widening of eyes had been at the sight of him, but apparently the sword grabbing and steely determination had been caused by this fellow's approach.

These fellows, he corrected himself, as he spotted a second and third man moving around the battling couple. Blake automatically reached for his own sword, only to find he'd left the bloody thing at the campsite. If his memory served him correctly, it was leaning against a log near where he had been building the fire. He hadn't thought to grab it before heading down to the loch's edge. Why would he? He hadn't thought he'd need it to simply check on the women.

Bloody hell, Blake thought with disgust even as his eyes skittered over the area. He spotted a good-sized branch nearby and snatched it up. It would do little against a sword, but was better than nothing.

Blake had raised the branch in hand and braced himself for the attack when Aeldra, naked and still wet, raced past him, yelling a war cry as she ran. The woman might be small, but her bellow near ripped the ears off his head.

Bloody hell, he thought again as the little Scot stopped the two men by engaging the first in battle. Blake stood and gaped for a moment at the sight of the two beautiful, naked women swinging their swords so skillfully. Fortunately for him, the third man also was momentarily stunned into stillness. As were the other three men he now saw behind them. There were six in all, it would seem. And other than the two presently receiving a fighting lesson, they were all rooted to the spot at the sight of the two women battling their compatriots; one raven-haired and tall, one blond and small, both seeming completely oblivious to their own nudity.

The men definitely were not. Their eyes were wide and hungry as they watched the women swing their swords overhead, the movement seeming to lengthen their torsos, drawing out their already flat stomachs and, lifting their firm breasts. It was a hypnotic sight, even for the men battling them it would seem, for either they were completely unskilled warriors or they were too distracted by the women to fight properly. Seonaid and Aeldra had no trouble taking advantage of their distracted state. Seonaid dispatched the first man she engaged within three blows; Aeldra was not far behind. Then both women turned to the other four men on the edge of the woods.

The men looked so entranced at the sight of the two naked women facing them, Blake half-expected them to drop their swords and pledge their fealty. One even had a silly grin on his face, as if he'd wandered into a bevy of bathing beauties offering to bed him rather than behead him. But what they would have done would never be known, for the silence of the clearing was suddenly broken by the snapping of twigs and the thunder of footsteps as a great herd of beasts crashed through the woods toward them. Seonaid and Aeldra immediately backed away from the four men, forcing Blake to back up with them. They kept their swords pointed at the four they had yet to finish, but warily noted the direction the sound was coming from as they gave themselves room to be able to fight off attackers from either direction.

When Little George charged out of the woods with Rolfe and a passel of knights on their heels, Blake realized that Helen's scream must have been heard. Relaxing, he turned his attention back to the attackers even as the women did, only to find the spot where they had been was now empty. They had fled during the distraction and had even taken their wounded with them.

"Oh, dear."

The soft murmur of dismay drew Blake's gaze back to their would-be rescuers, who were all now standing still, staring at the naked women, just as their attackers had. Bishop Wykeham was the speaker, and even he seemed unable to tear his gaze away from the sight. Blake scowled and moved toward the group of men, but couldn't resist glancing back over his shoulder as he did. The sight that met his gaze gave him sympathy for the other men. The women were still frozen in battle stance, legs slightly parted, swords up and at the ready, pale skin pulled tight over taut muscles. They could have been Roman statues. They were a beautiful sight to behold.

And everyone was beholding them.

"We were attacked," he announced grimly, his voice sharp enough to draw every eye his way, though some came very reluctantly, he noted. "They ran off as you came stomping into the clearing."

Silence met his announcement, but Blake couldn't

help noticing the way every man's eyes kept slipping past him, then back, then to the women again.

"What are you waiting for?" he snapped with irritation, snatching his sword from Little George. The man had obviously noted its presence by the fire and had the foresight to bring it to him when they'd heard the scream. "Search the woods. They cannot have traveled far while they are dragging two wounded men with them."

"Two dead men," Seonaid corrected, and Blake glanced over his shoulder again as she relaxed her stance and moved unhurriedly toward her clothes. "At least mine was dead."

"Mine too," Aeldra announced, following her in the same relaxed fashion.

Seonaid nodded, as if she'd expected as much, then said, "Now, if ye've all done enough gawkin', could ye no go away an' let us dress?"

Blake forced his eyes up from watching her as she walked and cleared his throat as he turned back to the men. "Come. Move back into the woods and give them privacy."

"Do you think we should?" Rolfe asked. "What if the attackers have not gone far? They could return."

It was a valid point, but Blake couldn't help noticing the way Rolfe's gaze kept skittering out toward the loch where Sister Helen still huddled. She had moved closer to shore, but had apparently dropped to her knees because the water covered her up to her neck. She might have thought she was preserving her modesty, but the water was extremely clear and they could see a good deal of her upper body even underwater.

Blake had never imagined a bride of God in the nude, but he also would never look at one again in the same light. God's toes, becoming a nun did not leave a woman a dried-out husk, as he had always imagined. Sister Helen had as lush a figure as any of the women at court. It was as beautiful in its own way as Seoanid's.

"We will stay close enough to hear if you shout," he announced to the women, forcing his gaze away and gesturing for Rolfe and Little George to back off into the woods. The bishop was already walking away, and the other men had heeded his orders and headed off to look for the men who might still be milling about in the forest. Though he would not have been surprised to hear that they were searching very close at hand, close enough to keep an eye on the women as well.

"Oh, aye. Thanks fer that," Seonaid said dryly in response to his words. "Ye were ever so helpful the first time they attacked, it does my heart good to know yer near enough to help again should they return."

Blake winced, but merely sighed and ushered Rolfe and Little George ahead of him.

Chapter Eight

"He had no sword," Aeldra murmured as she snatched up her shift to pull it on.

Seonaid grimaced as she tugged her shortened shift over her head. Her cousin had ever been fair and was quietly rebuking her for embarrassing her betrothed with her parting words.

"He had no sword an' grabbed up a stick to try to help us fight," the woman persisted.

"Aye, I ken," Seonaid admitted reluctantly. She'd almost yelled at him to get the hell out of the way and let them get on with it. She'd been a bit distracted, trying to keep an eye out to be sure the man didn't come bulling into the group of men with his branch. Fortunately, he had appeared as dumbstruck by the scene as their attackers were. Though she would never admit it, it had been terribly embarrassing to be caught unclothed and then be forced to battle that way. But it had also been rather handy in one respect, as it had clearly given them the advantage. Seonaid wasn't foolish enough to imagine it was their advanced skill with the sword that had so enthralled everyone. Nay, it was the fact that they'd been naked that had set the men back on their heels. Most women would have at least pulled on their shifts before storming into the fray. Their lack of modesty had no doubt dismayed the men as much as the sight of them had seemed to mesmerize them. But when it came to battle, who gave a damn what you were wearing? It was definitely not a time to consider fashion.

Seonaid was aware of Aeldra's continued stare as she pulled on her braies, then picked up her plaid. She tried to ignore the eyes boring into the back of her head as she gave the material a shake, then laid it on the ground to pleat, but found it impossible. It didn't help that her own conscience was pricking her for the unfair insult.

"Oh, all right," she gave in with irritation. "I'll apologize to him later."

Aeldra's mouth quirked at the reluctant words, but she knew her too well and asked, "When?"

"Later. When the time is right." Seonaid straightened her shoulders bullishly as she answered. She would not be pushed into giving a date and time for the apology. She'd give him one when she bloody well felt like it. Of course, Aeldra was kin, carried the same blood, and could be just as bullish. Fortunately, she didn't get a chance to force the issue. Helen had made her way out of the water and now rushed over to join them, snatching up her own clothes along the way.

"Seonaid, we have to go," Helen blurted, tugging her shift on as she spoke.

Seonaid paused in her pleating to peer up at the other woman with surprise. "Go where?"

"Anywhere. Away from here before those men return."

"They'll no return, Helen," Aeldra said reassuringly. "An' do they, we'll take care o' them again."

Seonaid wanted to agree with her cousin, but there was something about the woman's panic that gave her pause. "Did ye recognize them, Helen?"

"Aye." The redhead bit her lip. Her gaze moved around the trees surrounding them, as if expecting them to come running out of the trees again at any moment. "They were Camerons."

Seonaid expelled her breath on a sigh, then her mouth went firm and she turned back to her plaid and began pleating more quickly. Despite the way her mind was now racing, she sensed when Aeldra moved away to collect her own clothes.

"I thought I recognized one of the men when we passed them this morning," Helen added, anxiety heavy in her voice. "But we rode by so quickly, I was not sure."

"This mornin'?" Aeldra asked as she returned with her clothes and began to don them.

"Aye. Do you not recall the party we passed on the road this morning? There were six of them; three dark-haired, two blond, and a redhead, just as these men were. They moved to the side to make way for us. I thought I recognized one of them from Cameron's men, but I did not get a good look and, in any case, I was not close enough to see any of them very clearly," she admitted. "It must have been them, though. They must have recognized me and followed us."

Seonaid raised her head and took in the agitation in Helen's jerky movements as she tugged on her clothes. Seonaid had a vague recollection of passing a small party of travelers but had been rather distracted with the way Blake's arm had been rubbing against the bottom of her breast as they rode. He had tightened his hold on both her and the reins at the first sight of the oncoming party, presumably in case he needed extra control should trouble break out. He had also urged his mount to a faster speed so that they had passed quickly. Seonaid hadn't really caught more than a glimpse of the party as they passed, though it could have been the same men. There *had* been six, if she recalled correctly, and it did seem to her that there had been three dark, two blonds and a redhead in the party. A coincidence? Or had they followed them, waited for them to make camp, then snuck up on the women while they were bathing?

On the women and Blake, she reminded herself. They had entered the clearing directly on his heels. Of course, they might have been preparing to make their move when Blake had appeared, and seeing that he was weaponless and no threat, had attacked.

"Aye. 'Twas the same men," Aeldra murmured as she knelt to pleat her own plaid. "We passed them early this mornin'. I got a pretty good look at them then an' again just now while we were afightin'. 'Twere the same men."

Seonaid nodded slowly. If Aeldra said it was so, it was so. She had excellent vision. So, Rollo's men had passed them by chance this morning, recognized Helen—despite Sister Blanche's outfit—followed, and attacked.

Helen was right; they would have to head out immediately. Rollo would be desperate to see the redhead dead. Seonaid was as aware as he must be that if he didn't kill her before her father caught up to her, he would lose his chance, and once it became known that he had planned to kill her . . . Helen was English. Her father was wealthy, and wealth usually meant power. Her father could put pressure on his English king, who would put pressure on their Scottish king, and Rollo could very well lose his head over the matter.

"Was Rollo among the men?" she asked suddenly.

"Nay, he was not among them." The woman was just starting to relax at that realization when Aeldra spoke up.

"He wouldn't be foolish enough to be among the attackers, in case the plan failed—as it did. He wouldna have wanted to be recognized. 'Sides, he probably has several parties out lookin' for her."

"Aye," Seonaid agreed. Finished with her pleating, she donned her plaid over her braies and the shortened shift and stood as Aeldra completed her own dress. Seoniad patted an anxious-looking Helen on the shoulder, then took her arm and turned her toward camp. "Come. We should leave at once. We'll ride for Dunbar an' the safety it offers."

"Surely you do not think they would attack again?"

Helen said with alarm. "There are only four of them left and we have the king's men traveling with us."

"They'll no attack right away," she reassured her. "But three of them will stay nearby to trail us while the fourth rides to Rollo an' tells him where you are an' how many men we have. Then he shall bring twice or thrice that many back to attack."

"He will?" Helen was goggling.

" 'Tis what I'd do," Seonaid answered with a shrug, then urged her into the trees. " 'Tis best we get to Dunbar 'ere he returns. Once we're safely there, we can send a message to yer father. Though that shouldna be necessary. Once we reach Dunbar, Rollo will ken he has lost, an'—if he's any sense at all—will disappear."

"But—" Helen tripped over a tree root, managing to keep her feet thanks to Seonaid's hold on her arm, then said, "The men will not be willing to leave now. They just bedded the horses down for the night."

"We'll have to tell them the truth o' things," Seonaid decided. "Explain that ye're no a sister, an'—"

"But what if they do not believe you?" When Seonaid paused and peered at her blankly, she went on. "We have tried to escape them at every turn and have even poisoned them. The only thing we have not done is lie. Well, we have lied about me, but they do not know that. If you admit that we were lying about me, they may not believe anything we have to say. They may think this is simply another attempt to escape, part of some greater plot. Can we not just slip away and—"

Seonaid stopped her with a hand on her shoulder. The woman was in a panic. "Trust me," she said solemnly.

Helen hesitated, then slowly nodded. Satisfied, Seonaid turned and continued into camp. Her gaze shot between Lord Rolfe and Blake as she entered, but finally settled on Lord Rolfe. He seemed more likely to be willing to listen to her. He was eager to see this wedding done and be about his business anyway, so he would hardly mind rushing to Dunbar. He merely needed a good excuse to do so.

"My lord?"

Lord Rolfe and the bishop both stood as they approached them at the fire.

"Aye, Lady Seonaid?" Rolfe asked politely, but she noticed his gaze was skittering to Lady Helen—or Sister Helen, as he thought she was. Interesting, Seonaid thought, and stored the knowledge aside for later consideration.

"It'd be wise to leave now an' ride night an' day until we reach Dunbar," she announced bluntly.

Lord Rolfe's jaw dropped at this suggestion, and she supposed she couldn't blame him. Until now she'd done everything she could to avoid returning to Dunbar and tending to the wedding, yet here she was suggesting they hurry there.

"Is there a reason for this sudden suggestion?" Bishop Wykeham asked when Rolfe continued to gape like a fish out of water.

Seonaid turned to the holy man and nodded grimly. "I fear we're like to be attacked again. We passed those men who attacked us earlier this morning. 'Tis obvious they followed with the intention o' attackin'. I fear they'll try it again."

"But you and your cousin defeated them," the bishop pointed out. "They are two less men now than they were to start with; surely they will not be foolish enough to try attacking again."

"No by themselves," Seonaid agreed. Her comment appeared to help Rolfe's mind to start to function again.

"You think they will fetch more men to come back and try again," he said, and Seonaid nodded. Rolfe considered this, then tilted his head slightly to ask, "Did you recognize the men? Do you know who they could be?"

Seonaid hesitated. After what Helen had said, she'd rather not tell the truth, but part of the truth would be all right. She chose her words carefully when she finally said, "Our clan has many enemies. The Cameron keep is no far from here."

"The Camerons?" Rolfe looked surprised.

"Aye. A fouler lot of scabbies ye'll never see. They've had a grudge against us forever. If 'twas them . . ." Seonaid shrugged and let the sentence trail away.

"We can handle a couple of Camerons," Blake announced, making his presence known. Apparently he'd been made curious by the little huddle taking place and moved to join it. Seonaid glanced over her shoulder and found herself staring at his chest. She actually had to tip her head up to see that he was smiling down at her with reassurance. Having to look up to meet someone's eyes was a new experience in itself, but one she rather liked. It was nice not to tower over everyone for a change.

"Lady Seonaid was just saying that she thinks those men who attacked will go fetch more men and return," Rolfe explained to Blake.

"Nay," Seonaid said. "I doona think they will, I *ken* they will. They'll fetch back the rest of the clan; then the Cameron club shall come down on us like a great foot. They'll slaughter us good an' proper, at least the men. The women will wish they were dead."

"Oh, dear," Bishop Wykeham murmured. "Perhaps we had best saddle up and head for Dunbar."

"Aye," Rolfe agreed, his expression grim. "We could be there by late tomorrow evening or early the day after if we leave now. At any rate, it would put us ahead of the Camerons, and that is good enough for me."

Seonaid relaxed as the Englishman turned away and began shouting orders, but when she turned toward Helen and Aeldra it was to find Blake in her way. He was watching her with a narrow-eyed look that stunk of suspicion, and said that he suspected she was up to something. Seonaid didn't care. So long as they got Helen safely to Dunbar, she didn't really care what the Sherwell thought.

They rode through the night and most of the next day, forced to go at a slower pace than Seonaid would have liked because of the three horses carrying two people each. She found it rather frustrating, but Blake would not give in to the idea of the women being given back their mounts and Lord Rolfe, after a hesitation, had agreed with him. It seemed the king's man believed her enough to want to move, but not enough to risk the women being able to slip away again.

Seonaid forced herself to accept the situation. There was little else she could do. But it had been a long, tense ride, with her sitting as stiff and erect as a soldier the whole way in an effort to keep any part of her body from touching any part of Blake's. When midafternoon rolled around and Blake decided they should stop to let the mounts rest, she was most relieved. Helen was obviously not. The moment Lord Rolfe lifted her down off his mount, she rushed to Seonaid's side.

"Should we be stopping?" she asked, grabbing up her skirts to trail Seonaid down the sloping hill toward the trees.

Blake had decided to stop on a hilltop that allowed a clear view of the surrounding area. A watch would be set in place while everyone rested. No one would be able to approach without being spotted, at least while it was light. She suspected the moment darkness fell, Blake would have them back on their horses and riding again. At least she hoped he would. It was not much farther to Dunbar. They could be there by midmorning the next day if they left again as the sun set.

"The horses need rest," Seonaid said in answer to Helen's question as Aeldra caught up to them. "We'll no get far do the horses die under us."

"Oh, aye." Helen didn't sound pleased, but didn't argue the point either.

"We'd be at Dunbar by now had the men no insisted on our ridin' with them," Aeldra grumbled as they reached the trees.

"Aye," Seonaid agreed.

" 'Tis damned uncomfortable aridin' with that great lout Stupid George."

"Little George," Helen corrected.

The small Scot gave a sniff. "It should be Stupid George, if ye ask me."

Her words surprised a laugh out of Seonaid and she glanced at her cousin. "Givin' ye trouble, is he?"

"Aye. Ridin' with him is about as comfortable as ridin' on a great bouncin' stone."

Seonaid merely shook her head. She had noticed her cousin rode with Little George much as she rode with Blake, stiff and straight as a bow. Which made her wonder if her cousin found herself attracted to the large man in the same way she herself was attracted to Blake. But the image of the two together was so bizarre she shook her head. 'Twas like envisioning an Irish wolfhound and a Scottish terrier together.

"I find riding with Lord Rolfe most comfortable," Helen spoke up, drawing Seonaid and Aeldra's attention. "It feels safe and warm, and I find I doze off most of the time and sleep."

"That being the case, ye should be the one Sherwell posts as guard," Aeldra teased. "Yer probably the only one o' any o' us who's had any sleep in the last two days."

"That may be true," Helen said seriously. "Mayhap I should suggest it to Lord Rolfe."

Seonaid laughed at the suggestion as the women separated to find their own private spots to tend to personal needs, but the thought stayed with her as she tended to business. She had spotted Helen sleeping several times today and had no doubt the woman had rested through a good portion of the ride the night before. The small redhead had been curled up against Lord Rolfe like a cuddly ginger kitten, sound asleep and held in place by his surrounding arms. She probably *was* the only one of them in any shape to keep guard, or do anything else. Now, if Seonaid and Aeldra were to do the same when they rode out again that evening, when they arrived at Dunbar, they would be the only ones in any shape to do anything ... like ride straight out again while the men all rested and recovered from the journey. The very thought brought a small laugh from Seonaid.

"Somethin' amuse ye?" Aeldra asked curiously as the three women met up again where they had split. "I thought I heard ye cacklin' yer evil cackle a minute ago."

"Me evil cackle, eh?" Seonaid asked with amusement, then explained the thought that had amused her so.

"The women seem awfully cheerful," Blake said with some suspicion as he watched them make their way back up the hill. "What do you suppose they are up to now?"

"Probably nothing," Rolfe said, also watching them. "No doubt their good mood is because they are the only ones who have had any sleep."

Blake glanced at him with surprise. "Sister Helen slept on the ride?"

"Like a babe in its mother's arms. Did Seonaid not sleep?"

"Nay," Blake admitted, his eyes returning to the approaching women. Seonaid hadn't slept, she hadn't even relaxed; she'd been as stiff as a board in his arms the entire ride. Which had made it impossible for him to relax either. It had been a damned uncomfortable ride.

Turning away, he moved to find a spot to lay down and catch a nap. They wouldn't be stopping long. Four hours at most, and then they would have to be on their way again.

Seonaid blinked her eyes open and stared sleepily up at the handsome face bent over her own. A smile of welcome began to curve her lips; then her brain awakened as she realized who she was smiling at. She abruptly frowned and struggled to sit up as she recalled where she was. On horseback, very much in the lap of the Sherwell.

"Did you sleep well?"

Seonaid ignored the question as she forced herself upright in the saddle before him. She knew the man had been surprised when, on getting back on the horse, she had forced herself to relax and lean into him. Though she had intended to do so, she was still surprised that she had actually fallen asleep in his arms. But once she had forced her mind and body to relax, the lulling rhythm of the horse had sent her off to sleep.

"You seemed to sleep well. You were snoring," he informed her, adding helpfully, "and drooling."

Seonaid reached up, mortified to find that he was telling the truth—her cheek was damp. She wiped the drool away with irritation and sat a little stiffer before him as her gaze slid around the area they were riding through. They were ascending a hill, a very familiar-looking hill.

"We're home," she murmured with surprise as they crested the hill and Dunbar keep came into view. Seonaid felt happiness well up within her at the sight of the castle she'd grown up in. No matter why she left, or for how long, she always had this sensation on returning. Her father was here and her brother, Giorsal, and Aeldra's brother Allistair, and now her sister-in-law, Iliana, too. Her family.

The pleased smile remained in place until they approached the bridge over the moat and she spotted the charred and blackened bodies and rubble on the ground in front of the wall. Seonaid stiffened before Blake, desperate to know what had happened. She relaxed a bit when she recognized the men standing guard on the wall, and only then did her attention turn to scanning the area to see the traces of battle.

Dunbar had been attacked. Lord Rolfe, the bishop, and Little George urged their horses closer to Blake's.

"What think you?" Lord Rolfe asked.

"Greenweld?" Blake suggested as they rode across the bridge and entered the bailey. "It looks like there was a siege."

Seonaid wasn't really listening to the men; she could see for herself what had taken place. A siege was right. Someone had attacked the castle, catapulting burning missiles over the walls. There was quite a bit of damage to various buildings within. There were no bodies laying inside the walls, but then, there wouldn't be. Those would have been seen to first.

The bodies outside the wall would be seen to last, if their own people didn't beg permission to return to tend to the matter themselves.

Seonaid controlled herself as long as she could, but Blake had slowed his mount even further as they had entered the bailey and was now moving at a snail's pace. Halfway across the bailey, she could stand it no longer and tossed one leg over the beast to propel herself off the mount.

Blake let loose a sound of surprise and brought the horse to a halt to prevent running her over, but he didn't try to stop her.

Landing on the hard-packed dirt of the bailey, Seonaid broke into a run, racing toward the keep. The door opened as she started up the stairs and she glanced up to see wee Willie, the stable master's son, step out. A smile broke out on the lad's face when he spotted her.

"Seonaid!" he cried in greeting, and she stumbled to a halt at the sight of the bandages on the boy's arm.

"Willie?" She paused to run a hand over his good arm, her gaze locked on the bandages on his other one. "Are ye all right, lad?"

"Aye." His smiled widened. "Just a bit o' a burn," he assured her. "Lady Iliana took care o' it."

"Is everyone—? Was anyone—?" She stumbled over her own words, finding it difficult to ask what she wanted to know. "Father?" she got out finally.

"He took an arrow to the shoulder," he informed her, his little freckled face solemn.

"An arrow?" Seonaid echoed with horror.

"Aye, but Lady Iliana tended to it right quick an' says he'll be fine."

"Oh, good," she breathed the word, then asked, "a-an' Duncan?"

"He's fine. He was off tryin' to rescue ye from the Colquhouns."

"The Colquhouns?" Seonaid stared at him in confusion.

"Aye. We got news ye'd been kidnaped by the Colquhouns. Duncan took most of the men an' rode out to get ye back. But it was a trick. Greenweld was jest tryin' to lure the men out so he could lay siege to the castle. He planned to take over before the men could return to stop him. But Lady Iliana's smart an' she held them off. Gave 'em a good fight too."

"Iliana? What about Father?"

"Well, he took that arrow," Willie reminded her. "He's fine now, but fer a while there he was unconscious an'—" He shrugged. "Lady Iliana had to take over. She did a right fine job o' it too. Did us proud."

Seonaid nodded but was a bit amazed that her sister-in-law had managed to hold off Greenweld. Iliana was such a tiny little thing, which didn't mean much, she supposed, Aeldra was small too, but skilled in battle. However, Iliana wasn't. She was small and pretty and ladylike and knew all there was to know about being a wife, but the news that she had the ability to hold off an army set Seonaid to thinking. She had thought they

were opposites—Lady Iliana skilled at female things
while Seonaid boasted battle skills. It would seem, however, that Iliana was a far more talented woman. It was a
depressing realization.

"What about Allistair an' Giorsal an' everyone else?"
Aeldra asked, and Seonaid glanced to the side with surprise, not having realized that the other woman was
there.

Suddenly aware that Willie hadn't answered the question, Seonaid turned back to the boy. The expression
on his face and the way he was now staring at the
ground made her stomach drop. She could only think
the news was bad, and immediately suspected it was
about Giorsal, Aeldra and Allistair's aunt. Her cousins
had come to live with their mother's sister when their
own parents had died. Giorsal was a mother to them.
Whatever the bad news was, it had to be about her. Allistair would have been with Duncan and the other men.

"Is it Giorsal?" Aeldra asked, her thoughts apparently
running along the same lines as Seonaid's.

Willie shook his head but still wouldn't look up.

"Did Allistair no' go with Duncan?" Seonaid asked
and her stomach sank even further when the boy shook
his head again. If Allistair had been here and able, he
would have been the one to take over when Angus had
been felled. But Iliana had.

"Is Allistair . . . ?" Aeldra's voice broke as Willie raised
sad eyes to her. Whirling, the petite blonde raced down
the stairs and charged off across the bailey. Seonaid was
right behind her. Taller and able to take longer strides,
she could have easily caught up and overtaken her

cousin, but she stayed behind, knowing she was heading for Giorsal's cottage to find out what had happened. Allistair was Aeldra's brother, she had the right to know first.

She had nearly reached Giorsal's cottage when Seonaid was suddenly caught by the arm and drawn up short. Whirling to face her captor, she scowled to find Blake had run after her and caught up to her.

"Let me go," she hissed, glancing over her shoulder to see Aeldra disappearing into the nearby cottage.

"Nay, my lady. There will be no more running away. You—"

"I'm no runnin' away," Seonaid snapped impatiently. "Let me go."

"You are not running away?" Blake asked slowly.

"Nay. Something has happened to Allistair, Aeldra's brother. I think he may be dead," her voice cracked on the word. Rallying herself, she gave her arm a shake, trying to free herself of his hold. "Now let me go. Aeldra needs me."

Blake released her at once and stepped back, watching as she turned away and hurried after Aeldra. Seonaid almost expected the man to follow her into the cottage, but a glance over her shoulder before she slipped inside showed her that he was still where she'd left him, simply watching. Little George was approaching from the keep at a gallop. The man was large and strong but not overly quick, and was just catching up.

In the next moment, Seonaid forgot all about the two men as Aeldra's distressed cry drew her attention to the conversation she had walked in on.

"What? But Allistair—"

"He should have been laird," Giorsal hissed, interrupting the blonde. "As yer fither should have before him. Angus and he were twins. He had as much right to rule, and he should have ruled the Dunbars. And Allistair should have ruled after him."

"But Father didna want to rule. He was happy to let Uncle Angus—"

"They claim Allistair was killed by Greenweld," the old woman went on bitterly, as if Aeldra hadn't even spoken. "But it isna true, I tell ye. Greenweld would no have killed him. They were working together."

"What?" It was an almost breathless gasp of horror from Aeldra. "Allistair was with Greenweld? Why?"

"To get back what was rightfully his," Giorsal said grimly. "Greenweld was goin' to help him get Dunbar back."

"But what about Uncle Angus an' Duncan?"

Giorsal shrugged. "With them out o' the way, Allistair'd be laird."

"An' Seonaid?" Aeldra asked grimly.

"He wanted to marry her. He said it would strengthen his claim."

"So Allistair plotted with that vile Greenweld an' betrayed everyone?"

Giorsal nodded with satisfaction. "It was my idea. He didna want to at first, but I convinced him. Necessity makes strange bedfellows, an' I kenned Greenweld could help Allistair to gain possession of the keep an' the clan chief's seat. He deserved it. But he didna agree until I pointed out he could have Seonaid that way, that

Greenweld could send men out to kill the Englishman an' she'd be free to marry him, that in her grief for her father an' brother, she'd be easily led into marriage were he there to offer her support. It would have worked too," she said furiously, "but Duncan returned earlier than he was supposed to an' killed my baby."

"You convinced him to do this? To betray his own people?"

Seonaid's eyes had been frozen with fascinated horror on the old woman's bitter face up to now, but the flat sound of Aeldra's voice drew her gaze down to her. Aeldra had been on her knees at Giorsal's feet with her back to the door when Seonaid had entered. She still was, but where she had seemed like a collapsed doll then, she was stiff now, as if a stick had been slid up her back. Her head was erect and slightly lifted and her tone of voice was dead, but with an undercurrent of cold fury that made Seonaid's heart ache. Allistair had died while attempting to betray them all, but he had been led into doing so by Giorsal. Aeldra had lost both members of her closest family in a matter of moments, for while the old woman still lived, she would be dead in Aeldra's heart forever more.

"Betray who? That arrogant old bastard Angus? Who sat up in the castle while ye an' Allistair an' I lived here in this tiny cottage like peasants?" she asked bitterly. "We should have been in the castle! We should have—"

Seonaid didn't know who was more stunned when Aeldra suddenly slapped Giorsal.

Aeldra didn't say a word. She got slowly to her feet, turned her back on the woman who had raised her, and walked out of the cottage, neither slowing her step when she reached Seonaid nor even glancing her way.

Seonaid started to follow her, then paused and glanced back to ask, "How long ha'e ye hated us?"

Giorsal's mouth twisted bitterly. "Yer whole life."

Seonaid merely nodded and walked wearily out of the cottage. She looked around for Aeldra, but the girl must have broken into a run the moment she was out the door. Her cousin was nowhere in sight. Neither was Little George, she noted. Blake was still there, however. Seonaid debated her chances of avoiding him, but it seemed unlikely. He had that stubborn set to his shoulders she was starting to recognize.

That thought gave her something of a start. It was surprising that she was beginning to recognize anything about him.

"Your cousin is dead?" Blake asked the question in quiet sympathetic tones as soon as she paused before him.

Seonaid nodded. It was all she had intended to do, but suddenly she found herself blurting out what she had learned; Allistair's perfidy, Giorsal's hatred, and their plans for her and her family and even for himself. She finished with, "Aeldra is sore upset."

"Aye." Blake nodded, then added softly, "As are you."

Much to her horror, Seonaid felt tears rush to her eyes at those words and the sympathy he offered. She struggled to force them back, but they would not go.

"Oh, damn," she gasped, and tried to turn away from him, but he caught her arms and held her in place.

"There is no shame in grieving the deaths of those

you love," Blake said quietly and tried to pull her against his chest, but Seonaid resisted.

"He would have killed me father an' brother, an' you too even," she cried, and the words revealed her confusion. Part of her grieved Allistair's death; the other part was grateful he had died without succeeding at his plan. Was even grateful he was dead so she needn't hate him, a man who had been like a brother to her for years.

"I suppose you are sorry he did not succeed at killing me at least, though I doubt you would have seen your father and brother dead to escape me."

Seonaid's resistance had been weakening and she had slowly been allowing him to urge her against his chest, but now she pulled back with a shocked gasp. "I would ne'er—"

She paused as she spotted the faint twinkle in his eyes. He had been teasing.

"Would you never, Seonaid Dunbar?" he asked, and there was curiosity on his face. "You would not wish me dead?"

Seonaid shook her head and knew it was true. She did not wish this man dead. She didn't wish him ill at all. She wasn't even sure she wished not to marry him. Seonaid had been fleeing him for many reasons, fear, pride, anger . . . but mostly out of pride. Pride could be a terrible trial, and she had more than her fair share of it. Being betrothed to the son of a man her father hated had been hard enough to bear, but his tarrying in collecting her had been a shame she'd had to carry as well. The years in between had been confusing ones.

Life didn't appear to be getting any less confusing either, she realized as she became aware that his face was lowering toward hers.

"Seonaid." He whispered her name and she felt his breath on her lips. Her eyes closed, reopened, then almost crossed in an effort to focus on his mouth.

"Aye?"

"I am going to kiss you," he announced.

"Oh," she breathed, and was immediately cast into deeper confusion. He was going to kiss her. She should fight, she supposed, but Seonaid didn't have the energy to do so. She didn't even know if she had the will. She had felt so weary and lost on leaving Giorsal's cottage, and now those sensations were easing somewhat and she felt sure they would ease even more were he to kiss her. Maybe she could even forget for a little bit. She desperately wanted to forget. Seonaid did not suffer loss well, and Allistair's loss was twofold because of the hurtful actions that had apparently led up to it.

Her thoughts were brought to an end as his mouth covered hers. It was incredibly soft. He looked a terribly hard man—even his lips could form a straight line that appeared ungiving—but it felt soft, and he tasted as sweet as plum wine as his lips moved over her own. Seonaid's hopes that he could distract her from her thoughts were realized immediately. All she was aware of was the pressure of his mouth on hers, and the way his hands now moved up and down her arms, then slid around her back. His tongue slid between her lips and Seonaid released a small moan of pleasure as he invaded her, filling her mouth with the taste of him. All her senses seemed overwhelmed by him; his scent—one she had grown used to while riding with him—filled her nose, his taste was on her tongue, and she felt him everywhere their bodies met.

For the first time in her life, Seonaid felt completely and utterly female and didn't mind. She had always thought of women as soft and weak, but in Blake's arms, while she felt feminine, she also felt excited and powerful. She could have stayed happily locked in his embrace forever, and couldn't restrain a moan of disappointment when he broke the kiss and eased away to peer down at her.

"I am sorry about your cousin, but Allistair's death is not your fault."

Seonaid stared at him blankly, her mind slow to adjust. Allistair. Dead. His plans to kill her father and brother, marry her, and become laird. His betrayal. His death. Her fault? Had she felt guilty? Aye, she had. She hadn't had a clue that Allistair's feelings for her had gone beyond cousinly love. Certainly he had teased her and complimented her at times, and Seonaid had sensed that there was something. But . . .

But she was lying to herself, she realized. Aye, she'd known. She'd known his feelings for her had been stronger than they should be as cousin, but his attention had flattered her, and eased some of the pain Blake's neglect had caused. She had known and now admitted that she had even gently encouraged it. Seonaid had basked in his attention, using it as a balm to soothe her hurt pride. She'd told herself that Blake might not think enough to even bother to claim her, but Allistair thought she was brave and smart and beautiful. She hadn't felt the same in return, but she had encouraged him and unknowingly encouraged his traitorous intentions, aiding him in his downfall, and very nearly abetting the death of her own father and brother. And she was ashamed of herself, and mad as hell. But she wasn't just mad at herself. Blake deserved some of the blame. Had he come to claim her when she was sixteen as most men would have . . .

"Seoanid?" Blake was watching her face closely and concern now filled his features. "What are you thinking?"

Pressing her mouth closed to keep from speaking all the thoughts whirling in her mind, Seonaid shook her head and pulled away. He tried to catch her back, but she was in no mood to deal with him now. She was terrified she would start to yell at him for what she saw as his part in this ordeal. And she would cut out her own tongue and swallow it before she would allow this man to know how much his failing to collect her had hurt.

Evading his hands, Seonaid slid past him and broke into a run for the keep. She gave the effort all she had, stretching her muscles and pumping her hands to use up some of her anger. It worked somewhat, although it wasn't a great distance from the cottage to the keep, so perhaps her exhaustion as she mounted the stairs had something to do with the collection of emotions she had suffered in such a short time: shock, fear, grief, anger, and betrayal, even passion. After the strenuous

ups and downs of the last few days it was all too much.
Seonaid felt about a hundred years old as she dragged
herself up the stairs and entered the keep, far too tired
to deal with Lord Rolfe, whose voice was sounding extremely agitated as it reached her ears.

Chapter Nine

"What do you mean, the laird is unavailable? Is he all right?"

Seonaid let the door close behind her and eyed the bishop and Lord Rolfe. The prelate simply looked weary, but Rolfe looked frustrated as he questioned young Willie. It made Seonaid suspect that the lad wasn't being forthcoming with his answers. But then, she supposed he wouldn't be. Lord Rolfe was English. Scottish children were taught from birth to hate the English.

"I asked you a question, lad, and would appreciate an answer."

Seonaid sighed wearily and started across the hall. "Father was wounded in the siege. He's restin'; let him rest."

"Wounded?" Rolfe turned to her with a combination

of relief and alarm. Relief at finally getting his questions answered, she supposed. Alarm at the news he was hearing. "Is he all right?"

"Aye. He took an arrow in the shoulder. Iliana tended it. He's recoverin'."

"Oh." He relaxed somewhat. "Well, what about Duncan, then?"

Seonaid arched an eyebrow in Willie's direction.

"He's restin' too," the lad said. "With Lady Iliana."

"Resting with . . . oh." Rolfe scowled, but Seonaid smiled. She was glad her brother and his wife were all right. It also sounded as if they were getting along well, which made her happy. She liked Iliana.

"Well, perhaps we could speak to Lady Wildwood then, Iliana's mother."

"She's restin'," Willie repeated.

The bishop seemed to lose some of his sleepy air at this news. "She was not injured too, was she?"

"Nay. She's restin' with the laird," the boy explained with a grin that made Seonaid's eyes widen. Her father and Lady Wildwood? Resting? Together? The very idea stunned her. What had been going on while she was gone? If she was surprised, Lord Rolfe was positively horrified.

"What?" he exclaimed. "Well, tell them we must speak with them at once. We—"

"Let them rest," Seonaid chided, continuing across the hall toward the stairs. "It's been a tryin' time for all. Surely ye could use some rest too after our journey?"

"Lady Seonaid is right," Bishop Wykeham murmured. "It's been a long journey. Surely the morrow is soon enough to find out what went on here and who attacked the castle."

Seonaid stopped walking, her eyes fixing on Willie. It would seem the men hadn't got much information out of the lad if they didn't even know who had attacked. Either they'd asked the wrong questions or the boy was being difficult on principle alone. She suspected it was the latter but couldn't find it in her to be angry with him. They were English, after all.

"Greenweld sent a message claimin' I'd been kidnaped by the Colquhouns," Seonaid explained. "Duncan took most of the men and rode out to fetch me back. The moment he was gone, Greenweld attacked the keep and laid siege. Father was hit by an arrow and unable to lead those left behind. Iliana took his place and managed to hold the castle until Duncan returned." Seonaid glanced at Willie. "Is that no right?"

"Aye." He nodded and grinned.

"What happened to Greenweld?" Lord Rolfe asked.

"Dead," the boy said succinctly and with obvious pleasure.

"His men?" the bishop asked.

"Some fled, some are dead, and some are in the dungeons."

"Well." Lord Rolfe and the bishop exchanged glances and seemed to be at a loss as to what to say or do.

"Sleep, gentlemen," Seonaid said and started toward the stairs again. She had heard enough. Greenweld was dead, Allistair was dead, her father wounded, and Dunbar battered but not beaten. Anything else she could learn on the morrow. Despite her rest during the ride, she was so weary she could barely lift her feet to take the stairs. "Find one o' the women to show them where to sleep," she added to Willie as she slowly trudged up the stairs, leaving it to the boy to handle. For all she cared at that moment, they could sleep on the rushes on the great hall floor.

Seonaid paused at the top of the stairs and stared around with surprise. Duncan had started the changes abovestairs before she'd left. He'd decided to add rooms when his father had pointed out that the family was growing and that should Iliana's mother visit, she would be expected to have one of the three rooms abovestairs. He had then added that neither he nor Seonaid were giving up theirs, so Duncan had best be prepared to give up the one he shared with his young bride. The idea of sleeping in the great hall with his sweet young wife had been more than Duncan could stand. He had been in a panic to build extra rooms abovestairs. It appeared the deed was done. Certainly the upstairs sported twice the rooms it used to.

Seonaid hesitated, then moved to the door to her own room, or at least the room she used to sleep in, and presumedly still did. However, when she opened the door, she found it already occupied. Seonaid came to a halt in the entrance. It took her a second to recognize Helen sound asleep on her bed. Unwilling to disturb her and then have to answer questions, Seonaid backed out of the room.

" 'Tis sorry I am, me lady. But I thought it best to put the sister in yer room," the maid, Janna, explained as she rushed up. "The new rooms are no yet all properly furnished."

Seonaid waved the explanation and apology away. " 'Tis fine. I'll take one o' the other rooms. Lord Rolfe and Sherwell can either share a room or fight over who sleeps below. I am too tired to be polite and would not disturb Hel—er, Sister Helen," she corrected herself quickly. "Mayhap ye can go below to sort out the men and where they're to sleep."

"Aye, m'lady."

Seonaid watched her hurry off to the stairs, which was the only reason she saw Blake appear as he took the last few steps to the landing. When he spotted her and started forward, Seonaid turned away and hurried to the door of the first of the new rooms.

"Seonaid!" Blake called, his voice grim.

Not in the mood to talk, Seonaid managed to slip inside and shut the door before he reached her. She had slammed the bar into place across it just before his fist landed on the other side.

"Seonaid!"

"Go away!" she yelled through the door, then turned to survey the room she'd chosen. A grimace immediately made its way across her face. It had a bed, but that was all. There was no other furniture in the room. Neither were there tapestries on the wall yet, nor even linens on the bare straw mattress of the bed. Seonaid shrugged. She'd slept in worse conditions. At least she had a bed.

"Seonaid, open the door!" Blake pounded on the

wooden surface, but she ignored him. Removing her plaid, she wrapped it around herself like a blanket as she crossed the room, then collapsed on the bed to seek the oblivion of sleep.

Blake glared at the door with frustration and pounded on it again. "Seonaid! Come out here!"

"Here! What's all this racket? How's a body supposed to rest and regain his health with the likes o' you making all this noise?"

Blake turned slowly to find his intended father-in-law standing in the open doorway of the room across the hall from the one he had just pounded on. But it was the sight of his fine new braies on the man that made him scowl. The doublet was missing, but the bandage around the Scot's upper chest reminded Blake that the man had been shot in the shoulder by an arrow . . . and no doubt while wearing the gold doublet too. The blasted thing was probably ruined.

"Aye. What's all the racket?" Duncan asked, drawing Blake's attention to the next door down, which had opened to reveal the younger male Dunbar in a similar state of undress, though he wore only a linen wrapped around his waist. A damp linen. The man had obviously just come from his bath.

"My apologies, gentlemen," Blake said dryly. "I was merely trying to have a word with Seonaid."

"Well, have it another time. 'Tis obvious she's no interested in talkin' to ye." Angus's gaze slid past him to the door, then back, and a grudging smile curved his lips. "Managed to get her out o' the abbey, I see. That's a surprise. She must favor ye more than I thought, else she woudna have come out."

Blake snorted. "She came out because the abbess had unbarred the door to let us in. She thought it was safer to leave. We just got lucky enough to catch her. Then catch her again, and again."

Duncan gave a bark of laughter and moved away from his door to draw nearer, dragging the linen behind him as he came. "She's makin' ye run after her, is she?"

"Aye. The only reason we managed to get here now is because the Camerons attacked, else she would have made another run for it," Blake admitted grimly.

"The Camerons?" Angus's eyebrows flew up, and his gaze shot to Duncan before he glanced back and asked, "Well, what did ye do to make them angry at ye, lad?"

"Me?" Blake said with surprise. "They were not after me. Seonaid, Aeldra, and Sister Helen were bathing when the men attacked them. Seonaid said they were enemies to the Dunbars and it was best to get back here before they went for help and came back with a larger party."

Father and son exchanged another glance.

"Why would she lie about that?" Duncan asked his father, but the older man merely shook his head in open bewilderment.

"Do you mean to say the Camerons are not enemies to the Dunbars?" Blake asked, his eyes narrowing.

"Nay. We've no fight with the Camerons," Duncan told him.

"But she said you did."

"She lied," Angus said easily, not at all upset that she had.

"But she made us ride day and night to reach here for fear they would attack again."

"She made ye hurry back *here?*" Duncan asked with surprise.

"Hmmm." Angus pursed his lips and scratched the gray stubble on his cheek thoughtfully. "That *does* seem odd." Then he asked, "Did you say Sister Helen? Ye brought a nun back with ye from St. Simmian's?"

Blake nodded. "Aye. Seonaid had promised to escort the sister to England to visit her family."

"She did, did she?" Angus was looking even more thoughtful at this news.

"Aye," Blake murmured, then glanced past Duncan to a dark-haired beauty standing in the doorway. Blake had never met Iliana of Wildwood before, but if this was she, Duncan was a lucky beggar.

"Husband? Is anything wrong?" the woman called softly.

Duncan whirled toward her voice and shook his head as he moved back to her. "Nay. Everything is fine. 'Tis just that fool countryman o' yers causing a racket as he tries to woo Seonaid. He . . ." The rest of what he was saying to his wife was lost to Blake as the man urged her backward into their room, followed her, and closed the door without a by-your-leave to his father or Blake.

Angus was grinning with amusement when Blake turned back to him. No doubt his son's description of him as "that fool countryman of yours" had amused the man.

"Back to why Seonaid would lie about the Camerons . . ." he said grimly, but the older man cut him off.

"We'll sort that out when she emerges," he said, waving the matter away as inconsequential; then he tipped his head and asked, "Would ye care for a bit of advice on wooin' me daughter?"

Blake stiffened at the very suggestion. He had never in his life needed advice on wooing. He'd been a born wooer, wooing the local girls before he'd left the cradle. "Nay. I do not need advice on wooing Seonaid," he said stiffly. "Especially from you."

"As ye like," the old man said with a shrug. "But mayhap I should point out that I am wooin' Lady Wildwood . . . and verra well," he added with a grin. "While you appear to be makin' a mess o' it with me daughter." He allowed Blake to gnaw on that for a moment, then added, "Seonaid isna one of those weak-kneed, simpering idiots yer used to at court. Pretty words and fancy dress'll no impress her. It will take a strong man to move my girl."

Before Blake could respond, a rustling sound reached them from inside the Dunbar's room. Angus glanced over his shoulder, then turned back, suddenly all business. "Well, if that's all, I'm back to me bed. Took a terrible wound durin' the siege, ye ken." He raised a hand to cover the bandage on his shoulder and managed a sorrowful look as he backed into the room. "Need me rest. So keep the racket down." He growled the last in warning tones just before slamming the door closed.

Blake scowled at the door the Dunbar laird had just slammed, then at the door Seonaid had disappeared through, debating whether to pound and shout for her some more. He had just decided not to waste his breath or energy when the maid he had passed earlier appeared at the stairs at the end of the hall with Lord Rolfe and the bishop behind her.

"Ah, Blake." Rolfe nodded as they approached. "It would appear that there are only two rooms left. You and I can share one if you wish, and the bishop can have the other, or—"

"I shall sleep in the great hall," Blake announced, moving past the trio toward the stairs. That way he could keep an eye out in case Seonaid got it into her head to run again.

Seonaid didn't sleep long. The women had slept on the last part of the ride to Dunbar so that they would be wellrested when they arrived and could slip off again while the men recovered from the journey. She had only fallen asleep at all out of emotional exhaustion.

Rolling off the bed, she quickly rearranged her plaid, then moved to the window to peer down at the bailey and ponder what she should do. Her plan to escape once they arrived home no longer seemed viable. Helen was sleeping and Seonaid had no idea where Aeldra was.

Not that she really felt like running anymore anyway. It seemed to her that if she hadn't run in the first place, none of what had followed would have occurred here at Dunbar. Allistair never would have been tempted to treason because she would have been married to Blake when he arrived and wallowing in marital misery. Green-weld would have had no co-conspirator within Dunbar. Duncan and the men couldn't have been lured away by claims that she'd been kidnaped by the Colquhouns. The attack on the castle wouldn't have taken place, her father wouldn't have taken an arrow to the shoulder, the stables and several cottages wouldn't have been burned to the ground, Allistair would still be alive, and Duncan would never have been forced to kill him.

There was no doubt in Seonaid's mind that killing Allistair must have been one of the hardest things her brother had ever had to do. The four of them had been as close as peas in a pod as children, running the hills together, laughing and playing. Duncan had grown apart from the rest of them over the last few years, his time taken up with some of the duties he had to perform as he took over more and more of the laird's role. But still it must have been hard, and his suffering would be worse than hers and Aeldra's, because Allistair had died at his hand.

Sighing, she turned her attention to the problem of Helen and had been considering the matter for several minutes when a soft knock sounded at the door. Two raps, a pause, then three more. Recognizing Aeldra's signature knock, Seonaid moved to answer it and found both Aeldra and Helen in the hall. Stepping to the side, she gestured for them to enter, then closed the door behind them.

The three women milled about the room in an oddly uncomfortable silence for a moment, then Helen blurted out, "I fell asleep waiting for you to return. The maid who showed me to your room told me what happened. I am so sorry about Allistair."

Her gaze slid over both women as she said that, making it obvious that while Aeldra had found Helen in Seonaid's room, they hadn't really spoken yet, but had immediately come to find her.

"So am I. Sorry about Allistair, I mean," Seonaid murmured in Aeldra's general direction, too ashamed at the part she had played in his downfall to meet her eyes.

"Me too," Aeldra muttered.

They fell back into their uncomfortable silence again, then Helen said, "Well, are we going to slip off while the men sleep?"

"We'll have to take the secret passage," Aeldra announced. "Blake's in the great hall. He's sleepin' in a chair by the fire but wakes at every sound. He woke when I entered."

"Secret passage?" Helen asked with interest.

"Aye. It comes out down near the village. We can—"

"We arena goin' anywhere," Seonaid interrupted, and both women turned amazed faces her way.

"What?" Helen asked with disappointment. "You will not take me home to England?"

Seonaid shrugged away her guilt and said, "I was considerin' the matter 'ere ye got here, and it occurred to me that if Cameron has figured out yer disguise and followed us, he may be desperate enough that he could be waitin' outside the walls. If so, do we risk takin' ye back out, we could ride ye right back into his arms."

"Oh." Helen frowned. "I had not thought of that."

Seonaid shrugged. "Ye're safe here until yer father

can come to fetch ye. We'll send a messenger to let him know where ye are."

Helen nodded, then glanced at Aeldra when the blonde said, "So ye'll jest stay here and marry the Sherwell?"

Seonaid met her cousin's gaze but quickly looked away when she saw the solemn way Aeldra was watching her. Guilt was suddenly a suffocating blanket around her. If she had stayed put the first time and married Blake . . .

"Nay," Helen said firmly. "You need not stay here with me. If your father does not mind me staying, I shall be fine. You two should leave as you had planned."

Seonaid shrugged and turned to walk to her window. "Nay. We'll stay."

"Why?" Helen asked with amazement. "I thought you did not wish to marry Blake."

Seonaid shrugged but remained silent, her gaze fixed on the activity in the bailey below.

"*Do* you want to marry Blake?" Helen asked.

Seonaid scowled at her persistence. "Let us say I am resigned. I have known I was to marry him from the time I could talk." That fact had been drummed into her from childhood on, with confusing results. Part of her had loathed the idea of marrying him, but another part . . .

Angus Dunbar had spent years cursing the senior Sherwell, but other than calling Blake "that sneaky Sherwell bastard's whelp" had said little against the man she was to eventually marry. But any real information she had gleaned of the man she was betrothed to had come from other sources. There had been the occasional visitor over the years who had stopped in at Dunbar and, when it was realized that Seonaid was to marry Blake Sherwell, had often immediately set about telling tales of what he was up to.

By all accounts Blake had been a handsome boy, charming even as a youth. As he had grown, his charm and good looks had apparently grown with him, and the women visitors had raved about what a lucky girl she was. Then he had reached adulthood, earned his spurs, and she had begun to hear other things. That he was not simply waiting around for his father to drop dead so that he could claim his title and wealth as others in his position might do, but that he was ambitious. He had joined with a friend of his, Amaury de Aneford, and had collected a small band of soldiers together who could be hired out to anyone who had need of a strong sword arm. They were successful warriors, and the size of their party had grown until Blake and Amaury led hundreds and had earned immense wealth.

Then there were the tales of his male prowess. He was handsome and good with words and used both to his advantage to woo countless women to his bed. The wife of one visitor had even caught her alone so that she could brag to Seonaid about how she herself had been bedded by him, and that it was a treat she would not soon forget. Not ignorant to the ways of men *or* women, Seonaid had taken the lady's catty comments in stride and merely said, "He is a man and like all men shall bed all the whores he can, but he shall marry me." Leaving the woman gasping, she'd walked away. And that had been her attitude at first.

Young men were expected to sow their wild oats 'ere settling down to marriage. Many continued sowing them long after they were wed. But whatever the case, Seonaid could not take his activities with other women as a personal slight. She had taken them in stride and patiently waited for the time when he would come to marry her, and they would start a home and family together. After reaching puberty and becoming a woman, she had even had the occasional daydream about the future, about a handsome blond Adonis riding into Dunbar. He was on a white charger, of course. He rode in as proud as a Greek god, surveyed those here at Dunbar and—of course—his heart recognized her at once as his bride.

In her daydreams Seonaid was always practicing at swords with one of the men when Blake arrived. Her dream Blake was mightily impressed by her skill and talent. He leapt from his horse, took the place of her vanquished loser, and began to battle with her, giving no quarter because he respected her skill too much to hold back. In the end the battle was always a draw, neither beating the other. And Blake bowed to her, professing his undying admiration for her abilities and his pride in having her as his wife, and sometimes he even kissed her. Other times—if she was alone in her room and Aeldra was not snoring away beside her—her daydreams went further than a kiss. He might dare to touch her breast through her gown, and then they would begin to wrestle and roll around on the ground. Seonaid usually fell asleep with a satisfied little sigh at that point.

She'd had these fantasies with incredible regularity starting just before her sixteenth birthday, when everyone had begun to comment that the Sherwell would no doubt be coming to claim her soon. They had continued after her sixteenth birthday, and her seventeenth birthday. They, along with the predictions that he would soon come, had begun to slow a bit after her eighteenth birthday passed without his arrival, and slowed even more after the nineteenth. By her twentieth birthday, Seonaid's daydreams had changed somewhat. He still rode in, still recognized her, but their battle ended in her beating him, then his groveling for her forgiveness in tarrying so long and her eventually relenting and deigning to marry him.

By her twenty-second birthday, all predictions that he would soon be coming for her had stopped and people had avoided her eyes altogether when his name was brought up. They were embarrassed for her because he obviously wasn't coming. It was around that same time that Seonaid's daydreams had taken another turn. In a new one, he still recognized her and there was a battle, but she beat him to a bloody pulp, then spat in his face and said she wouldn't marry him if he were the last person on earth. No amount of groveling on his part made her relent.

When she had been informed that Duncan had agreed to marry Iliana only if Sherwell was forced to finally fulfill the marriage contract that had been drawn up between their families so many years ago, Seonaid had been a roiling mass of humiliation and fury. The man was being forced to come and collect her as if she were some poxy whore that no man would want for bride, and only a king's order could move him to do his duty. She had fled. With disastrous results.

"I think ye should make him suffer a bit more," Aeldra said grimly.

"Mayhap he should, but I'll no have anyone else suffer more with him; they have all suffered enough."

"I knew it!" Aeldra stomped over to her and caught her by the arm to turn her around.

"Knew what?" Helen asked in confusion. "What are you two talking about? Who else has suffered?"

Aeldra ignored the question and glared at Seonaid. "Yer blamin' yerself fer Allistair."

"Why would Seonaid blame herself for Allistair's death?" Helen asked with bewilderment.

"O' course I am," Seonaid snapped, also ignoring Helen. "And who else should I blame?"

"Me," Aeldra said firmly.

"You?" Seonaid gawked at the petite woman.

"He was my brother."

"Aye, but that makes ye no more responsible for his behavior than I am for Duncan's."

"Seonaid is right," Helen agreed quickly. "Neither of you is responsible for Allistair's behavior." She hesitated, then added, "I am afraid that Janna did not explain his behavior to me; she told me only that he is dead. What did he do?"

"Betrayed our people, snuck around helping Green-weld, planned to see my brother and father dead, then to marry me and claim himself laird of the Dunbars," Seonaid answered flatly, moving away from the window to sit on the bed.

"Oh, dear," Helen murmured, following and sitting on the far end of the bare mattress. "Well . . ." She shook her head. "That is awful, but 'tis his own doing. Neither of you is responsible for it."

"He was me brother," Aeldra said flatly, dropping onto the hard surface between them.

"If I'd stayed here and married Blake when he arrived rather than running off to St. Simmian's, none of this might have happened," Seonaid said at the same moment.

"But that is—You two are—Oh, this is just nonsense," Helen said with exasperation.

"Aye, 'tis," Aeldra agreed and frowned at Seonaid. " 'Tis no yer fault."

"I knew his caring fer me was more than that o' cousin, and it flattered me. My pride was so beaten down by Blake's neglect that I even encouraged it."

Aeldra snorted. "Not much ye didn't. Had ye given him any real encouragement, ye'd have been bedded and breeding by seventeen, Allistair was that crazy about ye."

"Ewww," Seonaid said as an image flashed through her mind of herself and her male cousin together.

"Aye." Aeldra grimaced, probably at a similar vision.

Seonaid sighed, then fell back to lay across the bed. She stared up at the ceiling as she said, "Still, had I stayed and married Blake rather than allow me pinched pride to send me harin' off to St. Simmian's—"

"Blake would probably be dead along with everyone else," Aeldra interrupted grimly. "Seonaid, had ye stayed and dutifully married Blake, Allistair would have seen him dead 'ere the wedding night. He wouldna have allowed it to be consummated. And who kens what might have happened next? He still would have had to see Duncan and Uncle Angus out o' the way to gain the title o' laird, and whatever way he tried might have actually worked," she pointed out, then shook her head. "Nay, ye canna take the blame. But I can."

Seonaid turned her head to cast a scowl her way. "Just because he was yer brother—"

"Nay, no jest because he was me brother." She sighed. "I kenned he was weak, Seonaid. And I kenned Giorsal's anger and the way she whispered it in his ear. I knew she was bitter, like fruit left to rot on the branch, and I just ignored her, but Allistair had no the character to do so. Ye ken he had no opinion o' his own. He would voice a belief, then someone would voice a different one and his would suddenly change. He was easily led and I kenned that. I should have realized that Giorsal's constant harping would affect him. I should have seen this coming and done something about it."

"Nay." Seonaid sat up and shook her head. "As ye say, I kenned he was weak o' mind too and easily led, yet I did not see this coming. Neither could ye be expected to." She kicked her foot in the rushes on the floor, then asked, "Did it anger ye that Father never gave ye a room in the keep? It truly never occurred to me, Aeldra, else I would have suggested—"

Her cousin interrupted her with another snort. "Seonaid, I practically do live up here in the keep. Ye and I have been inseparable since Allistair and I arrived here. I am up here at the keep from the moment I get up in the morning until the moment I go to bed at night, unless we are at an abbey or hunting with the men or practicing in the bailey," she added dryly. "Guid God, they called us 'the twins,' and that wasna because we look so much alike."

Seonaid laughed slightly at the old nickname, and her cousin continued. "And Uncle Angus treated Allistair and me as much like his children as a man could. He fed us, clothed us, and even supplied our horses and weapons at no small cost to hisself. Yer no the only one with the sword made specially fer yer size and strength, are ye? Nay, I have no bitterness with any o' ye. I've not, but gratitude and love."

Seonaid scowled. Her throat felt tight with the tears she was fighting back. "I'll take the love, but ye can keep the gratitude," she growled, then added, "And we love ye too."

"I ken," Aeldra said with a grin, and the two women hugged awkwardly, then pulled away, each of them clearing her throat and feeling slightly embarrassed.

"Well," Helen said with a pleased little sigh, "now that the two of you have settled that, you should both leave at once and make Blake give chase. Leaving you hanging about until twenty-four is shameful and he deserves to suffer for it."

Seonaid peered at Helen with amazement. "Yer no sounding much like a sister, Sister," she teased.

Helen grinned. "In truth, I do not feel much like a sister either. I wish I could go with you."

Seonaid glanced down at her feet again, feeling confused about what she should do. She wasn't completely over her anger with Blake, but the memory of his kiss was strong in her mind, blurring her thinking a bit.

"We do have to leave, Seonaid," Aeldra said suddenly. "And no jest to harass Blake."

She glanced at her cousin with interest. "Oh?"

"Has it no occurred to ye that Rollo Cameron is in quite a spot at the moment?"

"Aye. He's most like to lose his home and his very life over this does he no flee before Helen's father gets here, finds out what's about, and sends a message to the king."

"Aye," Aeldra agreed solemnly. "If Helen's father arrives here."

Seonaid frowned. "What mean ye, *if* he gets here?"

"Well, all Rollo's problems could be at an end if he could just silence Helen and her father."

"Damn," Seonaid murmured. Desperate men took desperate measures. And if he was willing to commit one murder, why not two?

"I do not understand," Helen said anxiously. "You think Rollo will go after my father?"

Seonaid stood and began to pace as she considered the problem. "Yer maid went to yer father. If she gets there, what will she tell him?"

"If she gets there?" Helen echoed.

"Aye. I'm presumin' Cameron had many men traveling with him?" When she nodded, Seonaid pointed out, "Well, he may have sent half after her, or even just a couple, and kept the rest with him to come after you. She may no have reached him at all. But if she did," she hurried on when Helen began to look upset, "what would she tell him?"

Helen hesitated, obviously distressed by the possibility that the maid might not have reached her father, something she hadn't considered. But then she appeared to force the thought aside and straightened. "She would tell him that I overheard Rollo plotting to kill me. That we escaped and I fled to St. Simmian's while she made her way home."

"And what would yer father do?"

"He would be very upset, furious. He would mount up at once and ride to St. Simmian's to hear it from me for himself."

"Alone?"

"Nay. He would bring most of his men. He would be angry and in a fighting mood. He would bring enough men to lay siege to Cameron's castle, if necessary."

Seonaid nodded. "Would he take the time to write to yer king first?"

Helen bit her lip as she thought, then shook her head. "Nay."

Seonaid sighed. "I suppose it doesna matter whether he would have written to the king or no. Either way, so long as Rollo kills you and yer father, he is safe."

"But Father would bring an army. He should be safe with all his men around him."

Seonaid shrugged. "They'll be lookin' fer you, no awatchin' fer an assassin."

"Assassin?" Helen gasped.

"Well, Cameron doesna need to kill yer father's entire army; he needs only to kill you and yer father and either make both look like accidents or attacks by someone else. Then he need only claim ye'd misheard him and it was all an error. He'd probably get away with it so long as yer father's no around to pursue it further. Unless ye have other powerful relatives, an uncle or a brother or some such?" Seonaid finished the comment on a question, but Helen shook her head.

"I am my parents' only child, and each of them were the only surviving children in their families. 'Tis why Father chose Rollo Cameron; he has an older brother who is laird of the Camerons. Father hoped he would wish to live in England and take over there."

Seonaid nodded and continued to pace and ponder. Helen and Aeldra waited patiently but looked expectant when she stopped and turned to face them. "Aeldra and I will away to yer father and explain all. That way at least he will be warned about what is happening and to watch fer Rollo. We can ride back with him and—"

"I will come with you."

"Nay. Ye're safer here, Helen."

"I shall not allow you two to risk yourselves for me alone. I will go with you," Helen said with determination.

"Nay. You—"

"Would you allow me to ride out on a dangerous journey like this while you stayed safely behind?"

Seonaid scowled, unable to argue that.

"Besides, if we were to take the secret passage Aeldra mentioned, surely we could slip away without Cameron seeing us. If he followed, he saw us enter the bailey, and he will be watching the gate to see us leave."

"She's right," Aeldra said quietly. "'Sides, we did promise to see her home."

"Aye." Seonaid sighed. "All right, we will all three of us go."

They were all silent for a moment; then Helen said, "What of Lord Blake?"

Seonaid smiled wryly and shrugged. "He dallied ten years in comin' after me, he can wait on me fer a change."

Helen nodded, then asked, "When shall we go?"

Seonaid exchanged a glance with Aeldra, then shrugged and stood. "Now. The men should sleep fer another four hours at least. That gives us a good head start. Come."

She led the way to the door of the room, opened it, and stepped out into the hall, relieved to find it empty. Gesturing for them to move quietly, Seonaid practically tiptoed along the hall to her own room and eased that door open.

"It is in here?" Helen asked in a whisper. The trepidation in the woman's voice made Seonaid glance curiously over her shoulder as she stepped inside.

"Aye. Why do you ask like that?"

"Oh, no!" Aeldra hissed as she followed the two of them into the room.

Seonaid's eyes shot to her cousin in question, then turned and peered at the wall Aeldra was gaping at, and her mouth fell open with shock. The entrance to the secret passage had been blocked off.

Chapter Ten

"I had the men block off the secret passage." Angus Dunbar stood in the doorway to his room, glaring at Seonaid irritably. She was glaring right back.

Seonaid had stared at the pile of huge stones stacked up against the wall of her room with shock, then whirled away and stormed to her father's door to find out what on earth was going on.

"Aye, I ken ye blocked it up. I just saw it. Helen was asleep in my room earlier, or I would have known then. What I'm wantin' to know is why ye would do a fool thing like that."

"Because Allis—" He paused abruptly, and seemed to change what he had been going to say to, "Because someone told Greenweld about the secret passages, or at least one o' them. So I had them both blocked off so they could no invade the castle."

"Damn!" Seonaid closed her eyes briefly, then sighed and told him, "We know about Allistair."

"Ye do?" His scowl deepened. "Who told ye? Duncan?"

"Nay. Giorsal."

"Giorsal?" He looked shocked. "How the devil did she ken?" he asked, then answered his own question. "Duncan must have told her. Only he, Iliana, and I ken the truth. Well, and Lady Wildwood, but she's no talked to anyone. She's been with me since—"

"No one told Giorsal," Seonaid interrupted. "She knew the tale o' Allistair's dying in battle was false because she knew he was plotting with Greenweld. She is the one who encouraged him to do so."

The air left Angus on a hiss.

"Ye may wish to watch her," Aeldra said quietly. "She's grown more and more bitter o'er the years, and this has jest made her worse."

"Aye." Angus ran a hand through his wiry gray hair, then told Aeldra, "She hoped to marry me, ye ken. When yer mother and my brother got together, Giorsal had hopes that she and I might make a match too, but I fell in love with Muireall, Duncan and Seonaid's mother. Giorsal never forgave me for it." He shook his head. "I'm sorry about Allistair, child."

Aeldra shrugged unhappily. " 'Tis no yer fault. Allistair made his own decisions, as does Giorsal. 'Tis kind o' ye to try to preserve his honor in memory at least by keeping what he was up to a secret."

"He wasna a bad lad," Angus said gruffly. "Must have been sufferin' a brain fever to have acted so. 'Sides, Duncan said 'twas obvious Allisatir's heart wasna wholly in it. He wouldna let Greenweld abuse Iliana and he couldna bring hisself to kill Duncan, but made the lad kill him instead."

Seonaid was grateful her father took the trouble to say that, whether is was true or not. Aeldra had needed something like that to hold on to. A rush of love welled up in her heart for the gruff old man, but dissipated when he turned narrowed eyes her way. "And why are ye so upset about the secret passage anyway? Ye werena plannin' to run off again, were ye?"

"Would ye care if I did?" Seonaid asked with a scowl, then thought to ask, "Blake's father hasna arrived yet, has he?" They would not hold the wedding without him.

"Nay, Sherwell hasna yet arrived," Angus said. He hesitated before adding, "The boy deserved a good set down after dallying so long in coming fer ye, and from what the Campbell told Duncan, ye gave him that." He grinned suddenly. "It sounds an entertaining tale too. Ye'll have to tell it to me at sup." His smile faded, his expression becoming solemn. "But ye'll have to marry the lad eventually. And 'tis a fine line between showing him the error of his ways and humiliatin' him to where he thinks he has to get some of his own back."

Seonaid frowned over those words.

"He's a lot like his father, mostly good-natured and honorable, but ye don't want to push him too far."

"Good-natured and honorable?" Seonaid gaped at her father. "Ye said the Sherwell was a sneaky English bastard, that—"

"Aye, well, I've been angry at him, haven't I? We had a falling out." He scowled, but the expression died abruptly as a lovely older woman appeared at his shoulder. "Margaret. What—?"

"I thought I would just go down and have a word with Elgin. He shall need to know there will be more for dinner this eve. I doubt Iliana will get the chance to warn him in time for him to prepare extra. Perhaps he could even manage a special treat to welcome Seonaid and Aeldra back." She offered a smile of greeting to the three women as she spoke, and all of them smiled in return.

If she hadn't looked so much like her daughter, Iliana, Seonaid would not have recognized Lady Wildwood from their first meeting. The woman was looking much better than she had on her arrival at Dunbar. Seonaid had only caught a glimpse of her then, but enough to know she'd been badly beaten; her face had been swollen, her eyes blackened, her nose broken. The rest of her hadn't been in any better shape. Lady Wildwood's face was completely healed now, however, and she was quite as lovely as her daughter.

"Oh, but . . ." Angus protested.

"Mayhap you should dress yourself, my lord," Lady Margaret cut him off with a gentle smile. "You should not really be standing about in front of *Sister* Helen like this. Do you not agree?"

Seonaid's eyes shot to Lady Wildwood's face at the way she said the word *sister*. She found her peering at Helen with a perplexed look before glancing at Angus Dunbar. Seonaid followed her gaze and found him peering down at himself with a frown. He had again donned the golden braies to answer the door when Seonaid had knocked but had not bothered with a tunic, so stood bare-chested in the doorway. Muttering something under his breath, he turned and moved quickly back into the room and out of sight.

Lady Wildwood smiled after him, then turned and held out a hand to Seonaid.

"Hello, Seonaid, is it?" Margaret asked.

"Aye." She hesitated, then placed her hand in Lady Wildwood's and found it drawn through the woman's arm as she stepped into the hall to join them.

"Why do you not come with me, Seonaid? Perhaps between us we can convince Elgin to make your favorite meal. What is your favorite meal?"

"Oh . . . er . . ." Seonaid glanced over her shoulder toward Aeldra and Helen.

Lady Wildwood glanced back too. "Would you ladies mind waiting for Lord Angus and explaining where Seonaid and I have gone?"

When both women nodded their heads helplessly, Lady Wildwood smiled. "Thank you," she murmured, then continued on, gently tugging Seonaid along with her. "Now, what was your favorite meal, dear?"

"I . . . er . . . colcannon, black buns, and haggis."

"I do not think I have tried the colcannon yet, though I have had black buns. Quite delicious," she pronounced.

"Aye," Seonaid agreed as she was led down the stairs. Her gaze swept the great hall as she walked. She spotted Blake dozing in a chair by the fire as Aeldra had said he was, and as she had said, he seemed to wake at the least sound, for he blinked his eyes open as they reached the foot of the stairs, and—spying them—sat up abruptly.

"We are just going to speak with cook, then have a little chat," Lady Wildwood announced when he got to his feet as if to approach them, adding firmly, "the sort of chat men are not welcome to join."

Much to Seonaid's amazement, Blake hesitated, then sank back into his chair and let them go on their way without interference. She peered at Lady Wildwood with new respect at this display of how to handle a man. Iliana's mother hadn't even raised her voice or had to make any sort of threat, and the man had behaved as beautifully as a well-trained puppy. Seonaid was impressed.

Once in the kitchen, the woman handled Elgin just as easily, greeting him with pleasure and gently flattering him until he was practically begging to do as she wished. Seonaid didn't know if she could emulate the woman's skill, but she was certainly impressed by it. Until Lady Wildwood said, "Perhaps we should see if Lord Blake has any dishes he prefers."

Seonaid scowled and suggested, "Rabbit stew."

"Hmmm. I think not."

Her tone of voice hadn't changed, but her smile had dimmed slightly. She'd obviously heard the tale of the poisoned stew. Seonaid supposed Gavin had blabbed about that to Duncan too and the tale had made its way to her father and then to Lady Wildwood. She wished it hadn't; she was suddenly feeling all squirmy inside with guilt under Lady Wildwood's solemn stare.

"I realize you were mightily offended by his delay in coming to collect you, Seonaid," Iliana's mother said gently. "And while I understand, I do not think you should take his actions to heart. After all, he did not know you, so it was not really *you* he was dallying over collecting, was it?"

"It wasna?"

"Nay."

"Then who was he dallyin' over collectin'?"

"You are being deliberately obtuse," she said with exasperation. "Surely you understand what I mean. Had he met you and known you before this, then you would have every right to be offended at his delay. But as he did not even know you, it is not you personally he was neglecting to collect, but your name. Your father's daughter. Now that he knows you, he is obviously pleased to marry you."

"He is?" she asked with amazement.

"Aye. Well, he did not need to chase you all over Scotland, dear. He could have gone to the king at any point after your battle at St. Simmian's and claimed he had done his part, that you were not co-operating and he wanted his freedom from the contract. In fact, the way you attacked him at the abbey would have worked to his favor in gaining his freedom had he truly wanted it."

"So, ye think he's awantin' to marry me?" Seonaid asked with interest.

"Aye. I do."

"Why?"

"Why?" she echoed with confusion.

"Why should he want to marry me? I ken nothin' about bein' a proper lady and wife. I canna sew, I canna run the servants, I—" Catching sight of Elgin edging closer and bending his ear their way to try to hear what she was saying, Seonaid scowled at the man and barked, "Get back to work on that colcannon else we'll have none fer sup."

The man leapt to it without question.

"Aye, well . . ." Lady Wildwood cleared her throat. "You could learn to have a gentler hand with the servants, perhaps, but you do know how to order them. As for sewing and such, Lord Blake will have servants to do those things."

Seonaid considered her words, then sighed. "I doona even ken what a lady is supposed to know. I only ken that I doona know it."

Lady Wildwood pondered the matter briefly, then said, "Aye, but you know other things most ladies do not. For instance, I understand you and Aeldra have been to battle with the men?"

"Aye." Seonaid smiled wryly. "And we just as often have to sew 'em up afterward too."

"You do?" she asked with sudden excitement.

"Aye. They're a great lot of babies about such things, ye ken. Most of 'em whine and whinge and flinch at the very idea of stitching up a wound or having whiskey poured over it, so Giorsal taught us how to tend them."

"But that is wonderful!" Lady Wildwood enthused.

"It is?" Seonaid asked slowly. "Why?"

"*Why?*" Lady Wildwood echoed with surprise, then shook her head. "Because, my dear, tending the ill and wounded is one of the most valuable skills a lady can have, and you do have it."

"Oh." Seonaid considered this with relief. She had one skill at least. It was better than nothing.

"And you also have many skills most ladies do not have. And you are very pretty, my dear. And obviously intelligent. These are all very good reasons for Lord Blake to be happy to marry you." Iliana's mother tilted her head to the side. "The question is, can you see yourself being happy married to him? For I feel sure that your father would give up your dower and cancel the wedding rather than see you miserable."

Seonaid considered the question seriously. She had always known she would marry Blake Sherwell, and had gone about her business on that premise. In fact, she had lived with the idea for so long that the possibility of not marrying him was almost alien to her. And from all she had heard—well, aside from her father's ranting, which the old man seemed to be taking back now—he was an admirable man; hard-working, ambitious, strong in battle yet fair.

Then too, there was what she had seen of him since battling in the chapel at St. Simmian's. Blake didn't appear to have a cruel streak. Another man might have beaten her on catching up to her at the barn after the incident with the stew. He would have been within his rights to do so. Actually, he would have been within his rights to do a lot more than beat her, she thought with a start. Poisoning others was against the law, after all. But he hadn't beat her; he hadn't even been mean to her since then. And this after she had already pushed his patience with her constant escape attempts, including the time she'd kicked him in the groin, then used her foot to toss him over her head. The man had the patience of a saint, to her way of thinking. She probably would have plowed him one herself for such a stunt.

"Seonaid?" Lady Wildwood prompted.

"Hmm." She sighed, then listed his positives, "He's smart, reputed to be good in battle, ambitious, patient, and I like the look o' him."

"You like the look of him?" Lady Wildwood smiled slightly.

Seonaid shrugged. "He's pretty."

Iliana's mother bit her lip, but nodded. "Aye. He is very . . . er . . . handsome."

"Well formed too," Seonaid informed her. "He has nice muscles in his shoulders and back, nice legs too, and I like his backside."

Lady Wildwood blinked. "Excuse me?"

"His backside," Seonaid repeated. "I havena seen many, but the ones I've seen all looked rather flat and saggy, but his is nice and rounded and—" Seonaid paused to thump Lady Wildwood's back when the woman made a choking sound and suddenly began to cough. When the coughing fit stopped and the woman waved her thumping off, she asked with concern, "Are ye a'right?"

"Aye." She nodded, but her face was terribly flushed. Still, she soldiered on, "So, you like him and find him handsome and he has fine . . . parts," she said delicately, then added, "I am sure I heard a *but* in there however?"

"Aye." Seonaid sighed, then admitted Blake's fault. "He has a huge cock."

Lady Wildwood began to choke and cough again. So

did Elgin, Seonaid noticed. There must be something in the air in the kitchen, she decided, as she thumped the lady's back again.

"I am all right; you can stop that." Lady Wildwood didn't sound all right. Her voice was practically a squeak of sound as she said, "But I do not understand how this is a problem, my dear."

"Perhaps I didna explain right," Seonaid decided with a frown. "The man is abnormal huge, from what I can see."

"You have *seen* it?"

"Aye. When he was bathing in the river."

"And you have *seen* others to compare his to?" she asked carefully.

Seonaid shrugged. "One or two while travelin' with the men. They're an immodest lot."

"Ah." She was nodding, but still flushed. "And you are worried that Blake is so large?"

"Well . . ." Seonaid frowned. "It seems to me with it bein' so large . . . well, if a normal man hurts the first time as they say, then Blake willna fit at all. Truly, my lady, he's almost the size of Elgin's rolling pin there."

Lady Wildwood glanced toward the object in question, as did Elgin. His eyes were wide and he was suddenly holding the thing away from him. Lady Wildwood's eyes went wide as well. "Well, that is . . ." She paused and shook her head, muttering, "And I was sorry I did not get to have this talk with Iliana the night of her wedding!"

Heaving her breath out on a sigh, Lady Wildwood took Seonaid's arm and urged her toward the door leading out into the gardens.

"Seonaid, you are blunt in your speech, so I shall be just as blunt," she said solemnly as they began to walk along the rows of herbs and vegetables. "You should not fear that Blake's . . . er . . . size will be a problem. You must remember that babies come out the same place he will be . . ." She paused, appearing at a loss for a moment, then struggled on. "It is not the size of the man that decides the discomfort the first time."

"It isna?" Seonaid asked with interest.

"Nay. We women are born with what is called a maiden's veil, and—"

"A maiden's veil?" Seonaid echoed, then raised her hands to feel her head and said, "What is that? I doona think I have one."

"Aye. You do," Lady Wildwood said firmly.

"Where's me daughter?"

Blake sat up straight in the chair he had been lounging in and scowled as Angus paused before him. "She is in the kitchen with Lady Wildwood."

"Hmm." Angus glanced at Aeldra and Helen, who were sitting at the trestle table. When he glanced back there was a thoughtful look on his face. "I've been thinkin' on what ye said about the attack."

Blake arched an eyebrow. "Aye?"

"Are ye sure 'twas the women they were after?"

"Aye. Why do you ask?"

"Because there must be a reason Seonaid lied about it being Camerons. And Allistair said that Greenweld had sent men after ye, and I was wondering if it might no be them and *you* were the true target."

"Me?" Blake sat up a little straighter. "Why would Greenweld send men after me?"

"For Allistair. To kill ye so he could marry our Seonaid," Angus explained, then shook his head. "But ye did say they attacked the women while they were bathing. So they couldna have been after you, could they?"

Blake said slowly, recalling the attack, "I had gone down to the loch to be sure the women had not made another run for it. I had just stepped out into the clearing when the men attacked."

"So, you were there too, and it could have been Greenweld's men after ye."

Blake shook his head. "But Greenweld is English, and these men wore plaids."

Angus shrugged. "Plaids are easy enough to find, and a smart Englishman would have his men don them if they were a smaller party and wanted to be able to travel the land without trouble. English dress is reason enough to stop and find out what they are about."

"Hmm." Blake considered the matter. The men had attacked after he'd stepped into the clearing. It could be that they were after him, not the women. In truth, if they were Greenweld's men, they might have thought the women little danger to them. "Are you sure it could not have been Camerons?" he asked now. "I do not understand why Seonaid would lie about it. I could understand had her lie delayed arriving here or allowed them to escape, but to lie to get here more quickly when she had been fighting the wedding as she had?" He shook his head, trying to make sense of it.

Angus again glanced toward the women at the table

as he considered the question. Blake followed his gaze. Aeldra and Sister Helen were huddled together, having what appeared to be a serious talk.

"Who is she?"

Blake glanced with surprise at the Dunbar laird. "Who is whom? Sister Helen?"

"Aye. Who is she and how did she come to be a member of yer party?"

Blake glanced back to the women and shrugged. "She is . . . Sister Helen," he finished helplessly. "Seonaid said she promised to see the sister to her home in England."

"Where in England?"

Blake glanced at him with surprise but had to admit, "I do not know. All I know is she is Sister Helen and left the abbey with Seonaid and Aeldra."

"Hmmm," the Dunbar said again, then turned away and headed to the trestle table. Blake watched him for a moment, then curiosity got the better of him and he stood to follow.

Seonaid's head was awhirl with information as Lady Wildwood led her back into the keep and through the kitchens. If she had been confused about Blake and her feelings about marrying him before, she was even more so now. Lady Wildwood had assured her that while the first time might be painful, it would not be due to his size, and in fact she might come to appreciate his size afterward. She had also assured her that—from all she had heard at court—Blake would probably make the bedding part of marriage very pleasurable for her.

Then there was his dallying about collecting her, the source of all her anger with the man. Unfortunately, she found unarguable the lady's suggestion that she should let go of her anger. Lady Wildwood insisted that it couldn't possibly have been a personal slight on his part since they hadn't yet met. With that in mind, Seonaid didn't know what she felt or thought about anything. All she knew was that she had made promises to Helen and felt she should keep them. And no doubt the other two women were waiting to hear what the next step would be, now that the chance to slip out through the secret passage was gone.

Seonaid wasn't sure. Storming off to her father's room after finding the secret passage blocked hadn't been the brightest move. They would be watching for an escape attempt now. Not that Blake had ever stopped watching for one, she conceded.

"Seonaid, dear?"

"Aye?" She glanced at Lady Wildwood curiously as she followed her out of the kitchen and into the great hall.

"Where is Sister Helen from? She looks terribly familiar to me. Perhaps I know her family."

Seonaid stumbled to a halt and opened her mouth, then closed it again, unsure what to say. It suddenly occurred to her that she had no idea where Helen was from. Not that she would have told Margaret anyway.

"Where exactly are ye from, Sister?"

That question from her father made her glance sharply toward the trestle tables where Helen, Aeldra, Blake, and her father were all seated. Helen's expression was a picture of panic. Excusing herself, Seonaid picked up speed and left Lady Wildwood behind as she hurried forward to forestall her father from asking anything else. Until she knew if they were going to try to sneak Helen home, it wasn't good to give them too much information. Although, after her conversation with Lady Wildwood, Seonaid was starting to think that she should let the men in on the actual events surrounding Lady Helen and let them help. But she would never do it without talking to Helen first.

"She is from St. Simmian's," Seonaid announced, pausing at the table to catch Helen under the elbow and urge her to stand. Aeldra was immediately on her feet as well.

"Aye. But where was she born, Seonaid?" her father asked. "Where is this family she wants to visit?"

"England," Seonaid answered succinctly, then rushed the women away before he could ask any more questions.

"Where are we goin'?" Aeldra asked as they started across the bailey.

"I am no sure. We need to go somewhere we can talk."

"That may be difficult. We have company."

"Aye. I ken," Seonaid admitted, aware that Blake had followed them out of the keep and was trailing them across the bailey. A moment later she glanced back to see that Little George had joined Sherwell. At this rate, it would soon be a parade. There would be no chance to talk.

The sight of Little George reminded Seonaid that

earlier in the day Aeldra had run out of the cottage and disappeared, along with Little George. She glanced at her cousin curiously. "Did Stupid George bother ye this morn after ye left Giorsal?"

"*Little* George," Aeldra corrected, then blushed when Seonaid glanced at her sharply. The nickname Stupid George was one Aeldra had suggested for the man just days ago. It seemed she no longer felt it suited. Interesting.

"He didna bother me," her cousin added, her face still flushed. "He—we talked. He was verra . . . er . . . kind."

Seonaid's eyebrows rose. Judging by the way her cousin was blushing, his kindness had probably not been dissimilar to the kindness Seonaid had enjoyed with Blake. She felt her own cheeks flush at the memory of his kiss.

"He is the strongest yet gentlest man I have ever met," Aeldra announced suddenly, and Seonaid peered at her in horror. She had never heard the smaller woman talk like this about any man. She sounded almost moonstruck.

Aeldra caught her expression and flushed further but said defiantly, "He is nice."

"Aye," Seonaid agreed quickly to soothe her, but was thinking with alarm that her tiny cousin was falling for the great brute. Of course, she was in danger of falling for Blake too. At least, his kiss seemed to plague her memory an awful lot. While Lady Wildwood had been explaining about the bedding that would follow the nuptials, Seonaid had been picturing Blake in her mind, remembering him naked, remembering sleeping pressed up against his chest, with his arm around her and his hand cupping her breast, and remembering his kiss and the way her body had reacted, the excitement, the budding passion, the—

"Seonaid!"

Slowing her steps, Seonaid glanced around, her face lighting with pleasure at the sight of the handsome dark-haired man walking toward her from the practice field. Ian McInnes, the son of their nearest neighbor, was about the same age as Duncan. He was also a friend, and she smiled happily at the sight of him.

"Ian," Seonaid greeted him with a laugh as he caught her up in a hug and swung her around before setting her down. Then he did the same to Aeldra. "What are ye doin' here?"

"I brought the men to help rout Greenweld," he explained, then grinned. "Ye ken I can never pass up the chance fer a good fight. No that it was much o' a fight." He shrugged. "I sent most of the men back after they helped clear up the worst of the mess, but I am staying until tomorrow morn. Mother will be put out if I return without the full tale, and I've yet to hear it all. Duncan and yer father havena been out of their rooms since shortly after it all ended."

"Ah." Seonaid smiled, then noted the way he glanced at Helen and introduced them. "This is Sister Helen. Helen, this is Ian McInnes, our neighbor and friend."

The pair greeted each other, then Ian glanced from

Seonaid to Aeldra expectantly. "Were ye comin' to practice? I could use a good workout."

Seonaid hesitated, but when she glanced back to see both Blake and Little George scowling to high heaven and hurrying toward them, she nodded firmly. They weren't likely to get a moment to talk anyway. She should have taken the women back up to her room to plan their next move and she would, after she'd had a little workout. Other than the skirmish in the abbey and then the one in the clearing, they hadn't had a proper chance to practice since leaving for St. Simmian's.

"Is that the English yer suppose to marry?" Ian asked as they walked to where several men were practicing their battle skills.

"Aye." Seonaid didn't bother to glance toward them. She knew Blake and Little George were still following, closing the distance between them.

"He looks put out, but then, I hear ye've been leadin' him a merry chase."

"Everyone appears to have heard," Seonaid said with disgust.

"Gavin told Duncan, Duncan told me," Ian said with amusement. He slapped her lower back and added, "Come on, Seonaid. Let's show him the fine lass he's amarryin'."

Moving in front of her, he drew his sword out as he turned to face her and immediately went on the attack. Seonaid was ready for him. She'd known Ian McInnes since she was a bairn and was used to his surprise tactics. In fact, she knew all his tricks, so found it easy to hold her own with him.

* * *

"She's good."

Blake scowled at Little George's comment as they watched his betrothed fend off the dark-haired Scot's attack. Ian, he thought he'd heard her greet him. She'd seemed rather happy to see him too. And he hadn't liked the way the man had embraced her and swung her around, anymore than he had cared for the way the man's hand had come perilously close to hitting her bottom when he'd slapped her back before squaring off against her.

But she *was* good, he conceded. He supposed he had initially noted that in the clearing when she had been doing battle with the men she had later claimed were Camerons. Unfortunately, he'd been a little too preoccupied with her state of undress to pay much attention to her skill with the sword. But she was more than just good, he realized now. Angus Dunbar had not wasted money on having the special sword made for her. She wielded it with expertise, using skill to counter the greater strength of her opponent.

A soft growl and the way Little George tensed beside him drew Blake's attention to the other two women. Aeldra and Sister Helen had been standing off to the side, watching the couple do battle. Now a burly red-headed Scot had approached them and, even as he watched, Seonaid's small cousin was moving out onto the field a little away from Seonaid and squaring off against this new man.

Blake wasn't surprised to see that the smaller woman was just as skilled. He *was* interested to note that Little

George wasn't happy about it and wondered if romance was in bloom for the pair. They would certainly be an odd twosome, he so large and she so tiny. But love came in many shapes and forms.

His gaze slid back to Seonaid, and he noted the way she was smiling and laughing, the flush of color that had come to her cheeks as she fought off the dark-haired man's attack. She was obviously enjoying herself, as was her opponent, and suddenly the battle almost seemed to take on the look of a courting dance. He had never thought of it as such while in battle himself, but the ritual was there in the way they moved in toward each other, swords meeting with the clang of metal against metal, in the way Seonaid whirled and spun away, and then back to meet his sword again. Of course, he supposed the fact that the image of her battling naked was imposing itself on his mind didn't help. He could picture the way her muscles would be stretching and moving beneath her clothes, the way her breasts would look in the afternoon sun.

Hell! Was there anything this woman could do that wouldn't excite him and make him think of bedding her? Wrestling with her on the forest floor had had the same effect, as had awaking to find himself curled around her like a blanket in the barn. Having her ride before him on his horse had put him in a terrible state, especially when she'd relaxed enough to fall asleep the last bit of the way and curled up against him like a sleepy cat. Now, watching her practice with swords put him in mind of wanting to tumble her to the ground right there and—

"Hell," he muttered with disgust. He had to get her wedded and bedded soon. In the meantime, he had some excess energy to work out himself. Drawing his sword, he walked out onto the field.

Seonaid raised her sword to deflect Ian's next blow and found it stopped by another's sword thrust higher than hers. Glancing to the side with irritation, she stared at Blake in amazement.

"May I?" he said politely.

Ian lowered his sword with a wide grin and moved to stand out of the way with Helen.

Seonaid glanced back to Blake, then abruptly lifted her sword to fend off the first blow from her betrothed. After that, Seonaid concentrated on what she was doing and found herself quickly winded by the ferocity of his assault. She knew Ian, knew what to expect, and found fending him off a relaxing pastime. She didn't know Blake, or the way he moved in battle. The man wasn't holding back either, and he kept her so busy deflecting his blows, at first she had no real chance to go on the attack.

It occurred to her that she had daydreamed about this very situation several times in the past, but when—after several moments of fighting him—she found her sword knocked from her hands and herself defenseless to his next blow, Seonaid merely gaped at him in shock as the sword came down, then stopped a breath away from her head. In her daydreams they had been equal in battle, or she had beaten him, but he had *never* beaten her. But in reality . . .

Bloody hell, he'd beaten her, she realized with dismay. She decided she preferred the daydream.

"You are very good with the sword, Seonaid." Blake bent to retrieve the weapon he'd knocked from her hand. "But you are not aggressive enough. You allow your opponent to take the lead and simply fend him off, waiting for an opening to make a killing blow. You should *make* an opening, else you are in danger of allowing your opponent to wear you out and win."

"I have told her that many times o'er the years. The lass jest willna listen," Angus Dunbar announced, drawing their attention to the fact that he, along with many others, had come to watch the battle. They had quite a little audience now, she noted with irritation.

Grimacing, she took her sword from Blake and moved toward where Helen and Aeldra stood.

"Ye'd best take yerself up to the keep, Seonaid." Her father's voice sounded behind her.

"That's where I was goin'," Seonaid muttered.

"Lady Wildwood is awaitin' fer ye in yer room. Go straight there."

"Why?" Seonaid asked warily, pausing to turn back.

"News has come from Sherwell. He's ailin' and canna come. The weddin' is in an hour."

Chapter Eleven

"There. You look lovely, dear."

Seonaid stared down at herself and cringed. It was her wedding night. That thought kept running through her head, over and over and over. Her wedding night. After all her running and fighting to avoid the wedding, she had gone to the slaughter without a whimper of protest. That fact was rather startling. But then, she hadn't had much of a chance to protest.

"News has come from Sherwell. He's ailin' and canna come. The weddin' is in an hour," her father had said. Then he had moved to stand before her and added, "I ken I have no behaved verra well over this marriage through the years. I was angry at Blake's father. But he is a good man, as is the son. Blake'll make ye a good husband, and I'm doin' this for yer own good."

"Doin' what?" Seonaid had asked.

For answer he had glanced over his shoulder and said, "Gavin, take four men and escort the women to Seonaid's room."

And that had been that. Gavin was one of her father's best men and he knew Seonaid very well. There had been no escaping his presence. He and the other men had escorted them to her room and into the care of Lady Wildwood, then had stood outside the door while she was bathed and dressed for the wedding. Then he had escorted her below, where the wedding had taken place.

Everyone had been terribly subdued. Aeldra and Helen had constantly looked as if they wanted to say something but had remained silent, as had Seonaid, leaving Lady Wildwood and Iliana to fill the silence with meaningless chatter and reassurances.

Then Seonaid had found herself standing before the bishop, Blake at her side and her father and everyone else there to witness. Seonaid didn't recall much about the ceremony—it was all rather a blur to her—but she must have said what she was supposed to. Then she had found herself seated at the trestle table with platter after platter of food passing under her nose until Lady Wildwood had tapped her shoulder and escorted her abovestairs, with Iliana, Aeldra, and Helen on their heels. The women had bathed her again, perfumed her, and dressed her in this confection of lace and almost sheer linen.

"Are you all right?" Lady Wildwood asked suddenly, eyeing her with concern.

Seonaid shifted from one foot to the other and shook her head.

"Oh." The woman looked taken aback for a minute, then released a little sigh. "I know it is frightening, dear. But it will not hurt for long, as I told you, and—"

"It's no that," Seonaid said quickly, not wanting Helen and Aeldra to think she was afraid of a little pain. She'd been to battle; a little pain wasn't that awful. At least, so she told herself. But in truth, it was quite odd, really. She wasn't a coward. Seonaid rode off to battle without a bit of fear. On the other hand, she didn't ride off into battle thinking she could be injured, or possibly killed. But tonight she *knew* she was going to be hurt. No matter what.

Lady Wildwood had said for some it hurt just a bit, for others a lot, and that one couldn't say how it would go for her. But as far as the woman knew, no one had ever had a painless first time. Or, she'd added a tad wryly, at least no woman she knew had admitted to not suffering the first time.

So Seonaid knew she was going to have pain. That wasn't something she was looking forward to. But she'd be damned if she was going to admit to any anxiety about it. Now, about her gown . . . that was another matter entirely.

She gestured to the thin white linen shift they had dressed her in. It was her mother's gown, one they had found in an old chest of her things. Fortunately, her mother had been tall like herself. In fact, she'd been much the same size apparently, for the gown fit beautifully. Seonaid stared down at herself. She'd never worn anything quite so lovely or delicate. And she wasn't at all comfortable in it. She felt terribly vulnerable.

"What is it, dear?" Lady Wildwood asked.

Seonaid glanced from the woman to Aeldra, Helen, and Iliana, then held her hands out helplessly and admitted, "I feel naked."

"Oh." When Lady Wildwood merely smiled gently, Seonaid's gaze skipped around the room.

"Where's my—?" She paused and moved across the room to grab her sword when she spotted it.

"Oh!" Lady Wildwood was at her side in a heartbeat, grabbing the weapon away. "No, no, dear. You will not need that."

"I wasna goin' to use it," Seonaid assured her. "I just want to hold it. I—"

"No," Lady Wildwood said firmly, and turned her toward the bed. "Just hop in and wait there. Everything will be fine. Truly."

Seonaid moved toward the bed, but when she glanced over her shoulder to see Lady Wildwood wasn't following, but had walked over to Iliana, she veered off to snatch up her *sgian dubh* from the chest where it had been set, then rushed to the bed. Unfortunately, Lady Wildwood happened to turn back as she was slipping the weapon under one of the cushions at the head of the bed.

"Seonaid!" She rushed to her side and leaned over to snatch that up as well. "No!"

"But I just want to have it near. I'll feel less defenseless," Seonaid protested.

Iliana's mother heaved out a breath and sat down on

the side of the bed. "My dear child, I know this is all new and alarming, but you do not need defenses." She patted Seonaid's hand soothingly. "Trust me. Everything will be well. Blake will be gentle and kind."

"I doona ken, Lady Wildwood," Aeldra said doubtfully. "Sherwell looked none too pleased at sup when Duncan was recounting what Gavin had told him of all that has occurred since he found us at St. Simmian's." She made a face. "He didna take well to everyone laughing at him. Mayhap ye should leave the *sgian dubh* at least."

"Aeldra, you are not helping." Lady Wildwood rubbed her forehead with one hand, a pained expression on her face. "Iliana, dear, perhaps you should take the girls and go see what is holding up the men."

"Aye, Mother."

"Thank you." Lady Wildwood waited for her daughter to usher the women out, then forced a smile for Seonaid. "While it is true Blake was no doubt distressed at being the butt of everyone's amusement, by all accounts he is a fair man and will not take it out on you. 'Tis hardly your fault that Duncan took it into his head to tease him."

"But had I no done those things, Duncan would have had nothin' to tease him with."

"Aye, but—" She paused when the door suddenly opened and Iliana leaned in to announce, "The men are coming."

Lady Wildwood was on her feet at once. She paused to pat Seonaid's hand reassuringly and murmur "All will be well," then hurried out of the room, taking the *sgian dubh* with her.

* * *

Blake spotted the women outside the door to Seonaid's room and tried to ignore the way they were watching his approach. Sister Helen and Iliana were looking slightly anxious, tense smiles pasted on their lips, and Aeldra was looking positively ferocious, glaring at him in what could only be warning. He presumed the little Scot was trying to convey with her eyes that he'd best not mistreat Seonaid. The message was coming through loud and clear.

He was almost to the women and the door they were guarding when it suddenly opened and Lady Wildwood slipped out.

"Oh!" She gave what sounded like a forced laugh and waved her hand vaguely as she said, "Here you are, then. Oh!" The last was gasped as she spotted the knife she was waving around with her gesture and quickly hid it behind her back. "She is ready for you."

Blake glanced from the arm that disappeared behind her back to the sword Iliana held and frowned slightly. The sword looked like—

"There ye are, then!" Angus Dunbar slapped him on the back and chuckled. "They've disarmed the lass, so ye should be able to get the deed done."

Blake's eyes widened incredulously. They'd had to disarm her? Good God. This was ridiculous. Women did everything they could think of to seduce, lure, or trick him to their beds, yet his bride had to be disarmed for him to bed her?

"Go on, then." Angus gave him a push toward the

door. "We'll be below fer a bit. If ye find yerself in diffi-culty give a shout."

The crowd began to move off. All but Lady Wildwood who, after a moment's hesitation, stepped closer and whispered so that the others could not hear, "I trust you shall be gentle with her? All that teasing at sup tonight was not her fault, and while the girl may seem strong and fearless, she is as overset as any virgin on her wed-ding night."

When Blake stared at her, too shocked to respond, she poked him lightly in the ribs with what he presumed was Seonaid's knife and hissed, "Promise me you shall be gentle."

"I promise," Blake said quickly.

"Good." She relaxed somewhat and smiled as she smoothed a hand over her hair. "Good night, my lord."

Blake stared after her with amazement as the older woman walked serenely down the hall after the others. If he had ever questioned what Lord Wildwood had seen in the woman—aside from her beauty—he no longer wondered. She hardly knew Seonaid yet acted like a fe-male wolf protecting her cub. She was obviously a spe-cial woman. Although he wondered if that did not reflect on Seonaid too. The woman had obviously seen something in his bride that made her worthy of such a reaction. He wasn't surprised. Blake had already come to the conclusion that his bride was a special woman too.

Blake waited until the hall was again empty, then turned to the door.

* * *

Seonaid stared at the door. She had heard her father's laughter and the murmur of voices, but silence had reigned in the hall now for several minutes and yet the door remained closed. Had he decided not to bother with consummating the marriage? Perhaps he had thought to have it annulled after all. Seonaid wasn't sure if that outcome would be a relief or not. It might be embarrassing, but she truly wasn't looking forward to the next few minutes of time. At least she thought it should only take a few minutes. She wasn't terribly knowledgeable about these matters, but between what she had seen when stumbling across couples indulging in the endeavor and what Lady Wildwood had told her, it did seem to her it shouldn't take more than a few minutes.

That was a positive point, she told herself. It would not take long. She should think about it like a trip to the smithy to have a tooth pulled. She'd had that done once when a blow to the face had broken a back tooth. It couldn't be any worse than that, she thought.

Actually, now that she recalled it, that *had* been pretty bad. And the smithy had made her drink a large glass of *uisgebeatha* 'ere doing it. The water of life, or whiskey as the English called it, could be good for numbing pain, but it hadn't seemed to help much that time.

Tonight Seonaid hadn't had a drop to drink at dinner. She should have drunk. What had she been thinking?

"Bloody hell," she muttered, shifting where she sat in the bed. Well, there was no hope for it now. It was too late for drink or anything else. It had always been Seonaid's motto that unpleasant things were best done quickly. So . . . she would ensure this was done that way too. If her husband ever bothered to show up to do it.

Seonaid blinked at her own thoughts. Husband? Good Lord, she was married now. She had a husband. She was a wife. Not that she felt any different. She didn't feel married, however that was supposed to feel.

Her rambling thoughts came to a dead halt when the door suddenly, finally, opened, and her husband entered the room.

His bride was seated in bed. Blake's eyes found her the moment he walked in. The sight of her made him pause in the doorway. Seonaid had proven herself full of surprises in the short time he'd known her. The memory of his first proper look at her still set him back on his heels: Seonaid in braies and a tunic. He'd never before seen a woman in braies. He was learning to like it. Long gowns were pretty enough on women, but they hid the lower body from view, and while every inch of Seonaid's skin was hidden by the pants she wore, they also revealed every curve she possessed. He liked watching her move in the braies. He had enjoyed seeing her fight in the nude even more. But this afternoon she had arrived—perhaps been dragged was the better description—to their wedding in a gown. Her hair—customarily worn carelessly pulled back—had been set free and left to soften her face and trail down her back. The sight of her dressed so had surprised him and taken his breath away.

And now she was a surprise again. Her hair was down still, brushed to a fine sheen and left to flow around her face and shoulders. She was wearing the thinnest of white gowns, one he could see the shadow of her nipples through. And she looked lovely. More than that, she looked luscious and desirable. That didn't surprise him, of course. What surprised him was that his Seonaid, his Amazon warrior, his beautiful, fiery, brave, strong battling bride, looked . . . terrified.

She sat in her bed, her eyes wide, her face pale, her hands fisted in her lap. She looked as scared as a child. Blake eased the door closed, then found his hands raising in the same soothing motion he would have used to approach a wild horse he wished to tame. But he didn't approach. He didn't speak either. He hadn't a clue what to say. What could he say? Have no fear, all will be well; I'm just going to come over there and give you a good seeing to?

Blake hadn't expected this. He hadn't known what to expect. Seonaid was a fighter, and he had half-expected a battle on his hands. In fact, he suspected he might still. Frightened animals often fought back when cornered, he thought, and was suddenly grateful they had taken her weapons away. While he had enjoyed the tussles they had indulged in until now—well, perhaps not the one where he'd gotten her foot in his groin—he thought that risking having his manhood cut off was a little too much spice for his wedding night.

"Well, what are ye waitin' for? Get over here and get it done so we can sleep."

Blake blinked in surprise at the gruff demand. She

had changed in the measure of a heartbeat. Gone was the wide-eyed look of terror. The woman facing him now was all grim determination. She was still pale, though, and had yet to unclench her hands, he noted, so he decided this must be bravado.

Forcing himself to relax—it wouldn't help her relax if he remained tense—Blake moved forward, his gaze moving around the chamber as he tried to decide how to proceed. He had no intention of walking over and "getting it done" as she so charmingly put it. He had no wish to hurt her, though he knew he probably would her first time. But Blake was used to seducing women, not—

"The bed is this way."

His head whipped around at her sarcastic words and he frowned at her slightly.

"Come on, come on, let's get this done," she insisted, tossing the linens aside to reveal the rest of the sleeping gown she wore.

"Seonaid," he said calmly, "I have no intention of just—Do you want a drink?" he interrupted himself to ask when she started to grow even more tense.

His bride let her breath out on a loud sigh of relief. "Aye. And lots of it. I didna think to drink until I was up here and 'twas too late. I wasna thinkin', I guess."

She got out of bed as she spoke and stomped past him to the door. Blake inhaled her scent as she passed. They had not just bathed her, they had powdered her too, and the sweet scent of flowers wafted off her as she moved by him. Oddly enough, Blake found himself a tad disappointed. Every woman he had seduced had smelled similar to this. Powdered, perfumed, and sweet.

Seonaid was none of those things by nature. Usually she smelled of fresh air and the woods, with a muskiness added that was her own scent. He rather preferred that, though he wouldn't tell her so, he thought, then grinned with amusement as Seonaid opened the door he'd just closed and bellowed into the hallway.

Seonaid slammed the door, took a deep breath, then turned to survey Blake. He was watching her with an odd grin on his face. It made her glance down at the gown she wore and grimace at the sight of it. She had never worn anything so delicate and feminine in her life and felt odd wearing it now.

"Lady Wildwood dug it up and insisted I wear it," she explained, resisting the urge to cross her arms over her chest to cover herself. She didn't know why she wanted to—he'd seen her naked when she was battling by the loch that day they were attacked. Still, this seemed different. She felt different. Seonaid was usually confident and sure of herself and what she was doing; but then, she usually *knew* what she was doing. At the moment she felt slightly out of her depth. And she didn't like it.

Grimacing, she stomped over to the chairs by the fireplace and dropped into one, then watched him and waited to see what he would do next. For a moment he didn't do anything; then his gaze dropped to the tub still sitting in the middle of the room, and he walked over to dip one hand in to test the temperature. Seonaid knew it would still be hot. It had been scalding when she had taken her bath, and that had only been moments ago.

Seeming satisfied by the temperature, Blake began to

undress, and Seonaid curled her legs beneath her on the chair and settled in to watch. She wasn't the least embarrassed to do so. Well, perhaps she would have been had he made a fuss of it, but Blake ignored her and simply set about his business. The plaid went first, and she hid a smile at the way his nose wrinkled as he removed the item.

Duncan had told her with much amusement that Blake had heard, and obviously believed, the tale that Scots wore their colors. He'd traded their father a fine gold doublet and braies for his plaid. They had all had a good laugh about that, for it wasn't true. Every clan had friends, and every clan had enemies. Only a fool would walk around wearing something that proclaimed your allegiances. It could see you dead. Perhaps one day there would be peace and they could do so, but for now they did not. If their clan all happened to wear the same design of plaid at the moment, it was because that was the design that Cailean Cummins had had colors for and had made. He usually did a great batch of one design, until the colors ran out, then did a different design for another great batch of cloth. But that did not make them their clan design.

She would have to tell him that some day, Seonaid thought. She didn't want a husband who was ignorant of such things and so easily made a fool of.

She forgot all about this concern as Blake next removed his tunic. Seonaid almost sighed aloud at the sight. The man was definitely well built and a pleasure to look upon. Except for the thing between his legs. She tried not to look at that monstrosity. It would just make her think about what was coming and the pain and blood Lady Wildwood had warned her about. Seonaid didn't want to think about that just yet, so she avoided peering below his waist at first and concentrated her attention on his chest and arms. He had a lovely chest, she thought, and had the oddest desire to touch it, just to rub her hands over the wide expanse and—

A knock at the door interrupted her thoughts, and Seonaid uncurled herself from the chair and moved to the door to answer it. It was a servant with the whiskey she'd yelled for. But it wasn't whiskey. It was wine, Seonaid saw, and frowned with irritation. "I yelled for *uisgebeatha*, Janna. What—"

"There is none at the moment," Janna said apologetically. "Lady Iliana used it all to hold off Greenweld when he attacked. She had them drop barrels of it off the wall onto the mangonel, then had the men shoot flamin' arrows at it to set it alight."

"Oh." Seonaid's eyebrows rose. "That was clever."

"Aye. She did us proud." Janna grinned, then asked, "Is there anything else ye'd like?"

"Nay. Thank ye." Seonaid offered a smile, then closed the door and turned in time to see Blake stepping into the tub. She stared at his behind with fascination as he moved and thought once again that it was the finest she had ever seen. Maybe she'd get to touch it later. She was curious to know if it felt as hard as it looked.

"May I have a glass?"

Blake's voice shook her out of her fascination and Seonaid started to move again. She set down on a chest the tray Janna had brought holding the mugs and wine and poured some for him, then some for herself, before carrying both over to the tub.

This afforded her a close view of his chest, and she had to bite her tongue to keep from whistling between her teeth with appreciation at the sight. If nothing else, she had herself a pretty husband, one it would be a pleasure to look at for years to come.

"Thank you," Blake murmured as he took the wine she offered. "Could you scrub my back?"

Seonaid hesitated. Her first instinct was to tell him to wash his own bloody back. She wasn't a servant. But then she realized she would get to touch all those corded, rippling muscles, and she moved around to kneel on the floor at the back of the tub. She set her drink on the floor, accepted the bit of linen scrap that had been brought up to wash with, and rubbed it over the soap, then paused with amusement. It was the flower soap Lady Wildwood had brought in for Seonaid to use. He would smell like a summer garden. She shrugged and continued to soap the linen. There wasn't any other soap to use. Besides, he would smell better than her father's plaid.

Setting the soap down, she contemplated his back, then grabbed her wine and drank it down before setting to the task. His back was hard and yet soft at the same time. Seonaid ran the cloth over his skin, then over it again, then let it drop away and used her hands, lathering the soap she had applied and massaging the skin with fascination.

"Mmmm, that feels good."

His murmur startled her. She had almost forgotten he was there. Well, not forgotten exactly, but—

"Can you do my chest?"

Seonaid stilled, her eyes locked on the back of his head. His chest? She thought of running her fingers over that wide expanse and her fingers almost itched with the desire to do so. Sitting back on her heels, she grabbed her wine, realized it was empty, and reached over his shoulder to snatch his out of his hands.

"Hey!" Blake glanced over his shoulder but just laughed as he watched her down it. "Thirsty?" he teased, and she scowled at his knowing look.

"I had a tooth pulled once," she muttered, setting the empty mug aside and shifting to kneel farther along the tub so that she could reach his chest.

"Did you?" he asked, his confusion apparent. "I am not following the conversation."

Seonaid retrieved the linen that was now floating on the water's surface and began to run it over the soap. "It was unpleasant and painful, but no nearly as unpleasant and painful as it might have been had I no drunk a bottle o' whiskey beforehand."

"And you are comparing this to having a tooth pulled?" He sounded affronted.

"Lady Wildwood explained what will happen."

Blake remained silent as she set the soap aside and began to smooth the linen over his chest. She could feel his eyes on her and sensed he wanted to say something, and so wasn't surprised when he finally said, "Seonaid, it does not have to be completely—Is that flowers I smell?"

Seonaid glanced up at his face and nearly laughed when he snatched her hand and drew the cloth to his nose to sniff it.

"Dear God, you are going to make me smell like a woman."

She did laugh then. He looked so horrified at the idea. "Too late, ye already do," she taunted and tugged her hand loose to continue washing him, but he immediately recaptured her arm in a bid to stop her.

"Nay, leave off with the soaping, then."

"Nay. I think ye smell pretty," she teased, grabbing the cloth with her free hand and started to run it over him again.

"Witch," Blake muttered, catching that hand now.

"Oh, witch, is it?" Seonaid asked, laughing at his sulky expression. He'd released her first hand to grab her second and she again switched the cloth to her free hand. Blake immediately tried to grab that hand, but Seonaid held it out of reach behind her back with a laugh.

"Give me the cloth, Seonaid." He had released her other hand again and leaned forward in the tub, both arms going around her to try to grab the cloth. Big mistake, Seonaid thought with amusement, slipping her free hand down to grab the soap from the floor where she'd set it. In the next moment she was rubbing it over his chest as he struggled to get the linen from her.

Blake gave an outraged squawk and gave up on the cloth to grab for the soap. Seonaid immediately started to rub the soapy, flowery-smelling cloth over his arms, chest, and anywhere she could reach. She was having great fun, until Blake caught that wrist as well. They began an odd sort of struggle then. He had her by both wrists and she was keeping her arms up to keep him from snatching the cloth or soap from her. Their struggle forced her forward on her knees. Her stomach pressed against the side of the tub, but her chest occasionally became pressed against his as she wrestled with him. He was trying to urge her hands together over their heads, but she knew he wanted to shift his hold so that he could capture both her hands together with one of his, then rob her of her weapons, so she was fighting valiantly against it. Unfortunately, he was stronger than she. When she knew the battle was about to be lost, Seonaid tugged away from him slightly and let the cloth drop rather than allow him to claim it.

She hoped that this way she might have a chance to retain the soap. At least she would if he released her to snatch up the linen as expected. But when both of them peered down to see where it had landed, they froze at the sight of it poking straight up out of the water like a tent. It had landed on something. Something sticking up out of the water from between his legs.

Seonaid's eyebrows rose. It seemed she wasn't the only one having fun, but she hadn't a clue why their wrestling was exciting him. Or did she? She asked herself the question as she glanced up, saw that his gaze had moved to the front of her gown, and followed it. The gown had gotten soaked in the brief tussle and was now transparent and plastered lovingly to her chest. It revealed rather clearly that her nipples were as erect as his member.

Hmmm, she thought. This was most interesting. She never would have expected it. Fighting, whether serious or in play, had never had this effect on her before.

She lifted her gaze to Blake's face almost reluctantly then, and he immediately took advantage of the act and swooped in to press his lips on hers. Seonaid started to pull back, an automatic reaction, but he immediately released his hold on her wrists and slid one hand around her back and the other to the back of her head to hold her in place.

Seonaid was not at all used to such masterful behavior. She was generally the one in control. She went still, her mouth opening on a small gasp, and then gasped in another breath of shock as his tongue immediately slid into her mouth. No one else had ever kissed Seonaid before. One boy had tried when she was very young, but she'd pushed him down and set about beating the haggis out of him. And that had been for just a peck on the cheek. She'd seen others kissing since then, but generally averted her eyes since it was usually when she'd turned a corner and come unexpectedly upon a couple. Seonaid had had no idea that tongues were involved in the endeavor.

She didn't struggle, but remained still under the onslaught, curiosity holding her in place. It was an interesting activity, this kissing business. His tongue was moving across hers and sweeping through her mouth as if in search of rotten teeth and—in her untried opinion—should have felt disgusting. But there was something about the taste and feel of him and the way he did it that was rather nice. His mouth was moving over hers, his tongue moving in her, his hand urging her chest back against his, and Seonaid had the oddest desire to stretch and arch her body.

When Blake's hand slid between them and closed over one breast, a moan was surprised from her and Seonaid did finally stretch, arching into the touch. Blake immediately caught one hand in her hair and tugged her head back, his lips slipping away to run down her throat. Seonaid moaned again, then closed one hand over the larger hand at her breast, urging him to touch more firmly. She liked what he was doing and wanted more of it.

Blake gave a rough chuckle at the demanding action, but instead of giving in to it, released her breast altogether.

Seonaid was just starting to scowl when he caught her around the waist and dragged her over the side of the tub and onto his lap in the water, positioning her there almost sideways. She did not squeal like a girl and thrash about. Instead she caught her hand in his hair again and tugged his face back to hers. He immediately satisfied her by kissing her again. Seonaid probably would have grabbed his other hand and pulled it back to her breast, but he beat her to it, catching the breast once more and squeezing it gently, then concentrating on the erect nipple, pinching it through the cloth and rolling it between thumb and forefinger.

Seonaid sighed her satisfaction into his mouth, quite

happy with the way things were going. She didn't even mind when he broke the kiss and ran his lips over her cheek to her ear. Seonaid found herself shifting and arching and twisting slightly in his lap as he explored her ear, her throat, and then ran his tongue along her collarbone and dipped it into the hollow there.

When his mouth suddenly dropped to catch the nipple he'd been caressing, she nearly leapt off his lap, but then moaned and caught his head by the hair again, holding him there as all sorts of interesting reactions flew through her body.

Dear Lord, this was good stuff. Why had no one told her about this? She suspected it might be even better without the damp cloth of her gown between them, but as she was new to this, she kept her mouth closed on the suggestion. Besides, Blake was distracting her, both with his mouth and with his now wandering hands. One of his hands was around her back, holding her in place, the other, the one that had been caressing her breast earlier, had run down her stomach, rubbed over her hip and along her outer leg, and was now creeping up her inner thigh.

Seonaid had never known that part of her body could be so sensitive. Skin that normally just lay across her bones in boredom was suddenly alive and almost leaping about on her body as his callused fingers brushed across it. She found herself spreading her legs to allow him more room, then she turned her head and clamped her mouth to his shoulder as his fingers brushed against the very center of her. Seonaid alternately sucked at the skin of his shoulder and nipped at it with excitement as he touched her. She was in quite a state of upheaval and in a quandary, wanting to demand that he stop, because a sense of frustration was rising within her, but at the same time not wanting him to stop because it felt so good. In point of fact, she didn't know what the hell she wanted.

Blake seemed to know, though, and for once in her life Seonaid was forced to give up the control of events and allow him to do what he saw fit. Until he suddenly stopped touching her and lifted his mouth from her breast too.

Seonaid released the shoulder she'd been unconsciously chewing at and blinked her eyes open to glare at him. "What?"

Blake merely chuckled at her scowl. He was already scooping her up into his arms and shifting to stand in the tub. Seonaid latched her arms around his neck and held her breath. She was a large woman, tall with solid muscle. Most men could not have lifted her so easily. Blake seemed to have no trouble, but still she held on as he stepped out of the tub and carried her across the room to the bed.

He set her down there and made quick work of removing her gown, then gave her a gentle push that sent her flopping onto the bed behind her.

Seonaid sat up and started to shift backward to make room for him, but she hadn't moved far before he caught her ankle to hold her in place as he climbed onto the bed next to her.

"Stay," he ordered, and Seonaid scowled. It sounded like an order you'd give a dog. And Seonaid was no dog.

"Doona think yer goin' to be able to boss me around jest cause yer me husband," she told him firmly. "I'm no very guid at listenin' to me father and doubt I'll be any better at listenin' to a bossy, arrogant English— aiyyeeeeee!" Seonaid half sat up in shock as he suddenly tugged the ankle he held farther away from the other and bent to place his mouth where his hand had been but moments before. She only half sat up, because Blake—without even looking—caught her with one flat hand at her chest and pushed her back down on the bed.

Seonaid was so shocked, she would have sat up again, but her body was having conflicting reactions and her hips were suddenly thrusting upward into his caress. It was hard to sit up with your hips thrusting that way. Besides, Seonaid was quickly losing the urge to sit up. Now she wanted to grab something and squeeze. His behind came to mind, but it was out of her reach. Most of him was, so Seonaid had to make do with catching the cushion on one side of her and tangling her fingers in the linens on the other as he did things to her that felt so good she thought she might just die from the sheer pleasure of it.

Seonaid wasn't capable of much thought for several moments, since what he was doing was driving the thoughts right out of her. She was aware that she was moaning and panting and making all sorts of indelicate sounds but couldn't have stopped them had she tried.

All her energy and focus was fixed on the excitement and tension he was causing inside her. Her body was writhing and thrusting as his mouth and tongue worked their magic, her muscles clenching harder and harder until she thought they must surely snap. At one point it all became too much and she tried to close her legs and force him to stop, but Blake simply caught his arms around her thighs and tugged them farther apart, then redoubled his efforts so that she was sobbing with desperation.

She didn't know what it was exactly he was doing, didn't know why, didn't know what she was supposed to do. She had never felt so out of control or helpless, nor had she ever experienced the tense pleasure-pain he was giving her. Her hips were thrusting into the action, but her head was twisting back and forth on the bed and she could hear herself moaning. That was when she felt something enter her. She didn't know what, because Blake wasn't in the position to do what Lady Wildwood had said he would do, but she didn't really care what it was; all she cared about was the sudden increased tension and pleasure it brought her. Seonaid drove down into the caress and finally felt the tension within her explode. Her whole body seemed to vibrate and shudder and she cried out with the strength of it, her fingers clawing at the bedclothes so desperately, it was a wonder she didn't rend it to bits.

She was aware of Blake straightening, but only on the periphery of her consciousness, as he shifted to move up her body. When he moved to cover her, her hands lifted to hold him of their own volition, just as her mouth opened beneath the demanding kiss when he claimed her lips. Then he slid into her and Seonaid stiffened, her body arching like a bow beneath him, and a startled cry slipped from her lips.

Chapter Twelve

Blake forced himself to remain completely still. He had thought that getting the breaching done quickly and while Seonaid was so relaxed in the aftermath of the pleasure he had given her would be for the best. But the roar that had just ripped from her lips made him wonder if he hadn't been wrong. Now he was encased in her warm, moist depths and his body was eager to move. He was listening to his head instead. It was a difficult task. She was so tight and hot around him, squeezing him, and he just wanted to—

"Are you all right?" he asked breathlessly.

Seonaid tipped her head back to peer up at him, and he noted that she had the audacity to look surprised at the question. "Aye. Why would ye ask?"

"You screamed," he pointed out in a tone as dry as dust.

"Oh." She shrugged beneath him. "It was surprise, and from what Lady Wildwood said I was expectin' pain."

Blake felt himself tense. "You mean you did not feel pain?"

She shrugged again. "No more than a pinch o' it. Nothin' worth mentionin'."

Blake narrowed his gaze on her, unsure whether to believe her or not. "Are you feeling any pain now?"

She raised her eyebrows, then wiggled about beneath him and flexed her muscles before shaking her head. "Nay."

"Thank God," Blake gasped and withdrew a little, then plunged back in again, making her gasp. He managed to make himself stop then and asked, "Now?"

"Now what?" she murmured, her hands moving to his back and holding him as she wiggled beneath him again.

"Are you experiencing any pain, or may I proceed?" Blake truly didn't mean to sound angry, but this was testing the limits of his control. She was so matter of fact and he just wanted to—

"Nay, no pain. It just feels a bit odd."

"Odd?" Blake asked, his eyebrows drawing together. "What do you mean, odd?"

Seonaid shrugged again. "Odd. Just odd. 'Tis all odd to me," she pointed out, then just seemed to realize what he had said and asked, "Proceed? There is more?"

Blake closed his eyes and held on to his patience. "Aye, wife, there is more."

"Lady Wildwood did no mention more," she muttered, then shrugged beneath him and shifted her hips, spreading her legs wider. "But then, she seems to have left out a lot."

"Seonaid . . ." he said through gritted teeth.

"Aye?"

"I cannot hold on much longer; pray tell me I may continue."

"Hold on to what?" she asked, then something in his expression must have warned that he was not in the mood for conversation and she said, "Go on, then. Continue."

Releasing his breath on a relieved sigh, Blake withdrew again and pressed back into her.

Seonaid lay still at first. The muscles in her legs, and everywhere in her body, really, were still trembling from what he had done to her before taking her maidenhead. And really, for the first few strokes she hadn't a clue what the attraction to this in and out motion was. Then he changed position slightly and changed the rhythm of his movements, and Seonaid began to take notice. Excitement was building within her again and her body began to clench. Catching her fingers in his hair, she drew his head down to hers, wanting a kiss. He answered the silent demand, fastening his mouth over hers and thrusting his tongue into her mouth in time with his body thrusting into her.

Seonaid kissed back just as aggressively, thrusting her own tongue out to tangle with his. She kept her hold on his hair but dug the fingers of her other hand into the flesh below his shoulderbone, urging him on. This was like nothing she had ever experienced. Seonaid had never realized there was anything as wonderful as this in life. Now she understood what all the moaning was about, and it wasn't pain. Dear God, this was better than riding a horse as fast as you could through the woods. It was better than swimming naked in a cold loch on a warm summer day. It was . . . well, it was even better than battle.

That was Seonaid's last coherent thought; then her body took over, overwhelming her with wave after wave of pleasure until she cried out with it, her muscles clenching around his and holding him in place. She was hardly even aware of his shout as he joined her there, then collapsed on top of her as they both lay trembling, gasping for breath. After a moment Blake groaned low in his throat and rolled off her to lay on his back at her side. He slid his arm under her as he went and lifted, catching her under her back and pulling her so that she lay half on his chest, her head in the crook of his arm.

Seonaid went unprotesting, finding his masterful behavior oddly endearing. They lay like that for several moments; then Seonaid lifted her head, peered at his supine face, and asked, "Can we do it again?"

Blake's eyes blinked open and he turned his head to peer at her with a rather shocked expression. Then a laugh slipped from his lips and he pressed her head back to his shoulder. "In a minute. Give me a chance to recover."

* * *

Seonaid woke as the sun rose. It was her usual time to
wake, but she opened gritty eyes to stare at the window
and scowled at the sunlight coming through it. She was
exhausted and had no idea why until a snore sounded,
drawing her attention to her other side.

There was a man in her bed. Not just any man, either.
Blake Sherwell. Her husband. He lay on his stomach beside her, his head turned in her direction. She stared at
his golden hair and sweet face in rest and felt an ache in
her chest. She wanted to comb her fingers through
those golden strands. She also wanted to smooth a finger over the forehead that was presently creased as if he
dreamed of something troubling. Then she wanted to
run it down his straight nose to brush it lightly over the
lips that had given her so much pleasure.

She also really, really wanted to squeeze his bum.

Seonaid grinned at the thought. His behind had fascinated her since first seeing it. It was so round and
cute. She was dying of curiosity to know if it was soft or
hard. Every other part of his body was solid as a rock.
Except for his lips, she acknowledged—they could go
soft when kissing her. But she wanted to know if his behind was as hard as the rest of him, or if it really was a
cushion for his seat.

Seonaid would have been embarrassed had anyone
known of her sudden fascination with the male behind.
But as no one did, and as he was now her husband, and
as he was splayed out on his chest with his butt in the
air, just begging to be touched—

Seonaid sat up and gently tugged away the linen covering his lower body until the two round globes were revealed. She then glanced quickly up at his face to be sure the action hadn't awakened him. Satisfied that he still slept, she leaned a little closer to the exposed area and tentatively reached out to place one finger lightly on the nearest cheek. The skin gave way slightly beneath her touch. It was not hard like the rest of him. Grinning, she allowed the rest of her hand to take position on the round surface, then gently squeezed.

Blake immediately murmured something in his sleep and rolled away onto his back. Seonaid was now faced with a frontal view of her nude husband. Much to her amazement, while he slept, his staff didn't. It stood as stiff as the king's flag. It still looked monstrous huge to her, but Seonaid was no longer afraid of its size. Much to her pleasure, Blake had proven time and again through the night that she could accommodate him. He had not needed long to recover from their first bout before proving ready for a second, and Seonaid had found that time equally pleasing. Afterward, she had drifted off to sleep with a smile on her face, only to be awoken hours later to Blake's lazy caresses and passionate kisses.

Seonaid glanced at his face and wondered if he might pleasure her again were he to wake up. The erection he was sporting seemed to indicate that it was a good chance. Perhaps if she lay down and pretended to be sleeping, then made some sort of sound to wake him . . .

Blake snuffled in his sleep and Seonaid almost

laughed aloud; then her gaze dropped to his manhood again. They had bathed in the tepid bathwater after the first time he'd awakened her, and she had awoken the second time in the throes of a passionate dream where he was bent between her legs, pleasuring her with his mouth as he had before taking her maidenhead, only to open her eyes to find that he *was* kneeling between her legs actually doing so.

Seonaid was not completely ignorant, but she hadn't realized a man might do that to a woman. She *had* once come across one of the servants on her knees doing something similar to a man. It was impossible not to witness such things when you lived in a castle and the servants all slept in the great hall at night. Seonaid distinctly recalled the bewilderment she had experienced at the time. She hadn't been at all sure what she had interrupted. She thought she knew now and understood why the man had been moaning like a cow about to give birth. And she had the sudden thought that it might be interesting to wake Blake so. She had certainly enjoyed the experience herself, and perhaps then he might not be grumpy with her for disturbing his rest, which might help induce him to pleasure her again.

The only problem was, she wasn't exactly sure how to go about it. She had a basic idea, but . . .

Seonaid had never let lack of knowledge stop her attempting something before this, and she had no intention of doing so now. Shifting closer to him, she contemplated the matter briefly, trying to decide how to start; then she reached out and ran one finger lightly from the base of his shaft to the tip, her gaze sliding back and forth between his manhood and his face, noting his expression as she did. It didn't change much. He murmured in his sleep and turned his head, but no more. Seonaid pursed her lips and wrapped her hand around him next, running it lightly up his length again. This time he gave a small moan and twisted his head the other way.

Shrugging, Seonaid bent forward, hesitated, then began to press little kisses along his shaft. She heard Blake moan and felt him shift slightly but didn't think he was awake yet. Probably a good thing, she decided, because she didn't think she was doing it right. Mary, the servant she had stumbled upon who had been on her knees servicing one of the visiting men, had had the whole thing in her mouth, her head bobbing forward and back as if she were greasing it.

She tried that next, taking him into her mouth and sliding it slowly up and down his shaft as far as she could. That seemed to get a reaction out of Blake; he moaned loudly, his hand moving to clench in her hair, his body stiffening with tension, but she still didn't think he was awake. Seonaid raised and lowered her head several times, but he was so large, she could not go far down the shaft before the tip touched the back of her throat and she had the instinct to gag. Frustrated, she closed her hand around the base of him and then began to move it with her mouth, hoping that would make up for the fact that she couldn't take him all in.

"Seonaid," he growled several moments later, and the

hand in her hair began to tug lightly, urging her head up and forcing her to stop.

Pausing, she lifted her head and glanced at him. "Am I doin' it wrong?"

"Nay, you were doing very well," he said between clenched teeth.

"Good." She lowered her head again, and Blake groaned as she continued what he had interrupted. After several more moments he pulled at her hair again, and Seonaid sighed and lifted her head to glance at him curiously. "What? Is there something else I should be doin' too?"

"Nay, but—"

"Well, then, stop interruptin' and let me continue," she ordered, and lowered her head again.

She was concentrating on what she was doing, experimentally changing her speed and the pressure she was applying to see what worked best, but the man was silent as stone now that he was awake and she could not tell if he liked any of it. Except he did seem to be getting a bit harder and seemed a little larger too, if that were possible, and a glance at his feet showed his toes curling. She thought that might be a good sign. Then he began to touch her.

Seonaid stiffened, her rhythm thrown off by her surprise when he slid a hand along her hips, then around and between her legs. She tried to get her rhythm back, but the man was proving a great distraction, to the point that Seonaid actually cursed around the member in her mouth. Straightening, she turned to glare at him.

"Stop that. I am pleasin' you now," she growled.

A slow smile spread across his lips at the way she was glowering at him; then he half sat up to catch her by the arms and tugged her on top of his chest as he lay back down.

"Hey!" Seonaid protested, pushing at his chest and trying to lever herself up. "I am—"

Blake silenced her with a kiss, claiming her lips, then thrusting his tongue in to keep her from talking. It was most effective, she admitted to herself, giving up trying to push herself back up for the moment. She would let him kiss her a bit, then go back to it, she told herself, letting her hands slide up his chest and into his hair.

He was a terribly good kisser. At least, it seemed to her that he was, though Seonaid didn't have anyone to compare his kissing skills to. But, comparisons or not, she suspected he was probably a master at everything to do with carnal knowledge. From what she'd heard, the man had got enough practice at it. And Seonaid couldn't help but be grateful for it, because it seemed to her that she was reaping the benefits.

She moaned a protest as he broke their kiss, then sighed as he moved his lips across her face. She felt and reacted like a cat beneath its master's caress, tilting and pushing her face into his hand, until he caught her firmly by the hair and turned her head so that his tongue could explore her ear.

Seonaid gasped and shuddered atop him, then became aware that his hands had not been still. They had started out holding her in place, but once she'd stopped resisting had turned from holding to caressing, moving over her back and arms. Now they slid down to her bottom and cupped her there, urging her tighter against his hardness. Seonaid turned her head and caught his lips again at the intimate caress, her legs slipping apart to increase the intimacy as he rubbed against her. When—after a few moments of this—it no longer seemed satisfying, she levered herself upward to sit on him, managing the task only because she took him by surprise.

Once straddling him, Seonaid slid her body back and forth over him, but while that eased her frustrations at first, it did not wholly satisfy her. She wanted to feel him inside her again, filling her to capacity and plunging in and out as he had done before. Shifting, she reached down and found him with her hand, then steered him to where she wanted him and eased herself down. A small sigh slid from her lips as he filled her, and she peered at him through half-closed eyes as she wiggled with pleasure.

Blake watched her, a small smile stretching his lips; then he suddenly sat up, caught her beneath the behind, and lifted and shifted her.

"Oh!" Seonaid gasped, her legs moving around his back of their own accord as their bodies rubbed together in a more satisfying manner. Then Blake shifted with her and dropped her on the bed. He came down on top of her, driving into her with the move and surprising a grunt from her. Seonaid caught her arms around him, her fingers digging first into his shoulders, then shifting beneath his arms to clutch at his back, and finally dropping to cup and knead his behind and urge him on as he propelled them both toward the release she was craving.

Truly, if she had realized what she was missing due to his dallying in collecting her, Seonaid thought she might have hunted the man down and dragged him back to marry her.

In fact, she decided, she would have a good talking to him later about all the time he'd wasted. On the other hand, she had already admitted that she was benefitting from the skills he had learned while neglecting her, and perhaps he would not have been so skilled had she gone after him. Perhaps everything had its time, and this was theirs. She determined to simply enjoy it and the fact that she had a husband who could do this for her. She suspected that this would not be as enjoyable with less skilled men, and that her father had done her a grand favor in betrothing her to the dreaded Sherwell. She'd keep that to herself, though. There was no sense giving her father a fat head.

Blake caught her head in hand, turning her to seal his lips on hers, and Seonaid suspected he had recognized that her thoughts had wandered. He now forced them back to him and what he was doing as he thrust his tongue into her mouth in time with his thrusting body, and Seonaid gave up thinking about anything as they both struggled toward and finally found their explosive release.

A knock at the door made Seonaid's eyes flutter open. Her gaze slid over the empty expanse of bed beside her, then she pushed herself up on one arm and peered around the equally empty room. She had apparently dozed off again. Blake had not. Or, if he had, he'd already awakened and left the room

A second knock made her growl, "Aye?"

The door opened at once and Janna entered, a bright smile on her face. "Good morn, m'lady."

"Morn," Seonaid grunted automatically, then opened her mouth to ask what the woman wanted, only to snap it closed again when several servants traipsed in behind her. Half of them carried empty buckets, which they used to empty the tub, scooping the cold water out and dumping it out the window. The rest of the servants carried bucket after bucket of fresh water.

"I didna order a bath," she said.

"Lord Blake ordered it, m'lady," Janna informed her. Then, as the last woman entered bearing fresh linens, she added, "He ordered the bed remade too."

Seonaid glanced around. She was naked as the day she'd been born, covered just by the sheet she was lying on, twisted up and pulled across her torso as if Blake had tried to leave her decently shielded. The rest of the linens and furs from the bed, as well as the cushions, were scattered willy-nilly on the floor. Even the base sheet was gone.

Rearranging the sheet twisted around her so that she wore it in the old Roman toga fashion, Seonaid stumbled off the bed and began tossing the furs and cushions back onto it as she searched for the bottom bed linen. She knew from when Iliana and Duncan had married that her father, Rolfe, and the bishop would soon arrive to witness the bed linen and the blood that should stain it, proving she had been a virgin last night. But the linen was nowhere to be seen.

"The bottom linen is missing," she said with concern.

"Aye, m'lady. Lord Blake brought it below with him earlier so yer father and the others would no disturb ye."

Seonaid grimaced. The stupid thing would be slung over the banister and hanging down into the great hall by now, for all to witness her innocence. At least, that was what they had done with the linen from Iliana and Duncan's wedding night. The idea actually made her squirm, but she merely grunted and walked to the tub as the last of the water was dumped in.

She hadn't been terribly interested in the idea of yet another bath on first realizing they were preparing her one. Preferring not to smell like a barn animal, Seonaid had never shunned baths as her brother used to before Iliana taught him the benefits of bathing. But four or more baths in two days seemed excessive. However, the moment she stood up and started to move, she'd become aware of the sticky wetness between her legs, and the idea of a bath was suddenly appealing. She saw many, many baths in her future if Blake continued to be as enthusiastic as he had been last night.

It had been considerate of her husband to think of it. She smiled softly to herself. He had proven himself very considerate indeed last night. Lady Wildwood had said that some women enjoyed the bedding part of marriage and some did not. Some women detested it, but she had found over the years that those who did not like it usually had selfish husbands who did not trouble to be sure their wives found any pleasure. She had added that from all she had heard of Blake Sherwell, Seonaid would not have that problem. And she had been right. The man had been most thoughtful. In fact, she was sure that she had found more pleasure than he last night. And this morning.

"Shall I stay and help ye with yer bath, m'lady?" Janna's question drew her attention to the fact that the servants were finished filling the tub and making the bed and were now filing out of the room.

"Nay. I—" Seonaid began.

"We'll help." Aeldra entered the open door, with Helen on her heels.

"They'll help." Seonaid dropped her sheet and stepped into the hot water. "Thank ye, Janna."

"Aye, m'lady." Janna slipped out, pulling the door closed behind her as Helen and Aeldra moved to the tub. Both women watched silently as Seonaid began to run the flower-scented soap over her body.

"Well?" Aeldra said after several moments had passed in silence.

Seonaid lifted her head and glanced at her in question. "Well, what?"

Aeldra tsked with irritation. "Well, how was it?" she expounded. "What was it like?"

Seonaid grinned at the question. How was it? Sweet Jesu.

Aeldra contemplated her expression, then began to grin as well. "That good, huh?"

Seonaid started to laugh. "Ye wouldna believe it."

"Judging by the mess yer hair is in, mayhap I would," she said with amusement, and Seonaid raised a hand to feel the back of her head, frowning at the rat's nest it had become. She was confused for a moment, then recalled twisting and thrashing her head back and forth on the bed and understood.

"You shall need help with that," Helen murmured, kneeling beside the tub. "Come, I shall wash your hair. Tip it back."

Seonaid did as instructed, tipping her head back as Helen picked up a bucket, scooped some water out of the tub and poured it over her hair, trying to avoid pouring any over her face. Once she had soaked her hair thoroughly, the woman began to wash it with what was left of the herbal vinegar from the night before, working her fingers through the knots as she went.

"Yer getting yer veil wet," Aeldra warned Helen and Seonaid smiled faintly as the other woman tsked with irritation. When the work on her hair paused, Seonaid opened her eyes and turned her head slightly to the side to see Helen removing her headwear to reveal her red hair pulled back in a knot.

" 'Tis annoying anyway," Helen muttered, setting it aside. " 'Tis hot and bothersome. I will put it back on afterward."

Seonaid said nothing. She merely smiled, closed her eyes, and tipped her head back again for the work on her hair to continue. They were all silent for a moment; then Aeldra said, "So yer no goin' to get more specific about what happened?"

There was a pause, and Seonaid supposed Aeldra was giving her a chance to speak up if she so desired, but she held her tongue. There was no way to describe what had happened last night. She could tell them what he'd done, but until they'd experienced it, neither woman would understand *what he'd done.*

Heaving an irritated sigh, Aeldra continued, "Then I suppose we might as well figure out what we're goin' to do next."

Seonaid smiled softly, her mind immediately going to Blake. She wondered where he was and when they would next get to—

"About Helen's problem," Aeldra added dryly, apparently reading Seonaid's expression.

She felt ashamed of herself. She had completely forgotten Helen's problem. Good Lord! How could she forget the threat to the woman's life and the possible threat against her father?

"Seonaid?" Aeldra said when she remained silent for several moments.

"Aye," she murmured, opening her eyes to assure them she had not fallen asleep. "I was thinkin'."

"What did you come up with?" Helen asked eagerly.

Seonaid started to give her head a slight shake but stopped right away as Helen began to pour more of the vinegar and herb mixture over it. "I am no sure what to do. I had decided yesterday that it might be best to go to Father with the problem."

"Your father?" Helen sounded unsure.

"Aye." She blinked her eyes open to stare at the woman. "He could arrange a proper escort, or send one messenger to yer father and another to the king. Aeldra and I might have been able to sneak ye down to England and escorted ye to yer father's keep using the passage, but without it . . ." She shrugged helplessly. "Yer chances are better with me Father providin' an escort."

"Aye," she admitted reluctantly. "But what if they attack your father's escort?"

Seonaid pursed her lips. "He may think 'tis best to send messengers and keep ye safe here in Dunbar."

"Oh, Seonaid." Helen sighed. "That is what he did for Lady Wildwood, and 'tis what brought about Greenweld's attack on Dunbar. I would not wish to cause such a thing to happen again."

"Well, he may come up with a better idea," Seonaid said quietly. "Father has lived a long time and seen much. I think we should let him ken the truth o' the matter at least and make suggestions. If he doesna come up with something we like, we can always sneak off again and try on our own."

"Oh, I do not think that is a good idea at all."

All three women jerked their heads around to the open door at Lady Wildwood's words. Iliana's mother stood in the open door, her gaze focused on Helen, an expression of recognition on her face.

"Forgive me for entering without knocking," Lady Wildwood murmured, pushing the door closed. "I was about to when I overheard what you were speaking of."

She crossed the room, her gaze fixed on the redhead still kneeling by the tub. "Lady Helen de Bethencourt. I thought you looked familiar when I first laid eyes on you, but the outfit confused me," she admitted.

Seonaid glanced toward Helen, who paused before speaking. "Lady Wildwood. I recognized you as well. You were a friend of my mother's."

"Aye." Iliana's mother smiled slightly, then glanced to Seonaid and Aeldra and explained, "Helen's mother and I were friends of Queen Anne's. We were often at court together."

"Ah," Seonaid murmured, then smiled at Helen with amusement. "Ye didna mention ye had friends in such high places."

"I do not," Helen said with a blush. "My mother was a friend of the queen's, but both of them are gone now."

"You still have influential friends, my dear," Lady Wildwood said gently. "The king is as fond of you as the queen was." She sighed, her gaze slipping to Seonaid. "You look very well, my dear. I am glad to see you survived the night."

"Thanks," Seonaid murmured.

"Now . . ." Margaret perched on one of the chairs by the cold fireplace and eyed them all expectantly. "Why do you not tell me how Helen came to be traveling with you disguised as a nun? Then we can decide how best to present this to the men."

Seonaid smiled wryly at the woman. Despite her phrasing, it was not a request but an order. Lady Wildwood was a woman used to getting her way, and this time was no exception. Iliana's mother sat patiently listening as the three women took turns explaining what had occurred since their meeting in the chapel at St. Simmian's. They left nothing out, revealing every step of the journey. By the time they fell silent, Seonaid had finished with her bath and donned her clothes. The three women then waited for Lady Wildwood to comment.

She said nothing for the longest time, but sat, her

face pensive. She was obviously deep in thought. Then she nodded to herself and stood. "Come along, then."

"What're ye goin' to do?" Seonaid asked as she followed her to the door.

"I shall take care of everything," she said simply as she opened the door, then paused to smile at Seonaid and reached up to brush a strand of black hair off her face in a gesture that smacked of affection. "You have had it very hard not having a mother, haven't you? Both of you have."

She had included Aeldra in her glance, and Seonaid's cousin opened her mouth as if to protest, then closed it again. Seonaid supposed Giorsal had not been much of a maternal replacement with her bitterness and anger. Of course, she didn't know why she herself had not protested that life had been hard without a mother. She was happy with the way things had turned out, was she not? She had not missed anything. In fact, Seonaid had more freedom than most women were given. And if she had watched other girls receiving hugs and affection from their mothers, and seen the way they were coddled and cared for and felt a pang, surely it was not envy.

"I shall take care of this for you," Lady Wildwood said. "Trust me."

She turned and started out the door, and Seonaid stared after her for a minute before turning to Aeldra and Helen. The three women peered at each other uncertainly for a moment, then moved as one to follow Iliana's mother below.

Chapter Thirteen

" 'Tis settled then," Angus Dunbar decided. "We shall head out the morn after next. Ye and Seonaid will ride with us into England, then split off and head to Sherwell."

Blake shifted with displeasure on the trestle table bench but did not refute his father-in-law's words. He really had no desire to travel with Lord Rolfe, the bishop, Lady Wildwood, Angus, Sister Helen, and the king's men, as well as the small army Angus was taking with them to travel into England but could think of no excuse to avoid it. He wished he could. Sleeping out in the open with all those people about was bound to dampen his love life.

He smiled to himself wryly at the thought. Much to his surprise, he was rather enjoying married life so far. Despite their ill-favored beginnings, he and Seonaid appeared to be getting along now. It still shocked him that she had not tried to battle her way out of the keep when it was announced that the wedding would take place right away, and his worry that she would had apparently been obvious, for Lady Wildwood had approached him to assure him all would be well. He didn't know what the woman had said to his betrothed, but whatever it was had worked, and Seonaid had stood silent and complacent for the ceremony. And as for last night . . .

Blake had discovered that, while Seonaid could be hard and cold as steel, there was a surprisingly soft and vulnerable side to her as well. In truth, she was turning out to be a fascinating mass of contradictions. She was also as uninhibited a woman in bed as he had ever met, which gave him hope that marriage might not be as bad as he'd feared. In fact, he was enjoying it so far.

Unfortunately, as uninhibited as his new bride was, he suspected even she would balk at engaging in anything with her father snoring but feet away.

"And after ye and Seonaid split off and head fer Sherwell, the rest o' us will continue south toward court," Angus finished with satisfaction.

"Until you need to split off from the group to see Sister Helen home," the bishop pointed out, and Blake wasn't surprised to see his father-in-law grimace at the reminder. He was fairly sure the man had no desire to take over Seonaid's promise to see Sister Helen home but was using the excuse as a way to remain close to Lady Wildwood for as long as he could. The man's feelings for the woman were plain for all to see.

"Aye," Angus said, disgruntled. "Wherever that may be. I wish Margaret—er, Lady Margaret," he corrected himself. "I wish she'd hurry about fetchin' the girl back here so we could find out where exactly that is. I'm thinkin'—" He paused suddenly and beamed a smile over Blake's shoulder. "Ah, there ye are. Thank ye fer fetchin' her, Lady Margaret. Now, Sister Helen, we're plannin' the journey into England and need to know where yer home is."

Blake glanced over his shoulder to see that Lady Wildwood had indeed brought the girl down. Seonaid and Aeldra also accompanied her. Blake's gaze slid over his wife, a small smile tugging at his lips as he examined her in her braies. She had a different pair on today. They were faded and worn and obviously several years old, the cloth fitting more snugly than the pair he was used to seeing her in. They outlined and defined every curve from her waist down and put Blake's mind to thoughts of dragging her back abovestairs.

It was going to be a long journey until they reached England and could separate from the rest of the group.

"Actually, my lords," Lady Wildwood said, drawing Blake's attention, "Lady Helen is from Bethencourt, and I fear getting her safely home may be trickier than you had thought."

Blake was slow to understand her words. His gaze slid to the nun in confusion, and it was only then, on his second glance, that he realized she looked different. She was no longer wearing her head covering. Instead, she had pulled her long red hair back into a knot similar to the one Seonaid wore.

"*Lady* Helen?" Lord Rolfe asked slowly.

"Lady Helen Cameron, nee Bethencourt," Lady Wildwood said, then settled on the bench beside Angus, and explained to the men how the women had pulled the wool over their eyes.

Blake felt satisfaction claim him when Seonaid settled herself on the bench at his side. He listened with interest to the tale Lady Wildwood was revealing. His gaze kept sliding to Lord Rolfe as the woman talked, and he grinned inwardly at the emotions crossing the other man's face. Irritation not that she wasn't a nun, but that he had been led to believe she was. Outrage over Cameron's intentions, and determination to see her safe. Blake suspected the other man was about as good as wedded to the little redhead. He had noticed the man's protective behavior to her throughout the journey here, and the way his eyes had always seemed to trail the little nun. He'd suspected the man was attracted to her and had pitied him, but now things had changed, and he wasn't surprised when Lord Rolfe said, "Then I shall be the one to see her safely home. The king is a friend of Bethencourt; he would wish it so."

"Now jest a minute there, lad," Angus interrupted grimly, obviously not wishing to lose his excuse to remain close to Lady Wildwood. "'Tis me daughter who made the first promise to see her safe, and I shall take on that burden, as I said. 'Tis me responsibility."

"Gentlemen," Lady Wildwood interrupted quietly, bringing silence to the party. "I think you are focusing on who Helen is and forgetting something more important."

"What's that?" Angus asked with a frown.

"As Seonaid pointed out to me abovestairs, there is the Cameron to worry about. He will hardly wish Helen to return safely to her father and tell all. His head will be on the block should she manage it. He will be desperate to stop her. The men who attacked in the woods would have trailed you all here, and by now there may be a small army of Camerons on its way, if they are not here already." She allowed that to sink in. "And then there is her father to consider as well. If Helen's maid *did* manage to ride all the way to southern England on her own, and he has heard what has happened, he too may be under threat."

"You are right," Rolfe said with concern. "I shall send a messenger to him at once. If the maid hasn't reached him, the message will inform him of what has happened. Either way, I shall instruct him to stay within Bethencourt and to keep any Camerons out until we reach him."

"*We?*" Angus asked grimly.

"Helen and I. As things stand, a large party would simply draw Cameron's attention. 'Twould be better if Helen and I were to sneak out on our own, perhaps with her disguised as a boy. Then we can head for Bethencourt."

Angus was frowning over this. Obviously his plan to use Helen as an excuse to remain close to Lady Wildwood would not work if Rolfe rode alone with Helen. On the other hand, taking the girl with the larger party would put Lady Wildwood and the bishop in jeopardy. They could take most of the men and brave an attack by the entire Cameron clan, as Duncan had done when he had ridden out after Seonaid, but after the attack and siege of Dunbar, he was reluctant to leave his home vulnerable again.

The sudden bang of the great hall doors slamming open interrupted the silence as everyone turned to see who had entered. Recognizing the messenger hurrying across the hall, Rolfe stood to meet the man and accepted the scroll he carried. He broke the seal on the scroll, unrolled it, and read the missive with a frown.

"The messenger I sent to the king with the news of Lady Wildwood's presence here 'ere we left for St. Simmian's arrived safely. He is ordering me to escort Lady Wildwood to court posthaste to discuss 'matters of great import.'"

"What *matters of great import?*" Angus asked suspiciously.

"And why the rush?" Iliana's mother asked.

"No doubt he knows Greenweld is dead by now too," Rolfe muttered. "News moves quickly."

"So?" Lady Wildwood asked warily.

"On Greenweld's death, you became mistress of both Wildwood and the neighboring Greenweld, my lady," Bishop Wykeham pointed out quietly.

"Aye." Rolfe scrubbed the hair back from his face with irritation. "And with Iliana as your only heir—and she married and installed here at Dunbar—he no doubt wishes to see you remarried. Preferably to someone with more than one heir to step in and take over each estate."

Margaret turned a horrified glance toward Angus. He stared back at her, stunned for a moment, then rose to his feet roaring, "The hell he will! *I am marrying Margaret.* In fact, I am doing so right now. Bishop, get yer Bible."

"Now just a minute," Lord Rolfe protested. "You cannot marry Lady Wildwood against her will."

"It is not against my will," Margaret said quietly. "I wish to marry Angus."

"But, I cannot let you marry him. The king—"

"Has not sent orders against it," Blake interrupted with amusement. He rather thought the pair would make a fine couple. Blake had noted a distinct difference in his father-in-law since returning with Seonaid and suspected it had to do with Lady Wildwood's influence. The two were obviously in love, and the woman was softening him. The Dunbar had even taken Blake aside to tell him that he intended to rectify the old rift between himself and the Earl of Sherwell.

"Aye, but—" Lord Rolfe began, and Blake interrupted again.

"He has not sent orders regarding anything except that Lady Wildwood travel to court. Does he have plans to marry her off, he should have said so. I see no reason they should not marry. Then the laird can take some of his own men, along with the king's men, and see his *wife* and the bishop to court, leaving you free to slip away with Helen and hightail it to Bethencourt," Blake pointed out slyly. "Then you two can collect her father and make your way to court to meet up with them."

"In fact," he added, "their leavetaking might be a good diversion for you. They can parade out of Dunbar slowly so that the Camerons, if they are hiding out there, will watch and eventually can see that Helen is not among them. Meanwhile you can take Helen and slip out through the secret passage in Seonaid's room."

"That may work," Duncan murmured, speaking up for the first time. "Lady Helen could leave disguised as a boy as ye suggested, and I could arrange horses to be waiting fer ye at the end o' the passage. Ye could slip away undetected."

Seonaid watched the men pack Lady Wildwood's trunks onto the back of the cart and shook her head in wonderment. She had no clue what all the woman had in them, but Lady Wildwood had insisted they were all items she would need at court. Lady Dunbar, she mentally corrected herself. Her father had married the woman the night before. She was now Seonaid's stepmother.

" 'Tis glad I am we're no travelin' with them," Aeldra murmured suddenly, and Seonaid nodded in agreement. She did not mind long journeys as a rule but was used to traveling with a small army of men, and without a wagon of trunks to slow her down. The cart of goods Lady Margaret was taking with her would force the party to travel at a snail's pace. Not that Seonaid supposed her father was in any rush to reach the English court. He would no doubt have to face the English king's wrath over their marriage, and there was nothing to rush back for. Duncan already all but ran Dunbar in deed, if not in name, and could tend it well enough in their father's absence.

"Seonaid."

She turned to find her father approaching and offered a smile.

"Lady Margaret and I will stop at Sherwell on our way back from court to see how yer gettin' along, and to tell ye how things went with the English king," he announced, his gaze shifting to the men preparing the wagon and horses for their journey. Then he glanced back. "I still think 'twould be better were ye travelin' with us at least til we reached England, but that stubborn husband o' yers refuses, so . . ." He shrugged, then turned away to yell at one of the men to make sure everything was tied down.

Seonaid smiled to herself while his back was turned. She and Blake were not traveling alone—Aeldra and Little George were to accompany them—but they would not be joining her father's party after all. The change had come about during her father's wedding to Lady Wildwood. Iliana and Duncan had been standing near Seonaid and Blake during the ceremony, and the smaller woman had commented that her father-in-law and soon-to-be stepfather looked very handsome in his newly cleaned and mended gold doublet and braies. The doublet had sported a hole from the arrow her father had taken until Iliana had taken care of it.

Blake had grimaced at the woman's comment and muttered that the man *should* look good in his doublet and braies; the outfit had cost him a small fortune. He had then turned to tell her what she already knew, that he had traded her father the outfit for his plaid, explaining that he had wished to wear the Dunbar "colors" while traipsing across Scotland to avoid as much trouble as he could while he hared after her.

Iliana had appeared confused by this news, Duncan had burst out laughing, and Seonaid had bit her lip briefly, then taken pity on her husband and explained that he had been misinformed: Scots did not have clan tartans. When he had argued the point, assuring her that everyone in England knew clans had specific tartans, she had sighed and informed him that everyone in England was wrong.

It had taken some talking to convince him, and then he'd been irritated to learn that he had been so foolish as to give up his new doublet and braies to her father under false pretenses. Seonaid couldn't really blame him—her father's plaid was rather malodorous, and she was always relieved when he took it off. Blake was rather relieved to be free of the thing himself. And before he could become too upset over the matter, Iliana had soothed him by offering to sew him a new doublet and braies for their trip home.

Blake had accepted the offer gratefully, claiming he would rather wear English clothing on English soil. But even with the small army of servants she had asked to set to the task with her, the outfit would take Iliana two days to create. This news hadn't seemed to bother Blake. In fact, she suspected it rather pleased him to announce that they would just have to wait the extra day and give up the chance to travel with the others.

Seonaid was not surprised that he would rather not journey with her father and the others to England. The two men got along much better now that the marriage was accomplished. Her father even showed some signs of liking her husband, but she doubted very much that

Blake wanted to be hampered by the presence of so
many people so soon after their marriage, at least not if
he wished to continue to bed her as they had since the
wedding. That thought was enough to ensure that she
had no desire to travel with the others. She couldn't
stand the idea of laying next to Blake night after night,
not being able to touch him for fear of waking everyone
with the moans and sighs she seemed unable to contain.

"Where is yer husb—Oh, there ye are," her father
said, and Seonaid glanced over her shoulder to see
Blake approaching. When he paused, he stood so close
that his chest brushed her back, and Seonaid was
tempted to lean into him but controlled herself. She
had not yet gotten used to the difference in their rela-
tionship. She had gone from battling and fleeing the
man to reluctantly giving up her injured pride at Lady
Margaret's urging to the intimacy that took place in
their bedroom of a night. She still had no idea how to
behave around him once they were out of the bedroom.

"Be careful on yer way."

Her father's solemn words drew Seonaid's attention
to the two men as he cautioned Blake.

"Remember," he continued, "Greenweld's men are
out there."

"Surely they would not still be after me?" Blake said
with surprise. "Greenweld is dead."

"Aye." Angus nodded. "But who is it ye think may
have told 'em that?"

Blake stared at him blankly, and the man nodded.

"No one. They're no likely to risk talkin' to Scots lest
they bring an attack on themselves fer bein' where they

doona belong. And they're no likely to come back to report to Greenweld that they have failed in the task. From all I've heard o' that bastard, he'd have skinned 'em alive for the failure. Nay, they'd no dare to return without seein' the job done."

"Aye, but if they have trailed us back here to Dunbar, then they shall surely see that Greenweld is not here and realize—"

"I doubt they've managed to get this far yet. They were several days behind ye and would have had to travel to the abbey jest as ye did. Had Seonaid no led ye sech a merry chase and ye'd headed straight back, ye'd have most like run into them on the way here. As it is, they are probably following the trail ye left in yer travels and are still several days behind ye."

Blake fell silent as he considered this information, and Seonaid suspected he was reconsidering traveling with her father and the others now that he realized they might be put in jeopardy due to his decision. It was too late for that, however.

"So watch yerselves when ye head out and keep an eye open," Angus finished.

Blake nodded solemnly.

Satisfied, Angus turned to Seonaid and chucked her under the chin. "Keep an eye on this one. His father will no doubt blame me if he gets hissel' killed."

Seonaid had trouble hiding her grin of amusement, but—aware of Blake's irritation over her father's words—she did her best. "Aye, Father."

"Guid. Now, find Lady Helen and get her up to yer room; we're almost ready to go. Let us know once they're on their way. We'll give them a few minutes to make their way through the passage, then set out. It should offer them enough distraction to ride out of the area undetected."

Nodding, Seonaid turned to move back into the keep, aware that Blake and Aeldra were following. They found Helen in the great hall, thanking Iliana for her hospitality during her stay there, and Seonaid smiled to herself at the sight of the former redhead. Helen had been transformed from a red-haired woman to a dark-haired young English lad. They had bound her breasts, dressed her in a set of Lord Rolfe's clothes that the women had taken in and resewn, then tied her hair back behind her head and darkened it with soot from the fireplace so that she now looked like a small, dark-haired lad. The transformation was remarkable.

Helen finished her thank-you as Seonaid, Blake, and Aeldra reached her. She turned to eye them and asked, "Is it time?"

"Aye."

Nodding, Helen fell into step with Seonaid as she turned toward the stairs to the upper level.

Lord Rolfe, Duncan, and Little George were already in the room when they arrived. The three men were working diligently at removing the boulders from in front of the entrance to the passage. They already had most of them out of the way.

"Why do ye no remove them altogether and seal up the passage?" Seonaid asked as Blake moved to help finish the task.

"Nay. I've no decided if the passage stays or goes,"

Duncan explained. "There may be a way to keep it from bein' opened from the other side. And I'd rather as few people as possible ken about it until I decide." He paused to glance around at those in the room. "I'm trustin' ye can keep yer mouths shut?"

"Aye," they all answered.

"Greenweld is dead," Rolfe pointed out as he picked up another boulder. "Surely the secret died with him and Allistair? Well, other than those of us here."

"Giorsal kens," Aeldra pointed out quietly, and the room fell silent again, no one wanting to comment and add to her upset.

"There," Duncan said with satisfaction, pausing to wipe his brow as the last boulder was removed.

Seonaid hesitated, then stepped forward and pressed one of the stones in the solid-looking wall, stepping back as the wall swung away, revealing a dark walkway.

"Ye'll need a torch," Aeldra murmured, and slipped out of the room, returning moments later with one of the lit torches from the hall. She handed it to Lord Rolfe, then moved to stand by Seonaid as Helen approached. The woman paused before them and Seonaid felt dread claim her. She didn't think she could bear it if the Englishwoman revealed her emotions. She was already feeling pangs of anxiety, fear, and sadness at her leave-taking.

"Thank you," Helen whispered; then she flung herself at Seonaid's chest, hugging her tightly, before turning to Aeldra and doing the same. With that, she turned and moved to follow Lord Rolfe into the passage.

"Remember, jest follow the passage. It exits into a

clearin'. James'll be awaitin' there with horses fer ye. Good luck!" Duncan called after them, then closed the passage again and immediately moved to begin returning the boulders to their earlier position.

"What if they come back fer some reason?" Seonaid said with a frown, thinking they were moving rather swiftly at locking the pair out.

"They willna return," Duncan said simply as Blake and Little George joined him in the work.

After a brief hesitation, Seonaid leant a hand as well, but she kept an ear open for any sound from the wall lest they did return. The job was done quickly with all of them working. Duncan lay the last stone in place, straightened, and put one hand at his back as he arched and stretched in an effort to work out any tension the exercise of bending and lifting, carrying and bending to set boulders back down had caused. Then he turned for the door announcing, "I'll tell Father they've gone."

Seonaid hardly paid attention. She was standing before the pile of boulders, her ears straining in case Rolfe and Helen returned.

"They shall be fine." Blake gave her back a gentle rub, then suggested, "Why do we not go practice in the bailey?"

Seonaid hesitated, then forced herself to turn away from the blocked passage. "Aye."

If nothing else, the activity would distract her, she hoped as she followed her husband out of their room. Aeldra and Little George trailed them to the practice fields and began to spar together even as Seonaid and Blake did. They worked in silence, Seonaid trying to be more aggressive and not let Blake wear her down. But she soon realized that Blake wasn't being aggressive in return. He had obviously suggested this purely to help distract her from her worry about Helen, and while she found it a thoughtful gesture, it made her think about it more. She was grateful when Blake called a halt and they went into the great hall for a drink.

Blake and Little George talked quietly about this and that as the four of them sat at the trestle table, but were she to be asked what they'd said, she wouldn't have been able to say. She wasn't really paying attention. Judging by Aeldra's silence, her cousin was just as distracted and worried as she.

When Blake suddenly set down his drink and caught her hand, Seonaid glanced at him with surprise.

"Come," was all he said; then he tugged her to her feet and led her abovestairs to their room.

The moment he closed the door behind them, Seonaid thought he must have brought her up for more loving. However, while Blake led her to the bed, he merely dropped onto it and tugged her over himself to lie next to him.

"Rest."

Seonaid stared at him. She was becoming more used to his assertive nature and the commanding way he took control of things, but it still startled her somewhat. While there were times she appreciated it and even secretly enjoyed it, she was not used to taking orders and at times found the way he simply assumed control a bit alarming. This was one of those times when she was slightly nonplussed. In truth, she *was* weary; they'd had little sleep the last two nights and it was starting to catch up to her, aided on its way by her anxiety and their physical activity. Still, she almost felt she should rebel for pride's sake alone.

Her gaze slid over him and she frowned at the sight of his booted feet crossed at the ankles on the bed. "Are ye no goin' to remove yer boots?"

"I am too tired," Blake said, then popped one eye open, a smile tugging at the corner of his mouth as he said, "You are wearing me out with your demands, wife."

"Wearin' ye out?" she exclaimed with disbelief. He was just as demanding as she.

"Aye. Wearing me out," was all Blake said.

Scowling, Seonaid sat where she was for a minute, then stood and moved around the bed to his side. Pausing there, she set to work on removing his boots.

"What are you doing?" Blake half sat up in his surprise.

"As yer so *exhausted*," she said dryly. "I'm helpin' ye with yer boots. Iliana would have fits did ye ruin her fine linens with 'em."

Blake hesitated, then flopped back on the bed, leaving her to it. She dragged the first boot off and unintentionally ran her hand over the bottom of his foot, which made him jerk upright on the bed and tug his foot from her hand. When Seonaid glanced up at his face with surprise, he relaxed back on the bed, but she noticed he kept his knee bent and his foot pressed flat to the bed surface, a good distance from her hands.

Considering this, she set to work on his other boot. This time when she dragged the boot off, she deliberately ran her hand over the bottom of his foot, and again Blake jerked and dragged his foot out of her grasp.

"Yer ticklish," Seonaid said with disbelief.

"Nay," Blake denied, but there was such panic in his eyes as he denied it, she knew he was lying.

"Nay?" she asked, an evil grin claiming her lips.

"Seonaid," he growled in warning, but she was already climbing onto the bed to reach his feet. He tried to swivel them out of her grasp, but Seonaid was quicker and managed to catch one. She immediately set to tickling the bottom of the foot she held, amazed when Blake began to laugh and struggle wildly. Seonaid held on like the claw of a lobster, locking her arm around his lower leg and holding him by the ankle with that hand, leaving her other one free to torment him. It was like trying to break a wild horse; he was bucking and jerking and thrashing about wildly. When that did not work, Blake had the presence of mind to sit up and grab her arms from behind. It turned into a wrestling match that had them laughing and rolling on the bed until Blake managed to trap her beneath him on her back, her arms over her head.

Breathless and panting, they grinned at each other; then Blake lowered his mouth to claim hers and they began a wrestling of a different nature.

"Sherwell!"

Seonaid blinked her eyes open and sat upright on the bed as the chamber door slammed open. She gaped at her brother with confusion. It was daylight, probably nearly noon, she realized. She and Blake had fallen asleep after their lovemaking and slept the morning away. And something had obviously happened while they slept, something that had her brother looking like thunder as he dragged Little George into the room, shoving the huge man about as if he were a pup.

"Duncan!" Aeldra rushed into the room on their heels. The petite blonde was flushed and disheveled; she was also angrier than Seonaid had seen her in a long time. "Let George go! Ye have no right!"

"Close yer mouth, Aeldra," Duncan snapped, shaking away the hand she had placed on his arm. "I have every right. Yer me cousin and me responsibility. Doubly so now that Allistair is gone." Turning back to the bed, he snapped, "God damn me, Sherwell. Wake up!"

"I am awake," Blake muttered, sitting up to survey Duncan with a frown. "What is going on?"

"I'll tell ye what's goin' on, I caught *yer* man on *me* cousin," Duncan announced grimly, releasing the man, but not before he'd shoved him toward the bed.

Blake looked nonplussed by this announcement, then glanced from Aeldra to Little George to Seonaid. Aeldra blushed and avoided his gaze and Little George stared at the floor looking rather chagrined. Seonaid was the only one to meet his eyes, but she did so with an expression as bewildered as his own.

"Duncan—" she began tentatively, only to have him turn his wrath on her.

"Not a word, Seonaid. This is men's business." His eyes turned back to Blake. "Get dressed and come below. We've some sorting to do."

Turning on his heel, Duncan stomped from the room, pulling the door closed with a slam.

The foursome left in the chamber were silent for a moment; then Blake tossed the furs aside and grabbed up his discarded tunic as he said, "You had best tell me what happened."

"Duncan caught us indulgin' in some *houghmagandie,*" Aeldra said defiantly. "And now he's up in arms."

"*Houghma—*" Blake had just bent to pleat his plaid, but paused at the blonde's words to glance to Seonaid, who was gaping at her cousin. "Seonaid?"

She closed her mouth and glanced at her husband, then cleared her throat and said, "They were . . . er . . . doing what we were doing," she finished helplessly.

"Sleeping?" he asked dryly.

"Nay, the part before the sleepin'," Seonaid said.

"Ah." Blake turned his attention back to his plaid.

"I am marrying her," Little George said grimly as Blake finished the pleating and donned the plaid.

"Is that what you want?" he asked as he stood, fully dressed.

Little George nodded abruptly.

"Well, we had best go tell Duncan and smooth things over then," Blake said and led his first out of the room.

Seonaid stared after them in amazement. Neither man had even bothered to ask Aeldra if she agreed to the marriage. And it apparently hadn't occurred to them to include the women in the discussion about to take place.

Muttering with exasperation, she tossed the linens aside and slid from the bed to begin dressing. "So?"

Aeldra glanced at her with a start. "So? What?"

"How was it?" Seonaid asked, amusement pulling at her lips. It was the right question, Aeldra's tension gave way to a grin.

"It was wonderful," she said enthusiastically, then added less cheerfully, "until Duncan caught us."

Seonaid nodded. "And do ye want to marry Little George?"

Aeldra smiled. "He'd already asked me 'ere we—" She paused and shrugged. "And I had already said aye."

"Good," Seonaid said with a sigh. At least she wasn't going to have to fight to keep her cousin from a marriage she didn't want. Finished pulling on her tunic and braies, she tugged her hair back, then strode to the door. "Let us go down and be sure Duncan doesna ruin things then."

A small laugh slipping from her lips, Aeldra followed her out of the room.

Chapter Fourteen

"Watch fer Greenweld's men," Duncan said gruffly.

Seonaid's gaze met Aeldra's and the two women exchanged amused glances as they mounted their horses. Duncan had been spouting warnings and sounding like an old hen all morning.

"We will," Blake assured him, taking his reins from Little George and mounting as well. "Your father reminded us to do so 'ere leaving."

"Hmm." Duncan frowned, his gaze sliding over the four of them with displeasure. While he had agreed to the wedding between Little George and Aeldra and had even sent a man out to fetch a priest back to perform it, he was still angry with the couple. Seonaid suspected it was mostly for show. He became more and more like their father every day.

"Mayhap I should send some men with ye, jest in case," Duncan suggested, but Blake shook his head.

"I can handle a few of Greenweld's men. We shall be fine. I shall keep Seonaid safe."

Seonaid glanced at him with surprise at the comment. She doubted very much that her brother was concerned with her well-being. She could take care of herself. Still, it was sweet that he wanted to take care of her. Her glance slid to her brother and she said, "And I shall keep him safe as well."

Duncan grinned at her words, and at the way Blake rolled his eyes at the claim. "Aye, well, jest keep yer eyes open. And travel as quick as ye can for the first little while. And send a messenger when ye arrive safely. And send one if ye've any trouble too. And look out fer the Camerons as well. Aeldra's of a similar height and shape to Helen, and they may mistake her for the woman and attack in error. They're no too bright. And—"

"Good-bye, Duncan," Seonaid said with amusement, turning her horse toward the gate.

Leaving him standing on the keep steps, Seonaid followed Blake when he turned his mount and started across the bailey.

They rode slowly over the moat and continued slowly as they crossed the clearing. Seonaid knew that Blake was trying to ensure that if the Camerons were nearby, they were given a good look at the small party and would see that Lady Helen was not among them.

The moment they reached the trees, however, he took the lead and urged his horse into a gallop. Seonaid immediately followed suit and fell in behind him. A glance over her shoulder showed that Aeldra had taken position behind her, while her husband, Little George, took up the rear.

Seonaid smiled to herself at the thought. It seemed odd to think of Aeldra being married to the great man who was Blake's first. He was such a giant, and Aeldra so petite, they made an odd pair when they walked about. Seonaid would not even contemplate the bedding part of their marriage. The very idea was almost too much to consider.

The first day of travel passed uneventfully. They were all alert, attending to the fact that even if the Camerons did not mistake Aeldra for Helen, they might try to capture them to try and learn where Helen was. The Camerons might even use one of them to trade for the Englishwoman. But nothing of the sort occurred, and neither were they accosted by the men Greenweld had sent after Blake. If either group were out there, they were keeping their distance for now.

Still, it might not have hurt that Blake set a grueling pace the first day, one that would put as much distance as possible between them and Dunbar and the trouble that might lurk in the area. It was late night when they stopped to make camp.

The spot Blake chose was nowhere near water this night, but it mattered little to Seonaid. Her concerns about traveling in the company of others proved not to be a concern in the end. She was far too weary by the time they had finished making camp, eating, and visiting the bushes to tend personal needs to even consider indulging in *houghmagandie*. She would not even have had the energy to bother with bathing had they camped near water. Seonaid barely had the strength to curl up next to her husband to sleep, and was only vaguely aware of the feel of his chest against her back and his arm around her as she drifted off to sleep on the cold hard ground.

They took it much easier the second day. Now that they were a distance away from Dunbar, Blake set a more leisurely pace, and it was only late afternoon when he decided they should stop. Seonaid suspected it was the beauty of the spot they chanced upon that made the decision. It was another clearing on the edge of a river, but this one offered a picturesque waterfall, which was a lovely diversion.

Seonaid and Blake set up camp this night while Little George and Aeldra visited the river to wash away the day's dust. They were finished and waiting by the time the other couple returned. Telling them they wouldn't be too long, Blake caught Seonaid's hand and tugged her to her feet, then led her into the woods.

Eager to wash away two days' worth of dust, Seonaid reclaimed her hand the moment they were safely within the trees and began to strip as they made their way along the path to the riverside. She finished undoing her braies as she stepped into the small clearing at the water's edge. Letting them drop, she stepped out of them, then bent to scoop them up and set all her clothes in a pile near a large boulder, which she used to lean against as she quickly removed her boots. Dropping those, she left Blake still working on his clothes and waded into the water. It was chilly at first, but Seonaid dove under and swam a distance out in an effort to allow her body to adjust.

She came up near the waterfall and stood to walk under it, noting that the water reached only to her waist here. Not that it really mattered with all the water pounding down on her from overhead. Smiling, she closed her eyes and tipped her head back under the spray, then tipped her head forward and simply stood like that for several minutes, enjoying the hammering of the water against the tense muscles of her shoulders and back.

Something brushing against her hip startled her, and Seonaid blinked her eyes open, relaxing when she spied the hand Blake was slipping around her back as he joined her under the cascade. He didn't say a word, but merely pulled her firmly against him with one hand, using the other to catch her at the base of her skull and pull her forward for a kiss. Though it had only been two days since he'd touched her, it felt like forever, and she went into his embrace willingly, sighing into his mouth when he claimed hers.

At first he just kissed her, exploring her mouth as if it were the first time; then his hands began to move over her body, following the trail the water was taking and smoothing across her shoulder then down her chest to capture one breast. Seonaid clutched at his neck when he suddenly broke the kiss and tipped her back to claim her nipple between his lips. She sighed and moaned and arched into his hardness, rubbing against him eagerly as he suckled.

When he started to back her up, Seonaid wasn't prepared and stumbled, nearly losing her footing, but Blake held her up and continued moving her backward until they were out of the waterfall and pressed up against the rock it curtained. It was like being cocooned in a storm, the water thundering around them, leaving a fine mist to make everything look soft and almost ethereal.

Seonaid ran her hands over her husband's chest, enjoying his strength and hardness, then let one hand drop to catch his erection as he bent to kiss her again. His own hands were not dormant, but moved over her body, caressing and teasing before seeking the heat at the center of her. Seonaid moaned into his mouth, her legs spreading farther apart to encourage him as he caressed her.

When he caught one leg under her thigh and lifted it to his hip, Seonaid was more than ready and lifted the other of her own accord to wrap around him. She shuddered, pressing back into the rock as he entered her, her eyes closing and a moan sliding from her lips. Seonaid loved it when he was inside her. His kisses and caresses were exciting, and when he put his mouth to her womanhood he could drive her over the moon, but she liked it best when he was inside, their bodies merged and rubbing together with every stroke.

Seonaid clutched the muscles of his shoulders and nipped at his ear as he made love to her. Blake immediately turned his head to kiss her and continued to do so until the very end, when he tore his mouth away and they both cried out as they found relief.

* * *

"Little George says we are in England now."

"Aye. Blake said we crossed the border shortly after noon," Seonaid agreed. It was the third evening of their journey, and again they had traveled at a more relaxed pace. Blake didn't seem to be in any hurry to reach Sherwell, and Seonaid didn't mind one wit. She was enjoying the trip.

Now they had stopped for the night along a river, and the men had offered to make camp while the women tended to their personal needs. Seonaid had been rather disappointed at the arrangement—she would have liked a chance to be alone with Blake again as they had been the night before. She'd not soon forget their sojourn at the waterfall.

Both women were quick about their ablutions and eager to return to the men. They reached the clearing just as Blake and Little George stepped out of the trees from another direction. Despite how quick Seonaid thought she and Aeldra had been, the men had apparently managed to tend to the horses and gather wood for a fire, then find a spot farther along the curving river and clean up in the same amount of time.

"I was thinking a rabbit might taste good over the fire," Little George announced as Seonaid and Aeldra joined the men.

"Sounds good," Blake said, setting his boots by a fallen log and bending to start work at lighting the fire he and Little George had built.

Little George grunted, then glanced at Aeldra. "Care to help me hunt one up?"

Grinning, Aeldra caught his hand in hers and rambled into the woods with her husband. Seonaid watched them go, once again marveling at the odd couple they made, then settled to sit on the log Blake had set his boots next to. Her gaze wandered from the boots to her husband as he worked, and she smiled slightly. Obviously he had not put them back on after his dip in the river. Her gaze dropped to his defenseless feet and her expression turned from a smile to an evil grin. She did so love tickling her husband. It always amazed her that the man who was proving to be so strong and commanding as a mate could become an almost paralyzed mass of helpless flesh when she tackled his feet. Did his enemies know this weakness, the man would have been dead long ago.

"There." Blake finished fiddling with the fire, brushed his hands together, and moved to sit beside Seonaid.

They sat in a companionable silence for a bit; then Blake mentioned that they were not that far from his friend Amaury's home, Eberhardt. Seonaid had heard the name before. In the week since their marriage, Blake had spoken of the man often during their quiet times. It was obvious he was a good friend to her husband, almost as close as a brother.

Of the many amusing tales Blake had told her about Amaury, her favorite was the one of how Amaury had been ordered by his king to marry Emmalene Eberhardt. Thinking her an ugly old hag whose husband had killed himself rather than bed her, Amaury had been less than eager to make the match. The man had dragged his feet about arriving to marry her only to find she was a beautiful, capable little blonde who could shoot an arrow better than most of the soldiers who fought under them.

Blake had spoken with admiration and affection about both his friend and the man's new wife, and Seonaid always enjoyed the tales he shared about them. She found that if she listened carefully, she learned as much about her husband as about the people he spoke of, so she encouraged his talking. As she did now.

But as fascinating as his story was, she again found her gaze sliding to Blake's bare feet, and eventually she found herself contemplating how best to tickle them without giving away her intention. She couldn't reach them from where she was sitting, but if she shifted to grab at them, her husband would be smart enough to suspect what she was about and whip them out of the way. She had gone after his feet every night at Dunbar after discovering his weakness. In fact, it had become something of a game. Seonaid would go after his feet and the tickling would turn into a wrestling match that ended with their making love. It was a game she rather enjoyed, and one she was sure Blake enjoyed as well, or he wouldn't leave his bare feet out to tempt her so often.

Blake had fallen silent for several moments when she made her move. In the end, she had no great plan to trick him; she merely counted on the advantage of surprise and launched herself toward his feet. As she had feared, Blake suspected at once what she was about and tried to shift them out of her reach, but she was quick and threw herself across his lower legs, pinning them to the ground with her weight as she reached for them.

She had Blake laughing and thrashing within seconds, but as usual that was all he allowed before grabbing her around the waist and rolling with her, having the presence of mind to move them both away from the fire. Seonaid put up a good fight, but there was no getting around the fact that Blake was stronger and soon had her pinned to the ground, both of them breathless and laughing.

"You, my dear wife, are an evil witch," he informed her, his body flat on hers and his hands holding her wrists pinned above her head.

Seonaid feigned outrage at the insult but found it more amusing than anything else. He always called her horrid names after a tickling session and she took it as her due.

"I think you need a good seeing to," he added, and Seonaid felt a slow smile stretch her lips. She did so love his *seeing tos,* she thought. Then movement drew her attention and she glanced to the side, stiffening at the sight of several men coming out of the woods toward them.

Aware of the sudden tension in her body, Blake followed her gaze and stilled. In the next moment both of them were moving. They were on their feet with swords in hand in a heartbeat, and instinctively putting their

backs to each other as they faced the men now surrounding them.

English, a dozen in all, Seonaid noted, and suspected
they must be Greenweld's men. If so, telling them that
Greenweld was dead might be enough to stop whatever
they had planned. Unfortunately, Seonaid never got the
chance to test this theory. Even as she was thinking it,
two of the men moved toward her, swords swinging. The
clang of metal at her back told her that Blake too had
been engaged; then she was kept too busy fending off
the attackers on her side to concern herself with anything else.

Seonaid tried to remember Blake's advice and not
simply fend off the blows coming her way, but it was difficult to be more aggressive with so many coming at her.
She had never had to contend with so many opponents
at once. She had never been in a battle where she was so
outnumbered and knew she did not have the skill, or
the strength, to keep them from killing her, were that
their intent. But it obviously wasn't, she realized after
several moments had passed. The three men attacking
her seemed to be more concerned with keeping her
busy than anything else—which convinced her they
must be Greenweld's men. They would have been ordered to kill Blake but not to harm her. Allistair had
wanted to marry her, after all.

She was well aware that the men Blake was facing
would not be fighting as lightly. He was the one they
were to kill. Concern for her husband distracted her,
and she found herself paying more attention to the bat-

tle taking place at her back than the one she was involved in. She was listening to the sounds and trying to glance over her shoulder to see how it was going for Blake when she tripped on something; a good-sized rock perhaps, or the root of a tree. Whatever it was, it put her off balance as she raised her sword to fend off another blow, and Seonaid cried out as she stumbled back and crashed into Blake, taking him by surprise and setting him off balance too.

It was then she heard what she had been listening for during the last few minutes: a surprised grunt from Blake as he stiffened against her. She turned to look, then glanced down in horror at the blade at her hip. It had either been driven through Blake's side or she had knocked him into it, but it protruded out of his back, his blood staining it.

Seonaid released a battle shriek of pure fury and, ignoring the men facing her, moved around Blake and slammed her own sword into his attacker just as he finished drawing his blade out of her husband.

Another battle cry echoed in the silence that suddenly descended on the clearing, and Seonaid glanced around in time to see Little George and Aeldra on their horses, driving them into the center of the men. Obviously, they had returned to see what was going on and had immediately gone for the mounts. Seonaid could have kissed them both. Instead, she grabbed Blake under the arm to help keep him upright when he swayed, and urged him toward the animals.

Aeldra released the reins of their mounts the moment she saw that Seonaid was grabbing for them, then joined Little George in hacking at Greenweld's men with both her sword and the hooves of her horse as she made the animal rear and paw at the earth before them. The sudden appearance of the couple, and the distraction they offered, gave Seonaid the chance she needed to help Blake onto his mount, then climb up behind him. Wrapping her arms around him, she caught the reins of both his horse and her own, then shouted at Aeldra and Little George before putting her heels to the mount they were on to send it charging out of the clearing.

Seonaid set the beast at a dead run and kept it up for several minutes before she became aware that Blake was leaning into her more and more with every passing moment. She had one arm around him to grasp the reins of his stallion, and was holding the reins of her own horse with the other to drag the beast along behind them. Seonaid suspected she would soon need both hands to hold Blake and control the mount they rode.

A glance around showed that Aeldra and Little George had followed and were hard on her heels. She only managed a quick look, but it did not appear as if either of them had sustained injury. Relieved, she shouted at her husband's first, who immediately rode up beside her. Seonaid tossed him the reins to her horse.

"Blake was hurt!" she shouted, once he had a firm grip on the reins.

"Aye, I know," he shouted back, and there was worry on the giant man's face as he eyed his lord.

"How bad is he bleeding?" she asked, unable to see for herself.

His grim expression was answer enough, and Seonaid almost slowed her mount. As if reading her thoughts, Little George yelled, "They are following us! And not far behind!"

Seonaid cursed. This was bad news. "We need to get him somewhere safe so we can stop and tend him!"

"We are close to Eberhardt." It was Blake who spoke those words, turning slightly to do so. The wince of pain on his face suggested turning was not a comfortable action for him at the moment.

"What did he say?" Little George yelled to be heard over the pounding hooves of the horses.

Seonaid wasn't surprised he hadn't heard. Blake's words had been faint enough that she had barely caught them. "He said we are close to Eberhardt," she called. "Are we headin' in the right direction? How close are we?"

"By my guess we are less than an hour's ride out," Aeldra's husband announced, then added, "and, aye, we are heading the right way."

Seonaid hesitated, then asked Blake, "Do ye think ye can make it that far?"

He gave a brief nod rather than try to turn again, and Seonaid frowned. She wished she could see his wound for herself; she didn't know whether to believe him or put his answer down to male pride and stubbornness. Men could be so foolish that way.

"Here!"

Seonaid glanced to her other side to find that Aeldra

had ridden up to join them and was now holding out a strip of cloth she had ripped from her own plaid.

"He's bleedin' badly," she said as Seonaid released Blake long enough to snatch up the cloth. "Bind him up or he willna make it far at all."

Seonaid nodded, then hesitated. She could hardly hold the reins, help steady Blake, and wrap the cloth around his waist as well. Little George solved the problem by taking the reins of their mount as well, as the riderless horse and leading both animals while she quickly and clumsily managed to get the cloth around her husband. She tied the cloth as tightly as she could, wincing at but not giving into, Blake's grunt of pain. She knew she was hurting him, but they had to slow down the bleeding if he was going to survive. Seonaid had caught a quick glance at the back of his doublet as she worked and the glimpse at the amount of blood he was losing had lodged a cold ball of fear in her chest. The knowledge that he would be losing just as much from the front had left her feeling sick.

"We have to move faster!" she yelled as she reclaimed the reins from Little George and urged the mount to ride as quickly as it was capable of moving. It was a dangerous thing to do. Riding at night was risky in itself—there was always the danger of not seeing some obstacle in the dark, or of the horse stumbling or setting its foot down wrong. But it was a risk they had to take. After waiting so long for him to come claim her, Seonaid would be damned if Blake was going to make her a widow now by bleeding to death in her arms.

Seonaid set a grueling pace, and one that might have

left their pursuers behind had Blake's stallion been able
to sustain it. But, forced to carry their combined weight,
the horse began to slow after a time. Little George and
Aeldra slowed their own mounts to keep pace, but
Seonaid soon wished they hadn't. While Blake was
slumping more and more against her until she was
wholly holding him upright and could not glance
around, the increasing frequency with which Aeldra began looking over her shoulder to the trail behind them
told Seonaid that their pursuers were slowly catching
up. When she began to actually hear the drumming of
their pursuers' horses, she began to think they would
not make it. Then the inky black of night in the woods
suddenly gave way to moonlight as they broke out of the
trees and onto the wide expanse of cleared land that
surrounded the castle they were approaching.

Seonaid almost released a sob of relief at the sight of
the castle ahead. Instead, she put her heel to Blake's
mount, urging the beast to one last burst of speed,
grateful when the animal responded.

They were halfway between the woods and the castle
walls when Seonaid judged by the fading sound of hoofbeats behind them that their pursuers had begun to
rein in and give up the chase. Still, her concern for
Blake didn't allow her to slow down. She kept the animal at a full gallop until she was forced to slow to a stop
by the fact that Eberhardt was closed up tight for the
night, its bridge up and gates closed.

Stopping at the edge of the moat, Seonaid glanced
back toward the woods in time to see the last of their

pursuers disappearing as Little George yelled up at the wall, identifying who they were and shouting that Sherwell was injured. Fortunately, whoever was on watch that night recognized the name and let the drawbridge down at once. Still, it seemed to take forever.

The moment the way was clear, she urged Blake's mount forward, trotting across the bridge, into the bailey, and straight up to the stairs to the keep before stopping. The moment she did, Blake began to slide sideways in her arms. Seonaid was straining to keep him from tumbling to the ground when the keep doors slammed open and a man almost as large as Little George came charging down them. Long dark hair flowing wild around his head and dressed only in a pair of black braies, the man had obviously been roused from his bed.

For all that, he seemed wide awake, and he rushed straight to where she sat holding Blake. Assessing the situation at once, he raised a hand to brace Blake, then ordered, "Let him go."

Seonaid followed the order without hesitation. The moment she did, Blake dropped sideways off the saddle, but the newcomer was there to catch him and ease him to the ground.

Seonaid quickly scrambled off the horse and knelt at Blake's side just as his eyes slowly opened. His gaze slid from her to the man on his other side, and he managed a weak smile.

"Amaury." His voice was barely above a whisper, and they both had to lean closer to hear. "Thought we would visit on the way home. Should introduce my wife," he added, and Seonaid frowned at the slur to his voice. "Wife, Amaury. Amaury, wife."

They glanced at each other, and Seonaid was not surprised to note the concern on the other man's face. She knew her own expression mirrored it.

"Blake!"

Seonaid glanced over Amaury's wide shoulders to see a short, curvaceous blonde rushing down the stairs toward them.

"What has happened?" she cried with alarm as she reached them and eyed Blake's bloodstained doublet. Then, before anyone could answer, she turned toward the servants gathering at the open keep door and roared, *"Maude!"*

"Aye, my lady?" A plain-faced servant started down the stairs at once.

"I shall need my medicinals!"

"Aye, my lady." The servant turned in midstep and flew back up into the keep.

Seonaid's gaze dropped to the man kneeling across from her, who grinned slightly.

"My wife, Emmalene," he explained.

"Ah. She . . . er . . . has a fine set of lungs for such a small woman," Seonaid commented, then winced as Lady Emmalene proved her words true with another bellow.

"Sebert!"

"Aye, my lady?" A male servant started down the stairs, only to turn and rush back up them when Lady Emmalene said, "Bandages!"

"Tell them to bring everything to the room Blake occupied on his last visit," Amaury ordered, slipping his arms under Blake and standing as he lifted him.

Seonaid scrambled to her feet and rushed along at the man's side as he carried her husband inside.

Chapter Fifteen

Seonaid watched as Amaury laid her husband on the bed; then she immediately moved forward, intending to remove Blake's tunic and doublet. But his friend started on it before she could. Telling herself that he was stronger and so would be quicker about it, Seonaid waited impatiently as the clothing was stripped away and Blake was eased onto his uninjured side.

Her mouth tightened when she got her first glimpse of the wound. It was an angry, jagged hole in the front that was echoed in the back. It looked ghastly.

"Here, m'lady." The servant Emmalene had sent for her medicinals rushed into the room, followed closely by the fellow who had been sent for bandages.

Emmalene accepted their offerings, then turned toward the bed.

"We'll need *uisegebeatha*," Seonaid said, then used the English word to prevent any confusion. "Whiskey. We'll need it to clean the wound."

Emmalene sent for the whiskey, then hesitated briefly before offering the medicinals and bandages to her.

As Blake's wife, Seonaid supposed it was her place to tend her husband, but she almost wished it wasn't; her stomach was roiling and she feared making a mistake. Considering this weak behavior, she straightened her shoulders and stepped forward to tend the task.

Seonaid had mended hundreds of wounds over the years, from small cuts that needed no more than a splash of whiskey and a bandage to major injuries like the one her husband sported. She could do this.

Seonaid sorted through the salves and other items Maude had brought in search of a needle and thread. Once she found them, she set to attempting to thread the needle, but much to her frustration, her hands—her very arms—were trembling so badly she could not manage the task.

"Emmalene, mayhap you should tend to stitching Blake up," Amaury suggested, apparently noting the problem. "Seonaid's muscles are worn from holding him in the saddle for so long, and her hands will tremble until they have had rest."

"Shall I?" Emmalene asked.

Seonaid handed over the thread and needle with relief. While her arms *were* weary from holding her husband, it was not entirely the source of her shaking. She was anxious and afraid for Blake. The injury was a deadly one, and she feared the ride here had been too long, allowing him to lose too much blood. He might not survive.

When the whiskey arrived, Seonaid poured it liberally over, and into, the wound, front and back. Blake did not even stir at the action. Had he been awake, he would have screamed in agony, for while the liquor cleaned a wound well enough, it was not called the fire of life for nothing.

Seonaid handed the whiskey back to Maude, then glanced past her, her attention drawn by a soft sob. There was a buxom blond servant standing by the door, crying softly. Seonaid eyed her for a moment, then asked her hostess, "Who is that?"

Emmalene turned to glance at the girl, then frowned and ordered, "Maude, you stay. The rest of the servants are to wait in the hall in case we need anything."

Once the other servants—including the teary blonde—had left, Emmalene turned back and set to stitching up Blake. She had neglected to answer Seonaid's question, but she let it go for now.

Once Emmalene had finished sewing up the wound, both front and back, Seonaid helped her spread a salve over the injury on both sides, then bandage him up.

"There," Emmalene said as they finished and both straightened.

"Will he live?" Amaury asked as he, Little George, and Aeldra moved closer to the bed.

Anxious to hear the answer, Seonaid waited for the other woman to speak. Seonaid herself felt his chances were poor, but they at least had some cause for hope. He'd lost a lot of blood and she'd almost feared he might die before they could stop the bleeding and stitch him up. But the fact that he had survived this far suggested to her that his chances were a little better than they had been on arriving. Every moment that passed with him still breathing made his chances better, but she feared she might be fooling herself and wanted to hear what Lady Emmalene had to say.

"He has lost a lot of blood," Emmalene said, her brow knitted with worry as she peered down at Blake's pale face. "But if he does not take a fever, he may survive."

Seonaid let her breath out on a whoosh. The possibility of infection hadn't even occurred to her. She would have to watch over him through the night. If Blake didn't show signs of fever by morning, he probably wouldn't have one.

"We will know better by morning," Lady Emmalene said, her thoughts obviously running along the same lines as Seonaid's.

Amaury gave an abrupt nod, then glanced to Seonaid, Aeldra, and Little George. "Have you eaten?"

Little George shook his head. "Aeldra and I were just returning with a rabbit to cook for sup. We arrived back to find Seonaid and Blake surrounded and battling."

"How many men?" Amaury asked.

"Twelve, I think."

"Aye," Aeldra said. "There were twelve o' them, but there are only nine left now. Blake had apparently dispatched two 'ere we got there, and Seonaid killed the one who put his sword to Blake as we fetched the horses to join them."

"Aye," Little George agreed. "There were nine left in the end."

"Who were they?"

Little George opened his mouth to answer again, and Seonaid left him to it as she walked to the fireplace to grab one of the chairs there and drag it back to the side of the bed.

"Mayhap we should move below so they can eat while they explain?" Lady Emmalene suggested, interrupting Little George.

"Aye." Amaury nodded. "Come, Little George. I would hear all that has taken place since you and Blake left Eberhardt with Lord Rolfe."

The two men moved out of the room, but Aeldra and Emmalene hesitated.

"Will you not come below and eat . . . Seonaid, is it not?" Lady Emmalene asked tentatively.

"Aye. Seonaid."

Amaury's wife smiled. "And I am Emmalene."

"Aye. I ken. Blake told me about ye and Amaury," she admitted, then gestured to her cousin. "And this is me cousin, Aeldra. She's Little George's wife."

The lady's jaw dropped and she gaped at Aeldra with amazement. "You and Little George?"

The woman's reaction startled a laugh out of Aeldra, as well as a smile from Seonaid. Some of the tension oozed out of her, leaving her feeling limp. "Shockin', isna it?" she commented with amusement, and Emmalene forced her mouth closed, then managed a smile.

"Nay, nay. I am happy for Little George," she said quickly. "He has had a most tragic time of late." She hesitated and cleared her throat, then asked, "Will you come below and eat? One of the servants can sit with Blake while you do."

"Nay. I am no hungry." Seonaid's gaze moved to her husband's face. A frown of worry immediately claimed her expression at his pallor. He was almost gray from lack of blood. If he died on her—

"I shall send some food up to you in case you change your mind," Lady Emmalene murmured, then turned to Aeldra and asked, "Will you come below and eat with your husband?"

Seonaid glanced to her cousin and, seeing her indecision, said, "Go on with ye, Aeldra. Eat with Little George. There's no need fer two o' us up here. 'Sides, 'tis sure I am Lady Emmalene would enjoy news o' her cousin, Lord Rolfe."

"Oh, aye, I would," Emmalene agreed, obviously pleased at the prospect.

"All right," Aeldra agreed reluctantly. "But shout if ye need me, Seonaid, an' I'll come runnin'."

Seonaid nodded, then turned her attention back to her husband as the other two women left the room. She stared at Blake's still face for a long time until she felt sure his features were burned so securely into her memory she could bring them up in her mind's eye at will for the next fifty years if necessary. She hoped it would not be necessary. She was too young and too newly married to be a widow.

* * *

Seonaid awoke in her chair, still seated upright, head tipped forward and chin resting on her chest. The moment she started to lift her head, pain shot through her neck. She'd apparently slept more than a few minutes.

Grimacing, she rubbed a hand at the back of her neck and slowly straightened, barely restraining a groan. A glance toward the window showed that the sun was rising on the horizon. Seonaid had pulled the window's tapestry aside during the wee hours of the morning to find it hid glass windows, and had been terribly impressed. Then she'd opened the window, hoping the fresh air would help keep her awake to watch over Blake. Silly as it might seem, she had a terrible fear that the moment she stopped watching him, he might develop a fever. She'd sat up most of the night, until exhaustion had claimed her.

By her guess, she'd slept an hour or two. It was early morning.

Turning back to the bed, she leaned forward and gently pressed a hand to Blake's forehead.

"Thank God," she murmured, equally glad that he was neither warm with fever nor cold with death. He was so pale, she would not have been surprised to find he'd died while she slept.

Seonaid sat back in the chair, then shifted uncomfortably. She was still tired, and now that morning had arrived with Blake still alive and showing no sign of fever, it should be all right for her to get a proper sleep. His having survived the night had been a big step.

Standing, she took a moment to stretch muscles aching from remaining seated in one position too long, then moved around the bed and carefully climbed in next to Blake. She arranged herself on the edge of the bed, as far from him as possible, to prevent bumping him should she roll over in her sleep. She closed her eyes and let sleep claim her again.

"Ye've been locked up in this room for two days." Aeldra stood, hands on hips, an air of determination about her as she glared at Seonaid from the other side of the bed. "And he isna even awake to ken yer keepin' vigil. Ye have to come out o' this room some time." Giving up her angry stance, she tried a more pleading approach. "Just come break yer fast."

"I already broke my fast." Seonaid scanned Blake's face for the hundredth time since waking up two hours earlier. He was regaining some of his color but was still pale and hadn't yet woken. It was worrisome.

"Then come out in the bailey with me and practice for a little bit," Aeldra coaxed. "Just for a little bit. Ye can come back up here afterward, and one o' the servants will sit with him. Canna they?" she asked, glancing to Lady Emmalene for support. The little blonde, about the same height as Aeldra but much more curvaceous, immediately nodded.

"Aye. Maude or one of the other women would be happy to take your place," Emmalene said at once.

Seonaid considered her cousin's suggestion and found herself tempted. She had been cooped up in the bedchamber for two days. Two long, wearying days spent staring at her husband's face and willing him to wake up. The longer he slept, the more worried she became.

He hadn't awakened for even a moment in that time, and if he didn't awaken soon and eat, she very much feared he would just fade away in the bed and die.

"Once he recovers, we'll be traveling on to Sherwell. What if we're attacked again? Ye'll need all yer skills to keep him safe," Aeldra added slyly, and Seonaid glanced at her sharply.

"Has Amaury no found the men yet?" she asked with a frown. Lady Emmalene had informed her the morning after their arrival that her husband had sent warriors out searching for the band of men who had attacked them. She hadn't mentioned the matter again since, and Seonaid hadn't really thought of them. Her concentration had all been focused on Blake.

"Nay," Lady Emmalene answered. "He says he thinks they have gone to ground like a fox seeking its hole. But he is sure they are still out there somewhere."

Seonaid frowned over this, then stood abruptly. "Aye. I'll practice with ye," she decided. She needed to be in top form when they left. She would not see Blake injured again once he'd recovered. If he recovered. If he didn't . . . She'd hunt the bastards down herself and send them to meet Greenweld.

"Maude!" Lady Emmalene roared, and all three women glanced to Blake's face hopefully, but her bellow did not even make him stir in his sleep.

Seonaid's mouth tightened at this added proof that his was not a normal sleep. She had already known that. She had tried to wake him several times to get him to eat some broth, with no success.

The maid, Maude, had obviously been waiting in the hall. The door opened almost at once and she slipped in.

"Please sit with Lord Blake while Lady Seonaid takes some fresh air," Lady Emmalene instructed.

The maid nodded and moved around to her side, and Seonaid hesitated, then got stiffly to her feet. She had been sitting too much the last several days and was stiff everywhere. Moving out of the way, she let the servant take her seat, then said, "Call me if he wakes."

"Aye, m'lady," the servant murmured as she settled in the chair.

"Call me if there is any change at all," Seonaid added.

"Aye, m'lady."

Seonaid opened her mouth again, but Aeldra grabbed her arm and tugged her toward the door. "Ye'll only be gone a little while. He'll be fine."

"Aye," Lady Emmalene agreed, following them out of the room and pulling the door closed before bustling along the hall beside them. "A little walk in the bailey, some practice with Aeldra, and perhaps a quick bite for the nooning meal, and then you can come right back up."

Seonaid glanced around curiously as she was led down the stairs into the great hall. She hadn't really looked about on arriving, her attention and worry had all been on her husband. Now she took in with interest the well-ordered castle with its small army of servants. "Why are the servants all wearing black?"

"Oh." Emmalene flushed slightly. "We were in mourning. Well, we still are really, or should be, but—"

She paused and shook her head. "My husband has only been dead a short while."

Seonaid's eyebrows flew up. "I thought Amaury was yer husband?"

"Aye, but I was married 'ere him, only my husband died and the king arranged my marriage to Amaury to keep me safe from—" She paused with a grimace, then said, " 'Tis a long story."

"Aye." Seonaid smiled slightly as she recalled Blake's telling her all this. "Blake told me. I but forgot for a bit."

"Oh." Emmalene smiled, then excused her. " 'Tis not a very interesting story."

Seonaid snorted. "It sounded verra interestin' when Blake told it," she countered, and it had—murder, a race to get the lady bedded, kidnaping, and a grand escape, it had been a very entertaining tale.

Emmalene flushed, but then her gaze dropped to the trestle tables and a small sigh slipped from her lips. "Oh, dear. Lady Ardeth is up."

Seonaid glanced at her hostess with curiosity. The woman didn't sound pleased to see the woman in question.

"She's a right bitch," Aeldra growled under her breath so only Seonaid could hear, and she raised an eyebrow at the words. Aeldra's only answer was a slow nod.

Deciding she would have to remember later to get her cousin to explain that remark and what the woman had done to so obviously anger her, Seonaid let the subject drop for the moment and accompanied Aeldra to the practicing field.

It felt good to get some fresh air and exercise after so long trapped in a room with an unconscious man. Seonaid stayed longer than she had intended because of it, and when she walked back into the keep and Lady Emmalene caught her and insisted she should stop to eat before going abovestairs, Seonaid gave in to the request, telling herself that it would only take a minute and would save the servants work. She supposed she hadn't been a very considerate guest, making Eberhardt's servants trudge up and down the stairs, bringing her food and drink when she wasn't the one ailing.

It wasn't quite time for the nooning meal yet, so the hall was empty, but Aeldra accompanied her to the table, and Lady Emmalene joined her as well. The three of them were just finished eating and were talking quietly when Lady Ardeth approached the table. It was only then that Seonaid recalled her intent to find out why Aeldra didn't like the woman. It didn't take her long to figure it out. She gave the woman the once-over as Lady Ardeth settled herself at the table, noting her fine facial features, voluptuous curves, expensive gown and head dress, and the artistically styled blond hair. She was a lovely woman. Until she opened her mouth.

"I saw you out practicing with your swords," the woman announced without preamble.

"Oh?" Seonaid said mildly.

"It must be . . . interesting for a man as refined as Blake to have such an Amazon of a wife." Her voice was full of derision and her pretty face was made ugly by the sneer pulling at her lips as her eyes slid over Seonaid's braies and tunic with scorn. "Tell me, does he substitute swordplay for foreplay to accommodate your unladylike tastes?"

Seonaid went still, aware that Lady Emmalene had released a little gasp beside her, while Aeldra had reached instinctively for her *sgian dubh*. Reaching to the side, Seonaid put a restraining hand over Aeldra's to keep her from removing the weapon. At the same time she patted Lady Emmalene's arm with her other hand, distracting her hostess, who had just opened her mouth, no doubt to rebuke the woman for her rudeness.

"Blake indulges in swordplay with me on occasion," Seonaid said calmly. "However, while he's a most accommodating lover, the only sword he brings to our bed is one I doona mind sheathing . . . again and again."

The fury mingled with envy that flashed across the other woman's face told Seonaid she'd struck her mark. But she couldn't resist twisting the knife. Aeldra had pointed out Lady Ardeth's husband to her while they were out practicing. The man was a tiny, fat, old man with a mean, squirrel-like face. Her first thought on seeing him had been that he was no doubt the sort who beat his wife and abused his servants. She would bet he was not a caring and considerate lover like her husband.

"I hope that ye were as lucky in yer marriage bed as I am," Seonaid continued pleasantly. "I realize how fortunate I have been and am grateful me father didna marry me off to one o' those sour-faced, wife-beatin' men like other women have been unfortunate enough to be forced to marry. Such a husband often makes the most lovely woman age before her time as she grows ugly with her bitterness."

Lady Ardeth's head snapped back as if she had been slapped, then she snapped, "Bitch!" as she got to her feet and whirled away.

Seonaid watched her storm off, trying to subdue the guilt that wanted to claim her. She'd hit her mark, all right. There had been no mistaking the misery and pain that had flashed across the woman's face before she'd controlled it and cursed at her. It was difficult to blame her for being bitter. Seonaid had noticed the faded bruises peeking out from beneath the woman's sleeves and had no doubt her life was an unpleasant one.

"I am sorry, Seonaid. Lady Ardeth is a most unpleasant woman. I blame it on her husband. I think he—"

"I think so too," Seonaid interrupted. "And ye've naught to apologize for. I should have been kinder."

"Nay. You were kinder than she deserved," Emmalene assured her. "And mayhap your comments will make her temper her behavior in future. She and her husband were at court at the same time as we, and while there I saw her reduce several ladies to tears with her cruelty."

Seonaid accepted this news with a nod, some of her guilt easing, then she stood. "I should return abovestairs."

Much to her relief, Aeldra let her go without protest.

Blake was still asleep when Seonaid got to their room. She hadn't seriously thought that he might wake while she was gone, but some part of her had hoped. She thanked Maude, then reclaimed her seat as the woman left to tend to whatever chores she had. Then Seonaid simply sat and stared at her husband's handsome face.

Refined, Lady Ardeth had called him, and her husband fit the description. He was intelligent and handsome and . . . refined. She could imagine him strutting around court. He had the manners, the grace . . . he probably even knew how to dance. He was nothing like her.

Seonaid blew out a little sigh. She would be a disaster at court, just as she had been in the abbey. Large and clumsy, she would knock things over and break things and embarrass Blake. Unlike Lady Ardeth, who no doubt wouldn't put a foot wrong at court. Or Emmalene.

And the woman's jibe about substituting swordplay for foreplay had come uncomfortably close to the mark. Though it was tickling and wrestling and Seonaid usually instigated it, and Blake definitely did not leave out other forms of foreplay for it. Still, she supposed other women were not so unladylike as to roll around on the ground with their husbands, laughing and squealing like children. She couldn't see Lady Ardeth doing it, and Seonaid didn't doubt for a minute that the cruel blonde was one of the women Blake had bedded in the past. The woman had been too smug and familiar. She also suspected he had bedded the well-endowed blond servant who had wept at the sight of his wound the night they had arrived. Then there was Emmalene. Seonaid didn't think he had bedded her—she was positive he hadn't—but when he had spoken of her it had been with great admiration and affection.

All three women were blond, voluptuous, and most

definitely feminine in looks and behavior: the complete opposite of Seonaid.

Her gaze slid to her husband again and she felt unhappiness tug at the corners of her mouth. She'd done a lot of soul searching the last two days while sitting here alone with him. The idea of his dying had shaken her up terribly. It was the idea of being alone again . . . which was a foolish thought, really. One was never alone in a castle, and Seonaid had always had Aeldra, Duncan, her father, and even Allistair before he had turned on them all. But it had been different with Blake. When they made love, when they lay alone together of a night talking, and even when they had traveled together and worked together to set up camp, it had felt almost as if they were a unit. One. During the attack, they had even moved as one, putting their backs to each other to face their enemies.

Seonaid supposed somewhere deep down inside she had hoped that eventually that ease of interaction, that oneness, would seep into other parts of their lives. She'd even gone so far as to admit to herself that she'd started falling in love with her husband; with his honor, his good humor, his strength, his consideration. She wanted him to love her too. But how could he love a great clumsy Amazon who knew nothing about being a lady or a proper wife?

"God's toes," Seonaid muttered to herself. She was sounding like one of those weak, whining women she hated.

If she wanted her husband to love her then she should do what it took to ensure that happened. She could do little about her height, or the fact that she wasn't a well-endowed blonde as he seemed to prefer, but she could dress more like other women and learn some of the skills they all seemed to take to so naturally. Once she set her mind to a task, she could do anything.

Buoyed up by these thoughts, Seonaid contemplated how best to go about what was necessary. Clothing seemed the easiest problem to tackle. She would approach Lady Emmalene and see if she could not aid her in that area. Blake had said the lady had ordered in a dressmaker and tons of material after marrying Amaury. Perhaps she had some cloth left over that could be made into a gown. And then perhaps the lady would be good enough to help her learn some of the skills she would need. Aye, Emmalene seemed her best bet.

A glance at Blake showed that he still slept the deep sleep that worried her so, and Seonaid stood to move toward the door. It would only take her a minute to have a word with Emmalene.

She was just reaching to open the door when it did so on its own, and Seonaid was forced to step back to avoid it hitting her.

"Oh, Seonaid," Aeldra said with surprise on spying her so close to the door. Then her eyes widened and her gaze shot to the bed. "Is he—?"

"Nay, he's the same," Seonaid said quickly. "I was just . . ." She hesitated, reluctant to reveal her plans to Aeldra. Her cousin would probably think she had lost her mind if she caught wind of them. Instead, she asked, "Is there something yer wantin'?"

"Oh." Aeldra hesitated, then blurted, "Lord Amaury

just suggested that as Blake will be a while recovering—
He seems sure he will, by the by," she interrupted herself to say, and Seonaid knew it was an attempt to cheer
her. "He says Blake is too damned stubborn no to, but
as 'twill no doubt be a while 'ere he does . . ."

"Aye?" Seonaid prompted when Aeldra hesitated.

"Well, he seems to think Little George and I should
go visit his family in the meantime so they can meet
me," Aeldra blurted out. "He seems to think Blake will
want to head home the moment he is better and we will
probably no be in this area again for a while, and—"

"Go," Seonaid interrupted, and Aeldra peered at her
uncertainly.

"Go?"

She nodded firmly, thinking this was perfect. For
some reason she felt better about attempting changes
to herself without her cousin here. Besides, Emmalene
had said the first night they were here that Little
George had suffered much tragedy lately, and Seonaid
knew from the nightly conversations she'd indulged in
with Blake since their wedding that the tragedy was the
murder of the man's wife. He wasn't the only one to
have suffered tragedy lately. Aeldra had lost her brother
and surrogate mother in one fell swoop. Here was her
chance to be welcomed into Little George's family.
Seonaid was happy for her.

"Ye wouldna mind?" Aeldra asked. "'Cause if ye
would, we could stay and—"

"Nay. Go and have a nice visit. There's no sense yer
sitting around here awaitin'. I'll send news when Blake
wakes up."

"Thank ye." Aeldra gave her a quick hug, and Seonaid frowned.

"What're ye thankin' me for? 'Tis no as if ye needed
me permission, Aeldra."

"Aye," her cousin countered. "We did."

When Seonaid started to shake her head at the non-
sensical claim, Aeldra gently pointed out, "Little
George is Blake's first. He serves him. With Blake unable to give permission, we needed yours to go."

Seonaid stared as she realized it was true. She didn't
like the idea at all, but it was the truth. Frowning, she
shrugged uncomfortably. "When are ye leaving?"

"Right away, most like."

"Well, go on with ye then." She gave her a push toward the door. "Have a good time."

"Aye." Aeldra started out the door. "Send a messenger if ye need me."

"Aye. Oh!" Seonaid said, and her cousin paused at
once to glance back.

"Aye?"

"Could ye ask Lady Emmalene to come speak to me
when she has a moment?"

"Aye." Aeldra grinned, then pulled the door closed,
and Seonaid turned and walked back to the bed, considering all she had to do and learn.

Chapter Sixteen

The first thing Blake was aware of was a terrible pounding in his head. It was bad enough that he nearly groaned, but—suspecting it would merely add to his pain—he managed to restrain the urge. Then he noted the unpleasant, pasty taste in his mouth and wondered what the hell had happened to him. He hadn't felt this bad since shortly after earning his spurs. Blake had celebrated the occasion with wine, women, and song—for three days. The agony he'd suffered afterward was enough to convince him that alcohol was a substance best indulged in sparingly.

Had he forgotten that long ago lesson and overindulged again? He didn't recall. The last thing he remembered . . .

Blake ran through the memories jostling about in

his head. He'd traveled to Dunbar on the king's order to marry Seonaid Dunbar, had chased her all over Scotland, managed to get her back to Dunbar, wedded her and bedded her—he paused for a moment to allow those memories to claim him. His wife was making him think that marriage would not be the boring burden he had always feared it would be. She was not like other women; forever acting demure and prissy. She was . . . fun.

Seonaid played with him; wrestling and laughing, not worried about her hair being disturbed, or her gown getting torn, or her nails being broken. And when they had camped out on the way to Sherwell, she had not fussed about the discomforts of travel, or stood cowering when he fought off their attackers. . . . Actually, he almost wished she had. Blake had been distracted during the fight, worrying about her battling at his back. It was part of the reason he'd not been able to keep his feet when she'd bumped into him, but had stumbled into—

Blake's thoughts came to an abrupt halt as he remembered the sword slicing into his side. The ride afterward was something of a blur to him, but he did recall they had been headed to Eberhardt. He suspected he had been sliding in and out of consciousness most of the way.

Well, that explained why he felt so awful, Blake thought, then blinked his eyes open and glanced to the side as a softly muttered curse caught his ear. He recognized the room he had slept in when last at Eberhardt.

He didn't, however, recognize the woman who sat sewing in the chair at his bedside. His first thought was that she must be a servant. Dark hair peeked out from beneath a head dress, but the woman's face was hidden from him, her head bowed, her attention on a bit of sewing in her lap.

The gown she wore didn't appear to be servant's garb, however. It was a plain style, but of a cloth too rich to be a servant's. He wondered who she was, and then in the next moment wondered where the hell his wife was. He had been badly injured. Would it have been too much to expect her to tend to him rather than leave him in the care of a complete stranger, lady or no?

Blake must have moved or made a sound, for the woman suddenly lifted her head to peer at him. Her eyes immediately went wide, and she tossed her sewing aside to shift forward on her seat, closer to the bed. "Ye're awake!"

Blake stared at her in amazement. It had taken him a moment to recognize the face framed by the circlet and veil she wore, but he knew the voice at once. God's toes! The dark-haired stranger at his bedside was his wife. In a dress. And she was sewing! Blake opened his mouth, closed it again, then opened it once more, but no words came to mind. He hadn't a clue what to say.

"Ye canna speak?" Seonaid guessed. "Doona try to, yer probably parched. Ye've had naught to eat or drink for days. I'll fetch ye some broth. They've been keeping a pot of it on the fire for days in case ye woke up. Doona go back to sleep, I willna be long."

●

Blake stared after her as she stood and hurried out of the room, the dark blue gown swaying with her movement. The only thought in his head was to wonder what had happened to his wife. It was a thought that was to repeat itself often over the next few days.

Seonaid pulled the door closed and rushed down the hall to the stairs. Blake was awake! She could hardly believe it. Her husband had finally woken up, and it had happened without the least bit of fanfare. She had glanced up and there he was, eyes open.

"Lady Seonaid, what—?" Lady Emmalene paused at the top of the stairs at the sight of a flustered Seonaid rushing down the hall toward her. "Is he awake?"

"Aye."

"Thank God!" Her relief was obvious but quickly replaced with an expectant smile. "How is he feeling? What did he say? Does he like your new dress?"

Seonaid blinked. She'd forgotten all about the transformation she'd been working on these last two days. Lady Emmalene had been more than enthusiastic in helping her. She'd set the servants to work on a dress at once, suggesting a plain style so that it could be done more quickly. The women had finished it but hours earlier, and Seonaid had donned the blue gown, then sat patiently while Emmalene had dressed her hair and arranged a matching dark blue circlet and veil on her head.

She felt uncomfortable in the garb but knew she would grow used to it in time. Seonaid also missed her sword, but Lady Emmalene had insisted she should not wear it.

That was not all Lady Emmalene had done. The woman was training her in womanly pursuits, such as how to direct servants, the ins and outs of managing a large estate, and sewing. Seonaid had been practicing the last skill when Blake had awoken.

"Seonaid? Did he not like it?"

"I doona ken," she admitted. "He canna speak. 'Tis his throat, I think; dried out from so long without liquid."

"Oh, aye, of course." Emmalene turned on the stairs and started back down. "You stay with him. I shall fetch some broth."

"Thank you." Seonaid whirled back the way she'd come and rushed to the bedchamber door, only to pause once there. "Doona rush or stride about," she reminded herself. "Walk like a lady." It was an oft-heard refrain as Emmalene had tried to help her become more ladylike.

Nodding, she opened the door and walked inside, forcing herself to take small, measured steps. It was a bloody nuisance, but Blake deserved a proper wife, and proper wives did not stride around with purpose like men.

Always try to smile serenely. Men have many trials and tribulations during the day and appreciate a wife who has a soothing smile.

Her hostess's voice echoed in her head, and Seonaid plastered what she hoped was a soothing smile on her face as she glanced to the bed. She was relieved to find he was still awake and had not dropped back off into his deathlike sleep again.

"Lady Emmalene is fetchin' ye some broth," she announced, trying to speak softly, as Lady Emmalene did. Well, as Lady Emmalene did when she wasn't bellowing.

Blake stared at his wife, noting the way she was talking and the softening to her voice. She looked beautiful, of course. The color of the gown suited her, but he did miss the way her braies clung lovingly to her slender curves. His gaze slid to her face and hair, and he thought she wore the circlet and veil well, though her hair looked just as nice pulled back as it once was, and he really liked it best when it was down like it was every night when they slept.

Aye, she looked lovely, but she didn't look like his Seonaid. And where was her sword? It was a question he kept to himself for two days while he recovered. When he did finally speak, Blake found that his throat was indeed sore. It took two days for it to get back to normal. But that wasn't why he didn't, at first, speak. It was just the excuse he used.

Mostly, Blake didn't speak because he didn't know what to say. Everyone else was busy talking most of the time anyway. Seonaid recounted their ride to Eberhardt for him, and their arrival, as well as Emmalene's sewing him up. Amaury told him about his search for their attackers and daily affairs at Eberhardt. And Emmalene chattered away about what had happened at Eberhardt since his leaving the last time.

No one explained, however, what had happened to

his wife. The change in her had not been confined to her dress. Her whole demeanor was different. She no longer practiced swordplay daily in the bailey as she had at Dunbar, but sat by him most of the day, insisting he rest and sewing whatever it was she was working on. And usually with the most awful grimace on her face. It alternated with a forced smile that she plastered on her lips whenever she looked his way. She now walked in jerky little steps and spoke in a hushed voice he had to strain to hear . . . when she spoke at all.

Blake fondly recalled holding her in his arms of a night, recounting tales of his youth, then listening to the few bits and pieces she was willing to tell about her own. In truth, he had done most of the talking, only occasionally managing to coax a story out of her. But now she didn't talk at all. She just smiled the most horrid, unnatural smile he had ever seen, and Blake watched her and wondered what had happened to his wife.

It wasn't until the third morning that he finally asked the question. Amaury stopped in to talk to him, and Seonaid excused herself to go below and speak to Emmalene. Amaury had started out telling him that they still had not found the men who had attacked them but would keep looking, and Blake nodded, then—unable to stay silent on the subject any longer—asked, "What happened to my wife?"

The question came out sounding slightly gruff, but it no longer hurt to speak. Much to his disgust, Blake had done little but sip broth for two days. But it had eased his sore throat and he had even been allowed solid food that morning.

"What happened to—" Amaury stared with bewilderment. "I do not know what you mean."

Blake shifted impatiently in the bed. Amaury had not known her before her arriving here and so might not realize there was a difference in her demeanor. Unfortunately, Aeldra and Little George, who did know her, were not there to ask. Blake had been informed that the couple were visiting Little George's family.

"Did my wife sustain a head injury in the attack?" he asked.

"Nay."

Blake frowned. "Has she been hit in the head since our arrival here? While I was unconscious?"

"Nay," Amaury repeated, looking mystified at this line of questioning.

"I see," Blake said. "Then what the hell have you done with my wife?"

Amaury stared blankly. "I—nothing. What—?"

"The woman is in a dress," he pointed out. "A *dress*, Amaury. And she is sewing. Or trying to. Dear God! What happened while I was unconscious?"

"I—Did she not wear dresses before coming here?"

"Nay," he assured him. "She was not wearing one when we arrived, was she?"

"Nay, but I thought perhaps that was for travel, and—"

"We were not carting about a wagonload of trunks that might be full of gowns, were we?"

"Nay," Amaury admitted with sudden realization.

"Well, there you are, then." Blake nodded, then informed him, "Except for our wedding day, she has not worn a dress in all the time since I met her in the chapel at St. Simmian's. Until now," he allowed. "Seonaid does not wear dresses. She does not sew. She does not take mincing little steps, she strides. And where is her damned sword?"

"I do not know." Amaury glanced around the room in search of the missing item. "What does it look like?"

"Like a sword, Amaury," Blake said dryly. " 'Tis special made for her and slightly smaller and lighter than a man's sword, but otherwise 'tis just like every other sword you have ever seen."

Amaury shrugged helplessly. "I did not notice it on the night you arrived; everything was so rushed and worrisome. And I have not seen her much since your arrival. Your wife has stayed up here most of the time, tending to you as she should."

"Well, surely Aeldra was not up here all the time before she and Little George left for—"

"Ah, yes!" Amaury exclaimed. "I did see Aeldra's sword. Very well made, and perfect for her size." He paused and eyed him with interest. "Do you mean to say Seonaid has a similar sword?"

"She not only has a similar sword but normally dresses in braies like Aeldra, and walks with strong, purposeful strides like Aeldra, and—The two are copies of each other, except that Aeldra is small and blonde while my Seonaid is tall and svelte, with that beautiful raven-colored hair."

"Ah." Amaury nodded slowly, then shook his head. "I have never seen her so. As I say, I did not much notice her on the first night, what with my worry over you, and she has been up here most of the time with you since then. She sounds fascinating."

"She is fascinating. Or she was, before we got here. Since I have awakened in this bed, she has been . . ." He sighed helplessly. She was turning into a girl. Like Emmalene. "Emmalene!"

"What?" Amaury asked with alarm as Blake sat up in bed.

"Emmalene," Blake repeated grimly. "Your little wife must be influencing her. She is turning my Seonaid into a girl."

Amaury's eyebrows rose. "Was she not a girl when you married her?"

"Aye, but—Oh, you know what I mean. She was a woman, but strong and fun."

"Emmalene is strong and fun." Amaury had begun to glare.

"Aye, but Seonaid did not fuss over—Where did she get the dress?" Blake interrupted himself.

Amaury frowned. "I think Emmalene had the servants make the dress," he admitted, then added reluctantly, "And I gather she had been spending time up here with Seonaid the last two days 'ere you woke."

"Ah ha!" Blake tossed the linens aside and shifted to sit on the edge of the bed.

"What are you doing?"

"Getting dressed. Where are my clothes?"

"Here." Amaury picked up a bit of white linen from the chair by the bed and tossed it to him. "Here is your tunic. Your doublet and braies should be here somewhere. But I do not think you should be getting up just yet."

"I have to." Blake snatched the tunic from him and began to tug it on. "I have to get Seonaid away from Emmalene before she completely ruins my wife."

"Ruins her?" Amaury's eyes narrowed and turned cold. "My wife is not *ruining* yours. Seonaid can only benefit from Emmalene's assistance."

"Seonaid does not need assistance. She was perfectly fine the way she was. I liked her the way she was!" Blake tugged the tunic into place, then stilled as he noted that one arm was longer than the other. One sleeve stopped midway between elbow and wrist, while the other hung past the tips of his fingers. Then he spotted the needle dangling by a bit of thread from the unfinished hem.

"Ha!" Amaury pointed to the needle and thread. "This is her work, is it not? See! She needs proper training. You should be grateful my Emmalene deigned to take the time to do so."

Blake glared at his old friend, then moved closer on legs that were so weak still that they were shaking. Ignoring that, he poked a finger into Amaury's chest and snarled, "I have servants to sew for me. My wife is perfect just the way she is."

"Blake?"

He glanced to the side to find Seonaid and Emmalene standing in the open doorway, staring at the two of them. He felt a moment's panic, worrying over how much of the argument she had heard, but judging by the smile trembling on her lips, he was guessing she and Emmalene had only just arrived.

"What are ye doing up?" She moved forward around the bed, her steps faltering as she took in the tunic he wore. A frown claimed her lips, and he thought he heard her mutter something about having more work to do on the top, but then she stepped between him and Amaury and urged him back to bed. He let her. It seemed better to get back into bed willingly than to have his legs give out under him.

"Ye must build up yer strength. Ye're recovering from a mighty wound."

"Aye." Amaury's voice was cold. "The sooner you recover the sooner you can go home."

"That will not be soon enough for me," Blake growled in response. The two men glared at each other for a moment; then Amaury turned and stomped out of the room.

Seonaid and Emmalene exchanged bewildered glances, then turned their attention to the matter at hand and saw Blake back to bed.

"Have ye been able to find out why they are so angry with each other?" Seonaid asked. She and Emmalene stood at the top of the steps of Eberhardt keep, watching their husbands stubbornly refuse to acknowledge each other below.

Blake sat his mount, expression grim and back stiff, deliberately not even looking in Amaury's direction, while Emmalene's husband stood grimly at the bottom of the stairs, arms folded over his chest, steadfastly refusing to look Blake's way. The two hadn't spoken to each other since Emmalene and Seonaid had walked into the room as Blake had snarled, *"My wife is perfect just the way she is."*

Seonaid had been too pleased with the compliment to notice that the men were glaring at each other until Amaury had spoken in such cold tones about Blake's needing to recover. Her husband's answer had sounded no more cheerful, and she had realized something was wrong, but not the extent of it.

At least, not then. But Blake had spent the last four days in their room as he recovered, insisting that she stay there with him. When she had tried to discover what the men had been discussing, he refused to answer.

During the few snatches of conversation Seonaid had managed with Emmalene since then, she had learned that Amaury was equally as grouchy and angry as Blake but would not say why. The women had vowed to figure out what was about, but the way Emmalene was now shaking her head suggested that neither of them had succeeded.

"Nay. He is being very unreasonable and will not even discuss Blake."

"Hmmm." Seonaid heaved a sigh. She and Blake were leaving for Sherwell today. Blake felt six days was long enough to recover and insisted they leave. Emmalene and Seonaid tried to argue for another couple of days at least before he risked the journey, trying to sway him by reminding him of his weakened state and the fact that Little George and Aeldra had not yet returned from their visit. But he would not be moved. And Amaury had not helped, pointing out that most of the warriors were back from the free time Blake had given them and so could escort them to Sherwell and see him safe. He had also pointed out that one of the men could be sent to Little George to let him know Blake was on the way home and to meet him there, rather than return to Eberhardt.

"Seonaid!" Blake scowled in their general direction. "Finish thanking Lady Emmalene and let us go. We have a half day's ride to reach home."

Seonaid turned to Emmalene. She considered hugging her but had never been very comfortable with emotional displays so only smiled. "Thank ye for everything."

"You are more than welcome, Seonaid." Emmalene patted her arm and walked down the stairs with her. "If you should find out what the men are so angry about . . ."

"I'll do what I can," Seonaid promised.

Smiling, Emmalene nodded, quickly caught Seonaid up in a hug, then stepped back to let her mount her horse. It was a tricky business for Seonaid. Used to riding astride her beast, she was clumsy and awkward trying to ride sidesaddle. Blake watched grim-faced, then tossed Amaury an accusing glare once she was settled and turned his mount toward the gate.

It was a long ride for Seonaid. Not only was she uncomfortable seated as she was, but Blake was silent and morose the whole way. Seonaid was quiet too. This was the last leg of the journey; within a short time she would be meeting Blake's father, and she was suddenly nervous at the prospect. What if he didn't like her? What if she forgot to hold her skirts up and tripped and fell on her face as she walked up to meet him? What if he hated her as much as he was reported to hate her father?

Seonaid tortured herself with such concerns the entire way so that it was almost a relief to arrive. Even if it was to be bad, it would at least be over.

Blake ordered the men to ride to the stables but led Seonaid directly up to the keep doors.

She glanced up warily as the doors opened and an older, slender man appeared at the top of the steps. Seonaid guessed by his pallor and frail appearance that this must be the ailing Earl of Sherwell. She was just screwing up her courage to meet him when her father appeared next to the man and took his arm to help him down the stairs. He was followed by Lady Wildwo—Lady Dunbar, she corrected herself—then Little George, Aeldra, and the bishop.

Most of Seonaid's nervousness left her. She no longer felt so alone and anxious. Besides, she was distracted with the questions running through her mind. There was no sign of animosity between the two older men, which suggested they had sorted out their differences, whatever they had been. And she wanted to know how the trip to court had gone, and how the English king had taken the news of Lady Wildwood's marrying her father.

She also wanted to know how Aeldra had found Little George's family. She hoped her cousin had liked them and that they had been kind to her.

Blake dismounted and moved to help his wife off her horse, but she slipped off before he could reach her and rushed to meet her cousin and new stepmother as Aeldra and Lady Margaret bustled around the more slowly-moving men to greet her. He watched the women hug, then clasped Seonaid's hands and turned to introduce her to his father. She greeted the old man politely, nodded to her father, then allowed herself to be dragged off by the women, who were both chattering away about what had happened while they were apart.

Blake sighed as the castle door closed on them. They looked like any three normal women. Even Aeldra was presently wearing a dress. His fascinating bride was gone. He had hoped that by keeping her away from Emmalene the last four days she would revert to her old self. Unfortunately, that had not been the case. Instead, she appeared to have redoubled her efforts to be more ladylike in his presence. She hardly even cursed anymore, which she had done on occasion during the first two days after he'd awakened.

Sighing again, he turned to glance at the four men still standing at the foot of the stairs. All four of them were staring after the women with differing expressions. His father looked curious, Little George looked bewildered, the bishop was smiling benignly, and Angus Dunbar looked horrified. Since that was something like what he had been feeling since awakening after his injury, Blake could sympathize.

He moved forward to his father.

"Father." Blake clasped the man's arms briefly in a

half hug and found himself frowning at the weight his sire had lost. The claim of being unwell had not simply been a way to avoid riding to Dunbar. The man had definitely been ill, and was still recovering by the look of it.

"She is lovely," the Earl of Sherwell said.

"Aye." Blake shrugged, resisting the urge to tell him he should have seen her in braies. "She—"

"What in the bloody hell have ye done to me daughter?"

Blake turned to find Angus glaring at him furiously. Shifting with irritation at being blamed for something that was none of his fault, and that he didn't even like, Blake scowled at him. "I did nothing. That is how she was when I woke up after the injury." He grimaced his distaste. "I think Emmalene influenced her."

"Emmalene? Lady Eberhardt?" the bishop asked with surprise.

"Aye."

"Nay." Angus considered Blake's obvious displeasure as he shook his head. "Nay. She has been around ladies afore without their turnin' her like this. It must be something else."

"Amaury admitted that Emmalene had put servants to the task of making the dress—dresses," he corrected himself, for Seonaid had left Eberhardt with three dresses and the promise that *the others* would be sent when they were finished. "And he even admitted that Emmalene had spent a good deal of time with her 'ere I awoke. It must be Emmalene." His expression turned grim as he added, "Though Amaury did not like my saying so. He took it as a personal slight that I was upset that Seonaid was turning into a taller, dark-haired version of his wife."

"Really?" Angus asked with interest.

"Aye. We almost came to blows over it." He grimaced. "We were not talking by the time Seonaid and I left."

"Hmm. It sounds no unlike the argument we had some twenty years ago," Angus said to Blake's father.

"Aye." The earl nodded. "And we waited far too long to clear it up. Do not make the same mistake, Blake. Sort things out with Amaury quickly; do not let the anger fester. He loves his wife, just as you obviously love yours, and you are both defensive when it comes to possible slights to them."

"I do not—" Blake began to deny he loved his wife, then paused and simply stared at his father. He liked her, respected her, and had from the beginning. He had also enjoyed her company very much since the wedding. Not just the bedding, but talking to her and playing with her, their wrestling and tickling and her cleverness and wit and . . .

Dear God, he was wearing the lopsided tunic. Seonaid had done her best to repair her handiwork, but it was still lopsided and he—who refused to wear garments that were not presented to him in perfect form—was wearing it. He *was* falling in love with his wife. Or, as his father suggested, he loved her already. And he wanted her back.

"I fear someone will have to explain how Seonaid was before this trip," the earl said. "She seems perfectly fine to me."

"Aye. She would," Angus muttered. "But then, ye've never met the lass before, have ye? She was very like yer Elizabeth 'ere today. She wore braies, no dresses, and she rode astride, no sidesaddle. I thought I'd fall over when I saw them ridin' up."

"Like Elizabeth?" Blake asked, starting at his mother's name.

"Ye willna recall her much, I'm sure," Angus said. "But yer mother was very like our Seonaid and Aeldra. She was a warrior. Beautiful and strong."

The Earl of Sherwell nodded. "Aye, she was. Beautiful and strong and still every inch a woman."

"That sounds like my Seonaid," Blake said. "At least, the way she used to be." He glanced at Angus. "I want her back."

The bishop cleared his throat, then asked, "Have you asked her why she has suddenly changed?"

"Nay. I did not wish to hurt her feelings."

"When did she change exactly?" the earl asked.

Blake shrugged. "She was wearing a dress when I woke up after the injury."

"So sometime while ye were unconscious," Angus murmured.

"She was still the same Seonaid 'ere Aeldra and I left to visit my family," Little George offered helpfully.

"So it was during the last two days 'ere I awoke," Blake said with a nod. "During the time that Amaury says Emmalene was spending a lot of time with her."

Angus Dunbar shook his head again. "I canna see it, lad. As I said, plenty o' ladies visited Dunbar over the years, including Iliana, and she tried to turn Seonaid into more o' a lady at my request, but Seonaid would have none o' it. It must be something else."

They were all silent, considering the matter; then Little George said, "Mayhap it has something to do with Lady Ardeth."

Blake's head shot up at this comment. "Lady Ardeth?"

"Aye. Aeldra was telling me that Lady Ardeth tried to insult Seonaid, but she put her in her place," he explained, then shrugged. "Mayhap something she said affected her after all."

"What did she say?" Blake asked.

"She said she had witnessed their practicing with their swords, then said something about it being interesting for you to be married to an Amazon and did you substitute swordplay for foreplay to accommodate her."

"Bitch," Angus said with distaste.

"Aye," the earl agreed, then murmured thoughtfully. "Ardeth . . . Did you not dally with her 'ere she married? You came home for Christmas the year you earned your spurs and she was here. She and her family stopped in on the way to her marriage, and I felt sure there was something between the two of you."

"Aye," Blake said and nearly groaned aloud. Lady Ardeth had a vicious tongue. "She is a viper."

Angus Dunbar shook his head again. "Plenty o' ladies have taken their talons to Seonaid over the years. She's always put them in their places an' gone about her business. Why would this be any different?"

"Mayhap because she loves Blake," Little George said, and Blake found himself turning to him sharply. "The way she reacted when you were injured was pretty telling. She would not leave your side, but sat up staring at you day and night as if willing you to live. She cares for you."

"And you think her loving Blake would make her change?" the earl asked.

Little George shrugged. "Amaury tried to be more like Blake to please Emmalene when they first married. Mayhap Seonaid thought being more like Emmalene would please Blake."

"Aye." Angus Dunbar nodded. "That may be the way o' it. In fact, 'tis the only explanation that seems likely so far."

"Well, there you are, then." The earl took Blake's arm and turned him toward the stairs. "All you need do is talk to her and sort the matter out. Tell her you love her just the way she is and she need not change. All will be well."

Blake helped his father up the stairs, his mind whirling with what he should say to his wife. By the time they reached the keep doors, the matter was settled in his mind. He knew exactly what he would say; he just had to find the chance to talk to her.

It was a task easier said than done. It seemed a number of their relatives had descended on Sherwell on hearing of his father's illness. With several aunts and uncles and cousins under the roof, as well as the bishop, and Lord Dunbar and his new wife, Blake found he did not even have his room at the moment. He and Seonaid had been relegated to sleeping in the hall along with the lesser guests and the servants.

* * *

"You are becoming very good at sewing, Seonaid. But would you not prefer to go practice in the bailey with Aeldra?" Lady Margaret asked gently.

Seonaid forced a smile for her new stepmother. "Nay. I am content to sit here with the ladies and sew," she lied. In truth, Seonaid was so sick of sitting around with the women sewing that she felt sure she would scream. Unfortunately, she found it hampering to practice with swords in a skirt. The stupid thing tripped her up at every turn.

"Seonaid," Lady Margaret said quietly, "your father is very worried about you. He thinks you are not happy."

Seonaid stared at the cloth she was practicing stitches on and grimaced. Her father was not wrong; she was miserable. But every time she considered giving up this ladylike business, she recalled Blake's yelling *"My wife is perfect just the way she is,"* and her determination to be what he wanted was renewed. She had been behaving this way for two days when he made that claim and was obviously well pleased with the change. It gave her hope that he might come to love her.

"Wife?"

Seonaid gave a start as Blake suddenly appeared at her elbow, then managed a smile for his benefit. "Aye, husband?"

"Come." Catching her arm, he urged her to her feet and began to lead her out of the great hall.

"Is somethin' amiss?" Seonaid asked, eyeing his determined expression warily.

"Nay, but I wish to talk with you," Blake answered. "I

have wished to talk with you since arriving at Sherwell. Howbeit, we have not had a moment alone since we arrived here, and as it does not appear that any of the guests intend to leave any time soon . . ." He shrugged. "I have decided we shall have to find someplace we can talk."

By this time he had led her out of the keep. Seonaid spied the saddled horses waiting for them and frowned. "Where are we going?"

"To a secret spot I know where we can be alone."

"Outside the walls?" Seonaid asked the obvious. They would hardly need the horses if this spot were within Sherwell's walls. "Do you think that's wise? What if Greenweld's men attack again?"

"There is little chance of that. Surely they have heard that Greenweld is dead and will have moved on by now." He didn't sound the least concerned, so Seonaid let the subject drop and concentrated on mounting and keeping her seat on the sidesaddle as he led her out of the bailey.

The secret spot was a little glen awash with buttercups. Seonaid smiled at the sight of the lovely yellow wildflowers carpeting the ground as she slid off her mount and into Blake's arms.

She almost protested that he shouldn't strain himself as he caught her and lowered her to the ground, but his strength had much improved in the days they had been at Sherwell. His color was completely back to normal, and Seonaid knew that he had been practicing with the men in the bailey, rebuilding his strength.

"Nice, is it not?" Blake asked as he retrieved a blanket and a small sack that hung from his saddle.

"Aye," Seonaid agreed as he took her hand and led her to the center of the small clearing. He released her then and spread out the blanket, then gestured for her to sit. Settling next to her, he opened the sack and pulled out some cheese, bread, fruit, and a skin of wine. He obviously intended on putting the talk off until after they had eaten, and Seonaid found herself growing nervous at the idea. He had sounded so grim and determined on approaching her in the great hall. . . .

"I thought ye wanted to talk to me," she prompted.

Blake lifted his gaze to Seonaid and noted the anxiety tightening her face. She looked much as she had on their wedding night, as if expecting something unpleasant was coming and wishing to get it over with. He hesitated only a moment, then nodded and set the food and wine aside. They might as well get the hard part over with first.

After briefly considering how to start, he asked, "Seonaid, why do you not wear braies any more?"

She looked startled, then opened her mouth, closed it again, and asked, "Do ye no prefer me in gowns?"

"In truth?"

She nodded.

"Nay," he answered firmly. "I prefer you naked."

Seonaid's eyes widened, then she grinned, and he continued. "Second to naked, I prefer you in those tight old braies that show every curve of your body."

She chuckled at his frank admission.

"I also prefer you happy," he said. "And while you may think you have a smile pasted on your face the day through, in truth it looks more like a determined grimace. You are not happy. I want you happy."

"I am happy," she said, but she was a poor liar.

Blake took her hands. "Seonaid—"

"And ye're happy too. I heard ye tell Amaury that ye thought I was perfect like this. So, we are both happy." She shrugged.

Blake was at a complete loss. He had no idea what she was talking about, when had he—*My wife is perfect just the way she is.* The words echoed through his head and he closed his eyes. That had been the last thing he'd said in his argument with Amaury, the one Seonaid had interrupted. And she—not having heard the rest of the discussion and having been rushing about in a dress for two days, doing her best to imitate a lady—had thought he'd meant he thought she was perfect as she was now.

"Seonaid, I meant I thought you were perfect the way you were prior to my waking up. As you were when I met you. As you really are underneath the silly wimple you are wearing and under all those skirts."

Her eyebrows flew up incredulously. "Ye did?"

"Aye."

"But I made ye chase me all over Scotland, Blake. I put my foot to yer groin. I—"

"Well, that part was not precisely what I meant, although it certainly made for an interesting courtship," he confessed. "Seonaid, I meant I liked the way things were between the wedding and the attack on the way to

Sherwell. I admired and respected your strength and skill and intelligence 'ere that, and I appreciated your beauty. But once the wedding was done and you stopped running, we matched beautifully. We got along well in bed, we lay in each other's arms of a night talking, we could play and wrestle and tease and tickle . . ." He shrugged. "I miss that. I miss the laughter and fun. You had relaxed with me and I miss that too."

He raised a hand to tug the wimple off her head, leaned forward, and kissed her gently on the lips, then whispered, "I like and miss *you*."

"I—Bloody hell!" She interrupted herself to roar.

Blake was just pulling back in surprise when she shoved him to the side and pulled her *sgian dubh* from the belt at her waist. It only took him a moment to see the problem. It seemed Greenweld's men had not given up after all. They were presently spilling into the glen.

"Bloody hell!" he echoed, leaping to his feet.

Chapter Seventeen

Seonaid moved instinctively to put her back to Blake's as the men moved to surround them, all the while wishing fervently that she'd brought her sword. Unfortunately, she hadn't worn one since donning a dress. That left her only with her *sgian dubh*. It wasn't much, but she assured herself it would be enough to at least guard Blake's back while he battled the men on his side. Besides, she reminded herself, these men were not likely to harm her; their orders had been to kill Blake. As long as she guarded his back, he only had to slay his way through nine men.

Brilliant! She had just had that thought when laughter drew her eye to the far side of the clearing as her father and his new wife came riding into the glen. Their merriment died the moment they spotted the trouble they had intruded on. But before either of them could react to what was taking place, Little George came riding into the clearing from another direction, Aeldra seated on the mount before him. Aeldra was sitting sideways in front of the man, pressing little kisses to his neck, but she stopped abruptly when the giant cursed and reined in his mount. Turning her head, she spied what was going on and stilled as well.

Seonaid's father and Aeldra acted at the same moment, Aeldra slipping from her seat in front of Little George even as Angus Dunbar dismounted. They both started to charge forward with Little George hard on their heels, but before chaos could erupt, Lady Margaret shouted, "Greenweld is dead!"

Seonaid's father, Aeldra, and Little George slowed in their approach but did not stop. Greenweld's men, who had noted their presence now and turned to face the threat they represented, stood hesitating. It seemed they didn't know whether to focus on Blake and Seonaid, the threesome now slowly approaching, or the woman still proudly sitting her mount.

"Greenweld is dead!" Lady Margaret repeated firmly. "He was trapped in the Dunbar passage while trying to invade the castle and fought to the death rather than surrender." She allowed a moment for that to sink in, then added, "On his death I became the soul mistress of Greenweld. You now owe your fealty to me."

Seonaid's father, Aeldra, and Little George had reached them but simply stood waiting, at the ready if necessary.

"I am aware you were only obeying Greenweld's orders in attacking Seonaid and Blake," she went on.

"And I will not punish you if you lower your weapons and ride out now."

When the men hesitated, their gazes searching each other out, Lady Margaret snapped impatiently, "You have lost three of your men already. Would you really all rather die here this day than serve me?"

Greenweld's men finally lowered their weapons and stood as if uncertain what to do.

"You are free to ride back to Greenweld and join the rest of the men there. And so long as you serve me well and loyally, we will never mention this again."

The men hesitated one more moment, then moved as one into the woods. Blake waited a heartbeat, then followed, with Little George and her father on his heels. The trio was back within moments, looking more calm.

"Their horses were not far away. They have ridden out."

Seonaid felt herself relax.

"Well," her father muttered, glancing down at Seonaid's feet.

Following his gaze, she saw that she had stood on one end of the bread when she had taken her position at Blake's back. Other than that, nothing else was disturbed.

"How did ye come to be here?" Seonaid asked, moving her foot off the bread as she put away her *sgian dubh*.

The Dunbar shrugged. "I found this spot some years ago while your mother and I were visiting. I recalled it today and thought to show it to Lady Margaret."

Seonaid nodded slowly, then glanced to Aeldra and Little George. "And you? How did ye two come to be here?"

"One of the men on guard told me about this spot when I mentioned wanting a bit of time alone with Aeldra," Little George answered.

Seonaid turned and arched an eyebrow at her husband. "A secret spot, is it? I think your secret is out, my lord."

Grimacing, Blake faced the other two couples. "While I appreciate the help you have been in ridding me of Greenweld's men, I would appreciate it if you would leave us to our picnic."

"Oh, now, doona be so inhospitable there, lad." Angus Dunbar sheathed his sword and moved toward the picnic. "What have ye got there? Wine, strawberries, cheese, and—"

"Seonaid and I were discussing her sudden desire to wear gowns and shun her sword," Blake said meaningfully.

Much to her amusement, her father stopped his forward momentum. Nodding, he turned on his heel to head back to his mount. He called out to Aeldra and Little George as he went, "Come along, ye two. Ye'll have to find another spot fer yer shenanigans. Me daughter and son-in-law have some matters to sort."

Aeldra did not have to be told twice. Grabbing Little George's hand, she tugged him back toward their own mounts. Seonaid caught the relief on her cousin's face and knew she would be pleased did she return to her old self. While Aeldra had returned from visiting her new in-laws in a dress, it had only been a temporary change in behavior. She had apparently donned the more traditional clothing for the meeting with his family but had shed it again once comfortable at Sherwell. Seonaid knew she had been waiting for her to do the same thing, and would be happy for her old sparring partner's return.

The two couples left the clearing as quickly as they had entered it, and without so much as a by your leave.

Seonaid glanced toward her husband once they were gone, but he stood still for several moments, head cocked as he listened to the fading hoofbeats. Once assured they were definitely alone again, he relaxed, then seemed to become aware that he still held his sword. He tossed it on the ground next to the blanket she stood on, still within easy reach.

"Now," he said, turning to face her, "as I was saying before we were so rudely interrupted—"

Blake moved to stand in front of Seonaid and clasped her face gently between his hands. "Seonaid, I like you just the way you are. There will be no changes. I want no simpering, sewing wife, for I will not wear lopsided tunics the rest of my life."

"Ye doona want me to sew and such for ye either?" She looked horrified. "But other wives do these things for their husbands and—"

"Then let them," Blake interrupted, "and they are welcome to it, but I have servants to tend to all of those things. I want you as my wife, not as a servant."

"But if I doona do those things, what can I do?"

"You can be yourself: strong, feisty, sleek as a cat, plain-speaking, smart, beautiful—" Blake stopped abruptly when he saw the tears welling in her eyes. "Are you crying?" he asked with alarm.

"Nay," Seonaid denied, even as she brushed the tears away, then she said helplessly, "yer complimenting me. And you have never complimented me before. I thought . . ."

Blake smiled wryly and brushed the tears away. For a man who was supposed to have such a way with women, he had certainly botched this up from the beginning. Sighing, he shook his head. "Seonaid, what I just said, those were not compliments. They are the truth. I vow to you I will only ever tell you the truth."

She raised her eyebrows. "And compliments are not truth?"

"Nay. Not the way I have always used them," he admitted. "They are an exaggeration, deliberate flattery aimed at gaining some end. I often have to think them up, or create them, if you see what I mean. But with you, what I say comes naturally because it is true. I respect and love you too much to sit about plotting ways to get under your skirt or—in future—into your braies."

Seonaid stared at him in silence for so long he began to worry and asked, "What is it?"

"Ye said ye love me."

Blake blinked. He had. He did, but he hadn't meant to say so. Now that it was out, however, and she wasn't laughing her head off at him, he decided to let it be. "Aye."

"I love ye too," she admitted, and Blake felt himself begin to grin, until she added, "But I doona think I like it."

That killed his smile. "What do you mean, you do not think you like it?"

"It hurts. Here." Seonaid pointed at her chest, then blurted, "And 'tis scary, Blake. I doona like being scared. Nothing before has ever scared me like ye do. Should I lose ye, or should ye turn from me, I . . ."

"That is a part of love, Seonaid," he said gently. "You only fear losing something when you have something of value to lose. And that fear shows that you know what we have has value. We love each other. We just have to work hard to be sure we never forget it and always act accordingly." He ran one finger along the side of her face. "I do love you. You are safe with me. You do not have to keep your defenses up, or be strong all the time while with me. And you do not have to change. I am pleased with you as you are."

Seonaid felt tears fill her eyes and glanced away with embarrassment, but Blake caught her by the chin and turned her face back. "I do not want you to fear being who you are with me. If you are afraid, or if you feel hurt by something, I want you to tell me, and between the two of us we shall do whatever it takes to see you are happy."

And between the two of us, we shall do whatever it takes to see you are happy.

Seonaid stared at him as those words echoed in her head. Between the two of them. Together they would see she was happy. As a couple, as husband and wife, as a team. They were two parts of one whole now, everything they did affecting the other. She had found her place, she realized. It seemed to Seonaid that she had spent the whole of her life trying to find a place for herself, trying to fit in, trying to earn the love of those around her. But Blake was saying that he wanted her as she was, softness and hardness. She did not have to change for him.

"Seonaid?" he asked with concern. "Are you well?"

Well? The question rattled in her brain and she almost laughed. Well? Aye, she was well. She was so full of joy it was almost bursting from her. Beaming a smile at him, Seonaid threw herself at his chest, hugging him so tightly she surprised a grunt from him. She then pressed a quick, hard kiss to his lips before pulling back and saying, "Aye, husband. I am verra well." She kissed him again, more gently this time, then pulled back solemnly. "I wish ye to ken, it goes for me too. If someone hurts ye, or ye feel afraid, or ye want somethin', ye must tell me, and together we two shall make sure yer also happy."

Blake grinned and hugged her to his chest, rocking her gently back and forth as he cupped the back of her head with one hand. After a moment the rocking slowed, and he pulled back to announce, "I want something."

"Already?" Seonaid exclaimed in surprise, then she nodded. "Tell me."

"I want to make love to you till neither of us can stand any more."

Seonaid blinked. "Ye . . . ?"

"I want to make love to you till neither of us can stand any more."

"Ah." Seonaid bit her lip to keep from grinning; then she hooked one foot behind his ankle and gave him a push that sent him tumbling backward to the blanket.

In the next moment, she had swung one leg over him and sunk to straddle him. "I think between the two o' us we can manage that."

"Do you?" Blake asked with amusement, catching several strands of her long hair and winding them around his hand to draw her down toward him.

"Aye," she answered, then she smiled and said, "Husband?"

"Aye?" he asked, his gaze focused on her lips.

"I think I am going to like this marriage business after all."

Blake's gaze shifted to her eyes with surprise; then he gave her a slow smile and said equally solemnly, "I think I will too, my love," before finally kissing her.

JENNIFER ASHLEY
EMILY BRYAN
ALISSA JOHNSON

Invite you to

A Christmas Ball

It is the most anticipated event of the ton: the annual holiday ball at Hartwell House. The music is elegant, the food exquisite, and the guest list absolutely exclusive. Some come looking for love. Some will do almost anything to avoid it. But everyone wants to be there. No matter what their desires, amid the swirling gowns and soft glow of candlelight, magic tends to happen. And one dance, one kiss, one night can shape a new destiny....

ISBN 13: 978-0-8439-6250-5

Alissa Johnson

"A bright star." —RT BOOKreviews

McAlistair's Fortune

To Miss Evie Cole, ignorance was never bliss. That principle had driven her to become quite adept at a most unladylike pursuit—eavesdropping. And it was while honing this skill that she heard her guardians' elaborate scheme to find her a husband. Too bad she'd vowed never to marry. At least she knew the peril they were planning to help entrap her was only pretend.

What she didn't hear would change everything. James McAlistair wasn't supposed to be part of the bargain. Not only was the retired assassin dark, silent and intimidating, but Evie also happened to know from an accidental encounter on a warm, moon-drenched night that the man was an exceptional kisser. Now the danger was real. Because now Evie might fall in love.

"Filled with rapier-sharp repartee, passion and espionage."
—RITA Award-winning author Sophia Nash on
As Luck Would Have It

ISBN 13: 978-0-8439-6251-2

GERRI RUSSELL

To Tempt a Knight

Brotherhood of the Scottish Templars

"Gerri Russell writes with a passionate intensity that will sweep readers straight into her richly imagined world."
—Jayne Ann Krentz

Sir William Keith owed allegiance to no one save the mysterious brotherhood of the Scottish Templars. But his task to protect the legendary Templar treasure brought him straight into the path of a bold lass who demanded he help find her kidnapped father, the treasure's previous guardian.

William dared not abandon Lady Siobhan Fraser to her enemies. She was his best hope for finding the holy artifacts—and a dire temptation to his vow of chastity. How long could he deny the ecstasy that awaited him in her arms? For he knew all too well it's the forbidden fruit that tastes the sweetest....

Coming this Fall!   ISBN 13: 978-0-8439-6259-8

✂ ☐ **YES!**

Sign me up for the Historical Romance Book Club and send my FREE BOOKS! If I choose to stay in the club, I will pay only $8.50* each month, a savings of $6.48!

NAME: _____

ADDRESS: _____

TELEPHONE: _____

EMAIL: _____

☐ I want to pay by credit card.

☐ **VISA**   ☐ **MasterCard.**   ☐ **DISCOVER**

ACCOUNT #: _____

EXPIRATION DATE: _____

SIGNATURE: _____

Mail this page along with $2.00 shipping and handling to:
Historical Romance Book Club
PO Box 6640
Wayne, PA 19087
Or fax (must include credit card information) to:
610-995-9274
You can also sign up online at **www.dorchesterpub.com**.
*Plus $2.00 for shipping. Offer open to residents of the U.S. and Canada only.
Canadian residents please call 1-800-481-9191 for pricing information.
If under 18, a parent or guardian must sign. Terms, prices and conditions subject to change. Subscription subject to acceptance. Dorchester Publishing reserves the right to reject any order or cancel any subscription.